COSMOS
INCORPORATED

COSMOS
INCORPORATED

MAURICE G. DANTEC

Translated from the French by Tina A. Kover

BALLANTINE BOOKS · NEW YORK

Cosmos Incorporated is a work of fiction. Names, characters, places, and incidents are the products of the author's imagination or are used fictitiously. Any resemblance to actual events, locales, or persons, living or dead, is entirely coincidental.

2008 Del Rey Books Trade Paperback Edition

Translation copyright © 2008 by Random House, Inc.

Published in the United States by Del Rey Books, an imprint of The Random House Publishing Group, a division of Random House, Inc., New York.

DEL REY is a registered trademark and the Del Rey colophon is a trademark of Random House, Inc.

Originally published in French by Éditions Albin Michel, Paris, France, in 2006, copyright © 2006 by Éditions Albin Michel.

Library of Congress Cataloging-in-Publication Data

Dantec, Maurice G.
 [Cosmos incorporated. English]
 Cosmos incorporated / Maurice G. Dantec ; translated from the French by Tina A. Kover.
  p. cm.
 ISBN: 978-0-345-49993-6 (pbk.)
 I. Kover, Tina A. II. Title.
 PQ2664.A4888C6713 2008
 843'.914—dc22   2008003019

Printed in the United States of America

www.delreybooks.com

9 8 7 6 5 4 3 2 1

Book design by Julie Schroeder

To Sylvie, and to Éva

To my parents

There is a Melancholy, O how lovely 'tis, whose heaven
is in the heavenly Mind, for she from heaven came,
and where she goes heaven still doth follow her.

—WILLIAM BLAKE

We bear witness to the fact that in counterpoint to the
darkening, the weakening of reflection in the organic world,
grace rises up ever more radiant and sovereign. But like the
intersection of two lines, where one side of the point meets the
other after having passed through infinity, or like the concave
mirror-image imposing itself suddenly upon us after having
moved infinitely far away, so grace emerges again when
knowledge has, so to speak, crossed an infinite distance.
It will appear in all its purity, simultaneously, in this
human body that is at once private and endowed with
infinite consciousness—that is, in the model, or in God.

—HEINRICH VON KLEIST

INPUT

UNITMANITY

> Every creature, and every single thing that is said,
> comes from but one Name.
>
> THE SEFER YETSIRAH

> *ZERO: CONTROL INTERFACE*

OFF/ON:

At the instant the world was born, it was divided in two.

On one side: light. Red. Red like the monochromatic beam cadenced at fifteen billion times per second, more commonly called LASER—*Light Amplification by Stimulated Emission of Radiation,* that which reads-writes data in all media using the Boolean encoding of binary numbers—an ember boring a single, enormous point; one that is colossal; titanic. So vast that its exact size is impossible to calculate, for, indeed, it is *all* space.

This is the 3 degrees Kelvin background noise that blankets the universe. It is the primordial light that precedes all creation.

On the other side: matter. White. White like the sclera of an eye, the organ directly linked to the human brain by the optic nerve—which is nothing more than an extension of the cortex to the outside—and whose diopter is scrutinized by the ray of red light, filling all the space the said organ can perceive. The refractive system of the human ocular globe is composed principally of an iris, behind which is a biconvex crystalline lens where air and cornea meet. Faced with light of such intensity, the iris automatically attempts to close almost completely, constricting the pupil to nothing—but the red light is still there, because a tiny, delicate mechanism of carbon-carbon veins linked to a minute frontal vacuum implant keeps the pupil open, keeps the eyelid from blinking, and then there is nothing but this red intensity, this red world, pure light etched on the white of the eye.

Between the two parts of the world there are luminous shadows, the shining shadows of the digital operation that turns both matter and light into a *number*. For millions of years, the human eye has captured light. From now on, light will be the captor.

Welcome to the Technological Genesis. Welcome to its beyond, its terminal horizon. Welcome to the world of the ubermachine. Remember that a machine is, above all, a network of disconnections.

The monochromatic ray reads the entire surface of the retina, gradually etching an image of the object it scrutinizes onto a cybernetic memory. This is its function. It controls.

The ray is ejected from a standard-model, UniPol-approved ruby microcannon, which is linked to a small data processor. This machine is linked in turn to the vast planetary information-storage network, and can compare the information encoded in the global control metasystem with the millions of nerve cells that make up each and every human eye in a matter of seconds. This is its task. The light has a job.

As does everything that exists today.

The light is a cop.

It's the same with the eye scrutinized by the machine. Yes—the eye, too, has a job. At this moment, its job is to fool the searching ray of light and the computer that acts as its brain. A brain that is, truth be told, superior to most of the human brains, with their optic nerves in contact daily with the light.

The organic globule is checked by the machine-light's reading. Its iris—which, like all irises, is absolutely unique—has an optic print that is as distinctive as a fingerprint. Its iris is, in point of fact, *wrong*.

In the UHU/RUS K-127 database, the machine control will compare this human iris encoded by the light-cop with its seven million counterparts kept on file by the Universal Police, and will find its specific identity.

In this particular case, the case of Sergei Diego Dimitrievitch Plotkin, born on September 19, 2001, at 10:17 P.M. in Irkutsk, eastern Siberia, to Carmen Lopez Chatwyn and Dimitri Vassilievitch Plotkin, this profusion of information conceals the fact that Sergei Diego Dimitrievitch Plotkin does not exist.

Or, rather, he does not exist yet.

On one side of the world, at the end of a ray of red light, electronic components transmit micropackets of energy along a network of logical operators that allow a specialized recognition program to draw matrices where the data received from the light-cop, on one hand, and the data stored in the Human Universe databases, on the other hand, are compared one-to-one at several million units per millisecond.

It is the culmination of an entire evolutionary cycle, and of several decades of rapid regression: a return to the primitive jungle, even to the Ocean Matrix; nothing is differentiated, nothing *can* be. All is in flux; the world never existed. In any case, at the moment, if it *does* exist, it moves in a spectral place whose distinguishing feature is that it always seems more real than reality itself.

On the other side of the world: the optic extremity of a brain whose standard-size cranium has a volume of around 1,350 cubic centimeters, covered with a layer of "natural"—that is, kept young via an organic capillary implant—black hair, which sits atop a human form 1.83 meters high and weighing 85 kilos and 202 grams. According to the available data, the biological structure just described is officially fifty-six years old, but several transgenic rejuvenation treatments have rendered its cellular age almost half that.

This human creature knows it exists, but just barely. It is hardly more self-aware than the white of the eye across which the red digital encoding microbeam glides.

The structure is dressed in a suit of gray Diacra with red-orange glints and a shirt of cloned cotton whose color falls within the range of pale yellow hues identifiable by the verification scanner attached to the automated security portal that has already searched the human creature beneath its clothing.

The human creature waits.

It waits for the light-cop to finish its job.

It remains standing, on one side of the world. On the side of the world reserved for those who are scrutinized by tubes of red light. On the human side of the world.

On the other side of the world, the machine side, they work. They compare retinal structures and ocular prints. They work very fast, because there are many optic prints stored, and every day there are many humans to examine.

We are inside Control Interface.

We have only just arrived.

We, he, you, I—it doesn't matter which. His personality is artifice. His ocular print is artifice. A large part of his body is artifice.

A large part of his existence is artifice.

For now, he waits.

He waits, like thousands of others he cannot see. Thousands of others isolated in their airlocks all along the concentric rings of the terminal's arrival arch.

Right now, he can see nothing but red light.

And he waits for the light to finish its work. For the light to check his ocular print. For the machine to compare it with the others in the database. For the system to identify him as Mr. Plotkin.

He waits for the system to be wrong.

Then, abruptly, the divided world is reunited.

The light disappears.

Reality replaces it.

And reality, in the first place, is a message transmitted directly to his optic nerve. His neurolinguistic implant, run by the Control Center, projects the words:

UNIWORLD
ONE WORLD FOR ALL—ONE GOD FOR EACH

In staccato pixilated letters, the airport control program's text scrolls across his retina:

SECURITY CONTROL BAR 18-H—PLEASE GO TO YOUR SECTOR'S BIO-DECONTAMINATION AIRLOCK—PLEASE FOLLOW THE ORANGE ARROWS

These appear on the cold neon-blue walls of the astroport's Grand Hall, which has replaced the still-fresh inferno of the newborn red world. The airlock door has just slid open.

In this instant when the world, it seems, is being born a second time, there is nothing but ordered chaos. Colors correspond to signs; signs give directions, behavior, the existence of foreign objects, spaces yet to be discovered.

Like the Bio-decontamination Airlock.

Control Interface, which regulates the international terminal's entries and exits, is in fact the only living organism in this place. This cybernetic organism was made to order for an average-size astroport and can process several hundred thousand travelers a day. It is a sociobiological brain that works nonstop; it divides and operates without the slightest discontinuity—except that of the digital.

Here, as you follow the orange arrows toward another floor of the Interface, you begin to see that the place is populated by human beings. A window-lined corridor leads from Ocular Identification Control to the Bio-decontamination Airlock. It is only now that you realize there are thousands of you, each in a sterile glassed-in tube, standing on a rolling walkway where an orange light shines, moving slowly upward in the direction of the next concentric ring.

The Bio-decontamination Airlock is a rectangular space whose walls, ceiling, and floor are uniformly white—so matte a white as to be nearly the gray hue of concrete. Blue-white light glares coldly from an overhead fixture. In the center of the room is a circle of white foam. Several anodized-aluminum machines gleam dully along the walls, their ashy luster reminiscent of weaponry. Above the white foam circle, which is etched with two human footprints—the universal symbol telling one where to stand—there is a wide tube where bluish filaments of light writhe and crackle along its honeycombed surface, seemingly sketching the outlines of a human body, the quantum shadow of he who must now match this icon of pure, searching radiance.

The instructions the Interface now sends to the optic nerve of the traveler identified as Sergei Plotkin are clear, concise, and imperative.

The tube, honeycombed with luminescence, descends from the ceiling until it lands upright, covering him where he stands on the foam disk.

Blue-white phosphorescence, like icy sunlight, dances and hums against his body. He feels tiny, invisible intrusions within him—brief stabs of heat in his pelvic area and upward along his spinal column to the base of his neck, an odd stretching sensation in his limbs, shivering cold in his fingertips and toes. Hot-cold, compression-expansion, limited-unlimited. Something is making a game of these paradoxes *inside his body.*

He knows he is being examined at the molecular level, even to the structure of his DNA.

They will know if he is transporting undeclared or illegal substances, orbital drugs, forbidden components, pirated software, microbombs or any other prohibited weapons, or viruses—digital or biological. Thanks to a bar code implanted in chromosome 13 by the Global Agency of Biological Resource Management—a bar code that cannot be copied—they will be able to tell if he is human, or a legal humanoid, or an approved combination of the two; or, indeed, if he is a renegade android escaped from one of the secret military colonies on the moon. They will know if he has falsified his gender or his genetic identity. *They* will know, the terrible *they* of the sociocollective brain. UniWorld. Present everywhere, detectable nowhere, they are able to know everything down to the EPO levels in your blood. They, *it,* can list not only every disease you have contracted since childhood but all the diseases to which your blood type makes you more susceptible as well.

The First Ring of the Interface determined whether or not the legal information contained in "your personal identification and privacy systems" was correct. To do that, of course, one part of your body—in this case, your ocular imprint—was selected, digitized, and meticulously compared to a billion-gigabyte stock of recorded data.

In the Second Ring, your whole body is used as the comparison "part." Here, the entire body becomes the general parameter from which vital functions are sampled.

PLEASE PLACE YOUR HAND BAGGAGE ON THE OBJECT SCANNER BELT
AND GO TO CONTROL ARCH NUMBER 18-H, FLIGHT 501-48A.
Merci/thank you/gracias/obrigado/spasiba,
Neuro-ocular software, Optrix @ NeuroZone Inc., Denver, CO.
UniWorld

Back to what is real now, via the unreal program of the astroport complex, a tiny cog in the giant metaprogram that governs the organic hominid lives distributed across the planet's surface by the Universal Economic Plan.

The message has just imprinted itself on the surface of the retina, etching itself directly on the optic nerve, and the voice has been redigitalized in his auditory implant—which has, naturally, been left in "open" mode, so as to transmit, again and again, reminders of the written and verbal ordinances that accompanied him during his voyage on supersonic Aeroflot flight 501.

The hall is three hundred meters long and one hundred fifty meters wide. Large windows of Securimax™ metaglass line the bay's right side; through these he can see the takeoffs and landings of hypersonics and zeppelins in the night sky. At the far end is the hangar, which his Russian aero-orbital enters slowly, a gray shadow covered with the sodium-gold zebra stripes of the projector lights that illuminate the arrivals, departures, and control areas in clusters. Red, orange, yellow, and green signal lights line the runways, streaked here and there with bands of quicksilver, whirling among the immense antennae of the Orbital Telecommunications Complex, which sits atop an artificial hill, a pyramidal stone cairn, carpeted by a lawn of identical leaves of grass.

His silhouette makes a vague translucent halo on the windows of the vast bay, beyond which the waning light paints the tall glass towers of the terminal with gold, glinting off the aluminum edges of the MagLev™ suspended monorail as it traces its old-chrome lines eastward in the direction of the high blue hills lining the horizon.

He walks toward the Checkpoint and Security Center; this is Arch 18-H. A small dose of endorphins to quell his anxiety is administered by his limbic nano-implants, which, since they are perfectly "natural" and legal, are not detected by the biophysical scans of the astroport's security system. Below the gangplank the runways form a network of charcoal gray lines where descriptive diagrams run from one end to the other on LED screens planted amid luminous blocks.

The sky is deep violet over a base of turquoise. Clouds split the residual infrared rays whose photons scatter aimlessly in the stratosphere. It is outrageously beautiful, he notes, as if the whole world might disappear in the same way, without the least fear, without the slightest shudder.

The orange arrows and moving walkway have deposited him in front of the airlock on the top floor of the Control Terminal.

Here, he encounters the first human operator.

The human operator is an administrative security officer for the international astroport. He is anonymous despite the fact that his first name, Gregor, followed by an identification number, is inscribed on the small plastic insignia affixed to the lapel of his yellow uniform.

As soon as he is seated in a chair facing the human control officer, who is behind a protective Securimax™ window, Plotkin sees the machine descend from the ceiling, looking like nothing so much as a huge, composite black spider, to grasp his head between its legs and insert a microscanner finer than a human hair into his occipital lobe.

He knows what it's about. His neuro-implants are continuously adapting his memory to the evolving world. The machine is an express polygraph; it will determine whether or not he replies truthfully to the questions the human operator is about to ask, analyzing the variations of the electric current passing through the cells of his nervous system, detecting the infinitesimal organic pulses that accompany his every thought. It is a by-product of the earliest studies on subvocal impulses dating back to the beginning of the century, when the first global control technology appeared with the war.

1) Are you now a member of, or have you ever belonged to, any of the following organizations: NSDAP (the Nazi Party), the Communist Party of America, CCC (Combatant Communist Cells), the Red Brigades, Islamic Jihad, the Armed Islamic Group, the Islamic Resistance Movement (Hamas), the Symbionese Liberation Army, the KKK, the Al-Aqsa Brigade, Jemaah Islamiya, the World Islamic Front for Jihad Against Jews and Crusaders (Al-Qaeda) or any related group (list available on request), the IRA, the Union of Christian Volunteers, the National European Bloc, the Russian Resistance Group, the Patriotic American Force, the Legion of King David, the Catholic Church, the schismatic Presbyterian Church in

America, or the Rebel Protestant Congregation? If yes, check all that apply.

2) Have you ever been found guilty of war crimes, crimes against humanity, or acts of terrorism?
3) Are you currently wanted for nonconformist religious proselytizing?
4) Did you enter American or Canadian territory with hostile intentions?
5) Did you leave your home territory with hostile intentions?
6) Are you the carrier of a virus, bacillus, or other contagious or noncontagious pathogen?
7) Are you transporting a weapon of mass destruction?
8) Are you transporting parts or plans for a weapon of mass destruction?
9) Are you transporting artificial intelligence whose sale is prohibited on land?
10) Are you transporting personal weapons of a type prohibited on pan-American territory?
11) Do you intend to remain illegally after the expiration of your six-month temporary visitor's visa?
12) Have you responded truthfully to all the questions I have just asked you?

NO. NO. NO. NO. NO. NO. NO. NO. NO. NO. NO. YES.

Subsidiary questions for religious control, UHU, Council for Ethical Vigilance:

1) Are you affiliated with a legal religious organization? If yes, which? *The Transnational Association of Worshippers of Nordic Faiths.*
2) Which personal God do you worship? *Ragnar the Viking, avatar of Odin, number A-128457, Official World Catalogue of Names of Personal Divinities.*

Everything here can be controlled, so everything is. In this world, there is no infinity other than the parameter that indicates the improbability of its appearance or, rather, the *probability* that is constantly nullified by the calculators of the human world.

But he passes the test with no difficulty. He does not even have to lie; the new express polygraph model used by the astroport's service cannot detect any abnormal neural activity at the fateful moment of response.

Because, for the moment, he still knows nothing. Or almost nothing.

And it is this fact that reveals that *all has been foreseen.* It has all been studied, planned, programmed.

And yet, in truth, in this territory that he discovers in simultaneity with his own self, none of it has been mapped out in advance. Here, nothing can be charted by the Control Metastructure.

He might be compared to pure white noise; he is simply matter to be molded, broken, corrupted, dissolved, invented. He is in that limbic state that occurs after birth but before the umbilical cord is cut. He is not yet *someone,* in the full sense of the word; that is to say, he is not an autonomous human, even though he possesses a name and a small store of information and emotion that allows him to pass for a living being.

For all intents and purposes, he is even more false than the world surrounding him, but this is what makes him the only *truly solitary* being among the millions of solitary beings that pass through here each day via the stratosphere. This, indeed, is necessary so that he can lie successfully in a world that has become expert in separating fact from falsehood. He must be completely innocent. If he is to deceive the Global Memory of the Control Metastructure, he must have no memory at all.

So it appears that while his false identity is in the process of becoming true, the real world has disappeared and a forgery has taken its place that is so true, so diabolically natural that, as in the Turing test, it is impossible to tell it apart from what was once the human world.

For the world, from now on, will be populated by machines—machines that call themselves men. Like the human security officer who has allowed him access, finally, to the Metropol Network Center, and is already waiting to question the next traveler.

He has left the Control Arch, but he is still under surveillance. The cameras are invisible, tiny devices the size of pinheads lodged in the walls, door latches, lighted signs, television monitors, plasma waste cans, escalator ramps, and elevator floors. They form the myriad facets of a single, monstrous insect eye that watches not so much the individual members of the hive as the entire hive; not so much the people as single sources of information, but the entire crowd as a statistical, relatively predictable system.

It becomes clear that there are other humans present here.

In very large numbers.

We are now inside the United Human Universe, also called Uni-World. We are inside Unimanity.

Everywhere, there are messages reminding us of the federative planetary slogan:

ONE WORLD FOR ALL
ONE GOD FOR EACH
UNITED HUMAN UNIVERSE

The Control Arch of the terminal was silent, empty, immaculate, seemingly peopled only by machines and signs. The kinetic, though, is a showplace of living beings passing through the Network Center en route to their various destinations on the North American continent. But are two places really as different as all that?

Security androids patrol beneath massive halogen-lit ceiling panels. There are some human agents among them, but it is practically impossible to tell them apart except for the insignia they wear—legal devices specifically intended for the information of the Universal Citizen.

Whatever he knows about this world, he does not know where it comes from—for he still knows nothing about himself. It is as if the purely mechanical cogs of this mechanical universe hold no secrets for him.

What he does know is that the Supreme Court is considering a case, Costello vs. Vermont, to determine whether or not a UniPol-approved android policeman can be considered human enough to read the rights of a person it has arrested.

He also knows that an Android Liberation Front has formed somewhere in orbit, that it has already claimed responsibility for a handful of assassinations, and that it is developing a clandestine network for the repatriation of androids in orbit or on the moon to Earth.

He knows, too, how the Collective Intelligence and Control Metastructure of Human UniWorld works; this Unimanity with which it surrounds itself by means of the now intramediary intermediary of its billions and billions of neuro-electronic connections, some of which can be found in this particular international astroport where transoceanic zeppelins, antipodean shuttles, and standard-line North American planes meet and mingle. Where, each day, millions and millions of people—millions and millions of *brains*—cross paths.

He understands all of this with a sort of hard, metallic clarity—an illumination even colder than the vast halogen lights in the aerostation ceilings: Machines have more of a soul than most of the men that swarm ceaselessly on this globe, doing nothing more than keeping those machines in service. They knew how to overthrow us so easily that it was done with a kind of gentleness, and before we knew it we had been dispossessed not only of our world, but of ourselves. And the most thrilling adventure to be had in a world dominated by such a paradigm is the rediscovery of what makes a man human, and of that which the machines so painlessly relieved us: our own *inhumanity.*

That is why he has come here.

That is why he has just left the final checkpoint of the Windsor, Ontario, aerospace terminal, and why he is now heading for the vast mechanical staircases that will take him to the magnetic monorail station and then on to the city of Grand Junction, with its private cosmodrome.

Yes. This is why he is never more than an identity in training. He is part of a secret greater and more terrible than himself. He is part of an infraworld that can be seen only in the traces of death he leaves behind.

He knows, now, why he has come. Come here, to this particular city.

The memory bloc falls together softly in his mind. Fragmented recollections reassemble, accompanied by feelings, simple knowledge, images.

It is enough to let him remember the basic truth: if he has come here, it is to kill a man.

> FIRST OPERATION

This is the MagLev™ suspended monorail.

The unifying slogan of UHU hovers like a huge protoplasmic cloud above the aerostation.

ONE WORLD FOR ALL
ONE GOD FOR EACH

A concrete ramp fitted with superconductive alloy coils traces a clean line away beyond the horizon; a pure geometric quadrant, etched on what looks more like a map than an actual piece of land, a rectilinear serpent, tetanized by an invisible flash, stretches across sixteen hundred kilometers under a spitfire sky, enshrouded by a cloud as dense as molten metal.

By magnetic train, it will take him an hour and a few minutes to reach his destination.

It is an endless thread that uncoils from the enormous complex of the Windsor International Astroport Terminal and winds, via its northeastern line, toward what is left of Montreal—largely abandoned now, thanks to the drastic population drop that has taken place over the last twenty years and the irreversible rise of the salt waters of the Saint Lawrence River—and through the private seaside towns of Labrador and northern Quebec to its terminus. In the other direction, it connects the cities of the Canadian West that were spared by the various chemical, bacteriological, and nuclear attacks of the

Black Years. The line forks, as far as he can tell, around a hundred kilometers northeast of Windsor.

He registers the layout of the local network in his memory. Departure destinations. Arrival schedules. Topological and histological organization of the system. He is still little more than a sponge, a giant antenna capturing every signal within reach.

He walks toward the open air now, across a vast concrete slab that leads to one of the aerostation's MagLev™ platforms, accessible via a number of lifts built into the immense dome that covers the rail station.

It is very hot. His neuroptic environmental analysis system, which posts an LED display on demand in the upper right-hand corner of his field of vision, informs him that it is 8:12 P.M. Eastern Standard Time, and that the temperature is exactly 40 degrees Celsius. His anti-UV thermofuge suit determines that the sun's rays are of the usual strength for this latitude at this time of year.

Everything is completely normal. The World is dissolving.

The high-speed train is a long, bronze-colored serpent of anodized aluminum. It is perfectly silent as it glides along the boarding platform. Its electric doors hum softly as they slide open; the tiny sound resonates in the vast subterranean hall, built to protect against nuclear attack.

Like all the technological objects he has seen since his arrival in this world, the high-speed train seems to represent a kind of paradox, a link, "the glue that holds the world together." Here, the more recent the technology, the older it seems; the newer it is, the less efficient it appears. There is a strange sort of reverse progress here, he notes. The older man gets, the less he knows how to do.

The high-speed train, for example, is around twenty-five years old. It represents a crest—a cliff—a summit in railway engineering. But it is *the last train;* after this one, there will probably be no more.

According to what the data sent by the instruction program tells him, almost no more serious scientific research exists that might help the technology to progress in the years to come. The high-speed train is, then, the apogee of human knowledge—a machine that is already nearly obsolete, with no successor in sight.

At top speed, the train will glide at almost six hundred kilometers per hour on its magnetically cushioned monorail. Such speed was an achievement twenty-five years ago. Soon it will seem like a miracle; after that, it will seem impossible.

During the voyage, the rest of his memory implants, which have remained deliberately inactive until now, will release their stores of information and thus complete the making of this Man who has come here to kill another man.

The first coil begins to unwind, and he learns that his Russian cortical nanocomputer, bought from the mafia, is a pirated derivative of the "secret defense" neuroprobe used by the combat team controllers of the United American Republics' Aerospace Force. Logically, the technology went unrecognized by the astroport's security systems. It passed the test. It is essential—and quite fascinating.

The next thing he learns is that, over the next few days, this biocomputer will autodevelop within his nervous system, giving him a complete ensemble of neuroportable weapons. The modifications will take place at night while he sleeps; he won't feel a thing.

The World—*in*. The World—*out*. His personality autoforms. Cortical *bootstrap* under the tungsten ramps of the magnetic train's corridors. He is Sergei Diego Plotkin. He just arrived at Windsor's international astroport en route to Grand Junction. He is carrying clandestine technology. And he must execute a man.

The compartment door slides open when he swipes his UniPol-approved intelligent travel card. He sits down in the window seat registered under his name.

Immediately, one of his nanomemory implants issues a warning. *The Order has ensured that your first-class, high-security, four-seat compart-*

ment will be empty. Do not talk to anyone, except in case of force majeure, during your trip to Grand Junction.

He has no idea which Order this refers to, but no matter. He knows that he will be traveling alone.

The wide glass windows give an expansive view of the world outside: an unlit, iron-gray sky supports the horizon-scratching high tension wires of Hydro-Québec; it forms an ashy dome over the remnants of an industrial-age aluminum city, long abandoned, with an enormous, oxide-scorched sign bearing the letters ALCAN on a rust-streaked blue triangle. The scene hovers in the foreground for an instant. A deserted road cuts a rectilinear line through its center.

The scenery of southeastern Canada unrolls in fleeting, overlapping lines, intercut by successive flashes of recollection, at almost three hundred meters per second.

The plains are blue in the twilight air. They quiver gently all the way to the banks of Lake Ontario, whose waves roll away beyond the line of the horizon, disappearing into the pale, green-lit sky.

Childhood. The courtyard of a dilapidated tenement for career soldiers, where the idle children of an unpaid army play soccer in the overheated August air.

"Boris!" cries one of the children. "Pass, Boris, pass!"

"Sergei, are you crazy?" replies the echo of another voice.

The second voice whirls in the glittering emptiness of a Catholic-school afternoon. It is a Catherine wheel of metallic spokes shrieking in tandem effort, while a ribbon of gray asphalt, seeming to fill every inch of space, unwinds in a long stone-colored spool.

Here he is, riding his old bicycle through the suburbs of Novosibirsk. He is twelve or thirteen years old. Tall metal chimneys, grouped in enormous tubular polypods, jut into the sulfur-colored sky. Petrochemical factories send their undulating flares toward the horizon like banners of war in an industrial crusade already lost. He is a Russian child; it is the beginning of the twenty-first century. He knows his country squandered everything during the preceding century. He knows his people are slowly disappearing. He knows that in this downtrodden world, big dreams don't have a chance.

Objective vision: an unused electronuclear power plant on the Ontario–New York state border. It has been abandoned for more than twenty years, like many industrial facilities in the area, a neural implant tells him knowingly. The postwar world is much like an interminable prewar one; all Unimanity seems resigned to the slow death of the globuscule. The ultimate depletion is so close that each individual thing shines with the intense light of extinction, just as stars glow brightest before going nova, then supernova. Nature may have been pushed aside by ecoglobal planning, but human cities are turning back into jungles: half-petrified virgin forests in the stagnant water of this unified human world, barely distinguishable from what remains of the natural wilderness around them, or from the out-of-control efflorescence running riot in the deserted streets, the silent highways; the empty buildings, shopping centers, and subway stations.

In these dead cities, cities abandoned by men, nature has become savage again, escaping the automated cycles and engineers of geo-global planning. It is the last vestige of liberty left by technology to the world of *Homo sapiens*. It does not lack a certain tragic beauty.

So, *he is* Sergei Diego Plotkin.

But who is Sergei Diego Plotkin?

Why is he here, on this train? *Why am I here, on this train,* he asks himself.

To kill a man, that is certain. But who? And why? For whom? *With* whom?

A flying advertisement has just plastered itself to the train window. The intelligent follicle of celluloid has somehow—he has no idea how—found its way here. It is a message from a Catholic station outlawed by the UHU's Council for Ethical Vigilance and cites the

words of the Gospel of John about the Antichrist in small lumines-
cent phrases that tremble a little in the prism of the Securimax™
glass: *He is king of the sons of pride.*

The clandestine prospectus is finally detected by the MagLev™'s
internal network, and a small electrostatic discharge breaks its hold
on the metaglass. It disappears as quickly as if swallowed by an abrupt
depressurization.

The UHU doesn't toy with that sort of deviance.

Plotkin orders a light meal on the compartment's console; a
young Filipino Amtrak employee brings it to him a few minutes later.
He swallows the pieces of transgenic sushi mechanically while the
console, set to automatic mode, shows him the news on a screen set
into the wall opposite him, part of the luxury cabin's internal network. It is set to CNN-MTV's *News of the Hour,* and text of the latest
headlines scroll laterally by in a translucent gray band while an ethically approved erotic video clip plays in the background; two adolescent girls, barely out of puberty, sing in the rain amid fences and
blank walls while an apathetic crowd watches. They are a revival of
the group Tatu, a pair of young, Russian, faux-lesbian girls produced
by Trevor Horn in the early 2000s. He is certain of all of this, down
to the smallest detail, without knowing why.

ONGOING NEGOTIATIONS FOR THE RATIFICATION OF THE TREATY
OF ODESSA REMAIN STALLED OVER THE SAME QUESTIONS, a UHU representative, Mr. Zordaiev, informs us from the edge of the Black Sea.
See Hyperpage 12-A for the interview with our special correspondent in Odessa. . . .

PRISCILLA PRESLEY III AND JENNIFER SLOANE-BARTOW, QUEEN OF
AUSTRALIAN WINE, ON THE BRINK OF DIVORCE, says the *Pacific En-
quirer.* Click to enter Hyperpage . . .

TURKMENISTAN SIGNS AN ACCORD OF COOPERATION WITH TEXAS,
New Petroleum Industries Syndicate said yesterday. . . .

MOROCCAN, LIBYAN, EGYPTIAN, LEBANO-SYRIAN, AND TURKISH
TROOPS EN ROUTE TO MARSEILLE TO AID EUROFEDERALIST FORCES IN

THEIR FIGHT AGAINST DISSIDENT ISLAMIC GUERRILLAS, Reuters-AP reports. . . .

ISLAMIC EUROPEAN FORCES HAVE ISSUED A STATEMENT FROM THEIR LONDON HEADQUARTERS THAT THEY WILL NOT ACCEPT ANY GOVERN-MENT OTHER THAN ONE THAT IS SUBJECT TO SHARI'A LAW; THEIR BEL-GIAN AND FRENCH COUNTERPARTS HAVE FOLLOWED SUIT, says our special correspondent in the United Kingdom. . . .

THE 3,227 UNCLONED CHIHUAHUAS OF FORMER TV STAR OPRAH WINFREY, NOW 100 YEARS OLD, HAVE BEEN SOLD TO AN ANONYMOUS WEALTHY COLLECTOR ON BEHALF OF A FOUNDATION TO PROTECT NATURAL ANIMALS; see link to *Century Stardom Magazine*. . . .

THE AUTONOMOUS COMMUNIST GOVERNMENT OF WEST NEPAL WILL FORMALLY JOIN THE UHU SOMETIME NEXT YEAR; the UHU's representative for Asia, Mrs. Chou Wei-Ling, has publicly expressed her happiness with the decision. . . .

THE WORLDWEATHER FIRM, WHICH HAS BEEN IN CONTROL OF GLOBAL CLIMATE FOR THE LAST FOUR YEARS, HOPES THAT ITS RECOM-MENDATIONS WILL BE FOLLOWED BY THE UHU'S SCIENTIFIC COMMIS-SION. According to Mr. Juan-Carlos Silverstone, president of the Planetary Climate Control Consortium, primary contractors should be allowed to choose their regional subcontractors without being subject to the bureaucracy of the Office of Governance. "A little flex-ibility in the system would probably prevent some of the malfunc-tions we have encountered lately," he asserts in a recent interview with *Forbes* magazine; see link to *Global Economics Review*. . . .

PEACE ACCORDS WITH THE VATICAN DO NOT MEAN THAT TRADI-TIONAL JUDEO-CHRISTIAN RELIGIONS WILL BE REAUTHORIZED. Mrs. Xenakis, the spokeswoman for the UniGlobal Department of Reli-gious Affairs, firmly dispelled these "unfounded and fantasist rumors" yesterday from her office in Singapore. "Only the agreement with the Islamic Conference will permit some UHU territories a degree of tolerable religious autonomy with UniWorld." Her statement was echoed by the Official Papacy of the United Human Catholic Church from its Holy See in San Francisco: "Simply because the Vatican and the traditionalist Antipope will be accepted at a few political conferences concerning the fate of the former Italy does not mean that we will accept a return of the Catholic Church to the dark days of the Inquisition and the Crusades. . . ."

ACCORDING TO GENERAL STATISTICS, THE AVERAGE FERTILITY RATE AMONG HUMAN MALES REMAINS FIXED AT AROUND 10% OF POTENT SPERMATOZOA. GLOBAL POPULATION SHRINKAGE WILL NOT BE STOPPED BEFORE THE END OF THE CENTURY, EVEN WITH THE MOST MODERN CLONING AND NON—Y CHROMOSOME FERTILIZATION TECHNIQUES. The scientific division of the Office of Governance confirmed in a report released yesterday that the global population will shrink by the record amount of around 1.5 billion people over the next fifteen to twenty years, returning global demographic levels to the same figures as twenty-five years ago. The percentage of males in the population is expected to drop dramatically to less than 41 percent of the current worldwide figure, or less than 30 percent. See link to *Science Global Review*. . . .

ADRIAN-LOUISE VON TIMBERLECK, ANDROGYNOUS HIP-HOP PORNO MEGASTAR, SELLS ITS SCOTTISH CASTLE, HALF OF ITS SHARES IN THE FIRM BIOTECH NEONICS, AND ALL OF ITS CALIFORNIAN, CANADIAN, AND HAWAIIAN PROPERTIES TO PURCHASE A HIGH-SECURITY FLOATING CITY IN ASSOCIATION WITH JOANNA-CAROLINE TRUMP AND THE CHINESE GENETICS TYCOON MR. WEN LU-CHAN. See Hyperpage 6 for the story from our special envoy to the Maputo naval shipyards. . . .

The world in a few minutes of magnetic ribbon. The world in a dozen sentences. The world in a few short paragraphs. After the news comes a short commercial for Amtrak; images of a silent train against the enchanting backdrop of the British Columbian Rocky Mountains. . . .

This, it seems, is the plan's predetermined signal. The signal to activate the last inactive cells. Another rhizome, another coil of memory, unwinds itself. Several million neurons are suddenly freed from his subconscious black box and unleashed in a spray of cortical molecules.

It is an entire library, one that was hidden away deep in his own brain. It is an entire life that now, finally, takes shape.

It is an entire network of meanings that combine to give what previously had been nothing more than a mass of organs the appearance, the structure, the *body* of a life.

It is an entire history placed suddenly in his hands, in the quicksilver fire of electric light and high speed.

First, the Siberian childhood in Novosibirsk under the steely post-Soviet sky is abruptly supplanted by images of a gripping underworld. These new memories are no less vivid than the earlier ones: light, neon, lead glass, stars in the electric night, alcohol, dope, dancing, nightclubs, cash, girls, sex, big money, power, more neon, more lead glass, more stars, more girls, more sex. The scene whirls in his head for several seconds; it is as if an entire life—or, more accurately, an entire postadolescence—passes before his eyes.

What was that? *Hello?* He wants to shout at the instruction program. *Rewind the tape; show me again—I couldn't quite catch all of it. . . .*

He heard English being spoken; he is sure of that much. Did he recognize parts of London somewhere in there? Hadn't he caught a glimpse of Leicester Square? And the cars—shit, they were Jaguars, weren't they, or classic Aston Martins? And the girls . . . typically British beauties at first; Celto-Saxons, brunettes with gray-blue eyes streaked with pale green, and the famous dentistry, teeth a bit prominent . . . and then—yes, the carnival had become more worldly; the scenes had been from all over: Latin America, South Africa, Central Asia, Iran, Russia, Japan . . .

Money. Drugs. Sex. The polar opposite of his gray childhood in the stricken Siberia of the 2010s. How did the boy of twelve, pedaling on his battered bicycle, become the young man of twenty, driving an E-type Jaguar down a Sussex country road with four supermodels along for the ride?

What *is* this?

His question hangs, unanswered.

An individual person is also a singular entity interwoven into the continuum of history, with a lineage all his own, but the instruction program's neuro-implants give him only scanty information in this area. He knows nothing of his parents other than their names, which are part of his basic ID file, and he has no idea if he has brothers, sisters, uncles, cousins. . . . Born in 2001, Sergei has known nothing but war: the Grand Jihad. It is the only thing in his memory that makes any sense—albeit in a detached, historical way. Dates, figures, events. Almost five hundred million deaths in four decades. Twenty-five metropolises razed by nuclear bombardment, six on the North American continent and a dozen in the Russian Federation. More than a hundred of the world's large cities destroyed in various ways: radium bombs, chemical attacks, bacterial warfare . . . not to mention the countless smaller towns and villages ravaged by the Great Planetary Civil War. Even now, on the periphery of the unified world, men are still being killed with machine guns, and with bombs, and by hand. Some countries were simply and completely wiped from the map. And only now were the tens, no, the *hundreds* of millions of indirectly caused deaths being realized, for as postwar spirits had risen, so had global temperatures, bringing their own insidious brand of catastrophe.

After finishing his studies, about which he still remembers very little, it seems that he joined one of the numerous paramilitary security and counterespionage organizations thriving on the postwar globe: the Red Star Order. Formed by former career Soviet and post-Soviet Red Army officers, and with bases in California and South America, the Order had quickly risen to the top of the ranks of high-tech transnational companies, renting the services of its cyborg samurai to paragovernmental shoguns and techno-mafiosi; they were moving shadows; barely detectable, elite mercenaries in tight digital flux; assassins in constant competition in the new planetary world created by the UHU—this new feudal world forged by the fires of the Grand Jihad, even after it was supposedly long over. In truth, the war had never really ended. It could not end. There was nothing now but a world slowly collapsing to the rhythm of its own technospherical unification, a world surviving only through terror, espionage, nexuses, and biological special effects.

The man had had his back turned to him for a long time now, standing in front of a large bay window dominated by a view of Lake Baikal. The waters were deepest blue, ultramarine striped with myriad shades of cobalt, and they filled the entire lower half of the window. Above them, the sky was a fiery, blinding yellow. The scene was as pure as a religious icon.

The man had turned toward him once more now, but in Plotkin's newly reawakened memory his face remained hazy, the distinctive features blurred by an encrypted neurodigital procedure. In all probability, he would never have been able to identify the face anyway, even with the aid of cortical nanosurgery. There are things one knows just by guessing them; it is what is generally called "intuition," but it is only the simple act of letting people figure you out.

"You will act completely alone until the time of your retrieval. You will receive a large bonus for it—*if* you are successful.

"Your client will pay a *very* large bonus just for him. You will need to be very sure that all the data is in order. If something doesn't match up, I will drop the whole thing immediately. I will keep the advance to cover costs and damages; you will keep the rest, and no one will be able to accuse me of breaking the contract. There, you've been warned. My lawyers in Micronesia have a copy of your papers; they'll take care of everything. You don't kill the mayor of a large American city without taking a lot of big risks these days.

"He's only an Indian, and it's not really *that* big of a city. You'll hardly even be on U.S. soil, really—or Canadian soil, for that matter. Consider it a sort of extraterritorial zone; they call it autonomous territory. Believe me, you won't do any better than seventy-five-thousand Pan-Am dollars plus expenses these days."

"If you want me to act alone, you'd better be prepared for a lot of expenses; I'm telling you that right now. I'm going to have to grease a lot of palms."

"You don't need to worry about that. You'll act alone, and you'll develop your own plan, but we'll be in charge of the overall scheme."

"What do you mean?"

"You'll receive one—*one*—communiqué during your trip. That will be your only help from the outside. I don't know what the e-mail will say, or when it will be sent to you. But I do know that it will give you a substantial advantage over the other guy's security system. Don't ask me any more than that. All the information is locked up tighter than a tomb."

"That's a good beginning. You know I'll be taking an antipod shuttle to the American East Coast, or maybe a simple supersonic—it doesn't matter—but then I'll have to get past more than one checkpoint in one of the highest-security astroports in the world, and I don't mean your stronghold. I'm talking about the Windsor Astroport Complex."

"I told you, don't worry. Everything's been taken care of. You'll see; you'll slide through it like a neutrino passing through a cloud."

"I'd like a more specific answer, if you don't mind. I guess I don't know as much about neutrinos as I should."

The man, whom he knows only as Vassily, had grinned widely at that.

The grin has stayed with him, suspended in the blank space of a face without an identity. Lewis Carroll's Cheshire cat seems vastly more human in comparison.

In his memory, the grin speaks again. "We've planned everything to make sure you succeed," it says. "We are prepared to pay you more money than you can possibly imagine.

"With your permission, we are going to remake you completely."

Later, as he walked through the city streets toward the great lake, he requested an optic download of several maps and video and photographic documents from databases in Canada. By the time he reached the lakeshore, he had, in the right corner of his stereo-optic screen, photos of the Great Lakes that identically matched what he would have seen with his normal vision.

As the high-speed train glides silently along on its cushion of air, a sudden realization strikes him: according to his newly reactivated memory, he had sat on a bank of the promenade lining the gray and pink pebbled beach, against the backdrop of hills ringing the bay with its crenellated cliffs and peaks, dotted here and there with old, half-ruined Soviet-era buildings and the new structures erected to support the tourism that had been revived over the past fifty years thanks to global warming and, more recently, the "official" end of the Grand Jihad. Now, as he superimposes the plains of the American-Canadian border, here between Quebec and Ontario, on the Siberian landscape of his recollections, the two sets of images seem almost identical. Or—are there really *four* images? Two split universes—two spaces, two times? There is the original one, implanted in his memory cells, which seems to unwind in tandem with the train's magnetic suspension track, but which also appears to contain the image of Lake Baikal that now imprints itself so strongly on top of the view out the window. And there are the new images too, the ones so unlike the view outside the train, that stem from the memories he has just remembered. . . .

His reactivated memory now allows him to access data about the world, data that the instruction program sent him several days earlier, but that has only now risen to the surface of his "awareness." It is an impossible paradox: through his memories, he is receiving information that he will only understand later on, and that will superimpose itself on the "real" world flashing by outside the train windows. It is called "inclusive feedback," the instruction program tells him, as it simultaneously incites the synthesis of a particular endorphin that will keep him from falling into a state of parapsychotic crisis.

The topological similarity between the two worlds naturally strengthens this reciprocal inclusion of reactivated memory and "real" world data. He moves as if interfacing between two barely distinct mirror images in space and time. There, in Siberia, sitting still on the shores of Lake Baikal. Here, speeding toward steppes newly created by global warming. And now, passing vast lakes, immense flat plains, forests of birch and conifer separated by wider and wider stretches of open space . . .

And the local Baikonur at the end of the journey.

While walking on the beaches of Lake Baikal, he had studied the data provided by the Corp—all the data available on the contract hit, down to the color of his boxer shorts, and everything about Grand Junction, the private city he ran.

But that he was not supposed to run for much longer.

His memory implants had downloaded the equivalent of an entire dictionary into his brain at superhuman speed, while he waited for Vassily and his men to take him to the Order's laboratory, where he would undergo transgenic reforming and the imposition of partial amnesia before being flown to Windsor, Ontario.

Now, while the outside world unfurled like a series of concentric waves of which he was the temporary center, the foundations of his personality appeared, tracing the specific topography of his psyche as if weaving a semantic plot ceaselessly reflecting this end of the limitless world.

The memories themselves are black boxes, full of secret operations, clandestine information, gestating crimes, and twists that defy common sense.

His personality itself, with the exception of the information planted there by the neuronal instruction program, is undoubtedly formed of a daring and inexplicable mixture of real and false memories. He has several lives in one, but none of them is complete. Nothing is true or false any longer. But there is at least a general schema in place now, shaping his view of the world and of himself.

He is a hired killer en route to Grand Junction, this city-cosmodrome, this vast Amerindian territory where spatial industry is in the hands of private entrepreneurs, insane businessmen, and the Amerindian gambling mafiosi.

It is the derelict Las Vegas of the Orbital Paradise, the last Free City, the newest Space Boomtown. It is the last private point of entry to the High Frontier left on North American soil.

He has been sent there to kill a man named Orville Blackburn.

Orville Blackburn is the Mohawk mayor of Grand Junction. He is rich, powerful, well protected. He will not be an easy target. But this man has broken some promise to the largest Russo-American mafia in the northeast.

He is a dead man.

The train is passing by an abandoned section of highway. A few grain silos stand in the distance like zeppelins vertically suspended by reverse gravity. The landscape is flat. The sky is deep indigo. Night is falling.

Soon he will arrive at his destination.

> *THE HOTEL LAIKA*

The Grand Junction high-speed-train station is a cosmopolitan shambles where the crowds throng like a human octopus in a city immediately reminiscent of Babel—that is, a mixture of Nero's Rome and Hollywood Boulevard.

He shuts down most of his multifrequency circuits almost at once, unable to deal with the onslaught of audible and inaudible signals of a million different types and from a million different sources.

In the few minutes it takes him to get off the high-speed train, reach the immense main hall via a series of squeaky old escalators, and pass through a teeming galaxy of humanity under the hall's vast neobyzantine dome toward the lot where the robotaxis are parked, he counts at least twenty-five different languages. He has met or seen thousands of people; seen smiles and smirks, lips tightly pursed or wide open in expressions of expectation, surprise, anger; faces stressed, impatient, neutral, and joyous. He has heard countless sorts of exclamations, laughs, quarrels, and idioms superimposed on one another in a strange Baroque symphony composed of every expletive on Earth.

The first thing he notices is the large number of "body tuners"—devotees of genetic transformation. His implant informs him that Grand Junction has a continent-wide reputation as one of the capitals of the biotech underground. Anything can be found there; anything can be bought. Or sold.

Especially bodies. Human bodies. For reasons the implant leaves unclear, the city and particularly a few of its "hot spots" serve as a refuge for all the body-tuning devotees who lack the means to obtain a true trans-G transformation cure in China or Australia.

If that is the case, they come here and are operated on—for still quite substantial sums—by charlatans and doctors speedily trained in barely approved African medical schools who end most months working for one or another of the local mafias. Perhaps unsurprisingly, there are more than a few "damaged" among the transgenic population of Grand Junction.

He passes several compact groups of international tourists duly escorted by their guides/bodyguards, noting among the atomized crowd the pointillist presence of "untouchables" in the terminal—the people who are not even allowed to enter the arrival area; they stand scattered and immobile, solitary in the midst of the interminable dance of humans in transit. He notes the recurring presence of genetic monsters among them—this time "naturals," born of chromosomal mutations caused by various changes in the environment and in man himself. These natural genetic monsters are considered lower than low in Grand Junction; even a body tuner whose seedy operation has been a spectacular failure is considered to be higher on the ladder, because his/her body still has some market value. At the Metabolism and Organ Commodity Exchange, genetic monsters born of this regression of humanity are not even rated as high as slaves— which is to say, objects—since in most cases their deformities render them virtually incapable of performing the smallest task. For a long time, Grand Junction's human garbage tried to survive in the darkest and most isolated corners of the station, relentlessly hunted by the city's sanitary police, before being finally shoved to the periphery, where, it is said, they all ultimately disappeared, kidnapped by some gang of renegade doctors or a mafia black-market clinic that quickly harvested whatever parts might be recyclable.

He also meets two very beautiful women. The first is a piquant brunette with green eyes and a Louise Brooks haircut, translucent frontal antennae, and pointed ears like Peter Pan. She loiters coquettishly on the balcony of a small cafeteria filled with newly arrived travelers, selling drinks laced with various meta-amphetamines that are legal in the autonomous Mohawk territory. He comes across the other girl a bit later, their paths crossing as he descends the wide escalators—whose green walls remind him, falsely or not, of an old swimming pool from his childhood—on his way to the enormous exit hall. She is a young blonde, hair knotted in an upturned plume, blue eyes vibrant with bemused intelligence, dressed sportily but with the grace of a woman who can wear anything and look good in it. She bears no obvious outward signs of transgenic modification, but that is meaningless—indeed, Plotkin knows this better than anyone.

Their eyes meet briefly, just for the time it takes for a bird to die of exhaustion in full flight. Then their paths diverge forever, like atoms scattered in outer space.

The city map is a prosthetic extension of his memory, superimposing itself on the concrete reality of the thousands of individuals who converge and diverge here, in a machine without even the slightest remainder of human tissue.

So he knows that the Grand Junction terminal is not the *real* terminal; not really the end of the road.

The real terminal is the cosmodrome itself. It's on the other side of the city—actually, the other side of the county. There are direct lines of communication between the arrival station and the departure astroport, but they are only for maintenance, security, or people possessing special puce cards approved by the Municipal Consortium that manages the city and spatial activity.

From the Enterprise train station, where, under immense holograms of the mythic *Star Trek* vessel as well as an enormous replica of the prototype shuttle with the same name built by the Americans in the late 1970s, the MagLev™ monorail line crosses paths with the old Amtraks of Canadian National, and from the Enterprise aerostation, where the giant zeppelins of the regular transamerican lines hover alongside electric airplanes belonging to this or that genetic-engineering tycoon, thousands of men and women stream each day. Of this teeming mass, very few will reach their true destination—the sharp point of their destiny. The cosmodrome. *Cape Gagarin.*

For it is not so easy to gain access to this Holy of Holies itself, even with tickets costing 75,000, 125,000, or even 250,000 Pan-Am dollars apiece, according to whether you choose to travel on an old, rebuilt Soyuz with an antique Atlas Centaur shoved up its ass or, even worse, a locally built fireball perched atop a fifty-year-old Japanese H-4, or an ancient American orbital shuttle purchased from NASA and partially refitted, or a Texican airplane-missile hybrid, or a good old Chinese capsule from the twenties coupled to a modern Brazilian launcher.

No, even before you obtain this ticket, the price of which is fixed according to a complex reckoning system approved by the UHU, you must often wait for years. Therein lies the guile of the economy that regulates the city. Some people have been waiting since the private cosmodrome opened, when the space industry had not yet been crushed by global terrorism, and when the Amerindian and Russo-American mafias, intelligently located in a transborder territory with lax legal standards, were attracting investors, capital, and research centers in droves. Even before the Windsor International Astroport was completed, more than thirty-five years ago. It might truthfully be said, in fact, that many people died before they were ever able to leave for the High Frontier.

He learns all this as he walks through the aerostation; he learns it while the topological network of the disaster sketches itself in his brain; he learns it as he travels toward the darkest night that has fallen on Earth.

The enormous discrepancy between supply and demand had

been amplified by the horrors of the Grand Jihad, its psychological consequences, and the progressive abandonment of "unused" space by bloated government bureaucracies.

There had been some who had tried to survive on makeshift boats, reclamation freighters, unused or pirated offshore platforms in international waters turned into shelters for stateless refugees of ethnic conflict, or even houses floating just off coastlines submerged by rising ocean waters. Others had abandoned the traditional large cities, riddled as they were with every type of civil disorder, for what remained of nature—but this too had soon been corrupted, full of knots of humanity; enormous, metastasizing shantytowns with ever-changing borders; nomadic colonies of Recyclo™ particleboard folding houses swarming like so many ants and devouring trees, earth, and water as they went.

And then there had been those who attempted to take their chances up there in the Ring.

Of course, not *everything* was entirely ruined here below, because UniWorld would have nothing left to manage if the world ended. But—and Plotkin asked himself if the feeling might possibly be shared by anyone else on the planet—the overall impression was definitely that *something had been seriously fucked up.*

Why had the giant cartels left the High Frontier? Only the military and the media sent satellites there now. Only the Global Control Bureau—the UHU militia—maintained a handful of stations in circumterrestrial or circumlunar orbit. True, aerospace companies had ended up developing supersonic planes, then transatmospheric ones that could fly businessmen and tourists from Helsinki to Buenos Aires in an hour, but all large-scale space-colonization projects had been frozen during the war, and never taken up again.

Only a few adventurous souls and mafia associations had persevered.

Space had become a true Far West, a *Far Sky,* a Frontier that the paltry legal provisions of the UHU Space Development Authority could never hope to regulate. By definition, the Frontier was marginal. It did not move; the margin would remain the margin, and the World was at no risk for change. And one could assume, without too much chance of being mistaken, that the World understood things would remain as they were for a long time to come.

The bureaucrats of the Global Governance Bureau, who were in charge of Unimanity and the institutions of the UHU, lost all interest in any subsequent development in the Ring. The only thing that mattered was that it did not interfere with daily civil and military operations, global telecommunications, or social and climatic control satellites.

It was strange, this feeling that in fact the twenty-first century was the first one in which not only had human history more or less stopped, it had actually begun to move in reverse. The state of the space industry, one hundred years after the launch of *Sputnik I,* was unequivocally characteristic of the state of everything, and in any case, there was no equivalent to the current atmosphere of decadence in the long history of human empires.

For UniWorld, a few eccentric billionaires and a pack of dingoes trying to shut themselves up inside a pressurized sardine can while continuing to pay taxes to the Universal Fiscal Agency might just as well have wanted to hold transsexual orgies on the moon; they were free citizens, after all, well informed of the dangers involved in any temporary or permanent move outside natural human surroundings. UniWorld disavowed any legal or moral responsibility, and serenely continued to tax them.

Order reigned, all the better for there being none.

Anarchy begins immediately outside the Enterprise aerostation.

He quickly realizes that this is the city's principal source of wealth, and that it is necessary to maintain the system of waiting and selection, as well as ironfisted control over ticket prices, in order to conserve the dynamic of this chaos, this inexhaustible source of power and money.

For in this state of chaos, as in all others, "freedom" is only a contingency of necessity. He doesn't yet know where this primal intuition comes from, but it makes his spirit tingle. When disorder is allowed to be society's guiding principle, the social engine ends by breaking down completely; both the explosive matter that initiates propulsion and the basic structure that maintains coherent operation fall apart. This permits rapid and very substantial gains—people depend on liberty, which is bound to necessity; people depend on voluntary servitude. People depend on *desire*.

It is volatile fuel to depend on, fuel that makes the world itself volatile too.

So here there is a blazing new motor—or, rather, the perfect appearance of one. It is really a simulacrum, where hundreds of thousands of human shadows move through a lovely cavern that hides the walls of an immense strongbox.

So this is Grand Junction. It sweeps you away in a flood of human desire; it is monistic, pure, terribly active, foaming in thousands of individual droplets and dashing itself against the walls of civilization. It is a huge brothel turned toward the stars. It is a lottery, a circus act that has become a true piece of the World. That has become a society.

Rapidly, letting his neuro-implants gather a few more bits of information as he navigates the different floors of Enterprise, he realizes that a "ticket to ride," as they say here, for an orbital flight is worthless in itself, even at the price of a quarter of a million on a high-security launcher. It is not for one of these that all these people have waited years, some until they died, crammed into capsule motels and collapsible shantytowns, luxury hotels and casinos, squalid streets and neoclassical villas; it is not for one of these that they are ready to steal, kill, humiliate, be humiliated, cheat, corrupt, lie, hate, love. It is for a document made of cloned recyclable cellulose, courtesy of UniGlobal Recyclo™, a piece of yellow paper called the Golden Track.

The Golden Track is an official document duly stamped by the

UHU—which of course keeps a copy of the number—that author-izes you to be a permanent resident in the Orbital Ring, and to apply for a flight to one of the lunar stations or Martian colonies that was lucky enough to gain autonomy during the Grand Jihad. The Golden Track lets you rent or buy, in cash, lease, or rent to own—with the amount and type of transaction clearly stated—a UHU-approved habitation module of one type or another, before you are assigned to one or another of the colonies of orbital stations grouped in star-shaped clusters that make up the Orbring, the Orbital Ring. Without this UHU-approved piece of paper, there is no point in leaving for the Ring; no one will be there waiting for you, and you will be automat-ically reshuffled into the waiting crowd. You must go through the en-tire corrupt bureaucratic, technocratic process before you can even hope to obtain one of these yellow slips; and if you want to make sure you have even a slight chance to get one, it is in your best interest to pre-buy your place right away. The waiting list is very, very long, you see, and that is how Grand Junction prospers so easily, by fixing ticket prices while interminably drawing out the process of getting one of these passports to the sky.

To the pioneers waiting to leave for outer space, for one private cosmodrome or another, this bright yellow paper with blue printing on it is also known as a claim.

The language spoken in Grand Junction is often translated into dozens of dialects from all over the world, but its basis is Anglo-Saxon, the lingua franca of the twentieth century and the first half of the twenty-first (after that, various bits of Chinese slang had entered the mix). In this language particular to the Cosmograd terminal, there are expressions from the frontier mythology of the mid-nineteenth century—that time of steam locomotives and Colt Single Action guns, and cowboys and Indians. The conquerors and the con-quered.

All around him, as he makes his way through the milling crowd at the aerostation exit, between vast concrete-composite pillars made to resemble Minoan columns, the name of that bright yellow paper with blue printing resonates in almost every language on Earth: the Golden Track. The *Sentier d'Or*. The *Pista de Oro*.

For Plotkin, the fact that Grand Junction had been able to flourish on "federal indigenous territory"—an Amerindian reserve covering the equivalent of several counties, and straddling the American-Canadian border, no less—was in no way the result of mere chance.

As he picks his way toward the robotaxi station, little by little the tableau comes together. Through the light evening fog, he thinks that he can make out the wavering bunches of city lights. He has an odd feeling that he has not yet been told everything about himself or about this world. He knows, somehow, that this is only the beginning.

He knows that he is going to like Grand Junction enough to be able to kill its mayor without the slightest twinge of guilt.

You must pray as if everything depends on God, and act as if everything depends on us.

The words were those of Bossuet, a French Catholic author from the Great Century; some attributed them to Ignatius Loyola. Why had the instruction program revealed them to him? Why were they contained at all in a clandestine neuro-implant? Why had he remembered them only now?

It was an amusing enigma, like the face of a woman seen in an aerostation crowd. It seemed to have nothing at all to do with his present situation: the robotaxi gliding toward the city; the wide circular avenue running around the periphery of the county in three main branches, each bearing the name of one of the mythical early American space conquests. To the west, Mercury Drive. To the north, the vast curve of Apollo Drive. To the east, Gemini Drive, where he finds himself at the moment, a vast ribbon of concrete regularly dotted with tunnels. The drive is, he notes, a good way to see various parts of the city, lit in successive sequences by the Toyota robotaxi's orange sodium lights. As they pass the head of Von Braun Heights, he catches glimpses of the cosmodrome itself, with its hangars and its three takeoff runways, one of which is currently awaiting the arrival of a rebuilt Russian Protron resting on its crawler, a sort of giant rover, moving toward the pad from its warehouse at two kilometers per hour.

The second platform is empty at the moment, though he can see the movements of human activity on it, and vehicles, and flashing lights—perhaps there has just been a takeoff? On the third and far-thest platform, a replica of a twentieth-century American shuttle points its black muzzle toward the sky, mounted bravely atop the bomb of hydrogen and liquid oxygen that is the enormous fuel tank, wreathed in plumes of greenish smoke that waver in the glare of the spotlights.

"Monolith Hills," he had told the robotaxi's verbal interface as he slid into the violet vinyl backseat, with its myriad tiny rips from which protruded nubs of piss yellow foam.

His neuroprogram had informed him of the exact address only a few seconds earlier, while he stood with his hand pressed to the taxi door's keypad decoder. The Toyota was orange, the color of the Grand-C-Cabs company, and an old Pink Floyd song, "Interstellar Overdrive," had started up along with the engine. Excellent choice, but it was a remake, not the original; a cover by a robotized Japanese chamber music quartet.

He had been surprised to discover this knowledge within him-self, unaided by the instruction program. Was it part of his original personality?

The remake wasn't very good—he was sure of that, in any case—and he eventually asked the robotaxi to either turn down the volume or find another station. A second later, the strains of a Sinatra tune had flowed comfortably through the car.

Now he is nearing Monolith Hills, where, he recalls, there is a copy of the famous black object from the Stanley Kubrick film.

"Do you have an exact address, sir?" the robotaxi's artificial intelligence inquires pleasantly as they approach the off-ramp, in a low-quality digital voice.

"Hotel Laika, 38010 Leonov Alley," he answers mechanically, prompted by the instruction program's memory bloc.

The Toyota takes the first off-ramp after the long tunnel from which they have just emerged and continues eastward, toward a succession of wooded hills forming a long promontory that rises above the city, along a winding road dimly lit by tungsten streetlamps. He has just enough time to make out a green sign indicating the name of the road—10 South—and several words, phosphorescent in the robotaxi's headlights, reading:

Cosmodrome—Grand Junction North: Exit 17
Monolith Hills, Voskhod Boulevard, Leonov Alley
To Heavy Metal Valley: Junction Road,
Nexus Road, Xenon Road
Drive Safely

The robotaxi zigzags among the hills, avoiding Voskhod Boulevard "because of traffic; there are road works in progress," the digital voice explains as it traverses streets bordered by scattered houses, before rejoining the *strip*. Leonov Alley.

The strip covers a little more than forty thousand numbers on the cadastre. It is around twelve kilometers long, following a sort of natural plateau leveling the tops of the hills, and it is here that nearly all of Grand Junction's shady and bootlegging activities of all types take place. Just outside downtown and the technological research districts of the northern suburbs, like the sordid neighborhoods adjacent to the aerostation, the Monolith Hills strip serves as a channel for frustration, desire, and crime. It is in a sort of orbit all its own: no longer inside the city proper, but not really outside it either.

The Municipal Consortium had probably not planned this situation, but neither had it done anything to prevent it. The Monolith Hills strip is easily accessed from the city; numerous roads cut through the wooded hills to connect with the streets that cross the long neon spinal cord.

The downtown area and its technological suburbs have remained relatively well preserved. They are more presentable to the international media and to financiers, but everyone, including the journalists, knows the Hills are the place to go to get their rocks off.

The strip is a long, seemingly endless stretch of motels, brothels, bars, nightclubs, sex shops, arenas for violent sport, auditoriums, and neuro-electronic game arcades. A motley crowd throngs the sidewalks and crosses the streets in packs in front of the robotaxi, which can legally do no more than blast its horn. It is a different crowd, though, than the one at the aerostation. But it isn't the same one that was huddled in the arrival area, either; there it had seemed like some of the people had never even left the confines of Enterprise.

This was a similar crowd, but it was not haggard with shock, ready to erupt into violence at the slightest provocation. No, this was the aerostation crowd in two, three, five, ten, thirty years.

Here is the core of Grand Junction's social security. Here is the jungle. The electric jungle. It is worse than a jungle. It is the secret heart of the city. Death reigns here, a living death.

For a moment, he feels his soul teeter on the edge of an abyss. Then he feels a burning onslaught of sensations and images, as if the instruction program has brutally taken over. Images. Sounds. Voices. High yellow grass on the edge of a vast stretch of brown earth. Men on horseback. Himself, running after a chestnut prairie pony dappled with white spots.

He is a young boy. Someone is calling him: *Diego! Diego!* He runs across the pampas. The sun is dazzling. Men on horseback gallop past him and the pony. The sun is blinding; its rays seem to devour everything. The light is right in front of him—it is terrible; it burns his retinas. It is like an overpowering spotlight shining down on a gladiatorial arena, whirling on its axis atop a pylon.

What is this memory?

Where does it come from?

Argentina?

The Argentina of the pampas? Patagonia?

During his childhood?

The memory is somewhat contradictory to his British recollections, but those took place a bit later on. Perhaps he had emigrated to London at some point? But there was no way he could have run across the vast grassy plains under the pearly blue skies of the Cordilleras at the age of twelve or thirteen while simultaneously pedaling his bicycle through the industrial suburbs of a large Siberian city. . . .

As the robotaxi continues smoothly down the strip, he is forced to admit, frozen with understanding, that his entire identity has been falsified. Something doubtlessly went wrong with the Baikal mafia's experimental program. It is even possible that most of his memories from that time are purely imaginary as well.

Perhaps nothing is true.

But it can't *all* be *false,* either.

The second idea is hardly less painful than the first.

After a few more moments, the Hotel Laika appears in the distance at the north end of the strip. It is an enormous structure built of tubular scaffolding and containing hundreds of orange-colored cubicles, around which are webbed corridors and fire escapes. Plotkin notices a double elevator on an external nacelle on each of the four sides of the building, each opening onto a portico leading to the hall and central patio.

It is a capsule hotel, but a most luxurious one as they go. It is part of the Municipal Consortium franchise, UManHome, which he knows finances the campaigns of the mayor and his party.

The hotel boasts two advantages: first, since it belongs to a financial group with connections to his target, Plotkin may be able to gather useful information about the internal workings of the Municipal Consortium; second, because of its position at the top of the wooded spine that forms Monolith Hills, it dominates the entire city.

The robotaxi deposits him in front of the hotel entrance, and Plotkin sees, coming toward him, the first real, living being he has encountered since his arrival on Earth, since his "rebirth" in this body at Windsor, Ontario.

It is a dog.

In the ashy light of the moon and the pale illumination of the streetlamps, the dog looks at first like a vague gray shape, barely distinguishable from the pavement beneath it. It is only because he had stood, mechanically watching the robotaxi drive away, that he had noticed it moving in his direction.

The Toyota has surprised it for a moment with the white glare of its headlights. It is not a "normal" dog at all. Identification parameters, lists of codes and figures, begin scrolling across a portion of his field of vision.

But he knows the important part already.

It is obviously not a normal dog. It is an old army cyberdog; its brain modified via transgenic mutation, implanted with countermeasure systems for electronic warfare.

The dog stays at his heels as he walks into the hotel. He shoots a glance behind him; it is like a gray shadow trotting on the concrete sidewalk that separates the hotel entrance from the street. Plotkin wonders for an instant why chance had decreed that he, of all people, should encounter a cyberdog from the American Aerospace Force in front of a hotel named for the first dog in space, whose holographic portrait, in the stylized fashion of the 1950s Soviet Union, turns slowly above the neon sign.

He knows that there is no such thing as chance.

Or, more accurately, that chance means nothing.

He guesses that the cyberdog and the name of the hotel are closely tied.

What he does not guess is that this tie is of no importance. What he cannot know is that other ties, even stronger ones, are already tightening, or will be very soon.

> THE MAN

"Are you here for the Centennial?"

The man is around thirty-five cellular years old, fifty in terms of legal identification. The data appears briefly in the upper right corner of his field of vision.

The man is fat, ugly, dirty: repellent. He stinks. When he opens his mouth, an odor reminiscent of the sewer assails the olfactory senses. Plotkin wrinkles his nose. He is sorely tempted to command his neurocomputer to initiate a cortical barrage against this horrid breach of his personal defense system by the real world.

At the slightest movement of the man's jellylike form, with its puffy face, tiny black eyes peering from between folds of flaccid flesh encrusted with festering pimples, and strings of bluish hair smeared with third-degree anti-UV gel, a wave of putrescent odor is emitted that is feebly and futilely covered by a mixture of eau de toilette, perfume, and other deodorants that add nothing but a note of cheap alcohol to the assault.

It is astonishing proof of Unimanity's ability to produce something so utterly vile. Plotkin is nauseated; he can hardly believe his senses.

He does not answer the man's question. He simply looks at him, this human manager of the Hotel Laika, as if observing a sort of marvel.

He forgets a bit of the information the program gave him during the taxi ride. "The Centennial?"

The marvel is a perfect example of the regressive evolution that has taken place in the biological species known as *Homo sapiens*. Five or six million years since the primates of the Pliocene era, Plotkin thinks to himself, have resulted in this. He cannot help wondering if the parable of the Fall did not actually refer to the moment when we dropped out of the trees.

Under the cold light of ceiling bulbs, the baleful eyes blink with a sort of morbid glint. The mouth opens in a thick-lipped grimace, shiny with spit. When he speaks, it is as if the words are oozing from a slimy cavern.

"Yeah, of course the Centennial. You aren't here for it?"

Plotkin stands paralyzed before this incarnation of humanity on today's Earth. His first category-three encounter, and it is with this specimen. He actually doubts—like a child; he *is* at that stage of life, after all—if they can both possibly be members of the same species. Impossible. He doesn't know why, but it is as if all the energy of a previous life has condensed into this figure of truth. He feels a profound, inexplicable sense of disgust, even beyond the objective aesthetic judgment. It is a wave of pure instinct, pure as a flame—but of course that is no excuse. *The habit makes the monk,* it says. *Judge the book by the cover, don't judge the look by the lover.*

Informer, it says. *SNITCH,* it screams. A direct line to the police.

It seems like part of the plan.

Yes, of course, it must be part of the plan. He's supposed to brainwash this big pile of shit, to make him swallow a giant lie that will travel through the esophagus of the whole structure of the Municipal Consortium, all the way to the stomach of the mayor himself, and his police.

The snitch watches him. He seems to be waiting for something.

Yes . . . the Centennial.

"Uh, no. That isn't the main reason for my visit, but it's part of it."

The man licks his lips, which are swollen and bluish—metananodrehynide, by the looks of it. "The Sputnik Centennial, on October 4. So you're here for a while, then?"

The evolutionary marvel licks his lips again. Plotkin does not answer. All his senses are wide awake, all his bio-implanted scanners fully operational. This is not simple, irrational personal antipathy—even if the man does seem to have been designed specifically to embody everything mankind finds supremely disgusting.

"All of Grand Junction will be at the festival. Are you going to the Starnival?"

Informer. Snitch. Rat. Narc. Bastard.

Smile; just smile. Don't forget: you're traveling on business; you work for a seedy Russian insurance company. "Sure, if I can. I'm always looking for a good time."

Message received. The fat man shows him a smile full of cavities and smeared with cosmetic-antibacterial gel.

"If you're looking for a good time, especially on that day, tell room service to let me know. There's nothing the Hotel Laika won't do for its guests."

The smile, with its rotten teeth, artificially white against the throat turned blue by dope, blackish, full of ink, flickers. The smile flickers and says, *"Girls for sale. Cheap."*

"I'd like a capsule with a view of the city, if that's not a problem."

He doesn't want to seem like a bullshitter, or to be marked out by the snitch, but he does want to sleep, and then to think calmly about his mission. It does not occur to him, just then, that the instruction program will probably send more information shortly.

The other man shakes his filthy head. "Not at all, sir. The Hotel Laika is at your command. Capsule 108. Faces full west; should be just right for you."

The man taps his fat, sausagelike fingers on the keyboard of his office nanocomputer. Plotkin takes advantage of the distraction to have a better look at the lobby. His attention is drawn to a small plastic plaque mounted on the wall behind the manager. It is the official authorization to open a hotel for humans, issued by the real estate branch of the Municipal Consortium. It is dull beige with grime—it must be white under the dirt—and inscribed with multiple languages readable by neuroscanner.

"I'll need to enter your personal identification code. It's law in Mohawk territory."

"I know. My encryption system is a bit special; it comes from a company in Russia. Do you have an encrypter that can read Cyrillic?"

The man looks at him scornfully, clearly thinking, *Where do you think you are, the Islamic Republic of Frankistan?* "Give me your disk, please. The Network informs me that you work in insurance?"

Plotkin hands over his personal identification disk, and the man inserts it into a slot in his reader and waits a few seconds, watching the dance of diodes. Red, green, red, green. He hands back the disk.

Plotkin takes it, wiping it surreptitiously on the sleeve of his suit jacket. It seems to be covered with an oily film. "Yes, I work for a Russo-Indian company that specializes in orbital flights. There's a niche for that here."

The man laughs. It sounds like a series of farts reverberating in an echo chamber. "A niche? You think?" The laugh dies away little by little in the bluish throat. "This is Grand Junction, my dear sir," he continues, as if he were speaking of the Parthenon, or the Grand Canyon, or Dealey Plaza. "That isn't *a* niche here, it's *the* niche. We're the only astroport still operating north of Texas, if you don't count the one in Las Vegas."

Plotkin smiles, as if realizing his mistake. *Never show an enemy the truth unless you can use it to destroy him,* says one of the Order's maxims. "Yes, that's why my company sent me here," he says. "We insure a lot of flights from Baikonur and Plesetsk. There's a *market,* is what I meant to say."

The man relaxes into a conciliatory smile—or his best imitation of one, in any case. "Well, welcome to Grand Junction, Mr. Plotkin. Take the west elevator and go left when you get out."

"Thank you," Plotkin says, turning his back, anxious to get away now.

"My name is Clovis Drummond. I wish you a good stay at the Hotel Laika," the fat man calls after him, adding a dry cackle of a laugh. "You've found yourself a good niche, Mr. Plotkin!"

Plotkin is already walking down the hallway with large strides, heading for the west elevator.

Two minutes later, the elevator doors open on the tenth floor, the highest in the hotel. Across from Plotkin, a mesh wall overlooks a square courtyard, which is surrounded by the hotel's panopticon. Through the grid, he sees the translucent bubble of the central patio where the cafeteria is located; above him is a loft whose tubular walls support an antiradiation protective dome that is obviously not up to code. It is full of visible holes and breaches where ultraviolet rays can stream through without the slightest barrier, in a vast shower of points of deadly luminescence, spilling across the roof and several cracked cement refractory slabs, down his hallway, and right up to the access door leading to the service stairway.

He walks down the corridor; his room is the third to the left of the elevator. He swipes his keycard in the reader and the door opens with a soft humming noise.

The room looks to be up to code: no parasite rays, residual toxic chemicals, ill-timed viruses, or pathogenic bacteria.

Not too shabby for a capsule room; not bad at all, for what it is. There is a Chinese-manufactured NeuroNet console. Upon verification, the water seems to be correctly filtered. The single-occupant room is a rectangle with rounded angles and white walls, its few bits of decor the vivid yellow-orange color characteristic of the UMan-Home franchise. It measures exactly 4.8 meters in length, 2.8 meters in height, and 3.8 meters in width. It consumes around one hundred kilowatts of energy per hour, is authorized to distribute between fifteen and thirty liters of water a day to its occupant, and is linked to local artificial intelligence by an ensemble of sensors legally approved by the city of Grand Junction. The mouth of a square junk-trap model trash bin juts out of one of the walls; linked to the room's network of sensors, it rapidly detects the various items of trash left by the occupant and can send out one or more specialized micromachines to retrieve the refuse and bring it to the retractable maw, which then sends it to the hotel's hydrogen reactor. In a corner near the bed, he sees the cubical stand of a UHU-approved universal altar. It is connected via the network to the NeuroNet console, and is standing by to receive the personal God program of the new occupant of Capsule 108.

It is all perfectly normal.

"WELCOME TO CAPSULE 108. THE HOTEL LAIKA IS HAPPY TO HAVE YOU AS OUR GUEST. YOU HAVE PAID IN ADVANCE FOR THIRTY DAYS, THE MAXIMUM ALLOWED, ON AN ACCOUNT REGISTERED TO CITICORP SIBERIA, NOVOSIBIRSK."

Standard-model hotelier artificial intelligence, Plotkin knows. Neutral, androgynous voice, neither male nor female in accordance with antidiscrimination laws, with very few emotive intonations. Rented software, probably on sale.

It isn't as bad as a village of particleboard houses, but it isn't the Ritz, either.

It takes him only a few minutes to undress and run a shower in the collapsible bathroom that unfolds slowly from the side wall. He is irresistibly attracted to the mirror, which reflects the ceiling light, a spray of fiery gold in the little rectangle.

He stands facing his own image.

And doesn't recognize it.

Which is exactly what he expected.

> CAPSULE 108

The image staring back at him from the mirror is that of a man with gray streaks in both his blue eyes and his black hair, thin lips, a scissor slash of a mouth, and a long face, somewhat triangular in shape. It tells him nothing at all.

At first glance, the man in the mirror looks to be around forty years old. That corresponds to his identity, and to his specific biomedical profile—two transgenic rejuvenation cures.

For long moments, he contemplates this stranger in front of him, hoping that the instruction program will pass along a few memories, or even a scrap or two of information. But nothing happens.

The program does not seem to react at all to what is happening, in fact. It seems completely indifferent to the fact that, while the re-identification process had more or less functioned smoothly up to this point, the mirror phenomenon has obviously caused some sort of serious blockage.

The retractable shower extends slowly behind him, its antiviral diaphragm releasing a tiny spiral galaxy that diffuses in a bronze-colored halo around his head. The machines obey; that is, they regulate the world they perceive. For him, a man whose identity itself is fabricated, nothing seems planned.

The humming of the electric motor stops. Plotkin stares at his image, itemizing every detail, while his ears take in the noises of Capsule 108 and of the entire hotel beyond it.

He is able to sort out the chaotic mélange of sounds in short order: There is the deep, dull infrabass rhythm that must surely come from the building's hydrogen reactor. It is a sine curve pulsation—rising, falling, rising, falling—with an unvarying frequency, barely discernible beneath the various other sounds filling all auditory space.

There is the noise of the suction pumps that distribute severely rationed water to the capsules. There are the small staccato sounds of electric, lighting, heating, and air-conditioning circuitry. There are the various individual noises of the active antimicrobial filters, antiviral diaphragms, ventilators, airlocks, and alarm and security systems. He also hears the clickety-clacking of the micromachines that burrow through the pipes and cables inside the walls, operating, repairing, tinkering. There is the characteristic vibration of the nacelle elevators as they move up and down the building's façade. Then there is the wind, blowing gently and causing soft quivers in the structure of polymetallic alloys, composite materials, and Recyclo™ concrete like a ship abandoned on top of a hill after the flood. And there are the crackles of the structure itself, thin threads of sound just barely audible when gusts of wind strike the hilltop.

He listens closely to the living sounds of this organic-mechanical structure; he listens, and he sees, and he hears, and he observes.

But he cannot recognize himself in the mirror.

Some people say—he doesn't know how he knows this—that life in Grand Junction's capsule hotels is the best training for life in space. As the last tiny droplet of water is vaporized from his body by the shower's atomizer, he begins to understand the truth of that phrase.

The retractable shower consists of a square cubicle with a sanitary system, closet, self-lighting mirror, chemical phosphorescent overhead lights, and the shower cylinder itself, which is hardly more than a meter in diameter and whose floor has a partially transparent bubbled surface behind which he can see pressurized water condensing in reservoir tubes before being projected out of the minuscule holes dotted all over the cylinder and into a hemispherical head placed just above his own. The soap is yellow biodegradable cleansing foam that is poured over him by the showerhead after fifteen seconds of water spray. A small rotating brush detaches itself from the ceiling and lowers itself on a thick steel tube; a green light goes on in front of him in the middle of the diaphragm, glowing LED letters informing him that he will be able to use the brush for the next sixty seconds before being rinsed by vaporization and then sprayed by antiviral eau de toilette.

Later, stretched out on the capsule's retractable bed, waiting for sleep that will not come, he contemplates the night sky of Grand Junction. His attention is caught by an abrupt flash of light that glances off the porthole window. He gets up and stands in front of the large circular pane of glass—it takes up almost the entire wall from floor to ceiling—just in time to witness the takeoff of the shuttle he noticed earlier on one of the astroport's launching platforms.

The fire is white streaked with dazzling molten gold. It forms a sphere as bright as a bit of the sun fallen to Earth and returning now to its birthplace. The shuttle itself is barely visible in the midst of the glowing gases; it is merely a tiny gleam at the top of the ball of sunfire, trailing flame as it shoots toward the high atmosphere. Then it is lost, somewhere in the direction of Ursa Major.

Suddenly, he understands why so many people are irrevocably drawn to this city, so many lost souls from all four corners of the Earth. He understands that even a slight chance to share your life with this dancing, meteoric dream could keep you here forever.

Nothing happens over the next few days. At night, his metacortical nanocomputer furtively organizes the networks within his nervous system. Bioprocessors self-replicate on ribbons of protein. The genetic instruction program scrolls its lists of invisible codes. His dreams are absolutely black.

He is content to stay in his room, eating trans-G sushi and nutrimedical pizza delivered by the hotel's room-service robots. The active vitamins, trace elements, and minerals are accompanied by several types of specialized antiviral GMOs (genetically modified organisms) that the console menu lists relentlessly every time he places an order.

The bathroom is programmable; it can serve as a shower, a water closet, even an emergency room if necessary. Twelve layers of intelligent poly-alloys are able to take on any of these three forms on command. It is an old system, one of the first of its kind, produced by General Electric in one of its last acts of brilliance before being purchased by a Sino-Japanese cartel. It takes almost twenty seconds for the programming to be finished and the facility configured for the desired use; the latest Fujitsu models open ten times faster, nearly instantaneously.

The cliché, it turns out, was true: a stay in a capsule motel like this one really was the best preparation imaginable for life in a pressurized box orbiting the Earth at an altitude of 450 kilometers, or en route to an agglomeration in circumlunar orbit.

It is also true that the power of UHU is obvious, even here on the margins—*especially* on the margins. The correlation between the presence of capsule motels and that of a crowd of lost souls longing to leave for the new frontier is purely economic. And yet, it is also as if the *economy* has created a mysterious link between these areas of temporary residence and the groups that gather there before departing for the moon, or perhaps Mars. Some of them do not stay, and come back to Earth. They resell their claims, their Golden Tracks, to the highest bidder, and thus the black market grows, the market of fake, real-fake, fake-real documents on which so much of Grand Junction's underground economy depends.

An interesting detail: in Grand Junction, the economy is underground by nature. Elsewhere, it is the opposite.

CATALOGUE OF NEUROPORTABLE WEAPONS

Cortical control metabolic nanoviruses, targeted cellular destroyers

Rapid-intrusion neurotoxic nanoviruses

Pathogenic metabolic nanoviruses, contagious pseudoviruses

Any of the following specialized neurovectors: neuroblocking
  neurovectors, prionic investigation and neuronal targeting agents,
  neuronic countermeasure and antiviral security systems, synaptic
  propagation retroviruses

Memory-controlling neuroprocessors

Neuroconnections with orbital telemetry and GPS surveillance
  systems

Integrated neuro-optic displays

Global language neuroencryption software

Programmable sensorial amplification

Plotkin vaguely understands that in this world where the rockets blasting into orbit are twentieth-century antiques, where cosmodromes are erected on rebuilt offshore oil-drilling platforms; in this world, which seems frozen in a sort of post-technical stasis, it is as if progress has reached its limit, as if it has buckled under the socially programmed repetition of its prodromes and has become monumentally inefficient. Yes, he realizes that the only real scientific progress here is the work of mafia organizations, or corporations of killers like the one to which he belongs.

It is incredibly pathetic, almost tragic. The sensation is one of absolute disaster and terrible beauty all at once.

The morning after the cortical computer finishes downloading the complete catalogue of neuroprograms into his brain, a list of them appears in transparent suspension in the corner of his field of

vision, only a few seconds after he awakes. He now knows, definitively, what he is: a living condensation of this black science, this science of assassins, this science of what remains of humanity.

He does not know the cause of the instruction program's block-
ages, but he has the feeling that this black science, dark as it may be,
contains a point of light. He cannot explain the feeling, but if this
point of light is not him, it is *in* him that it shines weakly.

For twenty-four hours, the entire third day, he remains connected to
the NeuroNet console in his room. He had located an intelligent
agent with the help of the nanocomputer, residing somewhere in the
anodyne peripheral memory of the Metanetwork. It is a neuroencrypted software agent; after a long and careful series of verification
procedures, it is activated in the digital world of the NeuroNet and
can appear within Plotkin's field of vision while remaining invisible
to outside eyes. It is a state-of-the-art neurodigital projection; its
World is the binary virtual world of the Metanetwork, which has become the regulator of the real World as well.

Its name is *el señor Metatron*.

In just a few seconds, it gathers for Plotkin the equivalent of an
encyclopedia on Grand Junction; the Municipal Consortium; Cosmos, Inc., the managing firm of the cosmodrome; the Enterprise
aeroport facilities; and the local history, geography, law, politics, and
media. Who hated whom and why; who dealt with whom and why;
who was fucking whom—and who was letting themselves be fucked
by whom—and why.

El señor Metatron can take an infinite number of forms. It says it
was designed for Plotkin years before, by a *yakuza* firm in the Republic of California. It says that Plotkin uses it for every mission. It says
he told it everything, before his cortical surgery in Siberia. Plotkin
sees in it an opportunity to find out more about his past; the neurodigital agent should have the memories of his previous missions.

But el señor Metatron, who has chosen this time to appear in the form of a pure gold flame with a dancing blue-violet base and every shade of red and orange flickering in its ephemeral body, tells him that since it is a projection of his own mind, he cannot hope for too much in that area.

Plotkin tells himself that he cannot stay in his room any longer. He must act. He must begin to spy on this world.

He begins to take an interest in the life of the hotel.

> CATEGORY-FOUR ENCOUNTER

The Hotel Laika is typical of Grand Junction's capsule hotels. These residential buildings were introduced at the beginning of the century in Japan, taking their inspiration from the modules under construction for the International Space Station. From the beginning, a mysterious affinity existed between the boxes men built for themselves on Earth and the ones they sent into space. They allowed people to reside cheaply in seminomadic tribes formed of millions of middle managers commuting within the conurbation each day. The astronomical rents in Tokyo and the rest of Japan's megalopolises provided capsule hotels with the opportunity to expand across the entire archipelago. Later on, the introduction of nanocomposite materials, then Recyclo™ multiuse particleboard resulted in the mass production of folding suitcase-houses, and several million Japanese workers used these to live in the streets even as the first thousand-floor megatowers were sprouting up like mushrooms.

In North America, the concept was taken up and adapted to fit local conditions. In Grand Junction, smaller-scale capsule hotels are the norm, as they are in most of Canada and the neighboring American states. Simply put, they are *the* motel of the twenty-first century.

This particular hotel was a quadrilateral-shaped building around sixty meters long on each side, with 110 capsules on each of its four walls; it was ten floors high, with a double-elevator nacelle and service, security, and maintenance capsules on each floor—the minimum legal standard for establishments of UManHome's ilk. The building

has a central patio covered with a pale pink resin roof six meters
high, at the four corners of which are wide columns in the neoclassical style typical of this area. These columns rise to support the antiradiation dome that covers the structure and is meant to protect
those within it from falling particles. A cement-composite and cheap
polymetallic alloy cubbyhole separates the antiradiation dome from
the rest of the building. There is a service staircase accessible via magnetic key; it is near the door to this staircase that Plotkin had been
able to detect the substandard holes and cracks in the ceiling, with radiation levels slightly above the norm.

There is, of course, a network of interior and exterior multifrequency surveillance cameras, standard-model, Ukrainian-made but
of good quality. Their small, globular, black-violet eyes are dotted
along the hallways and service stairways, in the elevators and corridors of the first floor, in the entryway and on the patio, in the reception office, and all the way out to the sidewalks, where an archway of
simple metal tubes tries feebly to replicate a Soviet flight tower.

The hotel is at almost the very end of Leonov Alley; the other motels are farther to the south, where the city's population is more concentrated. After the numbers 30–32000—as Plotkin noted during his
taxi ride—the strip changes little by little into a simple street lined
with conifer woods and groups of houses, several dance clubs, and two
or three more motels like his own, spaced farther and farther apart.

At the northern end of the road, Plotkin can make out an autobridge. It was from that direction that the cyberdog had come, when
he saw it for the first time.

A dense and black wooded abyss caps the street and fills the horizon. The autobridge spans it and joins, via an unfinished access road,
an old, unused municipal road. A billboard there reads, in yellow letters against a verdigris background: NORTH JUNCTION.

This dilapidated municipal road leads east between two long, up-
ward-sloping concrete ramps, then disappears among the emerald
fronds of a hill lit sporadically by ghostly bluish streetlamps.

To the west, the North Junction road descends Monolith Hills toward Gemini Drive and the downtown area, whose many lights create a glittering dome of brilliance that arches over the city and touches the cosmodrome to the north, spreading luminescence and various types of electromagnetic interference that render it not uncommon to see a missile transformed via malfunction into an exploding firework visible for a hundred kilometers.

Crossing the autobridge, Plotkin finds a staircase carved into the concrete ramp that allows him to access the North Junction road. Another sign at the bottom of the stairs bears an arrow pointing east toward the hills and the words: TO HEAVY METAL VALLEY, NEXUS ROAD, 6 MILES.

He briefly explores the area around the autobridge. There is only a peripheral surveillance system, a half-century-old panoramic camera set up by the Grand Junction Transportation Board; it has obviously been repaired twenty times and is still miraculously in operation, and sits atop an antique telephone pole whose wires were cut long ago. It emits an unpleasant metallic screeching noise audible for kilometers.

Plotkin heads back toward the hotel.

A rebuilt Proton rocket with its four passengers in a small Japanese-built capsule is just taking off into the dry, pure, monochromatic blue afternoon sky. He stops to watch the fireball follow a slightly oblique trajectory south, toward an equatorial orbit, a line of white fire as pure as a painter's sure stroke on the canvas of the world. He sits down on the side of the road in the grass, whose vivid green contains a multitude of subtle variations, and raises his eyes toward the zenith where this cloud of powder and fire has dwindled to an invisible point, its image now no more than an imprint on his retinal memory.

It is only then that he sees that he is being watched by someone beside and slightly behind him. That someone is the dog.

* * *

Plotkin watches the dog calmly, as it watches him.

The traces of several surgical operations and a number of biomechanical prostheses are visible on the surface of the dog's cranium. It is a Labrador-shepherd mix, or something like that; its coat is black, with a few tawny and gray spots on its belly and feet. Its hazel eyes are large and deep, with distant violet stars hidden in the irises.

He immediately feels a profound sense of empathy with the animal. Cyberdogs were invented in the 2020s, after all the necessary technology had been developed during nearly two decades of conflict.

Cyberdogs served as both scouts and patrollers, and thanks to transgenic manipulations of their cortices, the American and then Chinese armies had been able to turn them into very efficient bionic animal soldiers. As far as Plotkin can tell, this is an old Typhoon-class cyberdog, the highest class of them. It has a neurolinguistic center cloned from bonobo cells, with a vocabulary of around four hundred words—greatly superior to the current human average. Its surgically enhanced vision is greater than that of other canines—this area is not always so well provided for—and it can remotely control, via a GPS transmitter, certain security circuits in the hotel.

Hiring former army dogs to protect capsule motels is quite trendy these days. As a security guard, it is fully as intelligent as half the human goons that ply the trade, and it will work for the price of a little drinking water and a bowl of genetically modified food a day. Not even a German or Swedish immigrant worker can be had under such conditions.

He and the dog stare at each other. In the city below, half a million men go about their daily business. Another turn-of-the-century American shuttle, positioned on its pad, waits for an unknown signal for its transfer to the concrete runway, under the wide-open mouth of a hangar. The cosmodrome is empty, as is the sky. It seems that Plotkin and the dog are the only two beings in the world.

"You are the guest in 108-West, aren't you?"

The sound of the dog's digitized voice makes Plotkin jump.

Naturally, the dog does not possess speech organs. Techniques developed at the beginning of the century had used a little micro-surgery, a little genetic manipulation, and a little nanocomputer im-plantation to attain a yip that was relatively ill defined but remodulated by a phonatory control center bio-implanted in the larynx, which is-sued a partially digitized version of a voice. The end result is strange and, frankly, a little monstrous.

There he is, and the dog, and the world, and all three of them are monsters.

It is difficult to refuse to answer the dog, since that might be mis-interpreted. "Yes," he says. "And you're the hotel security dog, I be-lieve."

"Yes," yaps the dog. "My name is Balthazar. I was created for the Marine Corps on February 6, 2032."

Nothing in the instruction program has taught Plotkin how to act with an old Marine cyberdog from the era when the United States still existed, though not for very much longer. His barely formed person-ality is confronted with several possible choices; only his killer's in-stinct, lodged deep within his subconscious, has any idea of how to behave. He decides to let this somber and unknown part of himself act freely. He reconfigures his personality to the initial parameters of dis-guise: he is a Russo-American insurance agent who has traveled from Siberia to "assess the markets" on behalf of his company.

He turns to face the west, toward the depths of Monolith Hills and the vast takeoff zone north of Apollo Drive.

"Tomorrow I'm going for a closer look at the cosmodrome," he lies brazenly. "I have a feeling there are holes in the legal security net."

The dog does not reply. Plotkin throws a glance behind him. The dog simply looks at him, tongue hanging out, head slightly cocked to one side.

* * *

They stare at each other some more. The world, or what is left of it, seems frozen. The sky is blue-green; the sun dips slowly toward the horizon. The Proton rocket must be separating from its final stage by now. . . .

Plotkin's reconstructed brain works at full speed. Obviously, the dog knows all the hotel's security systems and, in all probability, the local network here in Monolith Hills, which means it knows all of Grand Junction. The animal seems to be in good shape despite the fact that it must be at least twenty-five years old. It has probably been all over the country—all over Mohawk territory—and has the aid of a biomilitary program that slows physical aging. It has lived through the Second War of American Secession and the height of the Grand Jihad—the Transpacific Great War, aftershocks of which were still being felt in the archipelagos of the Indian Ocean. It has known the prewar, wartime, and postwar worlds. It seems ready for whatever is to come next, whatever this world might still have the strength to propagate.

"What is this Heavy Metal Valley?" Plotkin asks.

He discerns an ephemeral sparkle of amusement in the dog's eyes. The bionic animal nods its head.

"It's on the other side of the hills. You take Nexus Road, over there."

It points its muzzle briefly behind it, toward the black mass of wooded hills and blue hollows illuminated by the North Junction road's streetlamps, but it has not exactly answered his question. It has only repeated the words inscribed on the autobridge signpost, only said *where* the valley is—not *what* it is.

Now the Order's instructions, the scheming and secretive killer's subconscious, the years spent as a master spy take over. His brain, still without any real identity, acts *as if* it has been told what to do. In an instant, he understands that the hotel dog has a relationship to this place, to Heavy Metal Valley, and that the dog wishes that relationship to remain secret.

> STARS IN FREEFALL

Back in his room, Plotkin orders the NeuroNet console to open an operating window for him in one of the walls. A UniScreen portal appears, a square of midnight blue in the midst of the computer network mesh that covers the walls of his capsule.

The console is a bit archaic. He has to juggle a few symbols just to open the pages of the various files, and more than once he encounters old 3-D routines that were in vogue thirty years before, in which he has to move virtually in a false universe inspired by this or that fashionable neurogame. Finally he approaches the core, the immense global neuroconnection tube, a gigantic ring coiling infinitely upon itself, a spiral of ultraviolet light whose gyrations are all linked to microimpulses in your cortex.

He wants to know everything about everyone who lives in this hotel. He wants a usable database, now. The dog may have a relationship with certain clients of the establishment. He also wants to know exactly what Heavy Metal Valley is. He wants el señor Metatron to get to work. Now.

So the neuroencrypted flame flickers into life. A pure digital translation of his soul, it erupts like a virtual rocket among the myriad optic cables interconnected with his own independent pseudoconscience. It is an illusion of digital voodoo—but the highest form of illusion.

Like a shooting star cutting through the intangible subterfuge saturating the world, this metabrain, built of digital copies of all the human brains that pass through it, has in a sense become the world it-self. El señor Metatron is not much in comparison to it. It can, if it wishes, appear to him in any form. In this sense, it is a devilish repre-sentation of the mind, and Plotkin knows this to the core of his being without knowing why, or how. It is a certainty that shines as brightly as the torch Lucifer himself uses when he descends into the darkness.

First: Heavy Metal Valley. Located around twelve kilometers northeast of the hotel in the Quebecois part of the independent Mo-hawk territory, it covers the equivalent of a county. It is a vast plain, faintly watered by a wadi, a small river that dries up almost com-pletely in summer. In the space of a decade, during which hydrogen motors definitively entered the global market in the context of the Grand Jihad, which would soon reach the height of its raging fury, hundreds of millions of gasoline-powered vehicles had been declared illegal and restricted to use only on closed and private roads. Enor-mous lots of cars, junkyards several kilometers long and wide, had accumulated on this plain, along the ancient bed of the little river. More than a million gasoline-powered vehicles had ended up there; the local residents themselves had built a vast network of roads on which one could, within the territorial boundaries of the HMV cor-porate authority, drive cars from the twentieth century or the early twenty-first.

It was a community of greasers, stalwart devotees of the combus-tion engine, stubbornly resistant to hydrogen-fed electric turbines. The dog must have a sweetheart there, simple as that. The greasers and all groups of their ilk often lived with hordes of animals, includ-ing dogs. Perhaps Balthazar had come from there? Or had passed a few years there before being hired by the hotel?

Heavy Metal Valley. So that's settled, for now.

Plotkin does almost nothing for the next few hours. The private fil-tering security camera observing him from the center of the ceiling watches him as he sits at the capsule's little desk, the lighted Neu-roNet console scrolling images from a legal Russian pornographic site while he scribbles a series of rough sketches on a digital notepad. In his falsified life there is still the indelible kernel that makes him the Man Who Has Come to Kill the Mayor of This City, and it is this ker-nel, barely possessed of a memory—only a few sparse recollections, more holes than real memories, and even those might not be real—it is this dark kernel that allows him to think about the various ways in which he might Kill the Mayor of This City.

Obviously, the instruction program knows how to keep the Proj-ect alive in his memory. The instruction program has made that the most vital part of his existence.

The strange thing is that he is acting exactly as this program has instructed him to, and he *knows it*. It is as if that fact has no real im-portance.

He knows enough about Orville Blackburn and the other Mo-hawks of the Municipal Consortium to avoid going anywhere that isn't useful. A small reconnaissance tour of the heart of the city—it should only take a few days—and perhaps a second one in a few weeks, should be more than enough. Thanks to el señor Metatron, he has a real-time view of the invisible city hidden beneath the visible one—the digital network and its security systems.

After that, he knows, things will move very quickly.

When an assassination is well planned, it is the preparation that takes time. The execution itself takes only an instant.

When amateurs get involved, the paradigm is reversed, and rushed preparation leads to a sloppy, slow execution—as unpleasant for the victim as for the assassin, and likely to leave traces leading straight to you and any possible accomplices.

One of his remaining bits of knowledge gleaned from the Order is that, when an assassin arrives at the scene of the crime, every-thing—or nearly everything—must already have been carefully pre-pared, organized, and planned. The killer may be left to choose certain operational or tactical details, but the general plot, and all the information and procedures relating to it, will have been determined long before. Of course, the assassin often knows nothing of his employer, and hardly anything of his victim—or, these days, of himself.

Plotkin wonders how many times he has woken up in this body, with false memories implanted in his head and a human target on his agenda.

Even that knowledge has been erased.

The instruction program is unable to give him any information about possible avatars under which el señor Metatron might already have been active in the NeuroNet. He is hardly aware that the base program even exists anymore. Plotkin had hoped to find out some information about his past identities, and perhaps find out which was the true one. But there, too, everything has been erased; the databanks are empty. There is nothing, other than a few snippets of information so vague that he is forced to admit that he will find out no more about himself until his return to Russia twenty-eight days from now.

He may not be able to learn anything about himself, but he now knows almost everything about the 135 current residents of the Hotel Laika. 135 residents, 440 rooms: the hotel is not functioning at even a third of its maximum profitability. In relaying this information along with the latest economic data on the region, el señor Metatron makes it clear that even here, in the best possible world, that of Grand Junction and its cosmodrome, things are far from perfect.

The data that el señor Metatron collects about the network makes it utterly clear that, in the euphemistic language of the communication firms, "We are beginning to see signs of a serious slowdown of business." Translation: there is a recession on the horizon.

As for the 135 current residents (not counting Plotkin), el señor Metatron is able to sketch general profiles of them thanks to pirated access to the hotel's poorly encrypted personal information banks and guest registry. Seventy-nine are there for express transits of only a few days; twenty-seven of these will already be gone within the next twenty-four hours. This seems to be the norm; thirty-one arrive tomorrow for stays of twenty-four to forty-eight hours, paid for in cash; only seventeen people are registered for relatively long stays like Plotkin's of at least several weeks.

That means that during the remaining twenty-eight days he will spend at the hotel, only 17 of the 135 current residents will be there for longer than two weeks. This is important information. It will allow him to refine his methods of monitoring comings and goings and, especially, to be virtually sure that at least 118 people will not remember his presence in the hotel during the week of his arrival.

If the current turnover rate isn't an anomaly, and the hotel makes its profit from express stays, only the seventeen long-stay residents might pose a problem for him. These are the people he will have to monitor; he must know everything about them, and as quickly as possible, before any of them are even aware of his existence, of the fact that he is there with them in the hotel.

He has not seen the manager, Clovis Drummond, or the dog, Balthazar, in forty-eight hours.

He must do everything he can to avoid these seventeen residents during his stay. He must do all he can to find out everything about them, down to the most intimate details of their bodies.

El señor Metatron has already gone to work. A few seconds later, the console hums and a tiny beep tells him that the complete listing of data is now in the memory banks. Plotkin commands the console to close the operating window on the capsule wall. He stretches out on the bed and falls tranquilly to sleep.

He is awakened by light and vibration coming from the direction of the cosmodrome. He springs out of bed half-naked and goes to the window, requesting maximum transparency.

It is the takeoff of the second big turn-of-the-century American shuttle, owned by one of the cosmodrome firms. To his knowledge, *Discovery* was bought cheap from the NASA museum by the Grand Junction Consortium twenty years ago; almost seventy years after it first became operational, it is still in good working order. Professionally speaking, because it is supposed to belong to this branch of the industry, each flight of the shuttle, in view of the repairs it must undergo each time it returns to Earth, results in an increase of at least 10 percent in insurance costs. However, falling numbers of clients are causing the Grand Junction Consortium to try to lower prices. This may mean several things:

That they still have a wide enough profit margin to absorb this type of financial shock.

That they have made a (no doubt barely legal) deal with the big insurance cartels to pay a kickback out of the profits in exchange for a false stabilization of prices. It seems certain that such insurance would do little to cover the costs of any real emergency.

The fiery spray emitted by the shuttle illuminates Monolith Hills below. The city and its lights look like pale, long-dead stars whenever this conical sun rises into the atmosphere.

I am come to send fire on the earth; and what will I, if it be already kindled?

The words of Luke, repeating one of Christ's most prophetic sayings, spring into his brain fully formed in his own language, and something—something he cannot understand—compels him to write them on a digital notepad affixed to the wall. Strangely, this something—which seems to him almost a some*one*—calls another sentence to his mind now, one that relates to the words of Christ and is cited by his apostle to the aged Old Testament prophet Jeremiah, to whom God said: *Now I have put my words in your mouth like a fire.*

Now this fire leaves the Earth each day despairing of its cause.

Discovery is a pure golden crystal shooting into the skies of the posturban night, while everywhere else on the planet, the cold visage of the Machine, with its sinister smile, obscures all human horizons.

Unimanity is fighting against itself, he thinks. Once this world has produced all the stars it can, and those stars have gone to join their sisters in space, then the worst monster of all will come. He has no idea where this strange intuition is coming from.

According to the General Statistics, the number of departing stars drops a little each year. Between the feudal and neotribal anarchies scattered over the globe and the Islamic emirates of Western Europe on one hand, and the motherly, terminal, and frosty world of the UHU on the other, the Devil had certainly given the choice to Unimanity. The UHU would undoubtedly finish by imposing itself on all humanity. The petroleum era was completely over. The cartels were restructuring themselves en masse in aquaculture, ecosystems, memory components, hydrogen motors, and nuclear fusion. Numerous Gulf and Central Asian states were left now with nothing more than a little blackened sand to sustain them. They, too, wanted a piece of the pie, and they wanted it more and more as they grew weaker.

People *dealt*.

The Arab Muslim nations, exhausted by nearly half a century of planetary warfare, now hoped to quietly eliminate the anarchical emirates that had so disrupted Western Europe, especially France, and to hand everything over to a global protectorate, under the control of one or another of the large UHU-approved government agencies.

That had worked fine, people said, for the temporary independent zone of Paris, and for thirty-five years! And they said that the European federal troops that surrounded the Vatican, who had themselves been surrounded for more than three decades by the various Islamic forces of the region, who were themselves at war with European nationalist groups of various allegiances, only pretended to be in agreement with one another until they could reach a "pacific resolution of the crisis." For more than forty years, the pontifical state had refused to sign the European Constitution from the beginning of the century, and for almost as long the Eurofederal troops, the Islamist organizations in their autonomous zones, and the various paramilitary groups had been fighting over the Western European territory. Everyone had had their turn at the punching bag. Nihilism always ends by exhausting itself.

Soon, the UHU will have all the power. It is the merit of the Grand Jihad that it precipitated its appearance. It is the greatest merit of almost half a century of global civil war to thus offer global peace as a *solution* that would even more certainly destroy humanity. There can be no doubt that the end of the world will come as it twists in on itself, like an old vinyl record scratched to the last groove. Dissolution disguised as the last solution.

Plotkin is surprised to hear himself humming a forgotten old tune by an American rock group from the 1970s and '80s called Pere Ubu: *I don't need a cure, don't need a cure, need a final solution.* . . . Just like his recollection of the Pink Floyd song title in the robotaxi during the trip from the train station to the hotel, this intimate knowledge of a song forgotten for decades, clearly stored in his memory, makes him think that at least a small part of his original personality must have been retained in this body. Yet he feels no particular attraction to music, other than perhaps a bit of Russian classical or jazz, or even a little mainstream rock—the same as everyone else. His fundamental personality itself seems to have been altered.

Discovery has left a fiery trail in the sky that he almost wishes would descend to wreak havoc on the Earth. He rereads the phrase from Saint Luke, sent by his unconscious and scrawled on a cellulose sheet attached to the digital network of the wall near the window. He does not remember knowing anything about the Gospels—or if he did, it was very little. Between dwindling Communism, post-Soviet neocapitalism, and the UHU's early prohibition of "intolerant" religions, and not counting what he knows of his previous activities, it is difficult to explain this unexpected appearance in his brain of a phrase from the Bible.

Something has malfunctioned in the instructional neurosoftware, and it is because *something else* has taken its place. Something parasitical. Something with an unknown objective.

He has no idea what this might really mean, but it seems very likely that things are not all going to go as planned.

> *HUMAN TERMINATION SYSTEM*

The first sign is the dream. The terminal dream. The original dream. The one that happened once and has simply continued ever since, all the other times, in all the other dreams. The one that accompanies all his crimes. The monadic dream of his new memory, the one that will, with two or three flashes, illuminate a few sad lengths of the great black labyrinth that occupies his conscience—that *is* his conscience, his being, whatever that is, or will become. His returning memory might prove to be a disaster. It is naturally disposed to be one. And when the Dream of his first identity comes tonight, assailing his sleep with a reality more real than any false digital universe or implanted memory, the secret memory of his personality, the black box of his past as a killer, he knows the real sense of the word *disaster*. The dream fills up an entire part of his memory, one meant to confine his existence to what he is. There can be no doubt of that.

And what he is, is this: a Human Termination System. An HTS.

He is an HTS. A *T-Excess,* in corporate-speak.

He is sitting with a guy named Van Halen, sipping martinis at a tiki bar somewhere in Australia. The bar is shadowed by a carbon antiradiation dome; the sky is too blue not to be dangerous. The sun is unbearable. They wear Hawaiian shirts of Fruit of the Loom cloned antiradiation cotton, Australian army shorts, retro luminous sandals, and anti-UV Ray-Bans. Both men are covered with a disposable, translucent, protective film that has been in use all over the southern hemisphere for the past twenty years. *Touristus universalis.*

The guy called Van Halen talks to Sergei in Dutch to avoid being understood by the crowd of vacationers around them. Plotkin's neurolinguistic center, a new technology at the time, works perfectly; it is as if he grew up in Amsterdam. He and Van Halen go over some important details of the plan. How to blow up the room located below the one where the target is staying?

More precisely, how to make sure that the sensors with which the target has filled his suite don't detect the electronic micro-impulse that controls the bomb?

They have already decided on the exact placement of the explosives: in the center of the ceiling. They have determined how they will illegally enter the room for exactly five minutes by the clock. They have chosen the type of explosives they will use—an antitank blasting mine. The modus operandi is set. Death is determinism.

Hidden in the ceiling behind an optical encryption screen, the bomb—made in China—buried beneath the floor of the space above, will unleash its deadly energy vertically. Its lethal contents, a combination of Ultrane aerosol gas and pulverized carbon silica, will be ignited by a second explosive blast. Any organic or inorganic material within forty cubic meters of the bomb when it goes off will be immediately reduced to ashes. After the time switch is activated, the mine will be set off the moment the target passes above it. The optical encryption console attached to the bomb will not only hide it from view, it will also ensure, thanks to a battery of specialized sensors, that it is indeed their target and no one else who trips the switch. It would be unacceptable to set off the device because of a pet, a hotel chambermaid whether human or android, or a hapless passerby. They are looking to blow the target's head off and no one else's.

They might have several hours or a handful of minutes to wait before the hit goes down. The neuroencryption system provided for this day by their backers, via a system of microsatellites, is not working too well. Their tests have shown its bandwidth to be quite limited. To make sure the profiling console works correctly, they have been forced to restrict the usage time and quality of the optical invisibility screen. Given his business, the German tourist might very well have an undetectable bio-implanted anticop scanner. They have no way of predicting his haphazard comings and goings. They have not yet figured out how they will get rid of him temporarily; that is one of the things they are discussing now.

It's the *temporarily* part that is the problem, actually. Temporarily, or permanently?

Plotkin thinks they should play it cool. No real reason to heap one more crime on the pile; it will be too much extra work to keep ahead of the police *and* kill the target, who is worth 100,000 Pan-Am dollars—of the time—to each of them.

Of what time? What year is he remembering? The dream truly is a black box of memory. His black box.

Input / Output. And in the shadows, reality.

Here, everything is recorded. He knows it is a few years after the end of the Second American Civil War. They work clandestinely for a secret agency of what is left of the American federal government. All of the thirteen original colonies of the 1776 Declaration of Independence, except for what is now Washington, D.C., are in Islamic hands. They are in Sydney to kill the young president and CEO of a free software company whose sales are skyrocketing across southern Asia and Oceania. The target is an Australian born with the name Sebastian Driscoll, thirty-two years old according to his birth certificate and a convert to Salafist Islam; he now calls himself Abdulaziz Ibrahim. A large part of his personal fortune, via various foundations and smoke-screen companies, finances Islamist groups, particularly those operating in Indonesia and Malaysia, where war with the Philippines, Thailand, and Sri Lanka is raging. He also supports the Islamic Caliphate of America, which emerged from the dissolution of the United States and occupies many territories, counties, and municipalities in what was once the Union.

They are there to kill the son of a bitch. "And I don't care if we have to knock off that pain-in-the-ass German tourist to do it," says Van Halen.

The pain-in-the-ass German tourist is a typical German tourist, born in the twentieth century, with at least five or six trans-G rejuvenation cures under his belt. He frequents Turkish baths, massage parlors, and especially the red-light districts, for visits to hookers of any sex. He is staying in the room just below the target's. The room where they need to put the bomb.

They've been following him for days, the stupid Kraut, and neither Plotkin nor Van Halen is about to be carried away by waves of compassion and pity. Plotkin just wants to avoid making a big mistake—like committing another crime. "I had to kill a bastard just like him in Brazil," Van Halen assures him. "Just before the Second American Civil War. A French pedophile, you know, serial rapist, violent asshole, with a custom-built personal neuroencryption mask and a top-of-the-line genetic depersonalization kit. He never left any identifying marks on his victims when he killed them, and even if he didn't kill them they couldn't recognize him. It was the family of one of the little girls he'd killed and mutilated that hired me, through a Chilean detective agency. All I had was a three-shot magnetic dart gun—you know, the little pseudometallic composite Glock Tridents. Undetectable by the cheap security systems at places like the fuckpad Dupont always went to, somewhere in Bahia, full of prepubescent girls. So I went out there. They welcomed me politely; I asked to see the second-floor girls and slapped five hundred dollars on the desk. They showed me upstairs like I was a fucking Saudi prince. There were a bunch of young girls waiting up there, all sitting on chairs around a big circular room with a multiscreen showing porno movies of themselves in action, with the clients' faces and voices scrambled.

"I told one of the girls I'd take her while I waited for number 13, who was busy sucking off the target, fucking redneck. So this kid and I go to her room, and I hit her right in the throat with a high-speed dart. Then I went into the other one's room. I killed the fat bastard with one dart in the spinal cord and another in the eye, and then I told the girl I was sorry that I probably wouldn't be back to fuck her later, and that she'd better shut up if she didn't want to end up like the other little whore in the room next door. I'd already reloaded the Trident; I just needed her to stay still for a second so I could fire. She opened her mouth when I pointed the gun at her, and a dart hit her right in the jaw. I finished her off with a second dart in the scruff of the neck, and unloaded the last one in the pedophile's skull. Mission accomplished. So I left. I'd asked a couple of young hackers from the Caracas barrios to break into the fuckpad's security camera system for half an hour, using a satellite that belonged to my backers. They punched in a few false sequences that made the cameras turn back and forth on a loop. A car was waiting for me on a quiet side street, about ten minutes' walk away. Then on the roof of the hotel there was a vertical-takeoff Chrysler. They had some bucks, my backers. The same night I was on the last flight from São Paulo to Chile; I'd used an ultraquick cosmetic surgery kit on my face during the ride to the airport."

Plotkin drew in his breath. "Shit, that must have made some noise, even in Brazil. Were the victim's parents okay with the collateral damage and all the hassle that came with it?"

Van Halen smiles. It is the smile of death at work.

"Those Brazilian fuckers? Not even Brazilian—Honduran, Salvadoran, Guatemalan, Colombian, Cuban . . . you're talking shit, Plotkin. The family that paid me was old money, from Venezuela. Oil, emeralds, electric energy, communications, civil war. Big money, nasty people; really hard-boiled. They'd been dealing with kidnappings for generations. Their daughter had been kidnapped and raped by that pedophile in Brazil while she was spending a school vacation with one of her friends near Rio, and the prick got the case against him dismissed because there was no concrete proof. No DNA traces, plus an alibi that seemed solid. He'd been hiding in France, and then cut out for parts unknown but influential. He disappeared for a couple of years and then turned up in Ecuador, in Quito, and went back to Brazil after that, with a false ID right out of *The Internet Catalogue of Pseudos for Pedos*. He found a place to stay; we followed him; we got him. And you know the funniest part?"

"No," says Plotkin, curious to hear the pearl of humor that would close this story, like the final nail in a coffin lid.

Van Halen. Van Halen's grimace-smile. The grimace-smile widens, filling the world with a luster that could chase away any divine shadow. "The funniest part is that five or six years later, just after the civil war, cops from the Free Midwestern Confederation found the real killer. The guy was living in Kansas; he'd been keeping a detailed journal of his crimes, and he'd just hung himself to avoid being arrested for murders committed there and in Missouri. I ran into a friend in China; he told me about it without knowing my part in the whole thing."

Plotkin is silent. He stares at the grimace-smile, which has taken over the universe. He guesses. The whole original-terminal dream knows it; all his being knows it: this ending has a moral. And the moral is this:

"I *am* sorry for the kids in the brothel, you understand, but they were all infected with AIDS. Not to mention all the new mutable sexually transmitted diseases; more than a thousand of those on the list now. They were doomed, no matter what. Plus, I mean, come on—that was a hot mess; a psychopathic killer settling accounts between gangs. The cops in Bahia really fucked that whole thing up."

Plotkin knows this moral. It is the moral of all assassins and spies. It is the moral of the World hidden underneath the World.

He also knows, though, that the grimace-smile isn't saying all there is to say. It is filling the world like a blinding truth—a truth that becomes invisible when brought to light. You need to have eyes used to seeing things in the shadows to bear such unknowable light.

This is the Batavian killer's moral:

"That French pedophile was a real prick. He was guilty, the bastard. Okay, not of kidnapping the little Venezuelan girl, or of the crimes committed by that asshole in Kansas, but he'd raped hundreds of minors, lined the pockets of human flesh peddlers all over the continent. You know just as well as I do that there are no innocent people in our game. Just guilty ones, actual or potential."

Plotkin remembers the World-grimace-smile. He remembers choking on the martini with its little fluorescent pink straw. The dream is entirely made of memory. The moment when he decided that he must always carry the plan all the way to the end. Exterminate the target, and kill the fucking German tourist.

Human Termination System.

We live in shadow. We never see the light of day; not even when we go out at dawn to kill a man; not when we drink martinis while planning the death of one or more targets under the burning sun of a southern afternoon, below a vast cracked mouth-dome screaming beneath the vanished ozone layer. Here, men talk in order to hide things. Here, men kill innocent people with the same cold tenacity as they exterminate the guilty. Here, you have to wonder if anyone is really innocent, or really guilty.

The dream takes him into another world now.

This time, it is night.

But it is the electric night of a Japanese metropolis. The interminable *daynight* of the endless city, looping in on itself all over the island and out into the ocean, where vast urban pseudopods shine their lights across the telluric abyss of the Sea of Japan.

This time he is with a woman, Mrs. Kuziwaki. They are in the offices of Mrs. Kuziwaki's holding company at the top of a high-security, two-hundred-floor tower belonging to her and her consortium. The top floor, a personal guesthouse reserved for Mrs. Kuziwaki and her guests, is overhung by a roof with programmable translucency; at the moment, despite the four-meter thickness of refractory composite above their heads, they are under what appears to be an open sky.

He negotiates the final terms of the contract with the Japanese woman—the Lady of Osaka, as she is called here. Mrs. Kuziwaki manages an immense network of legal businesses, and a group of illegal ones that is only a bit smaller. She is married to an English lord who fled Great Britain after the Shari'a took over almost 80 percent of British territory during the Franco-European Civil War. She also controls one of the large municipal parties in the region.

She has a rival, another businesswoman and head of a competing political clan, another queen bee. And now "there is no other solution."

We are the solution when there is no other solution, says one of the Order's maxims.

That is what he said to this lovely thirtysomething woman who wants to devour the world and anyone who challenges her, starting with that old bitch Mrs. Toshiro.

He said it to close the deal, and to show that his professionalism is not an empty promotional campaign by the Red Star Order, though he is still in the early stages of his promising career. They are at the top of the Lady of Osaka's tower. They are rising above the clouds of Olympus. They are overlooking a planet of light, stationary and mobile; it sparkles coldly, resembling the highly magnified motherboard of a computer.

They are like gods.

It is the definitive meeting of money and crime, Heaven and power, blood and truth. This moment, he knows, was a pivotal one; it made him what he now is. The contract is negotiated, initialed, and signed on the huge table of uncloned acajou that cost as much as a midsize house in Africa. It is a vast rectangle of natural obsidian, blackness marbled with green flecks like the water of an enchanted pond that lures him to the center of the room.

The dream images swim for a moment, then realign themselves like a series of ellipses.

There it is. A luxurious IBM-Chanel gown is half-ruined as it is torn from her body to fly like a black tornado across the room. Two pretty breasts, raised high by a bra of fine, natural silk lace in dark red, darker than the night that surrounds them, are topped by honey-colored nipples, amber points that quiver under his fingernails. Long black hair sways gently, like a vertical grid made of leaf veins, against skin more luminous than the moon, whose light spills gently across the ashy lakes in the blue-orange dark radiance of the city lights. This is what he is seeing, touching, caressing. Marveling at, with the sort of stunned curiosity children experience when their souls are still entirely free.

He takes her savagely on the emerald green table. Her thighs are spread wide; he lifts them high, feeling with his hand the heat and wetness of the dark bush he can barely see. He watches the young woman's delicate movements, her wrists curving toward the tips of her breasts while he, hypnotized, opens his fingers into a fan to gently rub the dark triangle of curls with its bittersweet drenching of moisture, the invisible aroma of her desire wafting around the two of them.

He tenses. Hard.

Here is your sex, sir.

An erection pointed toward the stars and the purple Osaka night. A tube of flesh so swollen it is nearly scarlet, straining to bury itself in the silver-colored flesh for which everything must be destroyed.

Because the beautiful Lady of Osaka wants to be fucked. Right here, right now. Immediately.

Under the stars and the purple night sky, at the summit of Olympus.

And she wants to be fucked, right here, right now, immediately, under the stars and the purple night sky, at the summit of an electric Olympus, because Plotkin—without even knowing it—has brought with him the explosive element that is creating these hormonal fireworks.

They have both come to screw the beautiful Lady of the Tower.

He has come here with his closest friend. He has come with Death.

As the soldiers back from the Second Gulf War said, these veterans he met from time to time when his career as a private killer was just beginning, death is the million-dollar question. It is worth at least that much. It is the question every woman accosted in a bar, every wanker you meet during a dinner in the city, every journalist who has never traveled farther than his own suburb, will ask upon learning that, one way or another, death is your business. If your job is to bring death, or, more precisely, to know how to sell death to the highest bidder, they will ask that question even if they can't lay the cash out on the table; they will ask to see, but they won't have more than a handful of coins. They will ask you without saying anything, but they will ask in such a way as to make equivocation impossible: Have you already killed? Have you already sold death?

And paradoxically, you will be able to hear the scream that sticks in their throats, no matter how drunk they are. "Shit, HAVE YOU ALREADY KILLED SOMEONE?"

Plotkin knows a guy in the Order, a Serbian, who always says that "Death is our whore."

It is the question no one asks, because it will not be asked. It hides. Its presence is only indicated by its apophatic revelation. There are a million ways to talk about death without ever mentioning it. There are at least a million ways to die. And the question, really, is worth its million dollars. Death is surely worth at least the price of a haute couture gown.

The dream has illuminated two time frames, two landscapes that reflect off each other, each reciprocating and intensifying the other. A vast ice palace might result from such a meeting, such feedback, such a Larsen effect.

Especially in a dream that holds such memories of experiences lived, whether falsely or not—which is of little importance now. The dream is there to incorporate those memories into his existence and his memory, and into what is called his identity.

There is, now, a third sequence that brings together all the points that emerged during the two original-terminal sequences. It is a long chain of violent images, murders, voyages in the night, men and women who scream or simply stare at him, paralyzed, at the crucial moment. Of cars that explode, personal planes plunging into the sea, cargo ships and tankers that are driven off course and then sunk. Political men killed by a long-range assault rifle with a telescopic lens mounted on its muzzle. Discussions like the one with Van Halen, or with other Order killers. Other solitary missions carried out as he climbed the ranks of the organization. Other landscapes, other lands, other plans to kill men. Or women.

Milan. The European Civil War has been frozen by the Peace of Sarajevo. In areas devastated by local outbreaks of the Grand Jihad, which would soon be heard again during these few years of false tranquility, this postwar that is never anything more than a preparation for the next war to come, an economy typical of this type of situation springs up rapidly, like weeds in a poorly cared for garden.

In Milan, during the various phases of the French civil war and the interminable European conflict that followed it, Italian nationalist factions stood in opposition to the regionalist militia of the Lombard Republic as well as Islamist troops from southern France and the Balkans.

There is a guy who wants to control one of the territories the Lombards have managed to retain: a big drug trafficker, Italian, but from Naples. For the Lombards, that means he is an Arab. When Plotkin kills him in the men's room of a very chic restaurant that just reopened its doors, tarnishing the fragile reputation of the establishment as well as the immaculate faience of the cubicle in which his target has just sat down—what was his name? Calvecchio, wasn't it?—he does so with the precision of a robot, the precision required to enter the world of the HTS, these authentic human supermachines.

He is hunkered down in one of the stalls when the target comes into the bathroom accompanied by his bodyguard. Plotkin could, of course, act as Van Halen does: fire first and think later—for example, wait for the target to sit down on his shitbowl while the bodyguard cools his heels in front of the entry door, which will have been locked to ensure the master's privacy. He leaves his own stall, kills the bodyguard—a high-performance silencer is less noisy than the fart of a new post-Italian-economy rich man—then kicks in the door and plugs the gentleman in question with the rest of the bullets in a gun that will be melted down within twenty-four hours.

But Plotkin has his own way of doing things. Something has already emerged in him that will set him apart from the others in his field.

He hides in the last stall, the one farthest from the door and the place where the guard will be. It doesn't matter much which stall the Neapolitan chooses. Thanks to a pocket scanner with neutrino tomography, Plotkin can discern—through three partitions and with the digital exactitude of a computer—the position of Mr. Calvecchio, the Neapolitan, or whatever his name is, who the Lombards want eliminated for one sick reason or another. On the scanner's screen, he sees the white, blue, and gold silhouette of the man sitting on a block that is vaguely cubical in shape and dark in color, like a negative of reality. The contours are very clean. The man is around eight meters away from him, separated by the climate-controlled air and something like three times two centimeters of Recyclo™ particleboard—in other words, nothing, for the high-velocity microammunition that the Sig Sauer magnetic unit will fire at four or five times the speed of sound.

He presses the gun barrel with its mounted nanocomputer against the partition wall to his right. Linked to the scanner, the pistol emits a tiny beam of telemetric light that points to the precise place where the mouth of the gun must be, and the exact angle it must have to be aimed directly at the unmoving head of the man who is currently emptying his bowels for the last time.

The high-speed projectile, the sound of which is absorbed by a long carbon-carbon tube made of several thousand kilometers of fibers rolled around themselves in a spiral, passes through the three partition walls without making the tiniest noise—sort of like a fiery fart—and causes a lightly smoking hole at the end of the gun barrel that is so geometrically perfect it might have been cut by a laser. The pocket scanner shows the man now sagging gently to one side, toward the opposite partition wall. His sitting position will keep him relatively stable for a few more minutes.

Plotkin dismantles his paraphernalia and stows it in a backpack made of antiradiation material (very useful against the optic-sensor glasses often worn by bodyguards) that hangs from the hook on the door, shining with the silvery sheen of Mylar. He flushes the toilet and leaves the cubicle calmly. He walks toward the sinks under the watchful eye of the big redheaded man who, dressed in a secondhand Armani-Apple suit, leans against the vast mirror next to the door and awaits his master's emergence.

Plotkin washes his hands—not too fast or too slowly—but with the eager speed of a man who has a pretty girl waiting at his table. He nods politely as he passes the big brute, who, sure of himself, unlocks the door for him. He is already on a plane that will take him to Finland.

Finland is only a transit hub that will take him in a myriad of directions, all leading to the murders he has committed on behalf of an Order of Siberian mercenaries.

Asunción, Paraguay, March 2028. Kraków, Poland, September 2030. Minsk, Belarus, January 2031. Cape Town, South Africa, June–July

2032. Tanzania, Senegal, Ireland, Panama, Singapore, Burma, Madagascar, Moscow, Krasnoyarsk, Irkutsk. Ciudad Juárez, Mexico; Baton Rouge, Louisiana; Portland, Oregon; Kamchatka, Estonia, Slovenia, the two Georgias (Caucasian and American), Morocco, Libya, Sweden, New Zealand. Southern China: Shanghai, Guangzhou, Hong Kong.

His life is a carousel of images, like an average tourist's photo album. Except that each postcard is written in human blood.

There is the local chief of the Global Unified Animal Liberation Front and Warriors of Gaia, whom a former member of the Ulster Freedom Fighters—Northern Irish Protestant loyalists—wanted dead for reasons known to himself alone, and he would never have used an Order mercenary for the job if his own organization hadn't refused to participate in the operation. Plotkin had only needed to follow the animalist guru for a week to precisely map out his habits. The man's security precautions are pathetically weak in the eyes of one who had been educated by the war schools of the Red Star. Boom. As the target comes out of the elevator in the apartment building of one of his mistress-groupies in his Dublin fief, Plotkin jumps out with a simple twelve-caliber Remington whose double barrel is conveniently sawed off. He opens fire two meters away, showering the man's upper body with buckshot. His head is instantly pulverized by an explosion of barbed-wire sand; his body distends under the impact, bucks, and begins to topple slowly toward the still-open elevator door. The second volley of double-aught buck, fired at the chest, paints the cabin floor with a spray of scarlet even before the corpse falls heavily to the ground. Mechanically, Plotkin sends the elevator back to the penthouse before leaving the building, singing an old Billy Idol song, "Dancing with Myself," the still-hot gun stowed neatly in his rucksack.

There is the wealthy Mexican businessman who begs tearfully for his life, promising untold fortune and pleasure, harems of women and entire federal reserves, brothel-cities and Olympic-size swimming pools filled with gold ingots. The man has himself ordered almost thirty assassinations, but he cries for his mother and seems ready to sign over the deed to Paradise rather than accept that his time has come, that the justice of the dark world has turned upon him. Plotkin and his men of the moment drag him out of the trunk of a big Chevrolet sedan and far into the southern California desert and the ravine that will be his tomb.

There is the private plane filled with an entire familial clan of Islamist guerrillas fighting the Catholics in the southern Philippines. There is the mobile firing station, an Israeli antiaircraft system, one of the technologies that proved so critical during the long siege of Jerusalem. There is the double-engine super-rapid speedboat used by members of the Catholic militia. There is the long flash of silvery powder that cuts across the night sky in search of a target he himself cannot see, then a sudden, enormous orange star—the explosion of General Santos's plane just off the coast, in the dense, tropical Pacific night over the pit of the Philippines.

Now dawn is breaking in an Asian city. Bangkok. It is suffocatingly hot, and Plotkin lolls on the banks of Chao Phraya, in front of the stylish, ultramodern, *made in Hollywood* Asian skyscrapers: extraterrestrial Burmese palaces; gigantic pagodas, tall crenellated towers curved inward in graceful convex lines, surrounded by huge billboards whose messages blink from Thai to Chinese to English to "International English."

The sky is a particularly intense turquoise blue all around the pale aura that rises slowly to the east of the East. The tourist-boat *Noria* operates twenty-four hours a day. He walks toward the quay at the end of a narrow street whose sidewalks are lined with houses made of Recyclo™ particleboard, displaying again and again the motif of survival in all its cruel nakedness—a filthy mattress, a case of local beer, and a cheap Indian television set. By the pier, the blue of the sky is even more vivid, the eastern aura whiter and more luminous. He boards a ferry and waits patiently for its departure on the pearlescent gray water of the river.

At the same time, at the other end of the city, a man starts up his big turbo-hydrogen 4x4, simultaneously detonating a powerful bomb lodged in the van parked in the neighboring spot. The luxury Range Rover and its occupant are blown apart in a fraction of a second, analogous to that nearly indiscernible instant of time when night is no longer night and day not yet quite day. That fragile and sublime instant he is living as the sun begins to rise over Bangkok and the waters of Chao Phraya glimmer with the pink-veined blue iridescence of dawn.

There is, in this dream, the *entire* catalogue of his crimes.

Even the ones that hold a moment of pure beauty in the terrible story of his life.

The moral of the killer Van Halen, and the ethic of Mrs. Kuziwaki, are stretched to infinity.

There is everything that can produce a world, then destroy it.

There is everything that makes him *him*.

The terminal dream affects his body like an endless series of white nights. A few minutes after waking, Plotkin finds himself as exhausted as if he has lived an entire lifetime in one night, and he knows that is, in fact, exactly what has happened.

That is why he does not ask the console for some legal amphetamine or another neural accelerator. He takes the time to swallow a bit of breakfast, then goes back to bed and sleeps for almost twenty-four hours.

> THE CARTOGRAPHY OF NOTABLE INDIVIDUALS

In the morning, the window lets through only a faintly pink gleam of light. The resin/cheap alloy furniture glows gently in the streams of pale sunlight. The list streams past in the air just within his reach as he lies on the helium bed, waiting for the automatic room-service waiter to bring him his breakfast.

The seventeen "special" residents are on the list, and everything about them is there too, down to the three billion sequenced pairs of nucleotides that form each person's DNA, down to virtually every hour of their lives, down to the memories that even they have forgotten. A second selection kicks into action now. El señor Metatron isn't just any intelligence agent. He was designed for an elite criminal order by the technological division of the California *yakuza*.

These seventeen people must be specially monitored in order for him to avoid them as much as possible during his stay. More importantly, el señor Metatron indicates, there are five that need to be watched even more closely.

For starters, two of them are androids.

The first is a sexed android of the female type, working as a legal prostitute in various autonomous territories analogous to Grand Junction. Like casinos and dope, this is quite a lucrative business in the areas around cosmodromes full of colonists-in-waiting, who knew they won't have a fuck for months, enclosed in their pressurized cabins, before—maybe—meeting their soul mates in the Ring

or on a lunar colony. To put it bluntly, the environs of private cosmodromes are little more than open-air brothels, mass cum reposi-
tories, that do as much business or maybe more than the simple space
industry. The android-whore is named Sydia Sexydoll Nova 280. Her
identification disk is perfectly legal, but two or three details ring
false. First, she leaves the hotel only rarely, and el señor Metatron
knows of no visits to her room, though he has viewed all the videos
recorded on the hotel's hard drives. Second, her DNA has a bizarre
print in addition to the official trademark of her manufacturer—in
this case Venux Corp. The strange print indicates the presence of a
transgenic operation whose main objective had been to cut all the
connections in her nervous system that would stimulate pleasure. It
is a legal operation in some cases, but sexed androids do not generally choose total and permanent neurocastration, because their
clients can feel it and don't like it. In this business, more than any
other, *the client is king*. El señor Metatron is formal: the operation
profoundly altered the basic bio-nano-cybernetic centers of Sydia
Nova 280's pseudocortex; it is irreversible. Never again will she feel
even a poor digital simulation of sexual ecstasy in a body initially programmed to give it.

The other is an orbital service android who has fulfilled its time
of service and who, legally back on Earth, is "looking for work" in
Grand Junction. It has a small pension from the cartels that employed
it during the first twenty-five years of its artificial existence. New
UHU laws regulating the "android proletariat" have imposed quarter-
century limits on "impersonal contract" service by androids to the
companies that have bought them. In other words, the legal age of
majority for an android is now twenty-five years, and until that
point, whether the android is paid for its services or not, it is not
considered a legal person. It is no longer a slave, but neither is it a citizen yet. Recent in-orbit attacks by the Android Liberation Front,
Flandro, are probably not unrelated to these legal changes in their
status promulgated by the Global Governance Bureau.

El señor Metatron points out two or three strange details about this one as well. In order of importance, they are: Several pirated rewrites are on its identification disk. The identity—only the name—has been changed. The rest of the information seems authentic. It gives its name as Ultra-Vector Vega 1024; its true name is Ultra-Vector Vega 2501. Just the series number was changed. Even before the android's return to Earth, from the looks of it. Then, even more strangely, el señor Metatron realizes that the android's departure coincides with the day of the last attack committed by Flandro, on the completely automatized Zero-G Industries freight transit station. The company specializes in the repatriation on Earth of used space materials. The attack took place eight weeks ago. The android traveled through Windsor, like Plotkin, and stayed there three weeks before arriving in Grand Junction around a month ago. Like everyone, or almost everyone, it lodged first near the aerostation, at the Hotel Manitoba on Aphrodite's Child, the town's red-light street lined with brothels. It then came up to Monolith, where it rented a furnished room near Nova Express before moving here a few days before Plotkin's arrival.

There is nothing positively linking it to the Android Liberation Front or the orbital attacks, but in view of the fact that its identity is false and also that there is no such thing as coincidence, el señor Metatron was certainly right to inform Plotkin of its presence. Best to file it under "potential problems."

Then there are the three humans: two men, one woman.

The first man goes by the name Harris Nakashima, but he too has a false identity, one that might possibly make it past the security systems in Grand Junction and the neighboring states, but likely no farther—not, in any case, past el señor Metatron's detectors. His real name is John Cheyenne Hawkwind. He is an American of Amerindian heritage, as both his real name and the photo on his universal ID indicate, though his mixed blood, a false ID, and probably a bit of cosmetic surgery allow him to pass easily for a Japanese American. He claims to have been born in San Francisco but is really from Montana, has lived in a dozen North American cities, both in Canada and in the Free American States—or at least those that are still members of the Union. He is forty years old. Like his alias, Nakashima.

El señor Metatron is firm: this guy is a dealer. A good one too. He sells prohibited metacortical drugs manufactured in zero gravity and therefore not in compliance with the bioethical laws promulgated by the UHU, which closely monitors the circulation of legal dope throughout the vast human territories it controls. The Governance Bureau has long since banned most orbital psychotropic drugs, citing them as "too dangerous" for the human psyche. The presence of a confirmed, experienced dealer near the cosmodrome, but in an area somewhat outside the city center and with a very reasonable crime rate for the region, suggests that a huge transaction—maybe several— is about to go down. The man has been to prison twice, but never for drug trafficking; he was arrested three times on drug charges, but released each time for lack of evidence. He must be really well protected by one of the mafias that share this territory. El señor Metatron thinks he might even be acting under the aegis of the Mohawk mafia—the one that you have to deal with if you want to deal anything around here.

For Plotkin, this one is immediately a PROBLEM. Not a potential one like the unemployed android. This guy has already had trouble with the cops. He's been in the cooler. He is also using a false identity undoubtedly crafted by the local mafia. Probably the Mohawks themselves. That last point is the most disturbing one. Especially since he arrived four days ago and will be staying for a month. Just like Plotkin.

Cheyenne Hawkwind, Plotkin muses, contemplating the man's face on the wall of images in front of him. *Piss off, Cheyenne Hawkwind.* He points his index finger at a virtual button and the Hawkwind problem disappears, to be instantly replaced by the next file. Somewhere over Plotkin's head, the bright bulb of el señor Metatron flickers in its spectrum between the visible and the invisible.

The double case Plotkin is now facing raises some questions even stranger and more troubling than the possible problems posed by the presence of a fucking dealer. He feels like he is being confronted with an enigma analogous to the malfunctions his neurolinguistic recombination center has been experiencing since his arrival at the hotel. It is as enigmatic as the words he wrote on the window's digital notepad.

Something.

Something unknown lives.

"What is it?" He asks the ball of light hovering between him and the various biomedical diagrams superimposed on the wall.

"That is the problem," el señor Metatron replies. "I have no idea."

This causes Plotkin no end of grief. For a specialized research agent like Metatron to be placed in a situation where it is forced to admit its incompetence is a kind of miracle. A reverse miracle, an antimiracle. Something completely out of character.

Though his still-limbic personality doesn't yet really know itself, his current identity—that of a Russo-American mafia killer—knows immediately what to make of this realization.

This is no longer just a PROBLEM, like with the orbital drug dealer.

This is DANGER.

Like the edge of the unknown. Like at the edge of the abyss of death.

There is also a couple.

Capsule 081. One of the motel's forty "double" rooms, corner suites on each of the ten floors. Jordan June McNellis and Vivian Velvet McNellis. Born in Auckland, New Zealand. Aged twenty-nine and twenty-seven years, respectively.

Legal papers? Yes, but part of their personal disks had been rewritten. Like with Nakashima, the work is shoddy; it seems temporary. The section of their file that has been rewritten covers a considerable part of their biomedical data. It seems that they suffer from a benign neurogenetic disease—these have become very common over the last half century—called retinitis pigmentosa, but Plotkin instinctively knows that this disease is more than just a trompe l'oeil.

Retinitis pigmentosa, version 2.0, to be exact, is a mutant strain that appeared shortly after the decryption of the gene responsible for the disease, the software agent tells him. The technical description provided by NeuroNet reads as follows:

http://www.nlm.nih.gov/medlineplus/ency/article/001029.htm#Definition: Retinitis pigmentosa is a progressive degeneration of the retina that affects night vision and peripheral vision. Retinitis pigmentosa commonly runs in families. The disorder can be caused by defects in a number of different genes that have been identified. The cells controlling night vision, called rods, are most likely to be affected. However, in some cases, retinal cone cells are most damaged. The hallmark of the disease is the presence of dark pigmented spots in the retina. As the disease progresses, peripheral vision is gradually lost. The condition may eventually lead to blindness, but usually not complete blindness. Signs and symptoms often first appear in childhood, but severe visual problems do not usually develop until early adulthood. The main risk factor is a family history of retinitis pigmentosa. It is an uncommon condition affecting about 4,000 people in the U.S. Symptoms: Vision decreased at night or in reduced light. Loss of peripheral vision. Loss of central vision (in advanced cases).

A disease of the vision. A congenital deformation of the retina, sometimes leading to blindness. An alteration of neuroptic cells, the presence of dark spots, loss of peripheral and then central vision . . .

This disease is a sign. A signal. A *code*. It is there to hide something else. It is there to mask the existence of some other disease, some other anomaly. It is evidence.

However, el señor Metatron is firm: there is nothing in their genetic codes that indicates anything other than this defective gene, and Metatron can discern nothing suggesting that they are carrying highly sophisticated countermeasure systems. However, their biodisks were rewritten with the obvious goal of hiding something.

Now here is an enigma. Something is not normal, that's for sure.

Here is a danger zone that needs to be contained, and fast.

Plotkin gets up, eats breakfast, showers, dresses, and decides it is time to go down into the city and conduct an initial reconnaissance of what will be his operating theater.

El señor Metatron has just brought up a detailed diagram of the hotel and its residents. "We have enough bandwidth on one of the Order satellites to be able to place the seventeen long-term residents under GPS surveillance," it informs him. They will all be traceable almost to the millisecond and millimeter.

While the bathroom gently collapses and withdraws and he gulps a scorching cup of tea in front of the window, he watches the city beyond the glass stirring and going about its business at the cosmodrome. In fact this too is a city that never sleeps. A decayed H-4 rocket prepares to launch a Soyuz recovery capsule—quite a high-risk endeavor.

As he prepares to leave the capsule via its exit airlock, el señor Metatron generates a wide operating window for his eyes only, a neuroencrypted display of a three-dimensional plan of the hotel, with graphics showing its occupants and their exact locations. Of the

135 residents, 98 are in their rooms and, given their relative states of immobility, are probably still sleeping. This means that 37 people spent the night elsewhere, most likely in some brothel or bar somewhere.

The nacelle elevator takes him directly to the first floor; the lobby is deserted. There is no noise from the direction of the patio. Only the surveillance cameras whir softly above his head. He knows that they don't really matter, that something in the plan will make sure they don't interfere. The only thing that counts is being seen by as few people as possible.

The patio is deserted—but, unluckily, the manager pokes his nose out from behind the counter.

"A little business trip, eh, Mr. Plotkin?" he smarms in an oily voice, a filthy smile crossing his visage.

Plotkin barely breaks his stride, throwing what he hopes is a friendly wave at the man, and tries to look like a Russo-American insurance agent. He only just manages to murmur a reply: "Just a little walk to stretch my legs, Mr. Drummond. Good morning to you."

He is already on the median strip between the motel and the street, walking toward the scaffolding of metal pipes above which the words *Hotel Laika* are scripted in twentieth-century neon tubing; a few of the letters have obviously been changed or replaced. He sees an orange shape coming up the street from the south; it is the robotaxi he ordered while waiting for the elevator. Turning his head in the other direction, toward the autobridge spanning the North Junction road, Plotkin makes out a black shadow that glides toward him over the asphalt. It's the dog, Balthazar. He has just come from the access ramp. By all indications, he is coming from the northwest—from Heavy Metal Valley.

As Plotkin steps into the car, the dog is several meters from the entryway, and pauses to note Plotkin's choice of destination—"City Hall, please"—before the taxi takes off. Their eyes meet: the bionic animal and the rebuilt human. In that instant, Plotkin realizes that neither of them is being deceived by the other's maneuvers.

Of all the hotel's residents, the dirty informer Clovis Drummond included, Plotkin tells himself, the one he needs to be most careful of is this dog.

> STARDUST ALLEY

KOROLEV PLAZA——MUNICIPAL TERRITORIAL SECURITY ADMINISTRA-
TION——YOU HAVE JUST ENTERED A YELLOW ZONE IN THE GRAND
JUNCTION CITY HALL'S SECURITY PERIMETER——PLEASE GO IMMEDI-
ATELY TO THE CLOSEST METROPOLITAN CONTROL OFFICE——FOLLOW
THE YELLOW NEURO-ARROWS ON THE SIDEWALK.

This is what happens when you pass the first security perimeter
that encircles Grand Junction's City Hall. Up to that point, you have
done nothing illegal. You can go into a "yellow" zone under the strict
condition that you must follow the neuroencrypted arrows transmitted by the city's UHU-approved system to the closest registration office, which will verify your ID and ask why and for how long you are
here.

If you stray from the yellow neuro-arrows for more than thirty
seconds, an imperious inscription will order you to return immediately to the "correct route"; if you persist for fifteen more seconds, a
final warning message will appear on your retina for five seconds.
Then there will be a numeric countdown from 10 to the ominous 0,
at which point the alarm will sound and the surveillance networks
will pinpoint your location down to the centimeter within a microsecond, and dozens of territory or city police officers, human and
android, will rush in to pounce on you.

El señor Metatron knows all this down to the smallest procedural
detail; all it has to do is enter the yellow zone and its organic backer,
Plotkin, receives a neuro-HTML page from the municipal depart-

ment; the *yakuza* software agent detects it in an instant, this funny living flame, gamboling joyously in the air, invisible to everyone but Plotkin. It hovers above the city's gray asphalt pavement, penetrating all obstacles that cross its path, human or otherwise, like a mass of neutrinos; playing with the neuroencrypted yellow line that marks—for the man named Plotkin, and for the crowd of thousands of humans that pass by the protected sector around City Hall—the shortest route to the closest metropolitan registration office.

For el señor Metatron, toreador of nanocomponents, sparkling keeper of the secret language of the pirate metacoders of the Unterbahn; for el señor Metatron, as powerful and invisible—or practically, at least—as the Word of God himself; for el señor Metatron, almost nothing is impossible when it comes to manipulating data, or the uninterrupted production of simulacrums meant to fool the simulacrum cops of the UHU network. All the immoderate pride of this clandestine intelligence agent passes through Plotkin's brain in a sort of flamboyant spray of pure ego, while words written in blue on a yellow background appear in front of him, floating above the sidewalk at the next street corner: TAKE KOROLEV-5, THEN VIKING ALLEY. NUMBER 456 NORTH, METROPOLITAN CONTROL OFFICE, STATION 14.

At station 14, he gets in line at window 3 and is welcomed by Jennifer CK2564.

It is law in all territories managed by UniWorld—about four-fifths of the planet—that any civil officer of a UHU-approved corporation must be identifiable by any UniWorld citizen. At the same time, an individual's right to his own "privacy" has led to a long legal battle that the Global Governance Bureau cut off by instigating the system of "registered first names." You have the right to lodge a complaint against agent John XX2000, but his anonymity will be preserved and you will have no way of bringing his "private life" into the fray. Jennifer CK2564 is a fat Mohawk woman, surely half-blood, who looks fairly agreeable in her brown Metropolitan Control Office uniform. Her muddy yellow badge indicates that her operational jurisdiction includes all the yellow perimeters in the territory of Grand Junction.

After a few minutes of discussion, Plotkin has learned next to nothing; the same is true for Jennifer CK2564; but el señor Metatron, who has come along like a sparkling torch to hover in the middle of station 14's ceiling; el señor Metatron, who glows insolently among the police station's surveillance cameras; el señor Metatron now knows everything about the various procedures, methodologies, organizations, and plans of Grand Junction's security forces. It—*he*—is undoubtedly the secret weapon Plotkin was told about in Siberia, the weapon that should let him—*if his memory works correctly; how ironic to think of that!*—override the enemy's security systems.

Plotkin's memory may not be the best, but el señor Metatron simply brushes that off as rotten luck. This bit of incandescent plasma would make child's play of security networks and countermeasures; he is sandwiched between two worlds, strolling on Plotkin's retina and neurons with no indication, even to the most modern scanners, that there is even the tiniest bit of suspicious cerebral activity. He is more false than all the false worlds that make up this one. More false than false—does that even mean anything?

That is why el señor Metatron was designed for the Red Star Order. To be clandestine now requires the ability to appear to a single brain, without even the Global Megabrain questioning what is happening. To be true is to be more false than the world itself.

In any case, this seems to be one of the surest ways to reach some kind of truth. It is perhaps Metatron—who else?—who is sending coded messages to Plotkin's brain; he might not even be aware that he is doing it. El señor Metatron is not just a simple program. He may not have a body to speak of, but he has a voice and a mind, things that he cannot understand in himself. It is undoubtedly Metatron—it must be—who sent him those unconscious messages about fire and its presence in the Bible . . . and in the rock music of the twentieth century.

* * *

Plotkin receives a temporary visitor's permit for the City Hall's yellow zone. Jennifer CK2564, the fat mixed-blood at the registration office, will only allow him three hours. *You came here what for?* she had asked him, in barely comprehensible English. He had explained that he was trying to contact a manager in the Municipal Consortium's financial department and that an introductory e-mail would be sent as soon as possible, but as a paid commission inspector, he had been sent to clear the way, et cetera, et cetera.

Jennifer CK2564 had cut him off short by handing him a dirty-beige token chip with the number 3 written in black in its center. *Three hours,* she had said, already signaling for the next person in line.

He had left station 14 well pleased, and begun to walk through the downtown streets.

Once he passes the barrier, he has full access to all the departments. He can go everywhere except the "orange" and "red" zones. He starts by taking Korolev-4, one of the large boulevards that divides Korolev Plaza into a star (it is modeled on the plaza with the same name in Paris); a venerable Korolev R-5, more than a hundred years old now and bought cheaply from the Russians forty years earlier, sits enthroned atop a grassy butte in the middle of the plaza, and large numbered streets form a vast eight-pointed star around it. At the corners of each arterial street, facing the antique rocket, tall buildings house various departments of the Municipal Consortium, linked by elegant circular walkways designed and built by a famous Indonesian architect in the 2020s when Grand Junction was at the peak of its power and could play with it as it wished.

Here, the crowd is very different from the one at the Enterprise aerostation. This is the administrative heart of the city; body-tuning-operation recipients have none of the brassy, cheap showiness of the trans-Gs at the aerostation or on the strip; with body tuning, the majority of modifications are internal and duly masked by nanosurgery.

Here, people look more human than natural humans—this has been the new trend for a good dozen years now. High-quality Versace-Motorola suits seem to be the norm for men, long Prada-Sony dresses for the women. Here, the crowd moves in lines cleaner and more fluid than the chaos that reigns at the city's gateway. Here, people work—or at least they work very hard at appearing to do so.

He turns off at the second circular avenue, called Mariner Street. It is a downtown typical of the short-lived 2010–2020 boom. The prevailing style is neo-Gothic with, toward the end of the period, the characteristic emergence of neoclassical styles that are still all the rage today. High crenellated towers overlook arches and naves in translucent composite or molded concrete in which statues representing pop stars, Gothic martyrs from the Middle Ages, famous Amerindian gods, and mythical figures from the space race are arranged in bas-relief or even built into the structure like gargoyles from an ageless age. These buildings are most often painted dark red, violet, mauve, or blue, cold and old-fashioned, while the more recent buildings—the ones from after the 2020s—duplicate the vivid colors of the palaces in Knossos or Babylon, complete with hanging gardens filled with lush, genetically modified bonsai jungles.

This part of the city is almost the oldest, if you don't count prehistory; it dates from the twentieth century, before private space exploration and before the Grand Jihad, when Grand Junction was still just a small town nestled alongside a Canadian National railway line in a Mohawk reserve partly located in Quebecois territory and partly in American—in the state of New York, within the borders of Vermont, and less than fifty kilometers from Ontario. Later, the "leopard spots" of the Mohawk reservations were partially united. The autonomous territory developed a triple border. Grand Junction itself was a bilingual city, and a large percentage of the inhabitants still speak French.

Well, Grand Junction French.

Here, humans are prosthetic extensions of urbanization. Each quarter, each street has its own dress code, which is more or less a

life code. Clothing brands are only the signs that point to urbanization as the utopian-atopian achievement of the human beings who
circulate within it. They are signs. They are urbanization. They are indistinguishable from the structure, the forms, even the topology of
the city. Born as the world began a steep decline, Grand Junction had
the time during its golden age to condense everything of the city and
posthumanity into a single matrix. Thanks to their off-center location, the autonomous territory and the zone of Grand Junction escaped the various waves of attacks that brought down North
America's metropolises during the Grand Jihad. Grand Junction was
even able to stay out of the conflict during the War of Secession; it
had the time to carry the urban phenomenon to the peak of success,
just before everything came tumbling down.

Men live here in a dream of total integration among machines
and society. Here and there are UHU-approved religious shops and
even legal interactive fetishes leaning against the walls of buildings, in
plain view on the sidewalks. Men or women can be seen plugged into
them, heads inclined toward the bluish haloes of the neuroconnections. Plotkin notes the presence of numerous Amerindian divinities,
pre-Columbian ones from Central America, as well as those from
Siberian shamanic rites and primitive slave and Nordic religions, and
even a few syncretisms that have risen from the mass of transcen-
dences supported by the magic of the UHU, whose federative slogan
appears each day at sunrise, written in clean white clouds disturbed
only by the dark oblong fuselage of an occasional passing zeppelin.
This is the source of the UHU's power, Plotkin muses to himself, again
without really understanding where the thought is coming from. *It
can swallow up complex singularities and unforeseen new innovations. It can
even admit differences, just like indifferences.* This world-machine is much
more intelligent than it appears to him—worse still, it is more intelligent than he can imagine. With the exception of terrorist groups
and "intolerant" religions—especially Catholic, Orthodox, and
Evangelical Christians, officially banned since the brief armistice of

the Grand Jihad and the "interim" concord with the circum-Mediterranean Islamic states and the American ones in Michigan, Atlanta, and Washington, D.C.—absolutely every possible and imaginable divinity existed in this new cosmopolitan Rome, the Rome of the End Time. Grand Junction, he knows (thanks to data acquired in Siberia—or had he acquired it somewhere else?), is regarded as a model of city living among the states federated under the aegis of the UHU.

He goes to 1044 Korolev-6 and asks to see Mr. Samuel Gerald M231, the deputy subcomptroller for the cosmodrome's general insurance department. They exchange banal small talk; Plotkin explains "why he has come" and is given two or three sheets of digital cellulose and a small disk, then advised to make an appointment. He insists a little, as planned, and obtains an express visit to the office of another peon named Jaggi S127, with whom the circus starts all over again. Plotkin acts like a complete automaton; he doesn't need to have anything to do with Mr. Samuel Gerald M231 or Mr. Jaggi S127 or their damn numerical prospectuses, strictly speaking, but it is part of the plan. On that point, at least, what remains of the instruction program was clear.

For three hours he acts like a robot, leaving dozens of traces in temporary and permanent files. False traces. Traces that won't be traces of anyone.

Traces that won't even be traces.

Then, he decides to visit the cosmodrome.

He plays the tourist—green zones, blue zones, no controls; just a few temporary traces in the tollbooths' files. He takes a robotaxi and pays cash. Grand Junction is one of the last places in North America where cash of any type is still in circulation. He pays with a mixture of yen and Philippine pesos, and receives change in rubles and various Eastern European pounds and crowns.

Apollo Drive marks the northern boundary of the city. To the east is Von Braun Heights, a simple rocky spine dotted with a few scraggly conifers, at the summit of which stands a tall bronze statue representing the German engineer, head inclined toward the stars, in the neo-Soviet style of the 2010s. Then there are the hills of Monolith Hills and their famous black monolith; then, farther still, the mysterious Heavy Metal Valley. To the west are two sprawling, posh neighborhoods where the bigwigs and local haute bourgeoisie live: Centaur City to the north and Novapolis just below it, separated by a small river with an Indian name. To the south of the city is first the aerostation and then, toward the water, several industrial and business areas, a handful of progressively shabbier residential blocks, and finally, at the southeastern tip of the county, the slum. The barrio. The favela. The human junkyard. Junkville. A line of eroded hills whose slopes are covered with clinkers stands over thousands of collapsible Recyclo™ particleboard houses and a few plastic bungalows and dilapidated mobile homes set on blocks for the more fortunate residents.

At the other end of the city, north of Apollo Drive, the restricted zone of the Municipal Consortium begins—only orange and red zones there.

Here the cosmodrome site begins. Here is the Holy of Holies, Cape Gagarin.

But it has never really been a cape; at least, not in recorded history. The last sea known to have existed in this region had receded by the beginning of the Cenozoic era. There aren't even any decent-size lakes except for Lake Champlain, to the southeast, toward Plattsburgh and Burlington, in what remains of American federal territory. Someone came up with the name, but no one can remember who it was. It goes back to the birth of private space activities in the area, some forty years ago at least. There are thousands of stories on the subject to be heard around Grand Junction; almost everyone has his own version.

From Junkville to the southeast, all the way to the vast natural plain of Cape Gagarin at the northern end of the county, is the secret dynamic that lies behind the entire economy of this territory. On one side is the Mud, the asshole of the World; there, outside the city, even before the aerostation and its connected industrial areas were there, is an indication that you would do better to leave, if that is even still possible, because you are already on the way to ejection—you are hardly more than a piece of garbage that cannot be recycled by local industry, or by a more base form of disposal, or even by the worst slut. On the other side is Cape Gagarin, the light of the stars, a vast plain bordered by hills to the east and west; an immense blue hole between two blue masses that press toward Montreal and above which, especially on particularly dark nights, halos of light appear like electric aurora borealises beyond the horizon, around sixty kilometers away. There, the launch center sends its blue and yellow pulsars into daylight that has become semiartificial, while its metal towers and the concrete pedestals of its launchpads, lit up by dozens of bunches of tightly packed spotlights emitting their blue and orange rays, serve as decoration for the nearly simultaneous takeoffs of the three different rockets on the tarmac.

Plotkin finds himself in the only "green" zone provisionally open to the public. It isn't even a blue zone; it is completely unrestricted. He is face-to-face with the Grand Junction Dream. To enter, you must punch in a red or orange code; then you will have a few hours to watch from a fenced walkway built for this purpose and called Stardust Alley. It is only a large, dusty alleyway several kilometers long, stretching alongside a high electrified metal wall that overlooks other perimeters of grids, some more dangerous than others.

It is at this moment that he realizes, with shock, that this area is populated by human beings just like him, at least in appearance. But since the beginning of his visit to the city of Grand Junction, it has been as if his perception program relegated people to the category of decoration, whatever their gender, race, or uniform.

He sees them, perhaps, all these humans, but he does not really *notice* them. Their presence fades in that of the terrible and manifest power of the city itself, its machines, its dreams.

Something has to happen, something unplanned, something outside the normal scope of life in the big city, for humanity to become visible even for a few moments.

For example, that bum over there—one of the aerostation untouchables that came to be here who knows how, facing his fenced-off, inaccessible dream, facing his forever-lost dream, facing the image of his ruined life.

Arms crossed, he shouts countless curse words in several languages and long roars that hang in the clear blue air, startling groups of fellow visitors who scatter, murmuring their shock and disgruntlement around him as he stands like a fulcrum, indifferent to their chaotic, fear-induced ballet.

He screams all his hatred, and all his admiration. Plotkin can't tell exactly what types of drugs he is on, but from the way his legs wobble, barely holding him up, he guesses that a lot of alcohol, probably legal, has gotten the best of his remaining synapses.

He belches; he shouts; he spits all his venom, the poor man, at the very face of the cosmodrome. He vomits out all his hatred of the city, of life, of mankind, of the stars . . . of God, who is not even there. Mixed in with his incoherent ramblings is a sort of barely audible poetry, an ode to what has destroyed him. An ode to the Holy of Holies. An ode to the cosmodrome.

A mobile Metropolitan Police unit is already arriving on the premises: two fairly old-model androids and a human chief. As they try a bit awkwardly to approach this big fellow dressed in rags, who continues shouting imprecations with his back turned to them, Plotkin sees him become aware of their presence via a sort of sixth sense and pivot slowly to face them and their old hydrogen MG. He offers them a smile so big he seems capable of swallowing them whole, as well as their old car and the whole fucking city they serve.

Then he screams, but it is also like laughing. It is a laugh that holds no mirth, a laugh so disturbing that it transforms him into a caricature, one that is frozen with terror.

"WHY DO YOU REFUSE TO SEE THAT WE ARE ALL DEAD?"

The untouchable's scream is only the vibratory prelude to his mechanical movement. He charges at the three cops and rams violently into one of the androids, who falls heavily on the hood of the MG. Immediately, the cop's robotic comrade and his human sergeant draw their nonlethal weapons from their holsters. Two small blue discharges shoot into the body of the big lug, who is turning on them, shifting from one foot to the other.

The dance stops abruptly, as the man falls unconscious. The human sergeant brings his GPS-radio bracelet to his lips and barks out a series of codes and instructions to the Central Police Bureau.

The crowd is already re-forming in small groups up and down the length of the fence. The problem is resolved. In five minutes, a municipal ambulance will come to erase all traces of the untouchable's presence. The cries and alcoholic odes to the cosmodrome are nothing more than an unpleasant memory, tempered by the icy presence of the police and the sound of radio voices in air ionized by the security grids.

Six hundred meters behind Plotkin, the Apollo Drive highway whirs with traffic; some of the cars, he knows, are defying UHU law with their combustion engines, whose noise and exhaust are poorly camouflaged by various homemade systems.

In the other direction, in front of him on the wide concrete expanse, the rovers advance with their mechanical, unrelenting, crushingly slow steps. Moving at barely two kilometers an hour, they seem almost to be standing still. The access runways leading from the storage and preparation hangars to the launchpads are between 2,500 and 3,000 meters long; it will take the rovers more than a hundred minutes to reach their destinations.

Plotkin sees the lights of the operations center, three control towers, and several long buildings that form a west-facing half circle against Centaur City, which has a clear view of the cosmodrome.

He stays where he is for a full hour, all the time allotted to him in the Stardust Alley blue zone. El señor Metatron sidles casually up to him; the security systems here are much more advanced than they are elsewhere in the city.

They are truly face-to-face with the Holy of Holies.

They are truly face-to-face with something like the image of the face of God fallen to Earth.

He summons a robotaxi and goes back to the hotel, filled with terrible, inexplicable doubt.

> THE MAN WITH THE DISGUISED LIFE

Thanks to el señor Metatron's GPS locators, Plotkin makes it back to the hotel without being noticed by anyone—except the manager, Balthazar the dog, and two tipsy Quebecois tourists hanging out on the patio in front of an antique video-game machine.

On the tenth floor, he barely has time to enter his room before the neighboring door slides open. According to the polymimetic flame, this capsule's inhabitant is a recently fired orbital cargo pilot. He works under the table on construction sites around the cosmodrome. He keeps a staggered schedule; they must have mistimed Plotkin's return to the hotel.

In his room, Plotkin changes and orders a breakfast of cereal and vitamin-enhanced yogurt—not too much nutrimedicine—with a diet soda full of Global Health Bureau–approved amphetamines. Then he asks el señor Metatron to show him a complete plan of the city's security systems and a general report on all operating procedures.

It takes more than an hour.

Plotkin takes a shower and is reminded once again that the image of his own face in the bathroom mirror tells him nothing, that the identities swirling around vaguely in his head do not seem the smallest bit consistent. Yes, he is a killer—that is the one thing he is entirely certain of—but for the rest, he has no doubt that the Order possesses genetic- and memory-reforming techniques that surpass human understanding, and that they have been used on him. What is all the more remarkable for being a rarity is the fact that the Order's techniques also appear to be incomprehensible to the highly sophisticated machines that have taken over the world.

Total amnesia would have been better; things would have been clearer—or a bit clearer, at least. One identity lost; one identity to rediscover. But his identity wasn't lost; it was falsified. One identity lost, ten to rediscover—all of them partially. His only oneness comes from this primitive duplicity between his identity as a killer with barely known origins and the many variables of his synthetic personality. His partial amnesia reveals only things that let him establish links among the false, the true, and the perhaps, like declassified files where anything important is blotted out in black ink. He is a man whose definition is chaotic, full of holes, a man who has too much memory. A fragmented man of the past.

He gets out of the shower. The rich afternoon light pours through the window; he stands nude in front of the large disk of glass. He can see that the first rover is now returning empty to its hangar; a Long March V rocket with a "handcrafted" capsule made in Alberta will probably take off within the next twenty-four hours. The second rover is nearing its platform, carrying a patched-up Atlas Centaur rocket. The third, with a French Ariane V from the 2000s, is only halfway to its launchpad.

Business was still good, despite the recession.

Could there be an intermediate state, or a synthetic one, between the two primitive qualities of Oneness and Multiplicity? He feels a strange yet "ordinary" sensation of single existence—of being part of a singular body in a singular place, in a specific era. He does not feel any of the side effects often associated with traumatic amnesia: no schizophrenia, no splitting of his personality. *He is terribly normal.*

His only excuse for a memory is a handful of half-false memories implanted in his cortex and a few shreds of true recollection stolen from the machine that controls his reality.

He is nothing. Or, *almost* nothing.

Maybe that is the "solution"—if, in him, the many can be one, and the one echoes throughout the many "hims," it is because he is nothing more than *potential*. He lets his mind explore a series of possibilities that go far beyond the few experiences he remembers. He envisions a line of infinite tension between the world and all the worlds within him.

He is undoubtedly a killer.

He has undoubtedly come here to Kill the Mayor of This City.

The instruction program is unequivocal on this point.

But though the past is dark, the future resembles a vast, luminous window onto an unknown more mysterious and sinister even than his own shadowy memory.

That night, he decides—against the most basic security instructions—to venture farther down the strip, down Leonov Alley, toward the plaza where a replica of the monolith from *2001: A Space Odyssey* stands. Urban legend claims that it is *the* monolith that was used during filming; everyone also knows that every private cosmodrome on the planet has its own monolith and that each one of them claims theirs to be the authentic one.

The Hotel Laika is situated at the northern end of the hills, almost right up against the cosmodrome. It has become a virtual northern suburb of the sort of long, linear city that snakes along the wooded plateau, a little more than twelve kilometers in length.

As far as he knows, the Leonov Alley strip stops short at the southern extremity, toward the 1400 block, just after it intersects Voskhod Boulevard. Part of the avenue and its environs had been replaced in the bygone days of the area's development twenty-five years earlier by a huge hydraulic basin that collects rainwater from the hills and directs it, in potable form, to other collection, processing, conservation, and distribution systems in the city. This blue gold, so necessary to the lives of Grand Junction's residents, is part of the primitive ecology of this corner of Canada, where the dryness of the American Midwest and the immense plains of Manitoba and Alberta is now infecting the north and east of the Great Lakes region, whose water table—despite the efforts of climatic agencies—has dropped almost 25 percent in the last fifty years, while more than a million of their glacial counterparts covering the surface of the country are already half evaporated and, like the Aral Sea in the previous century, are on the brink of vanishing from the map for good.

This war between man and water brought out the worst in each of them. Man not only needs water for himself, he needs exponentially greater amounts of it to proliferate, or just to survive under proper conditions—which are never anything more than a temporary plateau in the permanent struggle against entropy. At the same time, the more men and productive negentropic factors there are to consume energy, the rarer water becomes. Its rarity rapidly destroys the most basic growth and development factors. *If that isn't a war . . .* Plotkin thinks to himself. Only hydrogen engines, they say, are able to do the impossible—accumulate reserves of water while simultaneously increasing its consumption. It is said that the UHU is working ferociously to develop technologies that will result in actual water-manufacturing factories before the end of this century. It is said that certain branches of the Governance Bureau are looking to the private orbital colonies and their nascent savoir faire in matters of terraforming and astrochemistry. The lunar pioneers and Ring colonists have acquired, in barely thirty years, a great deal of expertise in the transformation of lunar rocks and circumterrestrial asteroids into reserves of oxygen and hydrogen, the two elements most important to extraterrestrial life. In the meantime, the war between men and water is not only continuing, it is intensifying, destroying ever more resources and individuals, just like the forty-five-year-long Grand Jihad, with its endless catalogue of abominations committed by men against men.

The Monolith South hydraulic reservoir is 1,200 meters long, 600 meters wide, and an average of 40 meters deep, half buried in the earth and divided into four equal sections. It is one of the best artificial hydrobasins in the Northeast for filtering and storage; it lets rainwater pass into the water table without any sort of artificial filtration. It is part of a Consortium eco-agreement: all new companies in Grand Junction, such as Hydro-Québec Waterplans, which manages the basin, are obliged to comply with it. The vast rhombus of concrete-composite, hemmed in by fences and security posts, cost a fortune at the time of its construction—but then, at that time, the Consortium was rolling in gold. The Mohawk and Russo-American mafias, as well as gangs of Canadian motorcyclists, had divided up the land. A few newer communities—like Junkville—had established their microniches in very specific areas and markets already abandoned by the huge local mafias. Business in the 2020s and 2030s was still booming, like it did in the heavenly Las Vegas of the American Golden Age. It is obvious, really, that the beginning, peak, and slow decline of the Grand Jihad have cemented the wealth of the city, the county, and the entire Mohawk territory. It is less and less certain that universal peace, only barely enforced by the UHU for the last ten or twelve years, will ever be as profitable.

While the battle against terrorism and expenditures for security and biogenetic research have taken up most of the public's money and energy over the last forty years—not without reason—*private* cosmodromes have been able to concentrate their efforts on the journey spaceward with the support of many countries and international agencies. The United States persevered a bit longer than the others in the space race, but the dream of a return to the moon was quickly extinguished by the double threat of terrorists wishing to destroy humanity at all costs and others just as rabidly desirous to preserve it.

Between the Second Civil War, the disunity that followed it, and the moral injunctions of all the lobbyists determined that taxpayers' money "would not be swallowed up by the infinity of space," it had only taken a few years for virtually the entire program to be frozen, as it had been in 1972. The moon was left to a few military companies and given up for the price of clumsy negotiations conducted among the various parties who had so recently come together.

Even with peace "restored," the UHU still does not seem ready to take a renewed interest in space exploration; there is always some urgent geopolitical program still to resolve, or a major ecosystemic crisis at hand, or a stuffy bureaucracy paralyzed under the eyes of ethical police and artificial legal intelligence. In a bar on the strip where Plotkin stops to drink a beer with an alcohol content that would be illegally high elsewhere in America (an imitation-British pale ale, outlawed since the application of the Shari'a in Great Britain; copies of English beers are all the rage in independent Amerindian territories, he is informed by a recollection that emerges from some unknown, dusty corner of his falsified memory) followed by an energizing cocktail typical of Grand Junction, he overhears a quartet of old gentlemen, all of them half-blood and speaking the local French—the details of which were imparted long ago by his instruction program. They explain, as they play cards in a corner of the smoky room, where a century-old jukebox blares twentieth-century country-and-western songs, that in a few years, when the Islamic emirates of Western Europe are more or less entrenched in the new Great Middle East, or in federalist Slavo-Russian Europe, when their fucking Odessa Treaty is finally signed, free cosmodromes will be regulated by "these damned bureaucrats and fucking big-ass maggots in the global government."

The artificial water table serves mainly Monolith South, a research center on Von Braun Heights, and Freedom-7, the only more or less "middle-class" neighborhood in the area, as well as the wealthy areas west of the city. It also provides a natural border with the southern part of the county, where the insalubrious Omega quarter and then the asshole of Grand Junction, Junkville, sprawl offensively. The entire perimeter of the basin is closely guarded: the border is, in fact, a high-security wall. Plotkin had the history and geography of the place inscribed in his memory in real time before he began his visit.

He is, in fact, *terribly normal,* like a supertourist.

Upon leaving the hotel, he walks through a galaxy of airtight whorehouses, a host of third-rate bars, small flea-bitten motels, capsule hotels like his own, deserted parking lots and shopping centers, numbered police stations, barely maintained parks (really just hilltops left in their natural state), and a few apartment buildings grouped in tight blocks, typical of the residential structures in Quebec and Ontario, Anglo-Scottish cottages in red and white brick, divided into two or three floors of flats and separated by long numbered streets with no names. These "rows" extend through the woods up to Gemini Drive. Back now below the 30000 block, he begins to feel the city become denser. There is more electric light. It pulses.

He walks past android-whorehouses whose neon signs blare the merits of their "girls from the sky." Indian casinos with names culled from Mohawk culture or the space race—or both—in this Franco-English mélange that is the official language of the whole territory, try unsuccessfully to imitate the giant Las Vegas establishments. Actually, this is a "freer" state than Nevada itself now, which had seceded during the first days of the Second American Civil War. Here, anything is still possible—even winning money at a casino.

Again, Plotkin is impressed by the incredibly fluid manner in which the instruction program can work—when it functions. It is like a living word processor implanted in his brain. As soon as any general, historic, or "academic" information becomes necessary, the neurosoftware and its linguistic nanocenter impart the desired knowledge so quickly that you feel you've always known it.

It is a residual morsel of the program, accomplishing its tasks without a hitch.

Continuing on, he sees a few exoskeleton-pedestrian shops, for people who want to walk faster. This phenomenon was a by-product of turn-of-the-century medical innovations in biomechanical prostheses for those who had been wounded, paralyzed, or had a limb amputated, and of military research conducted during the Grand Jihad. He notices that a large number of people are using these exoskeletons, sometimes mounted on wheels like Rollerblades, sometimes simply molded to fit their feet like orthopedic shoes from which several cables stretch up to the hollows behind their knees. The older models, which look like ski boots with shin guards attached to them, had never really gotten beyond the medical, military, or experimental phase. Now, nothing kept reengineering techniques from cobbling together for you—in less than an hour—a state-of-the-art biomechanical system and, if you had the money to pay for it, a portable system that could be incorporated into your own body and unincorporated from it just as easily—and, consequently, able to be sold or rented for a lot of money.

It is a struggle to keep the Orbital Ring in service, and only cosmodromes like the one in Grand Junction are still able to transport people there. Still, machines are constantly being invented that allow man to be less and less tired.

Plotkin walks through open-sky souks where various scavenged high-tech materials are sold. There are people selling cigarettes, which are illegal in 90 percent of the North American territory. He passes two or three neurogame arcades, where men openly sell versions of pedophilic, sadistic virtual-reality pornography that is outlawed almost everywhere else. Toward the north, near the hotel, it is still relatively calm. It is only when he crosses an enormous four-lane boulevard called Nova Express that he really passes beyond the border of the neighborhood responsible for the reputation of Monolith South: Ottawa Village. Here, your security level drops more than a few notches.

According to Grand Junction's internal ecology plan this Monolith Hills enclave south of the strip is part of the "low society," as it is referred to by General Statistics. In a way, a very certain way, it is closely connected to Junkville.

The paradigm is there, supervisible, in the form of blinking signs that indicate it like writing on a wall. In the PERMANENT INDEPENDENT ZONE FOR THE LOWER CLASSES—read: the poor—people exploit one another without the slightest qualm. Ottawa Village, fifteen kilometers to the south of Junkville, is like a predator face-to-face with its prey. In Ottawa Village, the cosmodrome pimps act like kings of the city and the Orbital Ring. *"Suck my cock, bitch, and I'll get you a visit to the Cape."*

Here, in this place that has managed to rise minutely above Junkville, throngs of procurers from the strip work the world like a job, feeding copious streams of bribe money into the Municipal Consortium's various black boxes.

In Junkville, you have only to look around to make a killing. Some people compare it to the intensive overfishing of the twentieth century, when there were still noncloned fish. Rumor has it that there are true open-sky recruitment centers there, and that they are never empty, day or night.

In general, Ottawa Village sits between Nova Express, in the 22000 blocks, and extends south to Pluto Street, 10000 numbers lower. This is the heart of the strip, with Leonov Alley as central Broadway, and dozens and dozens of streets where bars, brothels, nightclubs, arcades, fast-food places, and various cockfighting pits crowd together under the glacial polychromy of neon signs. It is here that one passes through the "solar system" with its nine successive streets bearing the names of our sun's planets. A veritable concentration camp for whores. All the diseased flesh in Junkville that is still capable of being used is gathered there. Especially the flesh of minors.

Past Pluto Street and the 9900 block of addresses, a vast area of electroneural arcades and gladiatorial arenas, whose flying saucer-shaped hulls seem to have only just landed between V1 Street and V2 Street, things grow progressively calmer. The start of Leonov Alley, at the corner of Voskhod Boulevard, may not exactly be SonyDisney-World, but it seems like nothing more than a trendy nightlife hotspot, with a few picturesque antique porno theaters (still working).

It is often said that the Devil loves to disguise himself, and will even dress up as Christ, if he must, in order to attract the damned.

He no longer needs to go to all that trouble.

The Devil's best camouflage, in this day and age, is the Devil himself.

The black monolith stands, obviously, in Monolith Plaza, at the corner of Mercury Street and—of course—Monolith Street. It serves as the symbolic starting point of the "solar system." It is only a poor slab of black carbon-carbon, three hundred fifty meters high, standing on a broad pedestal and facing, via Monolith Street, a long slope that goes down toward the valley and the lights of Grand Junction. Its hieratic presence in the middle of this square peopled with whores, pimps, and their motley clients, with crude noises and lights, is totally incongruous; it seems almost as obscene as it is ridiculous. It is as if some deity ended up on the wrong floor, and had never been able to get back on the elevator to Heaven.

Plotkin walks for hours, climbing from the 9900 block back toward the Hotel Laika.

The 9900 block alone contains a good hundred addresses; hence its name. It is home to one of the largest arenas on the strip; there, gladiators of all types face off against one another. Collectively neuroencrypted historical reenactments have been wildly popular for some time with the public, who gathers en masse in the rare places only partially controlled by the UHU to see "authentic" Roman gladiators, battles between superheroes, and famous battles that end occasionally, if not often, with actual deaths. Fractures, wounds, and amputations are the rule. The fights take place in beaten-earth amphitheaters with participants in the uniforms of Roman soldiers, Thracians, and retiarii; and in zero-G cabins where they dress as Superman and the X-Men. It is said that some directors of the UHU Governance Bureau admit that "violent sports, placed under reasonable ethical control, are an excellent substitute for imperialist aggressiveness and war." Plotkin hears wisecracks on this subject in the streets as he passes by groups of people loaded on some drug or another, legal or illegal—there are many for sale on the Monolith Hills strip. *Grand Junction's a model, did you hear? We're going to export the 9900!* He hears laughs and incredulous exclamations. But the more time that passes on this planet where he has apparently lived for fifty-six years, the more he understands that there is less and less sense in the claims of the UHU directors—the "masters" of the world.

No more frontiers to conquer; no more war to face; no more limits to reach beyond. There are good times ahead for the professional gladiators.

Bread and circuses.

The circuses, especially, are in for a brilliant ride, in these times when they are permissible and welcomed so much that they may well exceed their origins.

Back to the hotel now. Time to waste away in front of his neuro-quantum console.

* * *

El señor Metatron reappears just as he is crossing Nova Express.

ALERT.

The message blocks his view as he steps up onto the curb of a small street lined with third-rate cybersex shops. The words flash bright orange in front of an android-whore covered in black latex who strikes a series of lascivious poses in the front window of a specialty boutique.

The android Vega 2501 is there too. El señor Metatron recognized his genetic imprint on a cash machine a little further up on Moon River.

He must be avoided at all costs. Plotkin should take a left there, now, at the next corner (Alpha Street), but he does nothing.

He doesn't know exactly why he is acting this way—why he doesn't leap to follow the imperious instructions of the invisible light blob that is hovering above the pavement next to him, at the corner of a building, in front of a shop window, under a neon sign, a few inches from the aerosol-sculpted hairdo of a whore.

He walks calmly in the direction of Moon River. He walks calmly in the direction of the android. He walks calmly toward one of the possibilities that the instruction program did not anticipate.

The android is walking in front of him, heading north. Back to the hotel, no doubt.

The LED display in his right eye informs Plotkin that it is 2:18 in the morning. What has the android been doing in Monolith South, beyond Nova Express? Why here, in this neighborhood full of whores, illegal dope, and crime? Why the hell had he needed to get cash on his way back to the hotel?

Because he spent all his money on the strip between the "solar system" and Nova Express, that's why. Because he has plenty of cash. Even contracted androids get paid well by certain orbital corporations. And the strip is full of merchandise available for cash, and so is Ottawa Village.

Sexed androids are becoming more and more popular with humans. It seems logical that, in return, sexed androids would be attracted to *Homo sapiens*. And it is likely that, for an android who worked for almost twenty years in harsh lunar conditions, there is hardly any difference between a *biological human structure* aged twelve or fourteen years old and one twice that age. Male or female probably doesn't matter much either.

Something is pushing Plotkin to follow Vega 2501, or whatever his name is. El señor Metatron immediately makes his disapproval known, but the neuroinstruction program seems to be perfectly operational on this point. All the reflexes of a secret police agent are deeply and clearly ingrained in him.

He plunges into the crowd, never taking his eyes off his prey, turning away, bending to reattach a Velcro shoelace, or loitering behind a handy obstacle when, occasionally, the android half turns to look in some clothing or sex shop. He plays with his programmable clothing in an intelligent manner—that is, without overdoing it. He always keeps his distance.

His learning, the discipline acquired, the spy-killer training are so strongly embedded in his psyche that he is rapidly able to detect something abnormal in Vega 2501's maneuvering.

He is trying to determine whether or not someone is following him.

He is trying to spot a possible tail.

Have I already been found out? Plotkin wonders.

El señor Metatron suggests that he think about some information taken from the Moon River banking terminal. The identity of Vega 2501—the false identity—does not belong to anyone. More precisely, it is the identity of a person who died in the Ring, but for whom there is no registered death notice. This "person," an android like him, died on the eve of his departure from the Orbring—the eve of the Flandro attack on the Zero-G Industries facility. Yet his death has still never been officially announced, and does not seem to be recorded anywhere. Only the internal report of a hospital station mentions it. Vega 2501 undoubtedly had something to do with the Ring attacks. He is on the lookout for a possible UHU cop or one from some orbital corporation. Only an authentic NeuroNet genius like himself, el señor Metatron claims, would have been able to ferret out that grain of information.

Plotkin smiles to himself at the outsize ego of the brazier flaming with contentment at his feet. The little guy is very talented, he must admit.

Our "man" is hiding something. Something related to the attacks and the suspicious death of another android.

Something that has some relation to his "inhumanity."

It is clear now that at some point they must meet.

* * *

Past the 30000 block, around three or four kilometers from the hotel, the android goes into a bar. It is a place typical of this northern part of the strip, less noisy than Monolith South. There are the obligatory dancers executing their spins and outdated "sexy" poses around their everlasting aluminum bar at the far end of the large, dimly lit room. The tables are mainly occupied by middle-aged working-class men, probably punters from the nearby cosmodrome construction sites.

At the bar, there are one or two temptresses already at work. Calmly, the android heads for a free stool.

Plotkin knows that Grand Junction's bars are among the rare establishments in North America—on the planet, in fact—that do not refuse to serve "andros." That may explain why Vega 2501, after twenty-five years living in orbit and on the moon, in places where such segregation is not only useless but harmful, and is therefore banned, decided to come "find work" in Grand Junction. He is just another one of the pilgrims who come in the tens of thousands to populate the city, its strips and barrios, for a half portion of the dream, for a speck of freedom in its cellophane wrapper, for the more and more distant stars.

The best thing to do is be direct.

Plotkin sits at the bar and orders a beer; the barman hands him a sheet of memory cellulose listing alcohol of all kinds. Animated holographic advertisements pop up next to each choice. Plotkin glances distractedly at the menu, keeping his peripheral attention on the android, who orders a double scotch—perfectly legal in Grand Junction. When the barmaid, a nicely proportioned Anglo-Canadian redhead with green eyes that shine like phosphorescent lamps, comes to take his order, he again opts for a pale ale and gazes appreciatively at the young woman's body for a moment as she moves to the other end of the bar.

Plotkin notices that the android's attention is similarly focused; he likes women. Young ones—though this one is an adult at least, around twenty years old. He isn't a pervert, just an android who prefers to go to bed with *Homo sapiens*. Fine. Time to approach him now.

"Hello. Excuse me, but aren't you staying at the Hotel Laika?"

Plotkin doesn't budge from his stool; there are two empty places between them. He smiles pleasantly at the android, who turns to him, surprised, his face almost human save for the perfectly balanced features, the unnaturally bright gray-blue eyes, the bland smile and digitalized expressions, the too-perfect smoothness of his skin. There can be no doubt of his origins.

"Yes," he replies. "You too?"

It's as simple as that.

The waitress is Chinese American, a little pudgy, but whose voluptuous curves, accentuated by her black leotard, seem to provoke a good deal of arousal in the android's emotive sensors. She sets the two drinks down side by side on the corner of the table and takes their money, thanking them for the generous tip the faux human includes in the cosmopolitan Grand Junction currency. Plotkin and the android have moved to this isolated table in the corner of the room, lit only by an old neon Budweiser sign.

Plotkin plays his role perfectly, leading with his knowledge of the space industry. *My office is one of the best insurance companies in Russia, et cetera, et cetera.*

Later, it will be almost impossible for him to remember the exact chronology of events—or nonevents. It will be impossible to remember how long they talked, or what they talked about. He will, however, remember the waitresses.

And a few bits of important information gleaned randomly from a few sentences exchanged with the android.

Vega 2501, or whatever his real series number might be, worked his twenty-five years of orbital service for the Brazilian army, mainly on the moon. He then worked in several Ring factories as a security guard, among them Venux Corp, which manufactures—like all the companies in the field—orbital androids.

Plotkin remembers that Sydia Nova 280 was manufactured by Venux Corp. It was quite a coincidence. On the moon, during his contractual service, Vega 2501 had had high-responsibility jobs such as chief mission operator; he surveyed thousands of kilometers on the Hidden Face with the Wilcot-Volkov expedition. *The Dark Side of the Moon* was the Pink Floyd album that had marked the band's apogee and thus the beginning of its end, Plotkin is sure of it; he knows the group and its history by heart. It is part of the cobbled-together personality he is hanging on to as fiercely as if it were really his own.

It doesn't matter anymore what is true and what is false. *It doesn't matter,* he says to Vega 2501, smiling, who at his request is explaining the sexual customs of androids in orbit. It doesn't really matter whether he is an insurance agent or a professional killer, or whether he spent his childhood in Novosibirsk, or London, or Buenos Aires. None of these details really matter, do they? What counts is the fact that something totally unplanned is beginning, delicately, to take hold of him.

What counts is that he is beginning to live.

Later, when the bar closes, around 3:30 in the morning, they walk back up the strip together to the hotel. Plotkin decides to take a chance.

"Have you met the other android staying in the hotel?"

Vega 2501 seems genuinely surprised. "What other android?"

Plotkin knows he is treading on quicksand here. Yes, he has been drinking, but his reflexes and intuition are unaffected. All throughout the night, an antialcoholic filter has been dissolving and transforming the harmful sugars. He had half a dozen beers, but he feels as if he's barely had a pint. It wasn't even voluntary; this is part of his "organic" kit; as a good professional killer for the Order, it is out of the question to let himself be abused by any legal or illegal narcotic. The android probably has a similar device; he is walking quite as straight as Plotkin.

"A female android. I passed her once in the hall," he lies.

Vega 2501 seems frankly disturbed.

"A *female* android, did you say? So she's sexed? One of the new androids?"

"Yes; like you, but female."

They walk slowly but steadily, crossing Telstar Bridge, a simple twenty-four-meter expanse of steel and concrete spanning a millennia-old ravine carved into the hills. They can see the hotel on the horizon, with its holographic dog on the sign turning above the carbon dome, glowing eerily in pastel blue and pink.

"I've never seen her. A *female* android—you're sure? And you passed right by her?"

"Yes," Plotkin says, still hovering somewhere between a lie and the truth. "Definitely a female."

The words plunge Vega 2501 into renewed depths of confusion. He does not speak again until they reach the hotel. They part quickly.

"Well, good night, Mr. Plotkin. Thank you for the enjoyable evening," says the humanoid machine with a synthetic smile, before walking quickly toward the hotel's southern wing, where his capsule is located.

It's as simple as that.

Open and shut in the same way.

* * *

Plotkin crosses the lobby toward the west elevator. He passes the counter, and notices that the light is on in the manager's office. The counter and a good part of the space behind it, as well as a sort of attached cubicle separated from the main office by a partition and a little glass door, are full of all kinds of objects.

No. Only three kinds.

Exactly three kinds.

There is a pile of Recyclo™ particleboard boxes filled with packs of cigarettes.

There are translucent plastic Tupperware containers in which Plotkin can discern the distinctive color, shape, and smell of thousands of marijuana buds.

And there are boxes of children's neuroelectronic games made in India. One of the boxes is open, ripped partway across its width, near an ashtray made of a large crockery plate, in which several Camel and Marlboro butts glow orange in a pile of gray ashes emitting wisps of carbon smoke that fill the entire reception area.

Someone has been smoking cigarettes. Someone has piled boxes haphazardly. Someone has been very busy doing who knows what in the service office, and not for very long, by the looks of it. The delivery is dated earlier that night. Plotkin guesses that by dawn all of it will have vanished.

He obviously stumbled on this at a very bad time, but it is really a stroke of luck for him. The manager is probably in the middle of stowing the most compromising boxes somewhere in the office.

He shouldn't stay.

He makes a beeline for the west corridor and its elevator.

> NEXUS ROAD

He has chosen a moment just after daybreak. The eastern sky is pale pink; the air is already full of the warmth of the day to come. Violet cirrus clouds float high in the atmosphere. Above him, the sky is deepest blue, indigo really, full of the ghostly phantoms of stars, but already it is blurring little by little into the rosy edge of the sunrise.

During the night, Plotkin rented a car from his room, a ten-year-old Ford with a hydrocell motor, all in accordance with current standards.

After his expedition on the strip with the android, he slept all day. Then, at night, he started to think of his plan. His plan to Kill the Mayor of This City.

The android's presence might prove useful. He seems destined to serve as a scapegoat, a pigeon, a patsy, a pawn—the perfect Lee Harvey Oswald for this business. Plotkin's plan is a sweeping one: an attack on October 4, the day of the Sputnik Centennial, claimed by a phony abbreviation of the radical Flandro dissident sort. He will operate secretly from the android's room, leaving DNA traces there that will strengthen the theory of a conspiracy with local human ramifications. He will leave a few clues on Vega 2501's console—compromising documents here and there, and probably the weapon used in the crime, or maybe the portable organizer he will have used in developing his plan. *Vega 2501,* he thinks. *Vega 2501, the android with the false identity. A lovely career as a political assassin is opening up for you.*

* * *

At that moment, a sudden impulse moves him to write something on the desk's digital notepad.

IPSE
VOS
BAPTIZABIT
IN
SPIRITU
SANCTO
ET
IGNI

He stares at the words, written in all capital letters.

Another unconscious impulse, like when he wrote the phrase from the apostle Saint Luke on the wall near the window. What does it mean? Is it a code?

It is Latin, el señor Metatron explains, taken from a text by Origens, a third-century Christian writer. Again, the words are from Saint Luke.

"Baptism by fire?" Plotkin asks the software agent, intrigued.

"An old apocryphal tradition in both Judaism and Christianity. When you are reborn after death, you cross a river of fire that purifies the evil in you."

Why did he write these words on the desk's notepad? He knows no Latin whatsoever, and surely isn't familiar with any third-century Christian writers.

Something.

Something is interfering with his mind.

El señor Metatron detects nothing abnormal in the neurocircuits of the room's console. Plotkin asked the intelligence agent—who is, in the words of secret-network habitués, an "angel"—to proceed with a complete checkup of his own biocellular implants, with the very latest antivirus protection. Down to the tiniest immune-system nanomachine. It will take hours.

El señor Metatron doesn't find a thing.

If someone is trying to pirate his neuroinstruction program, or someone—or something—is trying to implant messages *encrypted in Latin* into his brain, they are doing it in a way completely unknown to him, or to one of the best personal security agents in existence anywhere.

A group of Catholic resistance fighters? Or Evangelicals? Hard to believe. There is no way they would possess technology so secret that it leaves no trace detectable by el señor Metatron's elite sensors. If they did try something, did attempt—for one mysterious reason or another—to control his mind, taking advantage of a moment of weakness in the program during his postamnesiac reconstruction, his guardian angel would have detected their maneuver, at least indirectly, after the fact if not at the time.

Plotkin goes to the window.

The cosmodrome's launchpads are empty. The stormy sky seems to be moving toward a monstrous abyss, with huge squadrons of altocumulus clouds lumbering like violet zeppelins whose black edges are edged with the city's lights as they float and whirl in the gusty night sky. On the console's weather channel, Plotkin reads that winds of at least eighty kilometers an hour will be blowing in from the west for the next forty-eight hours. WorldWeather explains in a communiqué that it was able to deflect part of the winds and the energy of these "super–jet streams" away toward the Great Lakes, but that the weather will still be unstable for the next couple of days.

There are forces at work here. Natural forces, social forces, forces of unknown origin. Forces that just may help him carry out his plan.

His plan to Kill the Mayor of This City.

He decides to leave the hotel.

* * *

The car is waiting for him as planned on the North Junction road, at the bottom of the autobridge staircase, facing east toward Vostok and Heavy Metal Valley. A map of the area is affixed to the car's computer, but Plotkin has no need of it. It is firmly etched on his mind: its graphics, its grid lines, its creases, its holes. The map is an integral part of him now, thanks to el señor Metatron, who appears periodically in a flash of wispy magnetic fire on the passenger seat before disappearing a moment later, as if breathed out and in again by the onboard computer.

The map is part of the land. The drawing seems to hang in front of his eyes at the same time as the actual streets flash past and the obscure network of all his electromagnetic systems—obvious and hidden—work in tandem to generate the changing images. The road is abandoned, but it is still part of the network. It is still part of the Municipal Metropolitan Consortium of Grand Junction, and part of the county.

They drive east through the hills for about ten kilometers. The road stops abruptly at the bottom of a hill wooded with tall tropical trees whose luxuriant, heavy masses and bunches of wildflowers with large, almost fluorescent green petals are familiar to him, as is the high, silver-tinted grass that undulates gently in the breeze like a vast carpet of velvet.

The road crosses a simple slope, or, rather, a semislope where the asphalt is laid in dashes several hundred meters long on the dusty, ochre-colored ground, then forks to the northeast and south. The sun blazes on bushes of pink and red-orange roses just behind the rocky butte directly in front of him. The sky is painted in slashes of gold, ruby, and flame.

HEAVY METAL VALLEY, XENON RIDGE: NEXUS ROAD NORTH.

NOVA EXPRESS CROSSROAD, NEON PARK, OMEGA BLOCKS, JUNK-VILLE: NEXUS ROAD SOUTH.

He turns north automatically, part robot, part human.

In front of him, the map spreads its wings of diagrams, its linear filigree. Xenon Ridge is eight kilometers high and overlooks the valley. It is an ideal observation point.

To reach it, he must leave the main slope of Nexus Road and take a lateral road—something that hardly even deserves to be called a path, actually—pompously named Xenon Road, which veers to the northwest and climbs sharply toward the summit of a mesa half denuded by the erosion of winds coming from the steppes of the Midwest, one of these southern Canadian maple-treed and wooded hills that are rapidly succumbing to global climatic chaos. From there, one overlooks the valley and Nexus Road leading from it. He notes the linguistic change; he must be just on the American-Canadian border, or very near it. "Rows" have changed to "rangs" and the signage is now bilingual, as is the onboard computer.

Historical diagram: This area has been around for twenty-five years, emerging when underground private astrobusiness was still booming despite—or perhaps because of—the Grand Jihad. The city of Grand Junction had grown considerably and already covered the equivalent, or nearly, of the entire county. The Municipal Metropolitan Consortium, which included the city proper of Grand Junction and all its emerging or fully developed peripheries, like the Leonov Alley strip and even Junkville, was thus created. They had decided to open a road from Gemini Drive toward the north of Monolith Hills, intending to go even beyond that to the eastern limits of the autonomous Mohawk territory near Lake Champlain. That was how North Junction came to be. Then Nexus Road, and then the access road with its autobridge to the strip.

Then everything stopped.

The Second American Civil War and the multiple confederations of free states that resulted from it had more or less supplanted the

planetary Grand Jihad, which had itself been detonated by the French
and European civil wars after a decade and a half of fiery attacks, just
as the Balkan conflicts had served as prologues during the century
preceding the war of 1914–1918. At the same time, or close to it,
like an ultimate historic Larsen effect, the entire Islamic world had
been enveloped in a religious and civil war so ferocious that, like a
bomb snuffing out the fires of every oil well, it had in a single blow
completely exhausted the planetary war that had been raging since
the beginning of the century.

That had been the moment when the UHU decided to make its
entrance.

Geological diagram: Xenon Ridge is a typical southern Quebecois
hill. Formerly covered with trees and bushes, it is now bare of anything but a few scrubby green oaks, dry shrubs, and mutant thistles
of astonishing size. Here, geological constraints have resulted in radical adaptation by the local vegetation. Xenon Ridge is in the process
of becoming an eroded monolith. Ancient schists cohabitate with the
granite pedestal of the Canadian shield; here and there, the terrain is
already grooved in places by the harsh winds that ravage the yellow-
brown earth, exposing bits of bare, hard rock like human skulls denuded of flesh in a thousand-year-old necropolis discovered by a keen
archaeologist.

Plotkin looks out over the low plain; it reminds him of a vast,
rocky amphitheater. Far away there are prairies and surviving forests
reduced to savannas; farther still, a few islands of greenery have been
planted here and there like atolls lost in an ocean of dust.

And in the middle of all this is Heavy Metal Valley. He has read
the descriptions, but now he can see it. Feel it.

He understands.

It is a city.

Legally it is part of the county, officially managed by the Consortium. But the general abandonment of expansion projects toward the east twenty years before has turned the zone along Nexus Road into a veritable *autonomous territory inside an autonomous territory*.

It is like a hole in time, and in society.

A million piled carcasses, ready for the scrap heap, the crusher, or the recovery yards of the various communities that share the plunder.

Plotkin is wearing special contact lenses equipped with a stereoscopy center and a powerful zoom, as well as an optional infrared mode. Legal, made in Chile, and of very good quality, they are part of his essential survival kit.

A million piled carcasses forming high metallic walls, often oxidized, in various states of crumbling disrepair; myriad makes, models, and colors, crisscrossed by an entire network of paths meticulously covered with clinkers. It is a vast maze of metal spiraling outward from its coliseum: an immense expanse of sloping concrete in imitation of the NASCAR racetracks of the Golden Age. Plotkin thanks his intuition for leading him directly to such a high vantage point. He thanks his killer's instinct for letting him admire the splendid dawn of this day; the azure of the sky is so intense it seems turquoise. He thanks whatever part of him ignored the *rest* of him to allow him to live this unique, memorable moment.

Heavy Metal Valley. A city within a city. An electric medieval fortress. He distinguishes well-ordered central avenues and smaller side streets that are a bit chaotic, and various rows superimposed on this tangled, discordant, and unimaginable tangle. It is like a slightly smaller copy of Grand Junction itself, but one made of metal, plastic, composite resin, and Plexiglas windows dating from the twentieth century that sparkle in the morning sunlight. Nothing here is newer than 2015 or 2020, in fact. And obviously, he realizes as the hours of watching wear on, the singular economy of this city within a city is based on century-old machines. In view of the derogatory statute of the private closed course granted by the Consortium for the duration of seventy years, the communities of Heavy Metal Valley have the right to burn rubber, gas, trinitrotuol—it doesn't matter what, he realizes, as long as it makes noise, smoke, and flame—right up to the end of the century.

Or, at least, right up to the end.

The city is also organized according to certain specializations. The basic types—cars, trucks, buses, and heavy and special vehicles (cranes, bulldozers, tanks, etc.) have their own reserved areas. By noon, he has begun to register the existence of a very complex economy, one that is far more sophisticated than simple dealing in used mechanical parts.

They are rebuilding vehicles.

They are remaking them completely.

And they are not content simply to build identical copies, though they do; often, they rebuild vehicles from different wrecks, creating new machines entirely, such as their own vision of the gasoline-powered automobile of the twentieth century, a time most of them are not even old enough to remember.

As the sun glides between banks of storm clouds, Plotkin discerns the repetition of one detail among the hundreds of subtle variations in the high piles of smashed cars—a recurring motif glinting all around an old school bus. In metal, in Plexiglas, in various plastics—everywhere, discreetly gleaming on the rearview mirrors of some cars and on metal plaques soldered to the chassis, as with the school bus.

Crosses.

Christian crosses.

There is nothing ostentatious. No really visible monument. No high symbol dominating the track. No figurines representing Jesus, though he sees a sort of crucifix inside the bus, planted in the wind-shield, the driver's area transformed into an altar.

Catholics? Secret Christians seeking refuge inside independent territory?

He orders his contact lenses to magnify his view fifty times, the better to see the vehicles upon vehicles where, half hidden in the masses, UHU-prohibited Christian symbols can be discerned. Some grilles have been redesigned to hold stained-glass rose windows, Celtic crosses, Maltese crosses, Lorraine crosses, Orthodox crosses . . . nothing that catches the eye at first glance, especially from afar.

Bingo.

Illegals.

Catholics.

Plotkin once again thanks his Order killer's instinct for having brought him here.

If a group of anti-UHU Catholic dissidents are living here, and if they are conducting various secret sabotage or recruitment opera-tions, then they must be behind the malfunctions of his instructional neuroprogram and the messages coded in Latin. A young Catholic hacker, a genius, living smack in the middle of Heavy Metal Valley?

In his head, the words *Heavy Metal Valley* flash scarlet.

If there is an unknown force looking to compete with el señor Metatron, the problem must be resolved immediately.

Yet, there is something—a flicker of good in the bad—like a glimmer of light in the shadows. He can easily imagine using all these forces against one another, to his own advantage.

Hopefully as part of his mission to Kill the Mayor of This City.

Past noon, a high trail of powder rises above Monolith Hills. A Texi-can rocket with a reusable Chinese capsule from the twenties and seven passengers is leaving for the Ring. A long strand of pale gold streams from its tailpipe. The white smoke from its boosters dissipates slowly in the sky in ethereal twists. After their ejection, nothing can be seen but a huge golden star glowing with radiation that is absorbed little by little by the gases in the ionosphere.

The atmosphere is growing more magnetic by the second. A storm is brewing. Obviously, the rocket took off at the last possible moment. The sky is ominously purple on the horizon, near Ontario. It is time to go back.

El señor Metatron, he is informed, visited a number of personal information systems of this city within a city while he stood watching from the overlook. He detected nothing really suspicious; most of the machines contained a number of legal irregularities, but nothing to validate Plotkin's theory of a young Catholic hacker lost in the valley.

Around six thousand people live here full-time, to which are added almost three thousand seasonal regulars and approximately two thousand travelers and transients at any given time. Altogether, the valley holds about twelve thousand people. Twelve thousand people for one million vehicles—probably, interjects el señor Metatron, more like one and a half million. That means a little more than a thousand vehicles per person.

Heavy Metal Valley must be considered differently now than Plotkin thought of it when he first set out for Nexus Road.

It isn't the strip. It isn't Ottawa Village.

It isn't the upper-class neighborhood of Centaur City or the downtown of Korolev Plaza.

It isn't the cosmodrome, or the Enterprise aerostation.

Nor is it Junkville.

It isn't any of those things, not even a monstrous mix of them.

It is something else. It is rich in things that are now worthless.

Everything seems turned toward the past, toward a disappeared era with high crystal towers, a morning from the first year of the century, and yet he sees it like the heartbeat of a future, a future that wants to be. It is as beautiful as the fading of a rocket into the azure midday sky.

He returns to North Junction a little before one o'clock in the afternoon. The sun is just a pale yellow disk in the sky now, behind the storm clouds that whip at nearly a hundred kilometers per hour across the heavens like enormous gray metallic flying saucers veined with purple and charged with electric energy.

There is a light to the west, and another farther north.

There, in the direction of Ontario, the sky is turning into a high blue-black wall, as if an enormous wave of Chinese ink is rising to blot out the western horizon.

Clearly, WorldWeather has decided to spare the megalopolises of the Great Lakes—where a lot of voters reside—and to refrain from shunting the winds and energy of the super–jet stream toward Michigan, Illinois, and Minnesota. Grand Junction will soon benefit from its status as an "autonomous territory."

The first drops of rain splatter on the car's windshield as the Hotel Laika comes into view. He leaves the rented Ford Nissan to autopilot itself back downtown and ducks under the metal-tube arch as the rain pounds steadily harder; an enormous flash of blue lightning crashes down on the horizon just then, sounding like some creature ready to devour the world. He strides quickly over the center divider leading to the hotel entrance as the monsoon grows even more violent and ducks into the lobby at the same moment as another peal of thunder strikes, closer this time. Shooting a final glance at the pouring rain assaulting the strip, he goes to the counter, finds it empty, and walks another few meters to the vast portico of white stucco that opens onto the central patio and its dome of translucent pink resin. Mechanically, he looks inside.

And sees her.

> *SYDIA SEXYDOLL*

It is the android-whore. He recognizes her immediately—even before el señor Metatron, that cunning little blue-orange flame surrounded by tiny sparkles, appears between him and the patio. His guardian angel warns him to be careful. "It was all right for the android from space, but for heaven's sake, not the Monolith Hills whore," the pseudo-intelligent creature begs.

"She might be useful," Plotkin replies in a whisper. "All of them, all five you told me about, might be useful to us. It doesn't really matter if they see me or cross paths with me. Actually, it might help to implicate them that much more in the authorities' eyes during the investigation. We're lucky—we don't just have one Lee Harvey Oswald. We have a bounty to choose from."

He isn't an Order killer for nothing. Intelligent agents have a reputation for being by-the-book, scrupulous sticklers. As a personal security metaprogram, it is el señor Metatron's job to watch over him; his zealous attitude is understandable. But though prudence is the mother of safety, as they say, an *excess* of safety can prove the worst imprudence. No, he needs to act quickly, like he did with Vega 2501 at the Next Frontier Bar.

The girl is at the farthest end of the cafeteria, standing in front of a table where a cup of coffee steams gently, and staring out the programmable window toward the valley, the city, and the technological zones of the northern suburbs. She is looking in the direction of the cosmodrome.

He chooses a table near hers but not too near, goes to the buffet, and serves himself calmly before sitting down.

She is around twelve meters from him. She hasn't turned since he came into the cafeteria. She didn't move one iota as he served himself at the buffet, sat down, and began to eat.

From where he is sitting, he can see that the cosmodrome, hidden behind an odd sort of white, drifting fog, is barely visible. The fog is truly strange: Mobile, like white pinpoints moving and covering the city little by little, coming from the north, from the direction of Montreal. White spots falling from the sky and floating lightly in the changing wind, sometimes almost horizontally. *Snow.*

The storm blowing in from the southwest had encountered a strong and probably unexpected current of cold air coming straight from the Canadian Arctic. In the space of just a few minutes, one of the most surprising climatic vagaries of the forty-second parallel occurs before his eyes: the quasitropical storm out of Dakota and Manitoba turns into a veritable blizzard. Between the time he got back into the rented Ford on Xenon Ridge and the moment he left it at the unfinished intersection of North Junction with the strip, the temperature dropped almost fifteen degrees. Ten minutes later, it has fallen below zero.

He immediately understands that this will be more difficult than the encounter with the android out to cruise the strip. "Clients" can chat despite superficial differences. Client and product, though— that is something else.

So he settles for a long, patient observation session.

She is an android of the very latest generation, no doubt about it—from a rear or even a three-quarter view, she is utterly indistinguishable from a human being. She breathes, moves, even stands still just like a human.

As with her "male" counterpart, Vega 2501, it is only the microdetails, which only a trained eye like Plotkin's can see, that mark this perfectly humanoid entity out as a nonhuman, a machine manufactured in orbit by Venux Corp, the global leader in sexed androids.

During all this time, el señor Metatron scans the network, all the way up to the mainframes of the Ring, to find out more about this "girl."

This is the time. Without a doubt. This is the time.

He feels strangely anxious just before speaking the banal opening phrase. The words are clumsy on his lips, as if his teeth are made of glass. He pushes the feeling away with a single thrust and says, loudly but not too loudly:

"The cosmodrome is lovely, isn't it?"

There is no trap more subtle than the truth. There is no trick more dangerous than authenticity.

The phrase, chosen after much reflection and the rejection of dozens of others, is simple—and, more importantly, it is true.

Completely true.

Plotkin too, in the core of his being, is beginning to feel singularly fascinated by Grand Junction, and especially by Cape Gagarin, where both the damned of the Earth and the richest dandies seek their assumption into orbit, into the chaotic, aristocratic, subproletariat of the Ring.

He too has stood at the window of Capsule 108, day and night, and watched the ballet of the rovers and technicians around the launchpads.

And so he too can utter a banality such as *The cosmodrome is lovely, isn't it?* with an authenticity all the more miraculous because he is living it himself.

And the truth is a trap so subtle that it functions inexplicably, whatever form it takes as a single incident. And the truth is so profoundly a total creation, an art, an apogee of artificiality, that in this way, like a gleaming rocket in the sky, it becomes free and closes in on its prey like a splendid carnivorous plant intoxicating an insect with its digestive juices, rendering it so drunk that it is unaware of its own annihilation in the midst of hybridic beauty.

He lures Sydia Sexydoll Nova 280 into his trap.

He quickly knows that he has done well, that his solid certainty, as well as his professional assassin's intuition, are good and that he was right to follow them, and that he must continue to follow them by seeing and introducing himself to all five "special residents" detected in the hotel by el señor Metatron—even if, by doing so, he incurs the displeasure of the solitary little flame sulking at the other end of the room. The impression rapidly swallows up "life," his "life" or what he calls his life, and this swallowing up is not closing it in— rather, it is opening it up wide, uncoiling it, unfolding it like a fruit peeled down to the core; even if the ribbon of his existence has more holes than whole places, more shadow than light, more goal than memory.

All at once, he knows that the trap of unassailable truth works. They find themselves side by side in front of the picture window.

On Platform 3, an Atlas Centaur modified with a "clipper" capsule, a reusable Russian vessel from the 2010s, is being readied for launch. Six people leave tonight for the colony of New Providence, somewhere in the Ring.

Just as quickly, after a conversation he consciously keeps very random—no premeditation, *ever*—they are seated across from each other at the table where her cup of coffee is no longer steaming.

Whatever his original personality was, whatever the various synthetic identities planted in his cortex by the Order's neuroengineers, his killer's instinct—his instinct as a man with an objective, of this body here and now—is shaping, each day, more and more, his real-time "personality." It is most likely one of the most secret components of the plan, one of the most clandestine mafia techniques used to reshape his brain, isn't it? Maybe there is nothing wrong at all with the instruction software. Maybe even the coded phrases and mystical messages have nothing to do with what he has until now thought of as accidental interruptions of the neuroprogram. Perhaps the two phenomena aren't even linked at all. Maybe the instruction program has just lost its usefulness.

Maybe he can finally begin to be sure, for good, about the emotions that are emerging inside him. Maybe he can be sure of his instincts as a spy, a killer, a man of secrets.

Maybe he can trap this "woman."

Yes, his deepest intuition tells him. You can trap this "woman."

And trap her he does. At the very moment when his jaws snap shut on her—like the bee caught in the juices that will devour her despite how much she wants to devour them—he understands the nature of the trap he has set.

She explains that androids like her are manufactured in orbit, but their use there is very regulated. She was manufactured in a weightless embryocell but, unlike androids created for the space industry, she was soon sent to Earth, where, for twelve years (the maximum time allowed by new UHU ethics laws for sexed androids) she worked for a Chinese escort company that had custom-ordered her from Venux Corp. For the last two or three years, she has worked solo.

She's lying, Plotkin tells himself, while listening with an outward air of interest. *She's lying; she isn't a prostitute anymore. She's been operated on; her sexual instruction programs have been erased. They even cut her neural circuits and took out her specialized microcomponents.*

She isn't a whore anymore. She can never be one again. She's lying to him. Why?

"With my resume," she is saying, "I'll probably never have the chance to get my hands on a Golden Track, even if I do have the money. I'm not even on any of the waiting lists."

Okay, okay, Plotkin says to himself. *So she isn't here to go to the Ring, and she isn't here to be a hooker.*

Then why?

His mind whirling, his intuition crackling like an electric spark at this android who watches him in silence while drinking her coffee, Plotkin changes the subject. It is a verbal move of desperation as he grasps for the time he needs to deal with the adrenaline coursing through him.

"Can you drink alcohol?"

Of course she can; he has known that since his night with the other android on the strip—but he didn't really ask the question hoping for an answer, just to gain some time.

"Yes," she says, chuckling lightly. "I'm a Venux. We're almost human. Really."

He smiles. The trap closes again, slowly. Impressions as precise and hard as knives assail him.

She isn't here to go to the Ring. She isn't here to be a whore.

Then what is she here to do? And how the hell is she living, anyway?

Knives, hard and hot, in his head.

The "girl" is, he must admit, very pretty. Long brown hair, firm body, oval face, fine, slightly upturned nose, violet eyes, and an astonishingly natural mouth—more natural than most of the puffed-up orifices on "authentic" women. The bionic engineers at Venux are incontestable masters of the feminine aesthetic; their reputation is impeccable. Next to her, any other make of android, even the new ones like Vega 2501, looks like a Japanese experimental biped from the turn of the century.

Who are you, SS-Nova 280?

Who are you, *made-in-space* Sexydoll?

Half an hour of observation, barely half an hour of conversation, plus everything he already knows—and these are the hard, hot knives penetrating his cortex.

An enigma. He is face-to-face with an enigma. His "trap" has caught a mystery he doesn't understand.

Nakashima/Hawkwind, the dealer: a problem.

The brother-sister duo in Capsule 081: potentially dangerous.

The android-technician from space: a pigeon.

But Nova 280: an enigma. And this enigma is still completely impenetrable as he goes back to his room.

The trap, it seems, is closing on *him*.

> MAPS AND DIAGRAMS

If such a thing as chance existed, Plotkin would never have come to Grand Junction.

If such a thing as chance existed, he would not be staying at the Hotel Laika.

If such a thing as chance existed, the conversation wouldn't have ended at the same time as the blizzard.

If such a thing as chance existed, he wouldn't have taken the elevator back to his floor at precisely twelve o'clock noon.

If such a thing as chance existed, he wouldn't have met the manager as he left the nacelle, while the fat man was carefully closing the magnetic door of the service staircase leading to the loft in the anti-radiation protection dome.

If such a thing as chance existed, he wouldn't be questioning the manager about his presence here now, in such a deliberately casual way:

"Have you been fixing the cracks in the dome?"

The man gives him a measuring look and slings a cloned-leather bag over his shoulder with a curt movement. "What cracks? You should mind your own business. If there were cracks, the security systems would raise the alarm about it soon enough."

Nearly nauseated by such blatant dishonesty, Plotkin gazes back at the bloated toad. *Sure,* he says to himself, *unless you regularly fuck with the sensors, which is exactly what you were just doing here.* "Ah—excuse me," he says almost humbly. "It's just that I have a pocket scanner that detected a few anomalies in your dome."

The man stares him down, a very unpleasant look in his baleful eyes.

"Is that so? Well, I've done a little research of my own, and that insurance company of yours is a piece of shit. Don't try to stick your nose in my business. You've got no right."

"I just wanted to help, that's all. Don't get excited," Plotkin retorts, shouldering his way past the man and going toward his room.

The manager smirks in a way that completely lacks mirth. "Don't try to help—it's a good way to get yourself in trouble. I came to repair the satellite antenna; the fucking blizzard damaged it. That's all. Have a good day, Mr. Plotkin."

The man is swallowed up by the nacelle as Plotkin slides his magnetic keycard in the lock of his capsule door.

Liar.

Cheat.

Snitch.

Squealer.

Informer.

Bastard.

Prick.

Nothing you say is true. Nothing about you is real. You are just you, in all your horror. You make me want to puke, Plotkin thinks, as he goes into his room.

Seated at his desk, he orders green tea and vitamin-enhanced medibiscuits to be delivered by the room-service robots. He is beginning to get a sense of the overall plan, an outline of the plot of this play, in which the final act will end with the Death of the Mayor of This City.

El señor Metatron chooses that moment to make his appearance, blaring with light like an ultraviolet flame smack in the center of the room. "There are anomalies under the dome. A lot more of them than we thought," he says.

"What kind of anomalies?"

"I'll show the sequences registered on the hotel's central disk—and what I've been able to see in the internal surveillance camera network. Or maybe I should say what I *haven't* been able to see."

"Okay. What do you mean?"

"It's very repetitive and boring, actually. Before I explain, I should tell you a couple of things. One, the manager sometimes goes inside the dome, often at night. He uses the secure service staircase. Two, the local network of cameras and sensors that are supposed to be monitoring this part of the hotel has been fucked with, to the point that whole parts of the dome and its loft are no longer visible."

Plotkin nods. That prick of a manager, that dirty snitch, is regularly sabotaging the sensors and cameras using some pirated technology so he isn't detected by the hotel's AI.

"But why?" asks his guardian angel. "For what reason?"

Plotkin chuckles at the candor that even these highly sophisticated neuroquantum machines use on occasion. "For the only reason anyone does anything here. Capital. Scratch. Bones. Scrilla. Money."

Now it is el señor Metatron's turn to laugh at such typically human shortsightedness.

"No, you're wrong. First of all, in Grand Junction, money, as you call it, is only an accessory. What counts is the Golden Track. Error number two: no one would risk getting caught by the Laika's owner and being fired by UManHome just to save a couple of measly dollars. Especially in a hotel where, remember, he's just a lowly manager."

Plotkin is ready to argue. "He wants to scam the insurance company. He must have something shady up his sleeve."

It is nearly impossible to describe the laugh of a digital guardian angel. Something like the whirring of radiation nearing critical mass, maybe.

"He's scheming at something, Plotkin, but it has nothing to do with insurance."

"Then what?"

"I have no idea. That's why he sabotaged the entire internal surveillance network of the dome. So nobody can figure out what he's up to. At least I can't do it with the electro-optic resources I have."

Plotkin doesn't say anything. He retrieves the orange plate room service has just deposited in the wall slot, pours himself a cup of tea, and nibbles a biscuit reflectively.

Then he asks his guardian angel to show him the images contained on the hotel's disk.

"If I understand correctly, only a human with the magnetic key to the service staircase can really know what's going on up there."

El señor Metatron doesn't answer. He hovers like a shimmering fountain of light above the center of the bed. His silence is enough to swallow up the whole world.

Undoubtedly, Clovis Drummond is hiding tons of illegal products in the gables of the dome. He takes delivery of them at night, stores them temporarily in his private office, then hides them in the most inaccessible part of the hotel.

No . . . that can't be it. According to the images on the hotel disk, he always goes upstairs with very little in his hands, sometimes nothing at all, and rarely even the small faux-leather backpack. Usually he takes the elevator to the tenth floor and goes directly to the highest section of the service staircase.

Watching the sequences from beyond the secure service staircase proves difficult; the images are blurry, since the cameras up there are only in use half of the time—often they are pointed aimlessly or mechanically blocked by some procedure or another. El señor Metatron detects the presence of a nanovirus in the sensor system, which has prevented the anomaly from being reported to the AI.

If the manager isn't hiding marijuana, or illegal cigarettes, or black-market neurotoys, what is he doing under the dome two or three times every week? Apparently there is now a sixth name to add to the list of "suspicious" residents in the hotel.

The next forty-eight hours are filled with intense planning.

First, they need to create a neuroencrypted zone that will continuously fool the private surveillance camera. El señor Metatron will execute a simulation routine each time Plotkin works on his plan.

The latter is taking form, in all senses of the world. Plotkin has food containing legal amphetamines delivered to his room and spends two days and nights at the console, configuring a three-dimensional model of the city: each of its neighborhoods, particularly Korolev Plaza, the Municipal Metropolitan Consortium building on Korolev-1, and all the surrounding buildings, each one corresponding to one of the specialized branches of the organization that manages the county and its resources. Thanks to the data secretly gathered by el señor Metatron, he is able to create an animated statistical reconstruction in real time of human movement in the city—in particular, the specific movements of the members of the Consortium.

Including those of Mr. Blackburn, the mayor of the city.

The mayor he has come to kill.

Any time, any day, any type of meeting or movement or security procedure—he now knows the real city well enough to be able to duplicate them easily in the false one. He knows the territory well enough to make a map of it.

And destroy it.

Only kill when it's a sure shot, says an Order maxim that comes out of nowhere to mingle with the curious mixture of English, Russian, and Argentine memories that are whirling at any given time in his brain.

Only kill when it's a sure shot. That means that a true professional assassin does not have the right to make a mistake. To kill properly, you must succeed with the first blow. The *only* blow.

It must be conducted like the launch of an orbital rocket. There is a takeoff window, a plan A, a plan B, and a plan C. There are hundreds of security measures to implement. Everything must be studied to the tiniest detail, like the bolts in a shuttle. No right to error. No glitches.

A priori, there are very few holes in the security system surrounding Mr. Blackburn. He has to admit it. There really aren't any at all—certainly none he can exploit. On this point, el señor Metatron and he are in complete agreement.

That is why they pick October 4, the date of the Sputnik Centennial and Grand Junction's huge Starnival.

On that day, there will be a hole.

On that day, Blackburn and all the members of the Consortium will be present on a code-red-protected panoramic dais to watch the takeoff of a large Brazilian rocket and a fairly new jumbo Chinese capsule carrying twelve occupants. They will be just above the control center buildings, and just below Centaur City.

But to get to this high-security area, they must cross a *yellow* zone alongside Stardust Alley. It will take them a few minutes.

For those few minutes, they will be vulnerable.

Those few minutes will be his takeoff window.

It appears that his assassin's intuition, despite his faulty memory, is to be trusted. The instruction neuroprogram, it seems, is useless except for maintaining a few basic routines.

It seems to him that everything is pointing to this decision; everything is in perfect alignment toward this plan: the Hotel Laika, from where he overlooks the eastern part of the cosmodrome, the access path to Platform 3 and the fallow lands that lie below Monolith

North. The area is unobstructed enough that he can see to the western hills, to Centaur City and the control center, and all the way to the observation gallery the Consortium bigwigs are having built. He can see the bustle of construction-site activity already.

El señor Metatron provides him with detailed plans of the gallery, with its Securimax™ windows that can deflect 20 mm light-uranium bullets and its firebrick roof that can resist temperatures up to 1,000 degrees centigrade.

The gallery itself will be untouchable. Besides, he is only supposed to kill Blackburn. Maybe his escorts, but not *all* the members of the Consortium. It is even probable that one of them actually ordered the assassination.

The gallery will be untouchable, but there is the small "yellow" portion of the route, below Centaur City.

There is also the fact that Blackburn will cross it in an armored presidential Lincoln that belonged to the White House in the 1970s.

The 1970s!

This is the ransom for glory; the ransom for being king of Grand Junction—Grand Junction, where the entire twentieth century is trying to exist in a condensed form, postmortem, to avoid being lost altogether. Blackburn will be riding in an armored Lincoln from the 1970s. With a few modifications, no doubt, but in the yellow zone it will not be enough.

Plotkin asks the console to display a few scenarios in the model city. The virtual human masses obligingly move in their various chaotic ways among the replicated towers. Black cars whose doors bear the official emblem of the independent Mohawk territory drive along the electronic streets, while el señor Metatron reproduces, thanks to information gleaned from the local initiative union, the various spectacles and street parades planned for October 4.

The cars come together every time toward the yellow zone.

There is an error in their security system.

There is, it turns out, a very good-size takeoff window.

He will have at least thirty seconds to Kill the Mayor of This City.

He will need something like an Oerlikon electromag rocket launcher, with its high-speed missiles that fly at five thousand meters per second.

The projectile should not be detected by the city's urban surveillance systems as it rockets toward the reduced-security zone, not at five kilometers per second. At that speed, and thanks to the special chemical components contained in its polymetallic alloys, the 13 mm minirocket will be in a state of superfusion and will be literally enveloped in plasma. Upon impact, a fireball equivalent to the explosion of a propane tank will erupt instantaneously. According to the initiative union's data, the yellow zone in question, bordering the cosmodrome's west fences, will be less populated than the city's large arteries or Stardust Alley, but there will be people there who have come from Centaur City and Novapolis.

Some collateral damage, though, will only reinforce the terrorist-attack theory.

He will blow up Blackburn's presidential Lincoln, and it will take part of his city with it.

He falls asleep in the morning just after dawn, while the model endlessly replays the trajectory of the digital rocket above the city's towers, until the moment when the ball of fire caps off the smoky line it traces for a brief instant in the replica's simulated sky. Then, during the night that follows, when he finally awakes from his long diurnal sleep and unfolds the collapsible bathroom to take a shower with an expensive extra ration of water, el señor Metatron appears in a corner of the room.

"Mr. Drummond has just graced us with his little nocturnal visit under the dome," he says.

> *UNDER THE CARBON SKY*

There, too, they have only one takeoff window. For just a second or two, Drummond's personal magnetic key will be inserted into the reader in the service staircase door. In that brief span of time, the data will be read, sent to an AI microcircuit, verified by an iterative component, then retransmitted with a positive access code to its sender. It will be el señor Metatron's opportunity to connect to the circuit, steal the card's code, and copy it onto Plotkin's keycard.

They wait. It is past one o'clock in the morning. They wait. Drummond still does not emerge from the protective dome; the cameras show virtually nothing: closed angles, blank walls, shadows, vague reflections. The sensors are paralyzed by the nanovirus. No sound, no infrared, no X-rays, no volume detection, no spectrography, no recognition of motion.

Nothing.

They wait.

Suddenly, the pyrotechnic angel dances beside the window, then all over the room. "I'm sensing something," it announces.

"What?"

"I don't know exactly. It's almost normal, but not quite. It's a sort of . . . a sort of vibration."

"What frequency?" Plotkin asks.

"Low, but not inaudible at the source. It's far away, stifled by ambient noise, but it's coming from the dome, I'm sure. I've set up a few trigs."

"An abnormal vibration, you said?"

"Yes—periodic but not linear. It stops for a long moment sometimes, then starts again. It started around twenty minutes after he went in. That's almost two hours ago now."

"By the sainted A-bomb, what the fuck is the bastard up to?"

"I don't know, Plotkin," the angel Metatron replies somewhat pathetically, hanging from the ceiling in a circle of flame. "I really don't know."

Drummond went up beneath the dome a little after midnight. It is now almost three o'clock in the morning. El señor Metatron copies the two codes—entry and exit—from his magnetic key and transfers them to the memory cell in Plotkin's. Then he suggests they wait a little, and pursue their initial investigation before going up into the dome themselves.

In the confusion of low definition and semidarkness, el señor Metatron has detected the presence, via the chance aiming of a camera lens at a mirrored surface, of two or three prohibited religious emblems.

"Like the ones in Heavy Metal Valley?" Plotkin demands.

His guardian angel's spectrometric analyzers show him the characteristic shapes of the symbols in question.

Yes. Like the ones in Heavy Metal Valley.

Christian symbols: a crucifix, maybe two, and a statuette of the Virgin Mary. He can also make out a small shelf of books, but the total absence of light makes it impossible to read the titles in the vague reflection on a metal surface.

Religious symbols. Books. Prohibited books. It could not be a more surprising find.

Drummond, an apostolic convert?

Was it the sound of his prayers that Metatron had detected under the humming ambient noise of the hotel?

The consequence is clear: maximum security. No going under the dome without taking every imaginable precaution. Drummond had been able to place countermeasures, traps, genetic tracers. He is probably the one behind the malfunctions in the instruction program. Maybe he is trafficking in clandestine technology beneath the dome. El señor Metatron will have to investigate. El señor Metatron will have to comb every disk in the hotel, including the ones archived in the databases rented from the Philippines and Paraguay. They need to nail this guy.

Then, Plotkin turns out the lights and goes to bed.

He sleeps dreamlessly, a sleep as gray as the color of the sky when he awakes, feeling as if he closed his eyes only a second earlier.

ON/OFF. He turns off and back on, like a computer. Between the moment of turning out the lights and the moment of the morning awakening, there is nothing. A simple digital skip. A blank page.

The day has the cold paleness of a Nordic dawn: the sky is leaden, metallic gray, ashy, with clouds pressing against the horizon. He gets up, eats, showers, dresses.

Then he leaves Capsule 108, goes down to the lobby, and waits for his usual rental car.

Why go back to Heavy Metal Valley? his guardian angel had asked him.

He hadn't known how to answer at first. Instinct, intuition, his killer's training. Something like that, anyway. Well, no. *He just wants to; that's all.*

Let's roll, el señor Metatron had replied, using the now-famous phrase. He wants to go back to the city of demolished cars, the city of lost metal, the oxidized Jerusalem of the last Christians.

The fact that Drummond is undoubtedly one of them, that he has probably installed a small altar and an illicit prayer room under his protective dome—which gives sense to some of his actions, but makes others even more confusing: the contraband cigarettes and undeclared marijuana, the trafficking of untaxed toys made in India, his lamentable hygiene . . .

Plotkin ends by concluding that perhaps—and that perhaps puts a lid on some troubling possibilities—if there is a cover-up, then the man's semilegal activities, as well as his official status as a capsule-hotel manager and a part-time informer are a perfect way of deflecting any suspicion that he might be a secret Catholic.

He drives, thinking that it probably wasn't Drummond after all that lured him to the northeast part of the territory, and Quebec, and Heavy Metal Valley.

Something in him, something that *is* him, but seems like it might be someone else at any moment—*some part of him* wants to return to Xenon Ridge. Something alive in him wants to live; something alive wants to act; something alive wants to break into ordinary language with blistering words. The impression that absolutely everything is *real,* especially *him,* simply because he seems to be able to think in parallel and cut through the world of illusory reality, is incredible.

This infinite tension between him and the world is pure, noisy like water fallen from the stars. It is as if the beauty of a ray of light has become like a perfume, or a needle lodged in his heart. His fingers seem to act of their own accord in choosing a playlist of rock and pop songs from the Great Century on the navigation console.

Why is it that the view of a few gray-purple clouds above an old abandoned Texaco gas station opens such gaping holes within his entire being, false, true, true-false, and false-true identities all together, while the pale yellow disk of the sun plays with the slivers of blue sky that let oblique columns of light pass through them—high glimmers, fixed and ephemeral, above the hilly land of southern Quebec?

Why—*how*—does he feel so *free?*

Because an instruction program is malfunctioning?

Or because something wants the fire to spout from his mouth?

He cannot compare this sense of freedom to any other concept or sensation, any known or transmissible abstraction or experience.

Why does he feel such a profound upheaval of his entire being when, very simply, the humming of guitars in an old song by The The fills the cabin and seems to fall from heaven like radioactive rain, like a larger-than-life reenactment of the London zenith? It dates from 1983, from the great album *Soul Mining. This is the day, your life will surely change, this is the day, when things fall into place* . . .

Then there are "Slow Train to Dawn" and "Infected," from the 1986 album *Infected.* Like a vision of an apocalypse with cold and delicate veins from some rainy island. The almost-rockabilly beat-up-beat seems to come from a bunker where the planes of Armageddon are lined up side by side, like beach huts in rows on the edge of an endless desert. The characteristic harmonies—Celtic-bluesy guitars, accordions, Irish fiddles, and harmonicas of groups from northern England, but with the addition of the electronics and violence of Cockney London—are superimposed on angular, hard rhythmic bases, with bridges that cut like glass blades. He has chosen these songs along with another audio file containing "Blue Monday" by New Order, dating from about the same time—the British mid-eighties—as well as "The Big Heat" from the album of the same name by Stan Ridgway. He is in a dark, strange area, somewhere beyond his own identity, a hollow space that does not belong to this century, or to this world, or to any of his false memories, but to which *he* belongs, with all his being.

He feels that he has been standing at the gates of something that his false English identity was created precisely to cover up. There are bagpipes whispering of the Irish Sea in the Simple Minds song "Belfast Child." There are the celestial guitar riffs of the Edge in U2's "Where the Streets Have No Name," and in The Silencers' "Northern Blues." There is the icy scansion of the totalitarian machine in Joy Division's "Love Will Tear Us Apart," and the views of the postatomic, sublunar world—so close to Plotkin's own—in "Rocket USA" by Suicide, which throbs with the contradictory colors of the end of civilization and the magnificence of sunset; black and gold, silver and red, like music written for meteors.

Why does it seem as if everything is on the brink of harmonizing even as it remains magnificently different, like a supreme collision by fire of the elements, the music, the car he is driving, and the words that are taking possession of his soul little by little? He becomes aware of—his consciousness is *assaulted* by—unknown diagrams that map out dazzling encounters between a violet cloud hovering low beneath the leaded dome and the guitar riffs of Johnny Marr, clear as glacial lakes and high as mirrors suspended between the sky and the Earth; by the image of oblique columns of light filtering through the clouds. There is the improbable shock of PJ Harvey's voice on "Rope Bridge Crossing" as if it is hanging on a barbed-wire horizon, with country guitar twanging in a postatomic desert, and the opening of a vast stretch of blue sky to the west as he turns onto Nexus Road. Yes . . . he feels as if he is touching with a fingertip something essential concerning his own identity, whatever its origins or method of creation: flashes of words, forming short phrases that cut into the emotional landscape of his mind, jarring in his brain, directly describing the experience he is living through now. Phrases like *Freedom is the point of being where it is consumed.*

Freedom takes up residence in a place of being where *encounters* can take place—collisions, accidents, implosions—outside the internal instruction program and outside the numerous routines shaped by the neotenic parameters of the totalitarian social structure in which he lives along with seven billion other human beings.

TOTAL COMBUSTION.

This place within him seems impossible to pinpoint, or describe, or define. It doesn't even seem possible to confirm its existence. If it is fire, its flame—its ethereal envelope—is barely visible. It is really as if, each time he tries to go back to the world of external and internal instruction programs that form "reality," this place vanishes abruptly from the maps, the diagrams, the land, the world—and even from himself.

This place, where liberty is burgeoning inside him, is, more than

anything else, the place where the terrible possibility exists of encountering another freedom. For that, he must pay the price—put
himself in danger—be confronted with his own nothingness. He
must let this freedom be subsumed into the other, in order to establish his paradoxical, but *vital,* existence.

He arrives within view of Xenon Ridge and follows Xenon Road to
the top of the mesa. He parks at the foot of a mutant cedar covered
with fuchsia-pink blooms and retraces his steps to find the same observation point he occupied before: a small, rocky ridge running parallel to the hill that, crowded with spiny bushes, hides him from the
view of anyone below.

Well, almost. It was a wise precaution.

But not wise enough.

He has just sat down when he uses the special program in his
optic lenses and neuroconnects to a small digidisk reader-recorder.
He concentrates on the activity in the little city within a city below,
on the life happening in the city of lost metal. There is a lot going on.
There is a lot of life. There are many things to see and to note.

He is so absorbed that he hears almost nothing until a voice orders him to remain seated and raise his hands high in the air.

The characteristic sound of a .12 caliber rifle cocking gives a certain weight to this suggestion.

> HMV

The small, dark room is warm. The man sitting across from him is a Canadian half blood called Wilbur Langlois. He has blue eyes and a short, natural gray beard, and weighs about two hundred pounds. He stares unblinkingly at Plotkin. A scavenged butane lamp illuminates his face and casts trembling flares of light here and there in the breeze that rattles the metal roof of the mobile home, where the little gas cylinder is hanging from a denuded cable.

Wilbur Langlois wears a silver badge shaped like a six-pointed star on the lapel of his midnight-blue uniform. He is flanked by four men who do not introduce themselves. The mobile home is a sort of tinkered-with bus—one of those, undoubtedly, that he saw during his first investigation. It serves as the official police station of Heavy Metal Valley. Wilbur Langlois is the sheriff of the community. The four men are his assistants.

Two of the men are the patrol officers that surprised him at his lookout point on Xenon Ridge and brought him here in handcuffs. The two others remain at the far end of the room; he cannot see much of them besides their impressively tall shadows, arms crossed, standing on each side of the gray steel rectangle of an escape hatch with its handle right in the center.

How had he made so many blunders in so short a time?

Going to the same place twice, only two days apart, only fifty meters the second time from where he had been the first!

Apparently all the poetic brilliance dancing like fire in his soul had led him—in this bloody world, at least—to the worst kind of danger. An error in *calculation*. "What are you doing in Humvee?" the man asks. He has already asked the question two or three times. This time, his tone hardens.

"HoomVey?" Plotkin asks. He heard "Hum-Vee" perfectly well, but decides to play the fool for a few precious moments, which he knows will really be worth very little.

"*Humvee*," repeats the Amerindian. "That is what we call it. Heavy Metal Valley: HMV. Humvee, like the American neo-jeep from the turn of the century. Okay?"

"Okay. Heavy Metal Valley: HMV. Humvee."

"Correct," says Wilbur Langlois. "Now, what are you doing here, eh?"

Plotkin has just realized that the conversation is taking place in French. American French. The base routines of his instruction program are functioning with the detachment of a dream.

Obviously, he can try to play the tourist lost in the hills, but stupidly, he has done anything but act like a clueless Japanese traveler with his neurodigital Nikon. No, he was surprised in the act of spying on something—he doesn't even know what. Or even why.

He will have to improvise, and fast. Let his killer's instinct talk. Let his professional assassin's intuition take over. But it is as if this part of his mind is frozen like an internal arctic circle. Instead, his mouth opens to let out a dart of pure flame that comes from who knows where, and manifests itself in the following words:

"I'm looking for something. Or someone."

"You're looking for someone? Who? And why?"

Again, the fire blazes from his mouth, and he can do nothing about it. He looks at Wilbur Langlois, the sheriff of Heavy Metal Valley, and is suddenly filled with strength neither inside nor outside himself. He cannot tell where it comes from—it is as if it's drawn from some entity in the interworld between him and the world. It is a highly magnetic strength that fills every cell in him. He smiles, and it is a smile that could light up the dark side of the moon.

"I'm looking for a man. Or a woman. Maybe even a child. And I'm looking for him because he, or she, is a Catholic. I mean, a Christian."

One of the men that captured him, a Nordic-looking fellow wearing round steel-rimmed glasses, brandishes his .12 caliber gun.

"This bastard's a UniPol bounty hunter. Where does he think he is, California?"

"Shut up, Florian," Wilbur Langlois growls. He turns back to Plotkin. "So you're not an insurance agent, as your ID claims?"

Plotkin uses the strength flowing through him to speak a truth that hides the truth. "My ID isn't false. I'm also an expert in technological risk."

He hopes his bravado is convincing. He does not betray the slightest emotion as he allows his Swiss-cheese memory to speak for him. Wilbur Langlois does not take his eyes off him. This is a true interrogation.

"Do you have a mandate from one of the American confederations? Or from Canada? Quebec, perhaps?"

The sheriff is obviously expecting Plotkin to answer in the affirmative to one of these choices so that he can inform him that none of these mandates have much power in independent Mohawk territory— and even less here in Humvee, an autonomous territory within an autonomous territory.

Plotkin, however, doesn't feel like playing games. Again, he feels it—the old talent of a human predator is still there within him. He feels it, he knows it, and he acts accordingly. Play straight; tell the truth. Or, more precisely, cover the fundamental truth with a truth of secondary importance. "I'm not a bounty hunter, I'm a journalist," he says. "I'm passing for an insurance agent. Since I actually am one, it's very simple."

Thirty seconds of silence pass. He can tell the guy with the .12 caliber would happily nail him to a post without further discussion.

"Ah . . . we have no resident that corresponds to your profile, Mr. Plotkin. I'm sorry. I don't know where you are getting your information, but it's incorrect."

Plotkin goes for broke, without even knowing whose table he has been brought to sit at. It is a blind blitz; he has no idea of the rules. He understands that the sheriff is lying through his teeth, a barrage of lies forming a Larsen effect—which explains his attitude, his words, his presence. He is there to cover up problems. He is there to shut up curious mouths. He is there to ensure that the law prevails. The law of Silence. The law of Heavy Metal.

"I have seen and made note of at least a dozen—probably even twenty—crosses, crucifixes, Virgin Marys, and other Catholic symbols that are forbidden within . . . Humvee. And you won't believe me, but I'm sure that at least one of the guests in the hotel where I'm staying on the strip is part of the network. Obviously, everything that happens here is neuroconnected to a machine whose code you couldn't break without about six trillion years' worth of calculations by the most powerful computer in existence."

"Our security systems—"

"—are worthless against my intelligence agent. Believe me, Mister Officer Langlois, you might as well quit playing games, like I have. It's better to talk honestly, man to man." *While the machines watch,* he adds to himself.

The young bloke named Florian fixes him with an icy, hate-filled stare. He notices that the blond lug is wearing a black bandanna knotted tightly at his neck; a metal charm dangles from it, its shape clearly visible in the *V* of the man's partly unbuttoned shirt. It is an Iron

Cross, a German military medal from the first half of the twentieth century. Definitely a cross, but Plotkin's memories—the ones from the Russian part of his identity—show him images of ruins, floods of men and women in rags fleeing burning villages while hordes of gray-uniformed soldiers whose lapels are also adorned with this famous Iron Cross advance between cohorts of tanks.

Chin resting on his hands, the sheriff watches Plotkin watch Florian, who in turn does not drop his gaze. Finally, Wilbur Langlois lets out a long sigh. "You aren't a bounty hunter, but you're not a journalist, either. Much less an insurance agent. So?"

"So?" Plotkin demands, facing him, abandoning Florian Iron Cross to his little macho games.

"So, who are you?"

I don't know, would be the correct response—but somehow he doesn't think it is appropriate under the circumstances.

"Let me remind you that I've committed no crime, and that your agents arrested me without cause. You should cut this conversation short before you infringe on my rights as a UniWorld citizen."

"First, you are in independent Mohawk territory," Langlois interrupts him, "a little outside the jurisdiction of UniWorld. Second, as for crimes, my dear sir, I can assure you that it wouldn't take me a minute to find fifty of them for which I could clap you in irons right now. You say you're looking for Catholics, but you have no legal mandate. You turned up on the ridge with spy paraphernalia and you think I'm going to swallow your bullshit stories?"

"It isn't illegal spy paraphernalia. I'm a freelance journalist and I'm investigating the underground Christian movement on behalf of a very confidential press agency. A few different things brought me to Grand Junction. That's it."

"What things?"

"I'm not obligated to reveal my sources. I'm keeping my mouth shut."

Then, Plotkin lets fly with the deathblow. "Are you protecting Christian rebels, Sheriff?"

He has no time to say anything more. The butt of the .12 caliber swings around to aim at him with incredible speed, while an indistinct oath clatters in his head as if uttered in some demonic echo chamber. The next thing he knows is a white flash of pure pain. He falls from the chair, unconscious.

ON/OFF. OFF/ON.

The pain is no longer pure light, a solar fracas, a shock of stars exploding in his head.

It has weight now. It has body.

His body.

He regains consciousness.

He hears vague noises, then voices, a little hazy, saying, "How is he, Dr. Brandt? I'm going to give that asshole Schutzberg two days in the brig." He opens his eyes. His vision is unfocused. His body is nothing but pain. His head, his cheek, and his right temple feel as if they have been branded with a white-hot iron; needles of pain are jabbing the entire top of his skull. There is a human silhouette in front of him. Something around his left arm is putting pressure on the vein, and crystallizes the cold sensation of a probe tucked into the crook of his elbow. The silhouette speaks.

"Contusions, a small concussion, scrapes and scratches, a large hematoma. Nothing really serious, fortunately."

"Finally some good news," murmurs Plotkin, not really expecting anyone to hear him—not even some random god that might be hiding in the corner.

The silhouette has grown clearer; it moves to the center of the room, toward the sheriff's desk and its butane lamp. It is a woman. She perches on the back of a chair, facing the big half-blood cop. Her voice is low, calm, smoky, like burning gases—the voice of a woman who has seen much.

"This man has the right to lodge a complaint against you. Your French assistant is an asshole. The fact that Alsatian Islamists exterminated his family doesn't give him a right to take it out on everything that moves." The sheriff says nothing. He stares at his boots.

"I inserted a polymedic probe and covered the hematoma with transcutaneous gel. He'll be back on his feet in a few minutes. Give him the tube of gel and the three remaining doses when he leaves. And take those handcuffs off immediately."

"Of course, Dr. Brandt," mutters the sheriff, humbly.

"You're lucky there are no fractures, Sheriff. Good-bye."

The woman turns on her heel; one of the guards hurriedly opens the emergency door at her approach.

"And don't forget to punish that prick Schutzberg. He won't bring you anything but trouble."

She stands in framed daylight for a few seconds before the heavy steel door closes behind her.

Plotkin stands up slowly in the light of the butane lamp and faces the sheriff. His bare arm, sleeve pushed up, is encircled by a strip of beige latex at the elbow. A black-and-gray microcomponent is embedded in the skin there; a small, luminous diode pulses gently. He can feel the presence of the probe under his skin with every movement he makes.

The two patrol officers are gone. Only the two guards are still in their places; Wilbur Langlois must have advised the edgy Alsatian to get lost for a little while, so that the affair could be settled as quietly as possible. The woman, Dr. Brandt, had not been wrong—Heavy Metal Valley's police station had been placed in a very delicate situation, legally speaking. Plotkin is fortunate, in a way, that the peon attacked him. He extends his arms so that the sheriff can unlock the handcuffs with a small metal key.

"Your car is in the parking lot," says Wilbur Langlois. "You're free to go—and to lodge a complaint against our department."

"That won't be necessary," Plotkin assures him.

"Good. Best to keep it among ourselves, I suppose."

Plotkin thinks hard. While he is still bumbling around this tiny office, rubbing his wrists, which are sore from the old-style steel handcuffs, he should continue playing the role of an investigative journalist
to the hilt. His core identity, that of a killer and professional spy, allows him to adjust his various fictional identities—and any new ones
he might need to invent at a given moment—as often as the situation
requires it.

"I won't bring a complaint against you," he says, "but I think I have
the right to some explanation. I told you that I'm keeping my sources
confidential."

*It is when you have been brought to your knees that you can achieve the
greatest victories,* says an Order maxim.

Driving back along the North Junction road, Plotkin surprises himself by thinking that it was all worth it. Getting clocked in the face
with a gun butt, losing consciousness, having his wrists chafed by
those fucking handcuffs, being temporarily but completely helpless—
all worth it. The sheriff had admitted that some Catholics, Orthodox,
Evangelicals, and even a few Israelites had fled the world after the
Third Destruction of the Temple and found refuge in Heavy Metal
Valley, and that they were tolerated there.

"Are you Catholic yourself, or a rebel Christian?" Plotkin had
asked the sheriff. The man had only smiled neutrally. So neutrally that
Plotkin had understood his message 100 percent.

"And your assistant, the one who knows how to handle a gun
butt?" Plotkin had persisted. "Is he a Christian too? You know, one
who strikes the left cheek after having struck the right cheek?"

"Listen, Schutzberg is a guy who generally does his job pretty
well. He was only six when his entire family was massacred at Col-
mar, in France. He might be a little too zealous sometimes, but he
protects his community."

"And the dog?" Plotkin had asked then.

"What dog?"

"The dog," Plotkin had sighed. "The cyberdog. The one from the Hotel Laika. I'm sure you've seen him lurking in some corner—around here, probably."

Langlois' face had lit up with comprehension. "Oh—right, the dog."

"Balthazar."

"Yes, Balthazar." The sheriff's smile grew distant. "Yes, he comes here sometimes. He likes to hunt in the hills around here."

"Don't patronize me," Plotkin had responded. "He comes here several times a week. To see someone. I'd like you to give me a little more of an answer about him. You owe me that."

The man had rocked back and forth a little in his chair, hesitating, then stopped suddenly, obviously making a decision. "The dog usually goes to see the Sommervilles and the Sevignys. I don't know why, but he's close to those two families."

"Are they Catholics?"

"Catholics and Protestants. I'll tell you again, this is a peaceful community. We don't tolerate armed guerrillas here."

"But they're still rebelling against UniWorld regulations."

Langlois' silence stretched for long moments as he pondered the question. Plotkin carefully recorded what he had just learned in his memory. Sommerville. Sevigny. Protestants. Catholics.

"Okay," Plotkin said at last. "One more question. Clovis Drummond, the manager of the hotel. How is he mixed up in all this? With Humvee and the Christian rebels?"

The cop's big face darkened. He fixed his cold eyes on Plotkin's and said coolly, "I can assure you that I don't know this Drummond. He has no relationship of any kind with our community, except that he is, I believe, the legal owner of the hotel cyberdog we were just discussing. Monolith Hills isn't part of my jurisdiction."

Plotkin had decided to let his maleficent killer's instinct decide, later, whether the sheriff was telling the truth or not. He certainly seemed sincere. That could mean that he was lying even more than he had been before, with even more sincerity.

He knew better than to push his shaky luck. He accepted the three twice-daily doses for his medical treatment probe and the tube of transcutaneous gel, and left Heavy Metal Valley with a brief handshake for the sheriff and a "Good-bye, gentlemen" for the guards who opened the door for him silently. He had hardly seen their faces; he had not heard their voices at all.

Now, as he drives along Nexus Road, he has to admit that everything seems to be going pretty well—right in tune with the plan, in fact. The plan that the instruction program had, in spite of being overwhelmed by his emerging personality, undoubtedly implemented without his knowledge.

The android conspiracy might very well have some connection to a clan of rebel Catholics.

And the fact that an entire "marginal" city on the outskirts of Grand Junction—the margin of the margin—and its police force had been infiltrated by this "conspiracy" gives a terrible appearance of reality to this theater of shadows: nothing like good old-fashioned territorial competition, a myriad of mystic financial conflicts, and a little gangsterism to give a highly political secret the appearance of an authentic frame-up.

True conspiracies are the coming together of interests that are often surprising.

At least for others.

> HOMO TENEBROSUM

Some incidents are bottomless pits, completely without sense or any hope of one's conscience ever enlightening what is lost in the void, like a handful of photons in a black hole. Some men are sinkholes, deep abysses like open trenches at the bottom of a deep ocean. They say that there is life there, but it is the life of sinkholes, of lightless chasms. The life of shadows.

It hadn't taken el señor Metatron long to run up against a wall of absolute blackness around—or, even worse, *inside*—Mr. John Cheyenne Hawkwind, alias Harris Nakashima.

There is plenty of information to which even an intelligent software agent cannot gain access. Even an elite "angel" like el señor Metatron. These are the darkest thoughts of men, who most likely do not even know them themselves—and if they do, it is a safe bet that they have done everything they possibly can to forget them.

Only a few human beings, very rare ones, know the secret, dark, wild, and terrible dimension that stretches infinitely within them. These men know and recognize each other immediately, even blind, even in a crowd. They know one another as well as they know themselves, but this takes more than a diagram of data, or a list of police information, or a bit of intelligent software.

Or, perhaps, it takes less.

All it takes is for them to meet each other.

It is enough for them to cross paths—then each one knows, in perfect synchronicity with the other, that they are both part of the same race. The race of shadow men—*Homo tenebrosum*—who know that conscience illuminates only a tiny corner of a labyrinth as vast as a planet plunged into darkness.

They are a highly dangerous race of men.

Plotkin meets Nakashima/Hawkwind, finally, upon his return to the hotel, as the incident in Humvee is just beginning to take shape in his reemerging memory. This time there is hardly anyone in the lobby; two or three new arrivals, lost souls from the strip, come to sleep off their cheap-wine hangovers or meta-amphetamine trips. Plotkin, desiring to avoid them, moves quickly toward the lateral corridor leading to the central patio.

The patio is not empty. There is a junkie there, staring vacantly at his empty glass; also two seedy middle managers sitting at a table face-to-face and, from the looks of it, discussing business. There is also someone who has obviously come to Grand Junction looking for a Golden Track, wearing a Hawaiian floral shirt and memory-form Ray-Bans—the "California look" from the beginning of the century— seated in front of a plate of trans-G tofu. And there is an old crone who looks to be in her seventies, apparently unable to afford any rejuvenation cures, shuffling a pack of tarot cards. A man wearing the uniform of a Municipal Consortium electronic repair company drinks a beer in complete, tangibly anguished solitude. A trio composed of two men and a woman—a whore from the strip—look as if they are only moments away from heading up to a room together; all that is left is to negotiate the final details of the "contract." Finally, two middle-aged women, visibly Latin American, gaze up at the wall-mounted television set to some neuroencrypted channel. The other two or three people in the room are dark, indistinguishable figures by the far wall. One of them detaches itself immediately as Plotkin enters the room. A silhouette. A face. Eyes.

A soul.

It is as powerful as a telepathic wave. It *is* a telepathic wave. A shock wave. It is the truth of one man exposed to the gaze of another, but also that of a man viewed through the filter of his identical other. Cheyenne Hawkwind looks at him. And at the other end of the room, Plotkin looks at Cheyenne Hawkwind. Each recognizes himself in the other. Despite the distance, the dimness, and the various distractions, the truth is there with such clarity and obviousness that both men know they are the only ones in the room who can see it.

For the first time since checking into the hotel, Plotkin feels something very like fear. Cheyenne Hawkwind is not a dealer like the others, or a trafficker taking advantage of local small-potatoes connections with the Consortium's Mohawk cops.

They have read each other easily despite the twenty meters' distance between them, like two decoding machines linked in a closed circuit. Hawkwind is a killer, as cold and organized as Plotkin himself. And Plotkin knows it, because he can see it in Hawkwind's eyes. He sees himself mirrored in the dark gaze, twin to his own, and the other man's message is crystal clear. *You're just like me, you son of a bitch.*

> DARK FIRE

It is well after dark, and Plotkin sleeps dreamlessly. A few sparse shreds of vague memory try to take shape in his slumbering mind—some of his past crimes, the only parts of his memory that form any sort of coherent whole, do their best to emerge, to be perceived by him as an image of a huge global neuroconnectional tube, an infinite spiral whose circular convolutions, woven in ultraviolet DNA biophotons, wrap simultaneously around his cortex and those of hundreds of millions of individuals and machines. He has the strange impression of dreaming, for a brief instant, of this same hotel room with the operations portal affixed to the wall, but it is so ephemeral that it is like something he might just barely remember, someday.

He is awakened abruptly by a voice audible only inside his head, via his auditory circuit, accompanied by a theta-stimulation neuroencoded order: EVERYBODY UP!

It is el señor Metatron, and he has information.

Information about the two residents of Capsule 081.

"What is it?" Plotkin demands.

The genetic file on Jordan and Vivian McNellis floats before his eyes, but this time the artificial combat intelligence does not say "Fuck if I know." Instead, he glows orange with nearly palpable contentment. "I've got it."

"Well?"

"The defective gene registered on their card is actually not the right one. I noticed the falsification when I saw an algorithm that seemed to correlate two sequences in their chromosome 4. They were able to do it thanks to a very simple mathematical translation; they just moved the error from the correct DNA strand to the one next to it."

"Which means?"

"Which means that they don't have a little degenerative retrovirus that can be controlled by transgenic transfusion; they don't have retinitis pigmentosa—the version 2.0 machinitis I was talking about the other day—at all."

"Well, that's good news, isn't it? What's the big deal?"

"Don't be stupid. You know very well what the big deal is. The gene next to the one with the degenerative disease initiates a noncoding DNA sequence, but it's the one that is really structurally modified; it's the one that shows serious anomalies."

"If it's a noncoding structure, then so fucking what?"

"That's exactly the problem, Plotkin. Why did they do it? I read on their registration card that they're trying to get a flight. They're on the official waiting list for Platform 2. A disease, even a relatively benign one like R.P. 2.0, drastically lowers their chances of passing the UHU-approved examination. Now do you understand?" The cryptovisible brazier seems impatient.

"Hold on," Plotkin says quietly, his brain still a bit sleep-addled. "Are you saying that the falsification is a decoy?"

"Well, not exactly. It's a bit random. They just did what they could, with what they had at hand, to be able to come here. With the help of a very clever little pirated translator, they moved the numeric data of their defective gene to the next gene over, which then became 95-percent-and-change susceptible to produce retinitis pigmentosa between now and the next fifteen to twenty-five years. They lost points and gained an insurance tax. Why, do you think?"

Obviously, the decoy itself is hiding another mystery. "Which gene opens the noncoding structure?" Plotkin asks.

"That's where it gets interesting. That's what the Global Biosecurity and Health Control Center inspectors in Helensville, New Zealand—that's north of Auckland—said. They spent almost two years there."

"What exactly did the inspectors say?"

"I was able to get a few bits of information from their optic disks—old machines, but in combination with the public reports and analyses I could legally get, it added up to a portrait that will let us understand why the McNellises are ready to lose points on the travel examination and pay more insurance tax to register."

"So what fucking disease do they have?"

"Nobody knows. Dr. Anderson, the head of their special unit, talks about 'neuroretrotranscriptase.' I wasn't able to find out exactly how that works, but what is certain, Plotkin, is that we're talking about some sort of neurovirus. And both of them are carriers. The man has the 'epsilon' type—it's regressive; he's a clean carrier. But the woman is 'alpha-omega'—a critical metamorphic carrier. They don't know if she's contagious or not."

"And they were able to leave the center in New Zealand legally?"

"That's what I don't understand. There's no mention of their departure anywhere in the center's records. It's like they didn't leave. It's really not clear at all."

"This is a damned catastrophe, is what you're trying to say," growls Plotkin.

"Not good news, that's for sure," agrees the guardian angel calmly, before disappearing in a tiny burst of sparkles.

Plotkin closes his eyes again, but he tosses and turns and doesn't fall back to sleep until dawn. Around five o'clock he notices gold-hued sparks refracting in the window, which is in seminocturnal mode; the Chinese rocket and its Albertan booster are taking off for the High Frontier. He watches the play of light in the glass, polychromatic glimmers of gray and dark violet filling the small, circular window. The sight finally lulls him to sleep, and he does sleep for a few hours before awaking in a hotel that seems to be dancing to and fro.

El señor Metatron soon appears to tell him that a hurricane warning has just been issued by WorldWeather Corp; it was urgently necessary, apparently, in order to counterbalance the effects of a violent hailstorm in North Carolina. WW has decided that a small tornado over Monolith Hills is worth the trouble; it is well-paid for, after all, and will not risk the peace of mind of the ten or twenty megacartels ready to swoop down at any moment on one of the most lucrative markets on the planet.

He spends the rest of the day being tossed around like a boat on a stormy sea, watching the hurricane's progression toward Montreal. Rain pours from the black-and-blue sky in whirling torrents, lashing the skyscrapers of downtown Grand Junction, the buildings lining Apollo Drive and Stardust Alley, and finally the cosmodrome, which disappears in its turn into the gray murk, a wall of water that hammers inexorably on the Hotel Laika like a tropical storm. Then, with a soft drumming like the sound of maracas, the rain tapers off.

This time, the dream is more vivid. Truth be told, Plotkin doesn't know anymore if it is even a dream.

His own body floats before his eyes, dismembered. A catalogue of organs, his biomedical file, opens on a wall like the one in his hotel room. It is his body—rebuilt, reengineered, on the midnight-blue background of the *spaceless space* of the Metanetwork. In this dream, el señor Metatron takes the form of a young woman. She is only a silhouette, but she is fiery. It is she who projects the catalogue of his organs on the midnight-blue wall of his dream. She smiles at him, and her lips part as if to blow him a kiss—but instead a spinning ball of fire shoots from her mouth to orbit around him, trailing a meteorite's blazing tail.

"Ha ha ha!" she laughs. Her voice becomes an exploding cloud of crystal shards. "You are completely free and you don't know it! You are the author of your own life, but you don't want to see it!"

"What do you mean?" he asks her, in this dream that seems so much like reality.

"It is time for the fire to be cast down to Earth."

At that moment, the entire hotel bursts into flames. His room is filled with fire. A stream of it runs up the wall near the door to the ceiling, clinging there like the rotten luck of an earthly sinner. The inferno spreads rapidly; the young woman laughs; constellations of rainbow crystal drops glitter in the flames. He runs through the hotel. Smoke snakes down the corridors, rises up to fill the elevator shafts, floats to the ceiling. Fireballs explode one by one in the capsule rooms; it is as if the entire hotel is being attacked by an overzealous terrorist or a crazy pyromaniac. Alarm bells ring, ring, ring.

They ring.

He wakes up.

The alarm bells are still ringing.

El señor Metatron hovers in front of him, a fireball escaped from his dream. "There is a fire in the hotel."

Plotkin sits up. So real events *had* directly provoked his violent, disturbing dream. "Where is it?"

The little flame seems to dance, oscillating like a candle in the wind. "You'll never guess."

Plotkin rolls his eyes. El señor Metatron displays the now-familiar signs of self-satisfaction—he shines as brightly as he can, in all his varied shades of red and orange. "In Capsule 081, idiot!"

His deepest instinct, what he considers the remaining kernel of his original personality, convinces him to take a risk. Armed with the small fire extinguisher from his room, Plotkin defies the security program's instructions and makes his way toward the McNellises' room, where, according to the little faux fireblob at his heels, the fire has now been contained by the capsule's automatic sprinklers. The blaring alarm fades to the softer alert mode, then stops altogether.

The neutral, androgynous voice of the hotel's artificial intelligence instructs residents to return to their rooms or to remain in them. He wonders for an instant if the order is meant for him personally.

Capsule 081 is located on the eighth floor, facing east and over-looking the street. As he walks down the access corridor, there is still a little smoke floating in the air at waist level. At the end of the hall where the double Capsule 081 is situated, he can make out an open door and sense movement within the room. He hears indistinct voices.

Beside him, el señor Metatron relays real-time information as it becomes available from the hotel disk concerning the damage to the capsule; it is displayed on a semitransparent screen suspended in front of him, where lists of figures unscroll on a vectorial plan of this part of the hotel.

Plotkin is already in view of the room when he sees the squat fig-ure of the manager profiled in the yellowish dimness of the security lights that are illuminating the entire floor. The man seems furious. He shouts:

"This goddamned fucking junkie shit will cost you plenty, believe me! I'm going to make sure you get kicked out, you nut job!"

Another voice replies, telling him to fuck off, that it was an acci-dent, and they will pay for the damages if they have to.

It is at this exact moment that Plotkin arrives on the scene, little red tube in hand.

Drummond swings to face him, his expression a mixture of in-credulity, fury, and pure nastiness. "What the hell are *you* doing here?"

"I heard the alarm and the security system told me where the source of the problem was. I thought I might be useful."

The man gives him and the small aerosol-powder fire extin-guisher a measuring, disdainful look.

"You're of absolutely no use here, and you're in violation of secu-rity regulations."

"Remember," Plotkin says, "I'm an insurance expert." The list of damages scrolls along on the room's open door; Drummond is keeping an eye on it without seeming to see it at all. He can't see the sparkling fireball whirling around him and absorbing the data being compiled in real time by the artificial intelligence managing the hotel. This cohabitation of two fires—one in the visible world, one in the invisible—causes all kinds of strange conjectures in Plotkin's mind. The barely tangible signs he has been receiving since his arrival in Grand Junction, which are visibly interfering with his initial instruction program, are now happening at a higher level.

"Would you mind if I took a look?" Plotkin says calmly, planting himself in front of the door frame with its list of damages. *The listing really has no idea of what has happened here,* he says to himself. *The real damage has only just begun.*

There hadn't really been any truly localized fire situated somewhere in the double room (two capsules joined but separated by Japanese-style partitions of composite alloy and synthetic cellulose). Yet there had not been a generalized fire either, as usually happens when a blaze begins at a single ignition point and ends by consuming everything it can reach.

Plotkin investigates the part of the room where the electric current seems to have been cut. Only a few biofluorescent lights at the level of the baseboards glow dimly with yellowish-green light. There are two people in the room: one is standing in front of him; the other is stretched out on a sort of sofa at the far end of the room near the window. He is face-to-face with a man—young, barely thirty years old, with black curls worn long in a neo-Musketeer style. This must be the brother; so it was the sister sleeping by the semitranslucent window. Black eyes are gazing at him, and in the low light they seem to shine with enough energy for an entire city.

Plotkin senses the manager's presence behind him. He turns

around. "I've got things under control here, Drummond," he says politely. "I'll come and see you in your office."

"These young assholes are going to have to pay for this, I'm telling you," the fat man grumbles, then leaves through the open door.

At the same moment, Plotkin sees the dog Balthazar coming out of the bathroom, which is unfolded from the wall. He is apparently conducting a professional survey of the room, all his natural and artificial senses in action. Their eyes meet as the modified animal passes in front of him to leave the chamber; Plotkin hears Clovis Drummond calling the dog from the hallway. Then he turns to face his destiny.

"My name is Plotkin," he lies while simultaneously telling the truth.

The young man doesn't move, nor does he respond to the hand Plotkin extends.

"I'm an insurance agent. Don't let that fat bastard Clovis Drummond worry you too much."

Now the hand moves forward and shakes his, a bit limply, without real conviction. "I'm Jordan June McNellis." The silhouette steps to one side and indicates the unmoving form on the sofa. "This is my sister, Vivian Velvet." The supine shape does not move. Plotkin studies the room's decor more attentively; now he can relate it to the data provided in el señor Metatron's listing. No, there hadn't been *a* localized fire. *There had been several.*

More precisely, it is as if an intense heat source had broken up and scattered all over the room—on the floor, walls, and ceiling, setting afire everything in its path. The bed in Capsule 081-A is marred by several brownish and black stripes, including one very deep one at the level of the pillow, which is entirely carbonized; this suggests the use of a welding torch or something like it. Plastic objects are melted; some of the retractable bathroom's components have been twisted out of shape by the fire and its circuits cracked, though it remains standing in the corner of the room.

The window itself, at the other end of the room where the unmoving and silent shape still lies gazing at the street and hills beyond, had also been attacked by the strange fire; a rusty line streaks from the center to the rim of the pane.

Plotkin looks at McNellis and sighs. "What exactly happened here?"

There is a moment of cold silence. Then:

"It was a simple accident." The words are said in an affronted tone.

In Plotkin's mind, the differences between an insurance agent specializing in high-risk spaceflights and a professional assassin are small, with or without his memory. The young man is a bad liar. The entire room is filled with contradictions to his statement. Even Drummond wasn't fooled—and the cyberdog certainly wasn't either. What would an insurance agent do in circumstances like these? What would a killer sent to eliminate the mayor of this damned city do in circumstances like these? Once more, he would need to let the part of him that didn't exist—at least not yet—do the talking.

"Don't give me the runaround. *Something* happened in here. And if I understand it correctly, maybe I can help you with Drummond and his insurance company."

The young man stares at him unblinkingly. "I said it was an accident. If we have to pay for it, we will."

Plotkin estimates the damage at several million Pan-Am dollars. If they have that much cash, why are they staying in a shabby capsule hotel in Grand Junction? If they've got so much money, why didn't they pay for a better forgery of their genetic disk? And if they're so rich, why haven't they had their defective gene fixed instead of attempting a shoddy modification of their biomedical file?

They are on a lambda waiting list for Platform 2 (the most primitive one). If they've got so much cash, why not try to get higher? It had taken him only a few seconds in Grand Junction to understand that everything, absolutely *everything,* is for sale—because it is really the cosmos that is being sold, parcel by parcel.

Plotkin looks the young man with the long black Louis XIII curls squarely in the eye. His killer's instinct, surely the only part of him that hasn't been reprogrammed, directs him to gaze clearly into the dark fire of the other man's eyes. His education as an assassin and spy, he knows, is traced in every line of his features; his silhouette, his general attitude—his organic structure itself—seems to have been affected by these changes in personality. "It wasn't an accident. I told you, I'm an insurance expert. Either you tell me what happened and I try to help you, or you deal with Clovis Drummond, in other words the city police of Grand Junction; in other words the bastards at Leonov Alley Station 40."

One thing is for sure: whatever happened in this room was not normal. Drummond thought it was some alcohol or drug crisis or a bit of traveler's insanity, but Plotkin has other ideas. It may have something to do with their genetic manipulation. And he needs to find out what, as soon as possible.

It would be out of the question for the Grand Junction police to come to this hotel. It would be out of the question to leave these two bizarre postadolescents to play with fire in a hotel like Keith Moon. It would be out of the question to let his mission be threatened by the damned big-mouthed manager of the hotel.

It would be out of the question to let everything get fucked up.

He needs to *know,* and something inside him is certain that he will go a very long way to do so.

If there is any real danger, Plotkin knows, he will kill this young man without the slightest qualm. The young man *and* his sister who lies there sleeping on the sofa.

"You're being an idiot," he informs the young man. "If the hotel needs to prove that you are in the wrong, all they have to do is watch the disk from your room's private camera and they'll know exactly what happened. You'll be arrested in the blink of an eye for willfully destroying property or something like it, and then you can kiss your trip to the Ring good-bye."

This brother and sister might have plenty of cash, but in Grand Junction they aren't the only ones. The real competition in this sordid world isn't between rich and poor; they never even cross paths, and the parallel lines of their lives stretch into infinity without intersecting.

Here, the poor compete with one another.

And the rich compete with one another too.

Then there are two other categories, where the competition is even fiercer: the *very* poor, and the *very* rich.

Grand Junction is a fractal of dislocated urbanism from the end of the Age of Cities. It is a crystallized piece of terminal AmeriWorld, a metamorphic condensation of several million lives ruined for the sake of a few more than seven thousand successful orbital flights. In the transborder world of Grand Junction, surrounded by three states, this middle ground between Earth and Space, with no more memory, identity, or stable benchmarks than Plotkin himself possesses, the complete cartography of this ecology of dreams and disasters is etched on every life. Here, however much one might want to, however hard one might try, it is impossible to preserve the invisible, secret, clandestine economy of the city, which feeds off its own darkness.

"What do you want, exactly?"

There it is. A beginning. Now they can talk.

"I want you to tell me what happened before the Grand Junction cops figure out your private access code and watch the disk from tonight." In Plotkin's head, he adds: *And before I ask my intelligence agent to do it illegally.* It is like a well-planned execution; he needs to take his time, and handle his prey carefully. After that, it should be only a matter of minutes. Enough time to draw a bit of inspiration, at least.

"Why?" asks the young man with the coal black eyes.

And that *why* indicates the meaning of the question like a xenon lamp illuminates the face of a prisoner in the interrogation room. That *why* really means, *Why do you want to bring this on yourself? Why do you want to help us?*

"Can't we sit down and talk about this calmly?"

It is the insurance agent persona talking, as if he were trying to sell a fire protection contract to a poor schmuck who just set his kitchen on fire. McNellis backs up slightly and gestures, hesitantly, through the open composite-paper sliding door at two armchairs facing each other in the neighboring room, Capsule 081-B. They head through the doorway together, a bit awkwardly, when a voice sounds from the sofa.

"Stay here. I'll tell you everything."

Which is already quite a lot.

But Plotkin understands that things are taking a completely unforeseen turn, one that not even the master spies of the Order could have predicted. In one second, the universe opens over an abyss. In this chasm, his body and falsified memory float toward a far-distant light. In this chasm is everything the instruction program did not plan for or anticipate. In this chasm is everything the Order's biotechnicians were unable to imagine. In this chasm is everything unattainable even for a being as powerful as his guardian angel.

Because he recognizes the voice that has just filled the room. It is the voice of the young woman of fire. The one from his dream.

BOOTSTRAP

CORPUS SCRIPTI

You have created two things, Lord: one close to you, which is the angel, and the other almost nothing, which is primary matter.

SAINT AUGUSTINE, *CONFESSIONS*, CHAPTER VII

> LIGHTNING

Now, here is the woman.

Her beauty is indescribable. Words would need to be invented, in fact *should* be invented, here and now, just to describe her.

She is flame. Or, she is the light of a newborn universe created by a very ancient fire.

Her hair is very short and of an ash-blond color similar to the lunar quicksilver of her complexion. She is starfire—the living manifestation of starfire. She is there, beside the circular window overlooking the human world, and she is as beautiful and pure as an icon.

Look at her eyes, says a voice inside Plotkin that has nothing to do with the instruction program. *Don't lose sight of her eyes.*

I saw her face
Now I'm a believer
Without a trace
Of doubt in my mind . . .

An old song from Britain's Mersey Beat era of the 1960s? Why did it pop into his head just now, as he stands transfixed by this gaze that seems to look into infinity? A double abyss that blends into a single one, looking into the frontal lobe of his brain, just behind the skin and bones of his skull, just beyond the barrier separating the visible from the invisible, and shining with a strange light that seems to absorb all other light around it.

Her eyes may be blue, but they are quicksilver. They hold the same dark flame as her brother's passionate gaze, but this flame seems somehow *infra*red: a point of dark red light, very dark, like a universe speeding away unimaginably fast; a point of crystal in the bottom-most depths of a well impenetrable even by the sun. And, bizarrely, it seems that her gaze is a negative—that it presents an inverted image of the normal ocular structure. A strange consequence of their bio-medical meddling with the gene for the degenerative retinal disease? Even more than that, he has the devastating impression that he is face-to-face with the organic materialization of a sort of *internal eye*.

At this moment, something happens deep in the heart of Plotkin's altered consciousness. Something that threatens to smash the relative integrity and delicate balance he has managed to maintain until now.

He is no longer completely a man, but neither is he an android or a machine. It is worse than that; he is all of these, a multiple whose unity rings false.

And there, all of a sudden, is *another.*

In a dazzling flash, it is as if his entire being has been plunged into the depths of a river of fire. A microsecond before, he had been in the Hotel Laika, in Capsule 081, in the presence of Jordan McNellis and his sister. Now everything that he *was* has been consumed, and an eternity separates this life from the previous one.

He is not only another, he is two others.

And the worst part of it is that these two others form a single, perfect unit.

And what keeps them bound so closely is the same invisible fire that now flows in his veins, his nerves, his bones, cartilage, cells. He burns and he is illuminated. He is illuminated and he burns.

He is another multiplied by two, which makes three—because of this fire that is allowing the two others that are him to remain as one, this fire that seeks and destroys; he is plunged into it three times before surging up again, dazed, into another reality. This fire is language. Or, it is the fire that smolders beneath language.

And this is why what he is going through now is moving into the supernatural terrain of an experience in which he is only an instrument, and whose goal seems to be the elevation of this instrument into a sort of superior reality—into music coming from another sphere. He is no longer Plotkin; he is no longer in the Hotel Laika, in the city of Grand Junction, in independent Mohawk territory, in North America, in the Human UniWorld. He is no longer a man. He is no longer a machine. Nor is he something better or worse than either of these. But he is another.

He is a *process ad infinitum.*

Just like at the moment when his consciousness rose to the surface during his passage through the Windsor aerostation checkpoint, he is again a new world, a blank page, a newborn, a brain without a past—but this time, something has come to write directly on the passionate slate of his fused memory; something has etched what is in the process of happening—these lives that are not his own, these lives that belong to another world, but one that he now inhabits.

"You are what I am," says the fire-woman who has just become his entire universe, a flaming substance swallowing and re-creating him.

"And I am what you are," she adds, while in the Hotel Laika she has just cast the merciful shadow of a smile at the man paralyzed in front of her.

YOU MUST NOT LOSE SIGHT OF THE FACT THAT YOU ARE ILLEGAL IMMIGRANTS CHARGED WITH A TERRORIST CONSPIRACY AGAINST THE CHINESE GOVERNMENT.

The words are imprinted on his mind in capital letters, as if by a megalomaniacal and paranoid typewriter.

And you, he thinks, *shouldn't lose sight of the fact that we are a little more than that.*

It was he who had thought the words. And yet *he* is *her.* Entirely. He/she knew it with his/her whole being, even while the heavy face of the medical officer swayed ponderously, his small, crude, homeopathic smile undulating between his fat lips, under the cold yellow light of the checkpoint's neon tube.

He/she is only one, like the human and divine parts of Christ are only one, while yet being synthetically disjointed. At his/her side, sitting on a rickety iron chair similar to his/her own, he/she sees his/her brother, Jordan June, eyes fixed on their interrogator. And the interrogator, a pompous Chinese military police major from Health Containment Camp 77 who, at the moment, is shuffling their files, printed on sheets of memory-cellulose, with a falsely careless air. Yes, Major Wu-Lei is a real son of a bitch.

He/she knows this all too well. He/she and his/her brother have been stuck in this camp for a week now. And in that seven days, the specific economy of Health Containment Camp 77, Hong Kong district, has been largely laid bare. Seven days has been more than enough to understand the genesis and operation of this humanitarian, UHU-approved concentration camp.

He/she has experienced it. And the still-separate part of the strange trinomial he/she forms with the fire that flows in his/her veins—between each of his/her cells, from one end to the other of his/her nervous system, even beyond his/her biological brain—the part that is still "him," the part that comes from another world, a world that does not yet exist, the residual part of his past/future memory, knows very well that it has now been absorbed by the fire that separates as it unifies, and unifies as it separates.

Fire. *Pyros.* That which purifies.

"According to what it says here regarding your identity in your personal report, Miss McNellis," says Major Wu-Lei in his military-school English, "you are guilty of several counts of computer fraud committed since your departure from New Zealand. At our request, the Sri Lankan police told us everything. You also manipulated data in your genetic code at the time of your entry into India, and that caused you to be deported to Mozambique. From there, both of you passed through Yemen, the Caucasus, Turkmenistan, and Burma. You then illegally entered Thai territory, and were subsequently forced to flee due to the war with the Malaysian Muslims, and now you are in your proper place. The New Zealanders never should have let you leave."

"There aren't any camps like this in New Zealand," he/she replies dryly. "We aren't criminals," he/she adds, without any real hope.

The officer laughs, a dry bark, the noise of a machine grinding in a freezing room. "Of course not, obviously not. That's why 250,000 of your compatriots died last year from a new mutant strain of Borneo bird flu. Here you are in the most secure territory on Earth with regard to health, young lady. It has been so for fifty years, despite all the wars. You should have known that before trying to play games with our mobile control centers."

He/she thinks, not without spite, that the major is right: one doesn't play *games* with the Devil.

"What are you accusing us of, exactly?" Jordan June McNellis demands furiously.

The major measures him up calmly; he tugs carefully on his sleeve in order to bring it back into precise, regulation alignment with his cuff.

"First, the manipulation of your IDs. Then, your illegal entry into the territory of the Asiatic Bloc Governance Bureau. As you must know, we now have a good idea of the basics."

"Our right to enter Hong Kong territory is protected by UHU laws concerning refugees—"

Major Wu-Lei's chuckle slithers from his mouth like a snake. "You are not refugees from any country on this fucking planet. And you know it."

"What do you mean?" his/her brother persists, adrenaline obviously pumping.

"What do I mean?" The man laughs again, with what might once have been sarcasm. "What I mean, my dear Mr. McNellis, is that you have tried to disguise the fact that you are Spacians; isn't that right?"

Spacians. The Anglo-Latin neologism coined for the first generation of humans born in orbit, in the Ring. *Homo spaciens.* He/she was born in the Ring.

He/she has always known it. He/she was born at an altitude of around 480 kilometers in an orbital colony called Cosmograd, which he/she left at around twelve years old with his/her brother, who was two years older, for southern Argentina to live with a Russian uncle after the accidental death of their parents during a mission on the moon.

The major continues without waiting for a reply, which in any case probably would not have been offered. "Then there is the fact that you are guilty of several infractions of the UHU's global traffic system. Your illegal entries into territories that are health-controlled by one or another of our agencies have been tracked by *our* services."

In his words, they feel—he/she feels, in unison with his/her brother—that this simple emphasis fills Major Wu-Lei with the pride of a servant of the state. In China, his/her brother had told him/her on the day of their arrival in the camp, they have a tradition in this sort of thing that stretches back thousands of years.

The major continues imperturbably, after a quick inhalation of breath: "And there is the fact that our health inspectors have decided to register you under security code orange while we wait for our genetics and biophysics laboratories to determine exactly what we are dealing with."

Another breath. This time he fixes each of them in turn with his little black bug eyes—flat and dull, the eyes of a man born to be a chief inspector.

"What you are dealing with?" his/her brother asks, almost too innocently.

The little black eyes linger on him, bored charcoal marbles, extinguished from birth.

"Don't play stupid with me, young man. We are well aware that you are both carriers of an unknown virus that is not listed on your UHU-approved genotype cards. We think it may be some new type of experimental neuroportable weapon, so we are very closely studying the analyses and samples taken when you entered Camp 77. If we have to, we will take others. We will find what we're looking for."

At that moment, the fire that is coursing through his/her entire being expands suddenly beyond its original boundaries, resulting in an intense surge in his/her energy levels. The light is no longer contained by shadows; it becomes heat that fills space and time, making the entire world his/her body. Next comes a violent increase in his/her body temperature; he/she feels more and more feverish. He/she fears the worst: *Is this a new attack?* But he/she continues to bear up under the cold stare of those eyes, lively as black holes, heavy as a dead moon settling onto his/her slender frame, exhausted in its chair. *And you, you fat slug, health police my ass; you don't even know what to look for or where to look. And neither do your so-called genetic specialists,* he/she thinks.

He/she is filled with radiant, negative certainty. No.

No, they can't guess a thing. They can't know, they don't know, anything. In fact they know less and less; it doesn't matter if they're Chinese cops or New Zealand doctors or global bureaus or local inspectors. UHU's approved genetic operative is more than a hundred years old. It dates from Crick and Watson; it dates from the Meccano biological era. It dates from before the conjunction of catastrophes and the convergence of biocidal vectors. In any case, it dates from before he/she was even born.

Science itself spent a lot of time frozen in posthistoric stasis before beginning to move again—backward. It is as if the 1983 Nobel Prize, awarded to Barbara McClintock, had never happened—as if the woman had never discovered that DNA wasn't a fixed "code" but rather a highly dynamic process open to the outside. It is like everyone decided to deliberately ignore the implications of a discovery as critical as that of mobile genes, called transposons, which are constantly changing their position in the genetic chain. It is like no one knows yet that RNA retroviruses are integrated into this same genetic base, continuously "retrowriting" vital information for the entire "code." It is as if no one had ever moved beyond the famous "standard model" of the genomic operative introduced by Mr. Crick in 1980. As if a deliberate decision had been made to stay there, to be able to clone in series, or to graft a pair of additional breasts paid for by social security.

Everything is frozen in the state it was in fifty or sixty years before. Ninety-eight percent of the genetic code is still considered to be noncoding, and thus "garbage," "junk DNA," white noise, useless information—but it is there, and he/she knows it in the core of his/her being—that the real "code" lies, the "metacode" that deciphers all others.

* * *

The only technical progress now tolerated is the kind likely to produce comfort, atomic-social equality, or pleasure. Fundamental research is concentrated in the hands of telecommunications, operative biology, robotic, and geoclimatic control agencies, as well as the various poles of military sovereignty tolerated by the UHU. And yet their famous genomic card serving as the means to identify every individual on the planet persists in considering 98 percent of our genes as noncoding! The fire laughs, a cascade of plasma that blazes within him/her while the fever rises even higher, a sure harbinger of an attack. This interrogation needs to be cut short, and soon.

But the tremors spasmodically racking his/her back, arms, and hands and the sweat beading on his/her forehead have already attracted the major's attention.

"Are you feeling ill, miss?"

The fire laughs again, and this time it comes streaming out his/her thirst-ravaged lips. "I'm wondering if the health conditions in your 'health camp' are in compliance with UHU regulations, Major. All I know is that your humid and poorly heated place seems to have caused me to come down with a sudden case of bronchitis. I'd like you to bring me a large quantity of aspirin and an electric heater, please."

The major makes a poor attempt at an apologetic gesture, but he cannot keep a tiny, cynical smile from turning up the corners of his mouth, a derisive relic of ancestral politeness. "Our civil war has caused us many problems, young lady, and now there is this eternal war in the Indian Ocean. Our funds are quite limited. The global economy, you know, has not been strong for many years. But I will do my best to get a heater for you. And Secretary Yu will give you an infirmary voucher for your aspirin."

This gesture of leniency is probably a sign that the interview is over, he/she says to himself/herself. In any case, he/she says, in a voice slightly weakened by the mounting fever that is like a fire, a rocket, an atomic reaction turning his/her body into a living battery, a living bomb: "I appreciate it, Major Wu-Lei."

Then he/she stands up as steadily as possible and says: "Good-bye, Major Wu-Lei."

His/her brother does the same.

The major has already relegated their health files to a pile by his right hand and pulled out another from the pile by his left. He does not look at them again, or say another word as they leave the room.

Now, the cell. It is next to Jordan's. The two rooms are actually in a reserved area, separated from the others by the most draconian health-security codes in all of Camp 77. They have been designated "code orange"; they cannot leave these cells unless the containment camp cops decide they can. Actually, it is easy to imagine that they will end up in the code red area, which no one ever leaves. The genetic labs of Hong Kong's health police won't find anything, of course. There is nothing to find. Because human eyes cannot read the invisible—don't *want* to see the invisible, even when it becomes visible, because if they allow themselves to see the invisible-cum-hypervisible, their entire pitiful world will vanish.

He/she is a form of mutating life. He/she condenses the production of a new human speciation into a single generation. It is alpha-omega; it gives rise to an infinite number of lines diverging from one another and all stemming from a unique, singular, and yet transfinite point. In the same metastatic movement, it encompasses all horizons that in the hyperbole of the possible may exist in this world, stretching beyond its own destruction.

The intimate structure, the thermodynamics of the phenomenon are impossible to describe by Euclidean means. The closest image might be that of a universe said to be in a phase of supercritical expansion from the quantum singularity that contains it in its entirety, and whose shock waves, like concentric circles made by a stone dropped into a pond of water, continually modify the creative process itself. This why each attack, each metamorphic stage, is more dangerous than the last. Like Empedocles, each step is a step closer to the red maw of the volcano, to the bottomless stomach of the black hole.

It was in this fire that she was born; she is the daughter of this fire. But this fire, as Saint John of Patmos, Denys the Areopagite, and Johannes Cassianus knew, remains invisible, behind an impenetrable fog. It remains in the shadows, though they cannot contain it. And this fire is a manifestation of Logos that articulates itself beyond Good and Evil, even beyond the Tree of Knowledge, because it is the eternal guardian in the form of a whirling sword, this fire that permits the creation of worlds—the writing of them, the narration of them, the giving to them of life. This fire of the World that causes Action is also the fire that burns, destroys, and consumes the bearer of this World.

The fire is both its own ontological limit and the infinite that stretches beyond itself. The fire is energy that devours all the so-called real simulacrums of the world and that endlessly carbonizes the global parameters of the machines that control the destinal matrix of every human on this planet. But it is also the differential that is ceaselessly resuming, and always on the point of creating, ontological danger—the part always ready for sacrifice, the already-written chapter of our own combustion.

He/she lies prostrate on this shitty, last-century hospital bed. He/she is alpha-omega.

This is why she is now *he and she.*

He/she has an idea.

He/she has a plan. Or, more accurately, a plan—a secret cosmic war—is being read and expressed through him/her.

He/she has simulacrums to destroy.

He/she has a world to create.

And to do this, he/she must create a man.

In order for any alchemical process to succeed, according to the precious wisdom of the Kabbalah, *one* must become *two*.

When you are ready to create a golem, when you are ready to replicate the divine gesture of Creation, when the fire of gnosis inside you is ready to consume itself for another life, you must be two. But in order not to produce a *hybris, an infinitely divided indivisible,* the presence of this sanctifying, reunifying fire is also necessary. You must be one to create. You must be two to divide. *You must be three to create.*

She knows this fire. She has known it for a long time. It was born with her, in her, in the hard, clean, blinding light of the sun as seen outside the boundaries of the terrestrial atmosphere—an unspeakable monster, burning its quadrillions of tons of hydrogen per second in the magnificent silence of the cosmos, that immense black ocean stretching across endless dimensions, dotted with white points without the slightest brilliance, the slightest radiance, the slightest optical illusion; semaphores perhaps already dead for thousands or millions of years before their light reaches us. This fire was born in her when she was playing children's games. She has understood it from earliest youth. It makes her something else, producing a line of infinite tension between her "I" and this "other." She had rapidly discovered the magnificent and terrible nature of her power—and realized that it would be considered the ultimate danger by the terrestrial society that strives to confine it.

Because you do not create worlds with impunity in this world that is for everyone, where there is one God for each of us.

During these attacks—these terrible moments of *superfusion,* while the network of mechanical disconnections in her being opens out and abruptly covers the star-filled space between her "I" and the "other"—all her transfictional narrative powers are completely sapped. One of the doctors at the center in New Zealand, who apparently read Husserl on the sly, had diagnosed it as an "intensified inversion of inversion" just before their flight across the Indian Ocean.

There is a moment—an "antimoment," really—when, as the mechanical network of her I-other tries to connect to the infinite line of tension separating them, rather than hollowing out a singularity that would fold this infiniteness over onto its differential gap, it separates from itself and swallows up her entire being. At the highest point of the attack, she is really nothing more than the abyss itself, a chasm of nothingness. She doesn't need to lose consciousness; that too has long since disappeared, and what seems to remain and evoke the idea of a "consciousness" is nothing more than a tiny kernel of pain surrounded by infinity. The maximum extension of the fold-over revealed to the "world," the suddenly formatted expansion of her "consciousness" within a matrix of content now coding only itself, provokes in reaction an infinite condensation of the rupture point, a moment when her entire body-spirit is at the point of breaking, a moment when the Nothing-Being that she has become cedes place to the overall invasion of the World, and of the suffering—the physical, psychic, absolute suffering—that comes with it.

This dark side of her state of being, this moment of chaotic superfusion, this moment when the gaps close again, this moment when the machine, coalescing with the World, becomes a program matrix, an antimonad opening to its own closure, this moment when the World takes possession of her, is the tragic other side of the human incarnation of the fire of Logos in her flesh; it is the double edge of the flaming sword that guards the Garden of Eden and the Tree of Knowledge. The fire tries to destroy her to purify her of herself; it separates her then brings her back together.

This dark face looks out upon the true Counter-World: the alphaomega phase, the unknowable moment when, brutally, her body-spirit becomes a metaliving, metacosmic, metaphysical generator/narrator.

It looks out upon the moment when narration becomes Flesh,

when the written word becomes the Body, and the Word becomes the Act.

The attack lasts two days, like always. It should really be understood as an anti-attack, since it is the devolving opposite face of the true, permanent attack on her body-spirit. She is the definition of duality incarnate. The attacks are the dualist reaction to her Trinitarian transcendence. They are not a phase of infinite division so necessary for the disjunctive trine synthesis to become operative and thus permit the emergence of the creative process. They are a phase of division separate from the process that folds all the other phases back on itself, all the other possibilities, in a devouring, reverberating, antiverbal phenomenon that promises to reunite everything—but on the field of separation, and to separate everything from itself, to cause fusion with the World. Vivian Velvet, and the He/She that she is becoming, can do nothing during the two days of Anti-Creation, the binary days of division looped back on false infinity.

Nothing. Not even sleep, not even thinking, nothing satisfies her so-called natural biological needs.

But when the attack finally recedes, and the third day dawns outside her cell—its light as pale as the face of a condemned man streaming weakly through the small, square Securimax™ window—she is now He/She.

Another can finally have a body. Another that was born here, in Health Containment Camp 77 in the city of Hong Kong, but who will not achieve existence until later, when he/she has decided to grant it—or, more specifically, when the narrative dictates it. Until then, he/she will carry him, in the deepest part of himself/herself, and thus he/she will integrate him into a world that is often cruel and pierces him/her to the core.

Because this Other now exists in him/her; he is the agent of a singular narration. He is the *he* of his/her symbiotic metamorphosis, but transmuted by the supermechanical device in which she is the *she*—that is, by the quantum leap represented in the incorporation of the Fire-Being, of the narration itself. This Other is becoming independent now. Neither a he nor a she. It seems most like the fire-spirit that tears them apart while encapsulating them. It is becoming the agent of a narrative that can predict the future, because this narrative is prophetic. It is formative. It makes Acts out of Words.

It is more than a "story" that she carries within herself—more than a character—more than a series of situations or more or less contingent intrigues. She carries a World, and she carries its Counter-World.

She carries a Man.

She carries the Man from the Camp.

The words of a book she read in the Ring during her late adolescence, shortly before her departure for Earth, come back to her in a flash of light, a lexical fire of shining glyphs glowing on the writing desk of her brain. The words are from the only book that gave her even a little understanding of the state of the world she was living in, the world she would soon be living in Down There. The book deciphered the central experience of the twentieth century, and demonstrated—with rare intellectual vigor—how this event was not a "moment" separate from all others, but rather the physical opening of an entire era, one that began to fade away at the same moment it was born. The one, in fact, that forged the world of UHU. The book put it this way:

> Our inability to claim the effects of our actions as *ours* is not only attributable to the excessive scope of these effects, but also to the outrageous *mediating* of our processes of work and action. The aggravation of the current division of labor means nothing more than this: we are condemned, working and acting, to concentrate on tiny segments of the whole process. We are enclosed in the phases of the work that affect us, like prisoners detained in their cells. Thus detained, we are stuck with the idea of our specialized

work, and therefore excluded from the representation of the machine in its whole; from the image of the work process as a whole, made up of thousands of phases. And most importantly, from the image of the result as a whole, in the service of which the machine is placed.

The book was called *We, Sons of Eichmann*. The author was called Günther Anders. It had been on her nightstand for months; she had read and reread it dozens of times, until she knew it by heart.

What I want to emphasize—I know this thesis may seem daring— is the fact that *our current world, as a whole, is being transformed into a machine. That it is about to become a machine.*

Health Containment Camp 77 of the district of Hong Kong, despite its humid cells, dilapidated from much use in a world that cannot even "progress" in a *technical* sense, is one of the most modern facilities of its kind in United China, the world's most important pro-UHU power. With one in three of the world's inhabitants being Chinese, the model planetary democracy of the governance bureaus and the planetary resource management corporations perfectly suits the system that China put in place at the end of the previous century. For the UHU, it is a bottomless source of managers, officers, bureaucrats, and specialists of every sort.

The globe's other great nations are important too, he/she knows perfectly well, but postnational breakdowns and Islamization have made them less competitive in the race for command posts. However, voluntary servitude is probably the only truly infinite strength man possesses, and most of these countries, even the ones still involved in more or less latent conflicts at, or beyond, their borders, such as the Islamic States of the Global Conference of Dar al-Islam, have accepted the permanent reign of the UHU over this humanity on its way to extinction.

It is as beautiful as an apparition of the Devil in his red velvet doublet. It is as beautiful as a dead young maiden stretched out on a bed of light. It is as beautiful as the end of a world. And where the Devil shows himself most ingenious is in the multitude of "rebellions" that are already brewing in the Human UniWorld. All of them, except the UNE, are in his service. In a rebellion, remember, the Devil is always one step ahead of you. You realize the extent of his power when you see that you are at least two matches behind him when it comes to control.

She must not think anymore. She must not even write on the poor-quality Indo-Chinese student tablets amassed in a humanitarian shop en route to Vientiane, or on one of the antique portable pods she managed to pick up at some souk or market in Maputo, or Mogadishu, or Aden, or Goa.

She must

Be

SILENT.

Silent.

Anyway, she cannot write, or talk, or think about the real meaning of her "existence," which is as paradoxical as that of the entity called Nothing, because to do so would be to negate her intrinsic and conclusive anti-existence, her absolute negativity. Nothing can be said, or sensed, or sketched about it without the Nothingness disappearing, without warping the meaning of each word, or thought, or dream.

The silence isn't passive; nor is the nothingness. Both of them are abysses, black holes. They are inaudible and invisible, but they can be detected by the energy disturbances they cause in their environment. They are, in a way, visible as negatives. They are lines that connect Being to Being via the absolute compression of her negation. This negation is not static, but neither is it dynamic in the sense of a "relative" and independent object across a space that is itself differentiated.

The negation is *metastatic*. Silence is the anticreative moment necessary for Creation. It is what precedes every birth and what hushes every noise. It is the acoustic and mental equivalent of the Luminous Shadow of the medieval Faith doctors. It is what contains the world without being able to hold it.

He/She is this silence. He/She is no longer. Anything.

Finally, as if after millions of years of petrifaction in the lithosphere of what is neither body nor spirit, but the residue left by their infinite division looping backward on itself, here it is—Illumination, Opening, Light. Freedom, the sensation of absolute freedom. Her absolute reality, the one that breaks down every wall of every cell in every camp.

She is there. She has risen from this metastatic tension between Being and Being, between her "I" and her "Other." She has risen not only from the nothingness, but also from the light that is contained in her at the bottom of the Abyss, the Light hidden in the Shadow, in the deepest depths of the black hole. And this freedom—this absolute faith in the Created World—this freedom is not a state, or a right, or a civil contract, or a gift, or a livelihood, or even a mania. This liberty is a weapon. A virus. A fire that will spread at the tiniest spark.

Now, he/she/I-other is in the process of incorporation. In her, the World is being born. In her, the World is becoming what it is. The template of a cosmodrome about which she is compiling information dating from the time of their flight across the Indian Ocean toward first South America, then Goa because of a half-assed smuggler. It is also what has come to impregnate this improbable surrogate, what has come to pass through this pregnant chaos-bearing envelope, thanks to the metahuman killer it is creating; thanks to this man who has come from the shadows of the world, this Man from the Camp.

He/She/Fire. A noncomposite trinity, synthetically disjointed. An infinity of disconnections that produce their unity through a total overall semantic reversion. A transsubstance via which her body becomes light little by little, at the moment when her spirit becomes fire. They need an assistant—an adviser—a joker. They will need someone else they can trust—that is, a supreme traitor in this treasonous world. A being without memory in this world that remembers everything. A being without pity in this *totally humanized* world.

The *I-Other* takes shape.

There, in Containment Camp 77, in the damp, cold cell in the "code orange" wing, she proceeds with the alchemy of the world her narrative will produce.

In the middle of the anonymous nowhere of this metanational state, she invents the Man that will come and kill the mayor of the city they must reach. She invents the fiction that will come to save her. She invents the Counter-Man from the Camp.

She already knows that it is this man who, soon, will invent her.

And that brings me to the basic concept of the global machine. What do I mean by that? Suppose, for example, that machines had actually succeeded in conquering the entire world, as completely as, on a smaller scale, Hitler conquered Germany—that is, in such a way that there would be nothing left but them and their fellows; nothing but a huge pen of completely mobile machines. What would happen to these different types of machines in these conditions?

We need to consider two things:

1) That without backup, none of these specimens would be able to function. No machine can take care of itself or feed itself, no matter how highly sophisticated it is.

It is at this exact point, she says to herself, that Günther Anders's ideas reached their limits, that his imagination reached its limit. He too found himself in the position of every human on the planet after 1945: imagining that the final result of our actions was already beyond the capabilities of most mere mortals, and even those of some exceptional men. It seems impossible to imagine that machines might one day begin to act on their own, to be independent enough to "feed" themselves by seeking out and consuming the energy necessary for their survival and development. But that is exactly what happened in the twenty-first century: the moment of freedom of the machine; the counterpole of the enslavement of humans, who became simply the "biological" operators of the machine-world.

Anders continued:

2) That among the ancillaries that will be available to these specimens, none will have survived that are not already machines themselves; in short, they will all be dependent upon one another. They will be limited on all points by the need to have access to their fellows, while each of them must try to help its fellows to function as well as possible.

"But what will such reciprocity lead to?" The German thinker who wrote this had asked, via two public letters addressed to the son of Adolf Eichmann—indeed, to all the sons of Eichmann of the era, not only his contemporaries, but future generations as well. *"To something extraordinarily surprising,"* he had answered himself. Since everything will be functioning like a well-oiled machine, as it were, some specimens will no longer be machines.

What will they be, then?

Pieces of machines. That is, mechanical parts of a single, gigantic "total machine" in which they will all be united.

And what will *that* lead to? What will this "total machine" be, exactly?

Vivian knows that here Günther Anders posed, in just a few lines, the most important questions of an entire century.

"What will this 'total machine' be," he asked.

When Vivian read these lines for the first time, she felt as if she had been struck by a bolt of lightning, a tornado of fire, because she sensed what was coming next.

"Think about it again. The parts that are not integrated will cease to exist. Nothing will survive in the outside. Thus this 'total machine' will be the WORLD.

"And here we are, on the brink," Anders had continued. *"We need take only one more step to get there. All we have to do is reverse the phrase, 'machines are becoming the world.' And then we get, 'the world is becoming a machine.' "*

"Your idea is a good one," Jordan said to her in a telepathic communication. "You need to expand on it. You need to respect—as much as you can—the sacrosanct rule of tragedy and psychological drama: unity of time, place, and action. We can't spend all our time running after him. Despite this *economy,* you have to cleverly organize a collision between us and the creature. You need to make an accident happen in the program."

"We can use fire," she said. "I've heard about the intelligent neurodigital agents UniPol uses. Apparently, clandestine spy corporations use a lot of them too. I incorporated them. This way I can be with him without making him suspicious, and I can write to him and bring him continuously into my world right up until the meeting point."

"And then?" her brother asked.

"Then—well, then I don't know. If I script it, the collision won't happen. If I prewrite it, the man won't be free, or able to consider the sacrifice calmly."

Now, imagine the following scene: He/You/I/She/Other, what you are, what we are; we are now an eye. An infrared eye. The eye of a panoramic camera placed in the center of the cell's ceiling. The camera detects violent fluctuations of heat in the body of the person it is programmed to watch twenty-four hours a day. According to the data transmitted by the local microprocessor, there was even a sort of photonic "illumination" that lasted several minutes, something completely atypical in animal—especially human—biology. The biophoton frequency range is close to ultraviolet. The camera's multifrequency sensors swallow and regurgitate entire lists of codes that come up with a single answer: *absolutely abnormal phenomenon.*

Major Wu-Lei is not happy. His dead-moon face fills her entire field of vision. The eye is no longer a camera; it is the camera that has become the eye. *Major Wu-Lei isn't happy,* she thinks. *Not happy at all.*

"YOU HAVE TRIED TO SABOTAGE OUR SECURITY SYSTEMS! YOU HAVE TRIED TO CAUSE A SOFTWARE MALFUNCTION IN OUR SURVEILLANCE SYSTEM! YOU HAVE TRIED TO CHEAT THE CONTROL SYSTEM!"

Not happy at all, Major Wu-Lei. Quite bothered, actually.

"But you cannot do anything against us. Plenty of others have tried," Major Wu-Lei adds in a voice of forced calm, coldly menacing after the frenzied guard-dog barks of a moment ago.

"There might have been others, you poor bastard. But none like us."

Her impulse is always to resist. It is a loop of fire, a flash that whirls between Heaven and Earth, an antiworld. An antiworld whose enemy is this world, the world of Major Wu-Lei and his fellows. The last world. The world of the last men.

She has no hope, she knows, of being left alone by the world of Major Wu-Lei and the others of his stripe. This is a war, without mercy, and there will be no quarter given or received. *No prisoners.*

"We have done nothing illegal, and you know it," she says. "Your cameras are malfunctioning. Your computers must come from

France, which means California. Your so-called mysterious phenomena of bodily illumination are just system-interpretive errors. We
have attempted nothing that might threaten the security of the camp.
It seems to me that you are breaking UniPol's police ethics code."

The dead man, king of this dead world, observes them with his
burnt-coal eyes, eyes that seem to have been mined in Hades itself.
He is the man of the moment. *He is in the right place at the right time.*

"You lie as easily as breathing," he tells her. "I think both of you
are extremely dangerous pathological cases, and you will not leave
here for a very long time, believe me."

We'll be out of here before you learn to believe in anything, he/she
thinks amid the fiery vapor that has taken possession of his/her body,
soul, and spirit both here and beyond. *We'll be out of here and you have
no idea. Even if you knew, you wouldn't understand. We'll be out of here because we don't exist, not according to the plan of your existence. And that's
why you don't exist for us anymore, either.*

She smiles widely at Major Wu-Lei, who is no longer looking at
them, his hand mechanically pulling the next file from the stack.

> INVASION—EVASION—DELUSION

I really am a neurobiological combat organism, she thinks, managing with difficulty to keep from laughing into the globular eye of the surveillance camera. *But not in your pathetic understanding of the world, you bunch of pigs. Especially your understanding of the word* combat, *you ridiculous toy soldiers. You're fighting in the Hundred Years' War, the Battle of Thermopylae, only now there are cyberplanes, drones, nucleotactical missles, neutron rockets, ionizers; and, shall we say, a single megaton bomb.*

The camera is built into the wall, which is built into the "code orange" sector, which is built into the camp, which is built into the world. The world of UHU. And in this World, men exist like the ones she is going to create. It will be enough to create him. And since the World is now part of her own spirit-world . . .

Now it is time to make the Names appear. Time to Name. The Name is the first thing that makes a being exist. The name of her maternal uncle, the one that lived in Argentina, on the pampas near Cordillera—where, he said, an English writer from the late twentieth century had once come on the trail of the legendary American West bandit-heroes Butch Cassidy and the Sundance Kid, and where they had filmed a western in 1969. Yes, the family name Dimitrievitch Plotkin would do nicely. She comes up with a few references . . . the writer-explorer Bruce Chatwin for his maternal family name, with images of the Patagonian pampas, a few sparse bits of memory, boys from the neighboring village, and her own memories of her uncle and her young cousin Sergei from Novosibirsk, on whom she would model the synthetic personality of her golem.

Obviously, the code-orange sector doesn't have any Internet access to the Control Metastructure. There is no connection in her cell, or in any of the cells at that security level—especially the wing reserved for her and her brother. But the camera is part of the camp, and the camp is part of the world. And the world is part of her.

They need to choose a place ahead of time. They need a cosmodrome, a private one. There are only a few of them left. UHU astroports are out. There aren't many viable options. They will need to flee very fast and get very far away from China, and then leave for the Ring as fast as they can. They need to get off Earth and back to Cosmograd, try to find whatever friends are still up there twelve years later, and then, most likely, flee again. Get as far away as possible from Human UniWorld, probably to the independent Mars colonies. If possible, even farther than that.

"It is especially important that you don't preplan too much of the world your golem will be coming from; you're absolutely right about that," her brother says to her one day via telepathic connection. "But you do need to be familiar with the microlocal universe where we're all going to meet. You need a plan, but the plan has to appear to necessitate his own destruction. The plan should only be the starting point for the story as it comes to life."

Her brother, whose phases had been stabilized at "epsilon" (as the New Zealand doctors called it) when he was a baby, does not have his sister's cosmogonic narrative powers. He cares little for religion or science; he is, rather, a connoisseur of European and American romantic literature dating from the Middle Ages through the twentieth century. In this age of books written by ethically controlled artificial intelligence, Jordan's library, inherited from their father, is worth millions of dollars. It is still up in the Ring, integrated into the library of Cosmograd's aged rabbi. Jordan spent their final year in orbit using the mental techniques of the *theater of memory,* a repertoire of mnemonic mechanisms based on Greco-Latin rhetoric that permits a person to retain thousands and thousands of citations, strophes, and verses and mentally register hundreds of books; Western universities pushed the art to the highest degree of composition, until the terrible twentieth century and its campaign to systematically destroy all true human power.

She, in fact, is the body-mind who directly integrated them into the theater of her memory, who made a neurodigital copy of all the libraries she had incorporated, sometimes without even desiring to. The models and techniques she uses to produce her world-fictions come from her brother's literary knowledge. The alchemical models and techniques of the Great Work come from her incorporation of the Ring's forbidden libraries. The power comes from this fire that combines all these characteristics and an infinite multitude of others besides.

"I know; I think I understand," she says to her brother, in this dream so identical to reality. They sit in their separate padded cells, but the beige-colored wall separating them has disappeared in a quantum, paradoxical manner, like a Schrödinger cat who doesn't know which box to choose; the wall is invisible yet concrete. "I think I know how to structure the narrative on Metatron's time—the open/closed time of angels. But now I just want to wait for the next attack; it should be coming soon," she adds. "I need to get it over with before I can do any more work. You know they always come in two waves. Hey, now that I think of it—are you still entitled to your legal Novatrix rations?"

"What for?"

"Well, you know our symptom is genetically similar to retinitis pigmentosa. Remember Dr. Dreisenberg—and Dr. Slavik and Dr. Anderson—said that if we didn't have any of their damned Trans-Epsilon vaccine, Novatrix would help a little with the symptoms."

"And you know that our little attacks are nothing compared to what you go through during your Dual Days of infinite division. There's no antidote for that. Besides, I don't think there's any point in drawing their attention to a neurojamming disease they've already classified anyway. As far as our supercoding gene, they're already snooping around down to our smallest mitochondria, our tiniest RNA strand."

"They won't find anything. The World Below is regressing even faster than we thought. I connected to the Net in my dreams, and found out that three-quarters of the libraries in Europe, digital copies included, were destroyed during their fucking Grand Jihad. In North America, the War of Secession completely broke up the research laboratory network. There are five confederations sharing that territory now, and that's not counting Canada and its independent territories. There are only a few centers still operational in Massachusetts, Texas, and the western states. The governance bureaus were betting on the Chinese, but they have the same problems as the rest of the world. So the UHU never stops having to fix things. Its metastructure of agencies and cybernetic machines is stuck in the twentieth century. They no longer have the technical, human, or mental means to keep conquering the world. The UHU isn't just an omnipotent police force that has the whole world in its claws. It's also what they don't know how to do—what they never knew how to do and never will know how to do. They don't even know what they're doing now, if you know what I mean."

"Are you sure about what you're saying?"

"This is confidential information resistance groups are circulating against UniPol's cyberbranch. Whatever the UHU governance bureaus' communications and public relations agencies might be saying, technology—*science*—hasn't progressed at all since 2030. Meaning, since the invention of controlled nuclear fusion, and since we were born in the Ring. It's like that technology started a complete shutdown of all scientific progress, and it happened to coincide catastrophically with the Grand Jihad and the global depopulation that went along with it. The UHU's military-humanitarians are dealing with the effects of more than fifty years of global chaos, and almost twenty-five years of real devolution. As for their so-called Ethical and Health Control Department, well, I'm figuring that one out. My mind-world is incorporating it, believe me. Every day I know a little more about them than they've ever known. They're only socialized atoms; never forget it, brother. *We* are *extra*terrestrial."

In the cell, the electronic eye observes the young woman, who seems to be back to normal. In the cell, the young woman observes the electronic eye, smiling as if it were some perfectly inoffensive pet. She could talk to this eye, which hears nothing but sees everything except the invisible. Maybe, like the HAL 9000 computer in *2001: A Space Odyssey,* it can read her lips? She could tell it: *There is a city somewhere in a sort of border interzone in North America, where a private cosmodrome called Grand Junction Cosmos Incorporated is still operating normally. This city was founded at the turn of the century, and it grew when the United States and some parts of Canada fell apart. It kept growing during the Grand Jihad and even for a while afterward.* And she has incorporated this city. Grand Junction is a part of her now. And she has incorporated Cosmos along with it.

Devolution is not a technical phenomenon. To describe it that way is absurd. Devolution is anthropological by definition, because it is a moment of infinite division of anthropogenesis. As long as it is attached to one of the *false infinities* the philosopher Hegel spoke of at the beginning of the nineteenth century, there will be UHU world and Human UniWorld, and Unimanity in all its splendor. There will be a moment when the false infinity breaks away endlessly from its own ending, and when the limits imposed by its incapability to conceive of creation as an eminently paradoxical phenomenon are reached, that will cause it to start moving backward. This progression, and its diabolical dynamic of infinite division tied to false infinity, when it is no longer in phase with other phases, in the Tri-Unity where each hypostasis is synthetically disconnected from the others—that of the sole Being and that of the trine Creation—continues mechanically during this phase of overall regression. It is its maker's mark.

The world does not go backward like a videocassette being rewound. The tape itself is affected. Physical time folds over. History becomes not only regressive, but evolution itself, its specific principle of regulation, is caught up in the overall anthropological reflux. This is *devolution*. It is something that will always end by becoming truly indescribable.

In a few years, the World of UHU will probably have sealed off the planet. Private cosmodromes like the one in Grand Junction, the one she has set her heart on, will be all but extinct. In a decade, perhaps fifteen years at the most, international laws will have abolished the last existing human adventure. Territories like Grand Junction will be outlawed, or regulated so severely that they will become UHU astroports serving suborbital flights of intercontinental shuttles.

The takeoff window is getting smaller every year, every month, every day.

Plotkin must be designed as soon as possible, and secretly incorporated into the World, and created when the time is right.

But they also need to get out of Health Containment Camp 77 as fast as they can. They need to get out of their cells, out of the code-orange sector, out of China.

They need to get out of this World.

"When do you think you'll be capable of that kind of conjunction?" her brother asks, during a dream connection.

"During the next anti-attack," she replies. "It depends on how fast I can integrate my golem into this World, and all of it into the Other World."

Her brother looks dreamy, sitting on his shitty beige humanitarian hospital bed in front of the reinforced beige security partition. The wall separating them has never really been anything other than a failed potentiality. Its symbolic simulation is the ultimate form of concretion possible in the quantum field of their two linked consciousnesses.

"You know I have only the equivalent of a nanosecond to make a connection between these two mutually exclusive worlds, to quote our dear Kabbalist Leibniz. The World Plotkin exists in is possible. The World he does not exist in is also possible. But the two worlds, Leibniz would say, are mutually exclusive. They are possible, but at the same time, their possibilities—like their impossibilities—can never coincide. That is the barrier between fiction and reality that only the power of Logos can cross. I must manage to short-circuit this 'grid' when the incorporation is finished. I can at least try."

"And what about getting us out of this camp?"

She smiles, in this dream more real than the image of her body stretched out on its prison bed, watched by the electronic eye of the surveillance camera. "The camp is in me now. Soon we will be completely outside it. The two 'parts' of the work are really just one.

"The camp is a world. An antiworld. Not an active 'counterworld' representing the invisible side of the Created World, but a non-place, a non-space, a non-time. It is an *ante-World,* really, because it is not yet a World. It is the stage that precedes all Creation, and it proves that in Human UniWorld, Chaos takes on a specific form, the form of a dual incarcerator/terrorist. The form of *Death at work. Death as a production process.*"

And yet the camp and its specific topology—its non-topology, since each "containee" only knows a tiny portion of this concentration/humanitarian camp he or she is stuck in for one reason or another—the camp, as a "real" antiworld, is also a *potential counter-world* for her cosmogonic narrative project.

Plotkin is the man of the UHU world—but his Counter-Self, his shadow self. He is the Man from the Camp. He is the intensified inversion of the incarcerator/terrorist. He is the master spy who manufactures his own personality out of multiple ones. The killer whose rebellion is extreme solitude. The shadow cast by the World of the Camp. And, in a most enigmatic way, he shows her more than a direction. He shows her a horizon.

Like two parallel lines joining in infinity, she and he, he and she, will collide in the outerworld that will short-circuit the fatalism of destinies, in the elsewhere of her own narrative, in this newborn city that is already dying, called—with the secret irony of prehistory—Grand Junction, when soon it will connect nothing at all.

Plotkin is the man of the End. Not a Last-of-Mankind man like Major Wu-Lei; he is even worse, more dangerous. He is his shadow, his secret, the absolute secret of the World of the Camp, the World Major Wu-Lei believes he knows, though he is only a servant, acting on behalf of a few shadows on the wall of a cavern he has been left to guard.

She knows.

She knows what is waiting for her.

"Massive DNA retrotranscription phenomena, with illumination and corporeal transformation, are described in numerous apocryphal writings such as the Gospels of Thomas and Philip and some esoteric passages from the Acts of John, as well as in the agrapha," Dr. Slavik, one of the brilliant biosemanticians of the Anderson-Dreisenberg team, had remarked once. "I have reports dating from around a century ago that are no longer tolerated by the UHU, but that clearly mention analogous phenomena being experienced by great saints and mystic visionaries."

She learned that in the Ring, by experience, when she was almost five years old, when the first manifestations of the Invisible appeared. What the New Zealand doctors called general neuroquantum retro-transposition. If the next anti-attack didn't follow the usual routine and ease up on the Third Day as it habitually did, but instead deepened the chasm of Infinite Division at the heart of the Darkest Night, then an angel would appear to her. She has known this angel, a creature of firelight, since her final days in Cosmograd. During her entire child-hood a procession of these fantastic entities had revealed themselves to her one by one. She had learned their names. When she was almost sixteen years old, shortly before the Ring's UHU humanitarian center had decided to repatriate the two orphans with their closest living rel-atives on Earth, she had been confronted with this unknowable, meta-morphic creature, this plasmic hyperlight that alone was capable, according to the others, of absorbing the glow emanating from the Face of the Real God, and thus hiding it from our eyes while at the same time making it perceptible in such a way as not to kill us. This creature, this angel of angels, called itself Metatron. They called it the Prince of the Face, because it was the face taken by the unknowable God in the Created World.

The "angels" are no brotherhood of picturesque characters with individual psychological qualities; they are each fields of metaliving frequencies of the Primordial Light, of which Metatron was basically the First Name produced, along with the Cosmos.

If each of them is a "person," it is in the hypostatic sense Chris-tian doctors of the ancient Church gave to the world. A single, yet triune God. A Multitude of frequencies for a Single Light. A cohort of Fire Names, Intelligence Fields, for a single original radiance.

"We come from the third world," they had explained to her. "Or, more precisely, the Third Time. There is a 'time' for God; it is His own Eternity. It was not created; it has neither a beginning nor an ending. There is a 'time' for Man too; this is the time of the World. Time, World, Life . . . they have a beginning, and they have an ending. We, the agents of the Name of Names; we, the angels of Meta-tron, Lord of all Powers; our time is that of the *Aevum*. A few Doctors of the Church, like Saint Bonaventure, Saint Thomas Aquinas, and Denys the Areopagite, spoke of this in writings that the rest of mankind preferred to throw away in oubliettes for the sake of a few sociology books! We have been created. We have a beginning, but for us there is no end. We are like cognitive cones, closed at one end but infinitely open to the Eternal at the other end."

"And me?" she had asked, with all the hauteur her eleven years could muster.

"You," replied Uriel, one of the great archangels, who had an-nounced the news of his Assumption to Enoch, "you herald the begin-ning of the Fourth Time, which is opening laterally, from its internal dimension. The Time of the ten energy plans of the Tree of Sephirot. You close the Trinitarian square: Enoch-Eli, Mary-Vivian. *You are the matrix, inverted and intensified*, a New Zealand doctor will say about you one day!"

Even the archangel's laugh was a *Logos spermatikos*. His fire, like a laser beam, wrote directly on her entire being, the ecstatic phase of her existence, this orbital hypercenter that cut and folded over mem-ory, world, recollection, reality.

She had always been a cognitive process laid bare. When the first hints of her power manifested themselves, the first books she "incor-porated," besides the scientific literature available in the Cosmograd network, were those of the circumterrestrial Catholic mission, just barely tolerated by the UHU in the Ring, and those of the private li-brary owned by the aged non-Orthodox rabbi who lived in one of the community's co-orbiting stations.

The angel of her sixteen years, this metaform called Metatron, was her human and transtemporal counter-face, or so it had been ex-plained to her. The first human transfiguration had been Enoch, a bib-lical patriarch, the grandfather of Noah. Just before the Flood began and Noah built his ark atop Mount Ararat, Enoch had been "taken up"

by a ray of light and, under the incredulous eyes of several dozen witnesses, had been drawn toward the sky and disappeared. An Ethiopian
book, of which there were also Hebrew and Slavonic versions, specifically recounted, in the epic, physical, and supernatural language of
very early antiquity, Enoch's exploratory and missionary travels
throughout the World of First Humanity, the one between the Fertile
Crescent and the Pillars of Hercules, the one between Adam and the
wrath of the Flood, until his sanctity led Metatron to choose him for
all time as his human face.

The angel of the Face had repeated the Sainted Act for the
Prophet Eli, who lived during the Second Humanity, the one after
the Giants and Demons born of the hybrid fusion of fallen angels and
human women, the age that followed the terminating Flood.

Then, of course, an analogous phenomenon, albeit absolutely unknowable, had accompanied the resurrection of Christ in the true
Year Zero, the central, absolute, transcendent fulcrum of human history.

Metatron had then served as the ladder of Assumption for the
dormition of the Virgin Mary at her "death" during the first century
of Christianity, which opened the age of Third Humanity.

The Assumption, like all metaliving phenomena created by the
Grace of the Metacosmic God, is not simply "levitation" animated by
an ingenious system of magnetic traction! The men of your century
have such small minds! The Assumption is a metamorphic elevation
of the body-spirit, which itself becomes Light little by little; not pure
"spirit," but *superphysical body-spirit,* like the Heavenly Body, where
Flesh and Light are simultaneously united and disjointed, like the divine and human natures of Christ.

In this process, Metatron was the highest and most powerful manifestation of the Unknowable God in the World Created by Him. He
was, so to speak, the cosmic energy plan closest to the Singularity.

The angel Metatron had only appeared to her once, but the cohort
of cherubim, sovereignties, thrones, archangels, and powers she had

learned to see came to her shortly afterward, while a UHU trans-orbital shuttle carried her and her brother toward a Chilean transit center. It was then that the Celestial Scribe had turned her brain into the biological platform for the illumination of her body-spirit. She would soon possess one of the miraculous powers that only Metatron, Scribe of all the Worlds, alone among all the other angels, held as well.

The power of writing directly on the World, and thus on the spirits of men, those worlds that contain worlds.

The power to draw a line of conjunction connecting several mutually exclusive, absolutely noncoincidable worlds.

She had the first seven Days of Creation inside her. She had the power of Most Holy narration.

Of course, she didn't possess them in the same way the angel Metatron did—his were infinite, encompassing all the dimensions of time and space ever created. But in her, there was now a spark of fire that burned without ever dying; a light that illuminated even the blackest darkness; an atom, a tiny morsel of the divine code. And because of this, sacrifice was, and is, never a choice. Whatever phase she is enduring—normal life, anti-attack, metamorphic crisis—each time she loses millions and millions of neurons. The fire that illuminates her, the nothingness that engulfs her, all of it takes a toll on *her body.*

So the Dual Day of infinite division occurs as planned. The world and its chasm of pain come together in her, and she assimilates them into herself. She is only a shell of nothingness. In her, time itself no longer has any meaning. It is suspended; it is no longer active; it does not exist.

In her, the world is an infinitesimal point, a quantum singularity that contains all the energy of a Big Bang, and yet though this world has been incorporated, it is also still there outside her biological envelope, outside of her, and thus outside of itself.

Inside her, everything is frozen. Icier than the worst fires of Hell, which is cold.

The phenomenon will take place just before dawn, the true realm of shadows, where in fact these shadows are contained in the Light that is to come.

Like during the discovery of the Exit at the bottom of the black hole with the creation of Plotkin, she now envisions the whole of the narrative as an antiworld in movement, an antiworld not only housed inside her head but also placed at the interface of all others. Men live surrounded by machines in their image and they are now cloning themselves in this image, yet they resemble men less and less, and machines more and more. There is a gradual loss of quality in each generation of copies. But this world of General Devolution, this world of machines and biopolitical falsehoods, this world of the global sanitary police, also points toward the horizon of its passing.

For Vivian now, a critical whole—or counter-critical—has been reached and will permit the disengagement of the Light buried in deepest shadow.

The Third Day has dawned above the chasm; the division looped onto its false infinity has resynchronized with the Created World, the Real Truth.

And Camp 77 is nothing more than a fiction now. And the consciousnesses of the men who populate it, or believe they lead it, are hardly anything more now than a handful of blank pages on which she can rewrite anything, everything.

"You only leave camp through the inside," she had said to her brother, paraphrasing a visionary Catholic saint. She could have said, like that saint, *You only leave the World through the inside.*

You only leave the World through the world inside it.

"I walked for a long time," she says, "on the chalk-white clouds covering the city lights. The Earth was a star, and the sky my cradle. I was the future echo of a very ancient dream. I was like a bush, burning in the bottommost depths of the abyss. I had fallen like a meteorite to the planet of men, and if the Light woke me I would have the gift of the Word; I would create the asymptote of our parallel lives. I would write on the world like fire on flesh. I would live by spirit, in a point of light.

"I am the atopic place of development. I am the place of the voice. I am what takes form in your mouth, in the name of everything that burns beyond its own combustion, of everything that illuminates you by allowing you sight of it and not blinding you. I am you, you are me; we are two, we are only one, and thus we are three. See how simple it is, Plotkin. You are in the process of being conceived, and you will soon appear, at the precise moment when we will disappear. We will leave the Camp-World through the antiworld contained in it— that is, by you, its Counter-Man. It is through your own genesis, your own production, that I will deterritorialize all these 'morsels' of reality and send them away to the infiniteness of my own imagination, and take form again in the world, elsewhere in the narrative.

"For me, the world is a machine to program. And the camp is only a chapter of the text I will transmute.

"Time has now become an appendage of the malleable hyperlight. It is modeled by her; its true form is that of a surplice covering our chromosomes. It can be manipulated by the hyperlight, which is the metaform of life. And the hyperlight is my friend. Better, it is my ally.

"You must first understand that my appearance on this Earth at this precise moment in man's history has nothing to do with chance, which is a very shadowy concept in itself. I have come at the defining moment of the fourth type of machine, the genetic machine, the chromosomic capital. But the mutations of the body-spirit come from metacodal DNA plan, the one we all call, in nice little mechanistic words, 'noncoding,' or 'junk DNA,' which might as well be the evolutionary garbage of their ape-savant biopolitics!

" 'Junk DNA is the "dark matter" of the ontology of the fourth-type machine,' said one Terry Bardine at the beginning of the century.

The metacode is the limit of the mechanistic vision of the living; it is beyond the machine, and beyond the living. So watch what happens, in your own head as well as in the 'real' world, this world in which we pretend to live, and which we endlessly escape by invading, by incorporating it into our own nothingness and separating us from its false unity. What happens is that your existence resembles that of an elemental particle, or the two quantum extremities of a 'supercord,' the rest of whose structure is located in other dimensions in the continuum. You are born like the imaginary Counter-Man in my brain, in the camp, and in the Camp in My Brain. You are born at the other extremity of the supercord, in the UHU astroport in Windsor, where we cannot appear, but according to a synoptic plan that links this place, this 'non-place,' to the city of Grand Junction, which seems almost to have been specially created for beings like us. You are being born at the mutually exclusive conjunction between two worlds. You are being born in the place of development of their disjunctive synthesis. You are being born like the Third Day of Creation incarnate in a non-man, a 'fiction.' You are being born between a world that is now inside me, and its replica that remains outside it. You are a line of convergence that stretches ever closer to its point of infinity as it gets farther away from its point of origin, and yet one and the other coincide.

"Because my narrative is cosmogonic. It is the hallmark of light of the angel Metatron, the scribe of God. It is what wrote you, and what has unwritten part of the world to do it. The camp gave birth to you; you are its child, its counter-child, because I am carrying it inside me. Now you must understand that nothing will ever be like it was before.

"Now that the ontological collision has taken place, now that the two mutually exclusive worlds have folded into each other, *into the space of a narrative,* now that a story has taken form in you, *now that you know,* now, you are no longer a non-man. You are no longer only the *Counter-Man from the Camp.* Now you are a free man. And you will quickly understand that there is no more dangerous condition on Earth than that.

"Because now we are there, all three of us, in Capsule 108 of the Hotel Laika."

> GHOST IN THE MACHINE

"We, the angels, are the *technology* of God. Created but infinite, our time is that of the Monad. We are the black box of God, cognitive induction cones, intellects-agents neither separate nor simple extensions of the Unique, but still synthetically disconnected from Him. We are closed/open. We are quantum fields whose individuation emerges only at the severance of all severances, like at the pivotal point of our time machine, where everything is numbers, everything is code; everything, paradoxically, becomes manifest presence."

This is what he is hearing, this voice that seems to be present in everything and nothing, part of every subject in Being. The voice is inside him, singing inside him, resonating to the other end of the universe. They are at the Hotel Laika, Grand Junction; Capsule 108, in *her* room. They have translated themselves here, and everything is surrounded by a halo of light, like the distant echo of a furnace, and he hears the voice. The voice—the voices—the multiplex of the Single— divine technology. And yet, here the most absolute silence reigns. Even ambient noise has been erased from the spectrum.

It is night. Through the vast window the three of them stand facing, Plotkin can contemplate the absolute darkness of the sky, pricked with stars *that do not sparkle*.

The stars are turning. No. It is the sky that is turning.

No. It is the entire hotel, pivoting on its axis.

No. The entire hotel is floating in space, somewhere in the Ring. And he, and Vivian McNellis and her brother, are floating weightless in the capsule. They are in orbit; they are at the junction of multiple worlds. They are in the Third Time.

"How are you doing this?" Plotkin asks, trying stupidly to gain his footing in the transmuted reality of the capsule.

"It is what I am. It is what I do. I am a living narrative," replies the young woman.

"So, you invented me. I'm not really a flesh-and-blood being, then? I'm . . . a simulacrum, like my own digital angel?"

The sparkling laugh makes his heart beat faster, and he does not really know why.

In this capsule shimmering with gentle starlight, the face of Vivian McNellis is almost indescribably beautiful. It literally makes him tremble. It seems easier to imagine killing a man—a German tourist, an Islamist agent, a Mexican mafioso—than to float gently halfway between floor and ceiling and face this otherworldly beauty. This beauty that comes from the Other World.

"Yes and no. You are a neuroquantum being, but not like your software agent. Because that 'angel' is only a mechanical, Earthly manifestation of some powers that Metatron, the true Metatron, has given me. I have been your guardian angel. I created it at the same time as I created you, modeled on the ones that exist in the World Below. I admit that, in a way, you are correlated, like the true Enoch and Metatron. You are both permanently located in the interface that joins the two mutually exclusive worlds. But you—you are the Counter-Man from the Camp; you are my fiction, and the golem of my own narrative. So I have incorporated you into this world. You are a line that continuously connects the real to the infinite. You are a paradox, an impossible truth, but you are compatible with all others. You have a real physical existence, yet you have never existed. Your body is real, and even your thoughts are . . . well, let us say relatively independent . . . at least right now. You are there in files, digital networks, databases; you are even there in the memory of people who you have actually never really known. Yet it is also true that they know you."

"Why have you done this?" Plotkin asks.

"Why? To get out of the camp. Your creation was an indispensable part of the process. I had to create a fiction-world capable of letting us break away in the black box where everything is being permanently recoded and rewritten. And here we are, now, and we are going to need you."

Things become clear again, just for a few moments. Clear like the mind of a hired killer. He is free, but he remains an instrument. An instrument in the service of angels.

Directly in front of him, floating in the ionized air of the hotel room, now permanently become a space capsule, this apparition of fire and beauty created by some unknowable miracle represents the truth for him, in a combination so absolute that it defies the impossible; it touches on the potential destruction of the Universe.

It is good that he is her creature, this girl fallen to Earth. No state—no other state—could compare to this raw, clean, incredible feeling. All the tiny flashes, each furtive intuition, the spectral apparitions of this sensation, an interior music in harmony with what hides in the presence of everything else, like when he drove toward Heavy Metal Valley in the early hours of the morning—all of it has become a concrete ontology, a mysterious presence manifesting itself down to the very depths of his being, all of him, flesh and light, fiction and reality, world and simulation.

It is clear that his freedom will consume him, and that it may claim his sacrificial existence if he puts himself completely at its mercy.

It is because he will be her instrument that he will become free.

Now everything in him has been incorporated. He is written. He is in the service of an angel. He will be free, and he will become what he is, no matter the cost. He will fight all the power of the reunited world, if he must.

"Take us back down," he says. "We will have to concentrate our strength against the World Below."

The young woman smiles. The sparkle in her eyes is lodged within him like the hard point of a volcanic rock newly ejected from the furnace. He knows that this point has been planted within him like the flaming sword in the Garden of Eden. It will only be extinguished with his life.

And probably not even then.

> *SEVEN DAYS*

On the First Day of Creation, God created the heavens and the Earth. In the same movement He separated light from the shadows. Spirit breathed over the Abyss opened by this single act, an act of initiation, of *fiat lux,* of the generating Word-Act-Light of everything.

It is a beautiful morning; the sun shines its golden rays on a childhood lost forever, filling the parallepiped room with amber light, full of joy generously dispersed by a whirl of pollen. The phrase is clean and precise in his memory: *The first act of any creation is to separate from oneself that which does not yet exist.*

No dreams. His habitual sensation of infinitesimal digital discontinuity. And the sentence about the First Day, written on the blank page of his morning memory.

He does not remember when or how Vivian McNellis and her brother left his room. He had simply fallen asleep at some point; he had lost consciousness; he had left the world to awake immediately in the morning, with a phrase from Genesis written on his memory. It wasn't simply an inscription on his mental screen; it seemed like the harbinger of more phrases to come. The words seem to reproduce not only Creation as a product, but the Creative Act as a production. A voice wishes to speak; it produces phrases in his mind without his even desiring it. For example, this one: *Man is the indivisible, infinitely divided.* Or, even simpler: *I am not; therefore I think.*

Even stranger is the fact that these Latin interjections and biblical phrases in his cortex, and on the room's digital notepads, have now been more or less explained to him by Vivian McNellis: when their two quantum-narrative fields "collided," since Plotkin's arrival at the Hotel Laika, moments of supertension have jumped from his brain to hers, and she has not been able to control certain neuroconnections between her own brain, the software agent, and Plotkin. On the day of the fire and the ontological crash, an *accident* had actually taken place, a brutal feedback effect. The software agent's flame had taken shape in his room, but in the form of a *real* fire. It had taken him several minutes to get this incendiary creature born of his own mind under control.

But, thanks to this paradoxical materialization of the false digital angel and his destruction, the meeting had happened—the overall swing of the narrative was in progress—and the destruction of the initial plan had happened as efficiently as if it were part of the only true initial plan.

Plotkin is stretched out on his helium bed. The model of the city, where the repeated beam of the rocket illuminates the dim room with rhythmical bursts of digital light, is set up in the neuroencrypted part of the chamber invisible to the hotel's security camera; it hovers very slightly above the bureau-terminal. It shines with a slight old-steel gleam, as if covered by a strange temporary patina, eroded by winds blowing from nowhere.

Everything seems to float. Him, especially; freed from a corporal envelope left four hundred kilometers below, but also objects that have completely lost their meaning as *objects,* like the persistent flame of the neuroencrypted agent hovering somewhere in the upper northwest corner of the room, and the replica of this city whose mayor he has come to kill, the replica of this city silently repeating, in the pure photonic scan of disaster, the crime he is preparing to commit.

Everything floats, even the crime, as if it is in a zero gravity chamber. Everything seems to corroborate it decisively; the link that joins Grand Junction and the Orbital Ring is indeed that of a secret, invisible economy necessarily lodged deep within the visible, official one. This secret economy has been revealed to him by what formed the "course of his life": his own birth, his entire existence makes no sense except as an organic support for this revelation. There is no longer any doubt that he is acting within the counter-economy of absolute freedom.

The light is probably there at his door. The Great Light the McNellis girl talked to him about in her speech—the speech within which he exists. But the light can shine only dimly without burning. The girl cited an ancient Christian writer, Denys the Areopagite: *Fire that does not bring light is not fire. Light that does not burn is not light.*

On this first day after Vivian McNellis's speech, on this first day after his transnarrative experience in the body of two other people in one, twenty thousand kilometers away, months before today, in Health Containment Camp 77 in the district of Hong Kong; on this first day after the re-creation of himself via the experience of another—his unitary re-creation via the experience of a multiplicity other than his own—yes, on this day everything is light, and it is all telling him that he must let it consume him entirely.

Fire, undeniably, is a recurring symbol. No need to consult a card reader in Leonov Alley to know that this is a sign.

A sign of great danger, and of very great freedom.

He decides to let the day break and pass, then fall into shadow. He does not sleep. He waits for the next day.

On the Second Day, God separated the waters from the sky. As it had been on the First Day, the Earth was unformed and empty. Spirit breathed over the Abyss. But already, just after the division of shadows from light, it was clear how the infinite division of God separated and unified at the same time.

At dawn, a phrase emerged from his half-sleep: *Any act of creation that does not divide its own divider can create nothing but itself.*

To create something different from himself; for a motor of repetition and difference to produce a world of simultaneities and asynchronisms, a world of events and variations, the creative act must divide its own division, its own disjunctive synthesis.

Vivian McNellis has transcribed Plotkin into the World via the narrative black box of Metatron, there where the network of disconnections reconvenes in the One. She has separated him from the Abyss to reunite him with the World. In him, she has separated light from shadow—but now, so that the process may act as Grace, as Freedom, what has been divided must be divided again, and so must *that which has done the dividing.* The gestating world must be separated once more from what it is, so that it will become what it can be. In the World, it is the World itself that initiates infinite division. It is the World itself that must divide in order to reproduce.

That is why the second divine process of infinite division consists of cutting the operator off from its own operation—of folding the World back in on itself—of causing the process itself to divide and the processor to become its own divider. Then, and only then, anything can happen. Cut off on the second day, infinite division can happen only according to the theological plan of Creation: the co-invention of Man by God, and of God in Man. It does not loop back on itself in infinity; rather, it creates a circumvolution that returns it from Infinity to Nothingness, to zero. It creates the possibility of life as an origin endlessly resumed and projected, as if *overstitched.*

The world of Unimanity resembles, feature for feature, this process of infinite division looped back upon its own false infinity. Human UniWorld has not been cut off by anything, even itself, because it is nothing more than the ghostly atomization of a world reduced to a horizontal, underground rhizome, its opening barred by its systematic opening, its total transparency a paradigm of new lies.

Plotkin understands that this knowledge comes as a result of his own genesis, of the destruction of the genetic operative program that served as the initial phase of Vivian McNellis's plan. It is the shadow cast by the knowledge that the girl fallen from the sky assimilated during her childhood in the Ring.

He is not the residue of experience; he has a crystalline form of his own.

He is free, because he comes from the camp.

He is alive because he cannot content himself with simply being a ghost, a golem with no language but that of Death. He is the *revival* of an ontological crash. He is the second coming of himself within another's experimental limitations.

The first sign of this freedom is an event that seems catastrophic at first: the ebbing flame of his software agent reaches the extinguishing point. It disappears from his neuroencryption field and he can do nothing to prevent it. But, after an initial period of anxiety, he realizes that there is nothing mysterious about it. The creature was a fiction even more fictional than him. It was the projection of Vivian McNellis's spirit into his consciousness.

And he believed himself to be spying on the other residents of the hotel! He realizes that the powers seemingly possessed by the digital replica of Metatron were really those of the girl fallen from the sky, converted to fit within the world of digital creatures and false angels of the World Below. In the World of Unimanity, Intelligent Software Agents are the mechanical equivalents of angels. They are intellects synthetically disconnected from the Unique—or rather, from its horizontal terminal representation, that of the Control Metastructure, the network of networks, the global cybernetic machine, the one that comanages the planet along with the governance bureaus.

Now, though, everything has changed. He *knows,* with all his newly minted being, that *everything has changed.*

The original plan contained the principle of its own annihilation.

In the conversations preceding their departure from the chamber, it seems to him that Vivian McNellis insisted on the real character of his fictive existence. He truly did agree to a contract with the Siberian mafia; his existence, however *created,* however artificial, was made possible in this world thanks to the miracle of Logos, to the infinite Folding, to the inductive cone of the angels, to Metatron's black box.

But what does it matter now, this mercenary pact with some part of himself he didn't even create? Who cares about this mayor of the city he came to kill? What does it matter, the initial plan, the plan to Kill the Mayor of This City?

The virtual replica of the city now displays the faded colors of several centuries; it looks like an ancient ruin that spent millennia in the crypts of a Sumerian video game. He stares for long moments at the digital copy of the city that disintegrates slowly now, gradually vanishing beneath coal-colored pixels, falling apart in fractals and polygons under the assault of desert simoons. The launch and explosion of the magnetic rocket are like the collapse of a dead star, a meteorite tracing slow-motion curves of anthracite, causing little more impact now than pale sparks and clouds of digital powder. The plan of the city is dying; the plan of the world, and that of his initial existence, are dead.

The plan of the city, just like the city of the Plan, the plan of the initial narration, the initial narration of the plan, are fading away. The Intelligent Agent has just left its last sparkle in a corner near the ceiling.

The neuroencrypted flame has gone out, because it became completely useless. It no longer had a reason for being, so it has returned to the digital nothingness it came from. Now the angel Metatron, the real one, is incarnate—however temporarily and quite partially—in the body of this young woman living at the Hotel Laika, this body-spirit that created *him.*

The only thing that counts is that the world is as new as he is.

He can let the day do its work and wait for the third morning.

On the Third Day, God continued His work of infinite division linked to His word processor. He separated the sky's lower waters from its upper waters, and in this way created the sky as well as the earth and the water as its by-products—themselves born of the separation-division of their matrix into its lithospheric and aquatic forms. The process was already that of a *cellular automaton*—from the moment of this triune separation of water, sky, and earth, LIFE appeared. Via this single divine enunciation, the first plant species emerged—that is, prebiotic proteins made their appearance on Earth. These *protocrea-tures* already contained all the information necessary for the creation of biological life: RNA, DNA—they were already programs set in intermediary stasis. An interface awaiting its *bootstrap*.

On the Third Day, then, God created life. The ontological operator of infinite division, folded during a third iteration, had obviously made a quantum leap: macromolecules in the form of simple, divine, cellular robots appeared. They did not yet have any specific space or time; they were born, lived, died, and were reborn again, each time being completely different and completely undifferentiated from the preceding lines, because they were not yet being born in generations—they were monoclonal structures. What differentiated them—their only differences—lay in the genetic "destination" of robots by natural selection.

He needs to see Vivian McNellis again. He needs to find her, because he senses something. He gets out of bed, showers, eats breakfast, dresses, and opens the door of his room. The girl is on the other side of it. She looks at him a bit timidly, brow downcast. Her presence seems the most natural thing possible at this moment. Plotkin doesn't say anything; he merely steps aside to let her enter. She walks to the far end of the room and looks out the window at the cosmodrome. It is his move. What is he sensing?

"You told me yesterday that from here on in, you are no longer directly in charge of the story. Is that right?"

The girl turns toward him, her profile outlined against the window. Her long silhouette is quicksilver in the dawn light, and she doesn't show the slightest pity for Plotkin. "Yes, that's what I told you. You're free. You have been, more and more, as the narrative of your creation unfolded."

"And am I really the only 'fictive' being that you incorporated into this world? I want to be totally clear on that point."

"Yes; what are you trying to say to me?"

"I'm trying to say that if I'm free, and if the other people living here weren't created by you, then what will ensure a coherent narrative from now on?"

Her laugh was like so many photons scanning the grains of a heap of golden sand.

"That which cannot be named. The true author of the World. I told you that you are free now, but I should have said that you are as free as the rest of us, we other humans."

"You are no longer entirely human."

"I'm not so sure. I think it's man that is regressing. We are just following the opposite curve. We are an ontic countermovement. We are *remaining* human, but under new conditions. The others are just adapting to the conditions; they're following the program of overall devolution. Not us. *We are beginning to teach ourselves, while unlearning everything that is known.* An old French writer said that about Cosmograd."

"Maybe so, but I need information."

"What kind of information? And to do what?"

"What exactly do you know about this World you created? *Rewrote,* I should say."

"I know everything you know, and everything your software agent could collect as data."

"What do you know about the Hotel Laika, for example?"

Vivian McNellis looks disconcerted. "I know everything you do. I told you."

"About the hotel manager?"

"The man—you mean Clovis Drummond and his little business?"

"Yes. And other things. And I want to talk about Heavy Metal Valley too."

The girl looks out at the cosmodrome. "Yes . . . the rebel Catholics. You were already slated for an independent existence, but I could dictate your activities thanks to the digital angel that was constantly observing you. This world is real, don't forget. I didn't create it; I just incorporated you into it."

"I know. I think I understand. But I'm the one who saw it. There is a connection between the hotel and that place. Humvee, as they call it. There is a connection between the Hotel Laika and that place, and you."

The girl stares at him, dumbstruck. "Be more specific."

"I can't. This is pure intuition. There's the Christian connection, obviously, but that is just an image, like a reflection. Something is telling me that there's a link even you didn't see. That's why I'm asking what you know about this world."

The silence stretches for long minutes. They watch the ballet of the workers on Platform 2. A crawler carrying a Russian Proton is on its way to the launchpad. Then, Plotkin hears words that she pronounces softly, as if speaking to the human ants milling around the last Titans on the other side of the window glass.

"I produced you. I wrote you, and then I incorporated you into the World of the black box. That's true. But all I do is reproduce the act of divine creation on a human scale. That is why I'm dying."

"Dying?"

"*Death is the way to eternal life,* as the great Novalis said. Yes, I am dying. The neuroquantum modifications to my body have affected its life span, which is now quite limited. I must get back to the Ring as soon as possible. And I created you to help me do that."

Plotkin can find nothing to say. He looks at the young woman fallen from the sky.

"And that is why I don't have the power to predict your death," she continues. "I transcribed you into the World, don't forget, with the help of the powers that the angel of the Face granted to me. You are physical and nonphysical at the same time. You are a fiction incarnate. You are, like the angels, created but infinite."

"I am immortal?"

"Not in the way you understand it. I want to be clear about that. You are immortal through the conjunction I was able to create between you and the infinite, in your fictional dimension—that is, in my imagination. Because you have been *written,* you are *alive.* You are still mortal—that is a possibility and a certain risk—but in you, I was able to make your destiny as a hired killer swerve toward its own resumption. Until our ontological meeting, I was the master—the *counter*master, really—of your creation. But now, neither you nor I are really in charge of anything. I have annihilated the determinisms of destiny; I have destroyed what you were, such as it was; I have cut you off from a past that never existed and thrown you toward a future that you will have to create for yourself."

"In other words, I'm free."

"Yes, you're free in terms of the matrix. Free in comparison with the world I bore to create you."

"Does that mean freedom monitored by something else?"

"No—or in any case, that isn't the problem. The problem is that all freedom involves an inevitable element of sacrifice. That's why you are at risk of dying too. As a gambit, as a man-sacrifice, the Man from the Camp."

"Why?" he asks, with a shiver he has never before experienced.

"Because I think the fire of narration wants it that way."

"You aren't sure?"

"I'm only its instrument. I too am only an agent. I'm just one of Metatron's sparks. I told you, I conceived you in the imagined camp, but you were really created in the divine black box as a being of flesh and blood, and one with a spirit. I am the temporary human form of the angel of the Face. Angels don't create anything themselves; they are also just instruments. Only God creates. That can only be what the poet Charles Baudelaire meant when he said 'the critic is the translator of a translation.' I am only a translator, really. It is through me that you were transcribed into this world, but you need to understand that I am not your Creator."

"Okay. But whoever it is . . . why would he want it?"

"I think . . . it's possible that this world I incorporated so you could come into the world, this world I wrote in my cell at Camp 77 . . . yes, it's quite possible that this world is continuing to act according to its own laws. There is a secret contingency at work behind everything that happens to us. A contingency operating according to perspectives I can't talk to you about right now."

"Why not?"

"You don't know enough yet."

And the discussion ends.

There is another night, and another morning.

The World has just been born.

In Genesis, the Fourth Day is unquestionably the most mysterious of all. God seems to repeat His first action: *And the sky was filled with light, in order to separate day from night.*

But this separation of day from night already took place on the First Day. *God separated Light from shadow, and called the Light day and the shadows night.*

What does it mean, this identical reiteration, when the trine day has permitted such a loop to happen?

The question haunts him until night falls.

In the cobalt postdusk light, the cosmodrome is empty. There is a bit of commotion on Platform 1, and all the hangars are lit up, but the launch sites are illuminated only by a few sodium projectors spaced along the access ramps. The calm of postindustrial desolation reigns. With the exception of a few purple shadows on the northern horizon, the night is black. The stars are out.

On the Fourth Day, God created the lights of the sky. All the lights; all the heavenly bodies—the stars, including our sun.

The Fourth Day was the first point of emergence of the divine operation into the *physical* world, he realizes suddenly. With the preceding day, the Third Day, it constituted an invisible quantum leap—a double interface between the visible and the invisible, the physical and the superphysical, and thus between microcosm and macrocosm. Plotkin's mind formulates a surprising hypothesis: all the Days of Creation were layered atop one another. Each had a relationship with all the others and a singular one with each of them individually as well. The Seven Days of the Creation are not exactly synchronous, and yet they do not simply form a banal succession. They form a diagram, and even, one might say, a program. They form a code. A metacode.

In Genesis, it seems to be a foregone conclusion that the sun is a star like the others; it is the great star, the one that lights us or burns us. When night falls, the shadows do not reign uncontested. The heavenly bodies—the stars, the moon—are there. Light continues to shine in the shadows. As plant life developed on Earth, an elementally identical process was taking place in the sky, filled with heavenly bodies, macroscopic robots for which the cellular robots of prebiotic life were like the rhizomic biological counter-form, nine-tenths submerged, microscopic. Now algae, plankton, and moss, whose horizontal proteic structures flowed in the primitive earth-water, regrouped, focused, and moved toward the light their *heads,* which in all plants is also the *sex*. The ontological process of infinite division is outlined here with the cleanliness of a physical form: a first ontic "bridge" is extended between the World Below and the one above, between created matter and uncreated Light, by the intermediary of this sensitive celestial light, by photosynthesis, the *photaïsmos* of baptism, the animated biophysics of life.

With the Fourth Day and the cutting of the Trinitarian division that began it, God takes the risk of life as a process. He takes the incredible risk of giving physical form to a Universe that has heretofore been in a state of pure genetic codex. And thus, on the Fifth Day, all animal, terrestrial, marine, and aerial life takes shape. And this risk leads, of course, to the greatest one of all—for on the Sixth Day, God creates man in His own image.

> THE EIGHTH DAY

On the morning of the Eighth Day, it seems, God invented writing.

Or rather, He caused His divine gift of narration to come together with the freedom of Man, in an infinitesimal quantity of time and energy. This freedom could not simply be a reflection; the poisonous propagator of the Fall, but its counterworld. Now the ontic bridge would be double: it would come from the light down toward Earth, matter, and flesh, but it would also draw up into itself, from its own light, its own flesh-spirit, *toward* the light.

Doing this required a very risky bet. To do this, the narrative codex of the light must be transcribed onto a material support by a human hand and mind. Men must be given the power to name and thus, on their scale, to create or destroy worlds.

The danger was extraordinary. There was absolutely no guarantee that *Homo sapiens,* only just barely capable of controlling physical fire, would be able to bear this torch and make it grow so as to light up their own fleshy and spiritual existence—to make from it a fire capable of saying something.

The Celestial Scribe, through whom God had narrated this universe, now had the delicate mission of entrusting men with a tiny parcel of colossal power—the gifts of supercoding and narration with which he had been provided—the Prince of the Face, the one through whom He showed himself in this world. In this spark was contained, like an active image of the Tree of Knowledge, Good and Evil. In this spark was contained the terrible effects of Judgment, for those who used language without respecting its sacred character, and this shadowy/punishing effect would prove, via a powerful paradox effect, the surest way to attain light through writing.

On the Eighth Day, God invented writing, and also its corollary. Prison. And God understood that it was neither good, nor bad, nor well, nor ill, that the Tree of Knowledge was contained, in an inverted form, in everything Man produced, above all his language.

A phrase emerges from this apparent paradox. A phrase that lodges in his mind like an executioner's bullet.

In the same instant, he awakes from his dreamless sleep, the sleep of a human computer.

And the phrase is this: *One can only write freely from the depths of a cell.*

Near him are stacks of paper, voluminous notes written in one week on Recyclo™ cellulo-paper with an old laser transcription pen from his nightstand. The pages are filled with phrases like aphorisms, the product of a brain in a state of incandescence. There are paragraphs on the nature of fire and of angels, as well as fragments of exegesis on Genesis. There are also plans, diagrams, maps, and strange codes pertaining to the Hotel Laika, the city of Grand Junction, the community of Heavy Metal Valley, and the characters he has encountered during this fiction-cum-world, some linked to others by lines of multiple conjunction. It looks like the design of a machine, where phrases, spurts of narrative, and aphorisms are the directions for use.

His intuition, which he shares with Vivian McNellis, concerning underground reports she may not have seen; his intuition, during the narration of his fiction-world; his intuition has taken, in seven days, the form of a vast piece of machinery made of signs, of words and pieces of forgotten dreams. It is much more mysterious than all these digital replicas of a city whose mayor he has come to kill; it is more dangerous. It hides, it seems, an even more terrible secret.

Aside from the extremely opportune visit of the girl fallen from the sky, he has been living entirely alone, cloistered in Capsule 108, for the past seven days. And in those days he has felt a sense of freedom he can hardly believe.

Vivian McNellis has the power to give a body to a being of pure spirit. She can make the life of a fictional character concrete, a character whose invention now comes from himself. Plotkin needed to be real, so she incorporated his fictive existence into the World Below. And she gave him freedom.

Nothing he had believed to exist, this *Human Termination System* with dozens of assassinations under his belt, was false—but neither was it real. And this apparent contradiction has nothing to do with any mafia "modification" of his memory. It all depends on the choices he makes now, the choices he has begun to make, and the choices he will make in the future.

Vivian McNellis spoke to him of a possible sacrifice, and has he not felt the mortal, anticipatory burning of this gambit, played among the stars?

She has gambled on his talents as a killer, master spy, and Man from the Camp.

She will have to throw in her lot, now, with the supreme chaos that reigns within a free man. She will have to throw in her lot with the man in Capsule 108.

> *DAY NINE*

On this morning, he wakes without a single word in his memory.

Pale sunlight. Yellow rays lancing through the room. The faintly ominous sound of the hotel's organ-machines. Something terrible will be born of this sublime innocence. He knows it, with the calm of a suicide commando. His mind flows from intuition to intuition, a machine forever evolving in its network of cuts. The McNellis girl used his mind and his body to create this exegetic business of Genesis. But in spite of it all, it was he who, now an independent human being, had created this genetic exegesis during seven full days in the Hotel Laika capsule. Quite simply, he realizes with alarm, it means that she and he are correlated in an unimaginable way: this whole operation was transcribed by and in the mind of Vivian McNellis, beyond the borders of space and human time.

This must be why one of the last aphorisms he wrote, on the night of the Sixth Day, said: *It is because I have two brains that I am one.*

He is in a strange world, a specific "time," this angelic induction cone whose terrible and luminous opening he senses in every particle of his newborn being. It is what lets him understand, instantaneously, that now she and he will evolve more or less simultaneously in this Third Time, the *Aevum*.

How far away it seems now, the time when his neuroencrypted software agent seemed ne plus ultra in the transfinite process of simulation! He was nothing but code in a mechanical machine; he was not code in a metamachine of light. Just like his fictive/real existence

as a killer, the digital angel represented the plan of the initial narration—it had been the fictive/simulated replica of Vivian McNellis's
powers in the digital world of angels below. It had been the mechan-
ical/human face of the Celestial Scribe—but, unlike the Scribe, it
communicated with men in the language of men. The real Metatron,
on the other hand, spoke *in* men by communicating *with* their language.

And now, Vivian McNellis is here.

Here.

In Capsule 108.

He knows she was also there at his origination, in her own chamber, but that means nothing. They are in the world of magnetic chants
and the rock 'n' roll of quarks, in the canticle of quantum bodies.
They are two cortexes falling toward each other like two galaxies in
perdition, and that is what saves them.

So she is here, physically present. It is no digital phantom, no
angel, no dreamlike projection made of fire.

The fire is her.

"Do you know the exegesis of Saint Thomas Aquinas on the subject of the *Aevum?*"

He does not know how to answer.

"Hmm. Obviously I didn't incorporate everything into your
memory. During a famous academic dispute at the end of the thirteenth century, Saint Thomas had to explain the Third Time. Was it
unique or multiple? If he admitted that angels, however purely ethereal, still formed a multiplicity, and not a unique Being—which only
God is—he would have to agree that each of them lived in a form
separated from temporality. Each angel had its own singular time.
But because they were a product of divine creation, and divine narration, they also formed an 'all'; they were linked to one another by the
intermediary of a specific time that Saint Thomas, in his luminous genius, called 'circumspect time.' It is a *noncontinuous* time, he said, because it is the line of *disjunction* among all the continuums. Without

knowing it, he had allowed Leibniz to conceive his own Theodicy, his Monad. Are you following me?"

"Circumspect time. Yes. Time that operates in discontinuity. I almost feel like the incarnation of this story."

"This time is the time of the Machine. The 'logical' Machine. It is the circumspect machine-time of electronic calculators. I mean, in this World. The World Below. You were a machine, a narrative machine. You were an operator of ontological division."

"And now?"

"Now we come to what will happen—the event. Now what was *retained,* but could not be *contained,* will happen. It is the circumspect time in which we can be copresent without being in the same place."

There is a deep silence. A silence between two temporalities that are asynchronous yet intermingled, linked by an invisible thread of light. The invisible made visible in the form of fire made flesh and named Vivian McNellis, whose very beauty seems to emerge from the chasm of silence.

He crosses the first part of the chasm. "How do you need me to act so we can get you back to the Ring?"

"I have a plan—a sort of appendix to the initial plan. On the Monolith Hills strip, there are all the sorts of traffickers that you might expect to find near a cosmodrome. We need a black-market claim—but a real one, an authentic one, just resold, not passed by the spatial governance bureau and its taxes. But we can't buy it ourselves—too much danger of being refused or noticed. We need someone safe, someone familiar with this sort of thing."

"There's one of these dealers living in the hotel."

"Yes, I found that out when I was your digital angel. Harris Nakashima, right? Do you think we can trust him?"

Plotkin's laugh is like an old, sarcastic memory. "You can never trust a dealer. In general, you should never trust anyone."

"My brother suggested something yesterday."

Plotkin's laugh trails off. He looks at the McNellis girl. He senses that something is careening toward the gaping maw of the induction cone and the infinity beyond. "I'm listening."

"He said he has noticed the carefully choreographed ballet of our friend the manager of these premises. I mean, his comings and goings under the dome."

"I'm still listening."

"Jordan thinks the manager is a dealer too. Not just in cigarettes and psychotropics and black-market neurogames—also in something that's right under the dome."

"Under the dome?" Plotkin remembers his night of spying with the digital angel, when Clovis Drummond spent more than three hours under the hotel's antiradiation dome. Something is going on up there, at the other end of the service stairways, where the sensors and cameras don't work.

"Yes, under the dome. Jordan thinks Drummond is trafficking in technological information. With the satellite antenna and a pirated device of some sort, he is regularly sending lists of codes to a firm in competition with someone here in Grand Junction."

"You've detected this?"

"Well, we only just talked about it yesterday. The next time he goes under the dome, I'll know more."

"You and I both know that the angel Metatron—I mean you—detected prohibited religious symbols under the dome."

"That doesn't contradict my brother's theory. He might very well be trafficking in religious relics too."

"Yes, and that's something we should talk about."

"What? What do you want to say?"

Plotkin does not hesitate. He is well versed in verbal combat. Something in him wants him to remain what he is. "The rebel Catholics and the Evangelicals, and the Jews in HMV. You didn't choose Grand Junction by chance, did you?"

McNellis laughs, and it is like crystal in the light. Something will keep her like this, always. "You don't get it. I learned about it while I was incorporating the Created World, in my cell at Camp 77. For me, it was even a sort of handicap at first. We cannot get ourselves mixed up with Christian rebels—we would be putting them in danger, because we would get them noticed fast, and vice versa. We need to keep our distance, and not have any contact."

Plotkin's mind goes back to his writings of the past seven days. He thinks of the plans, the maps, the diagrams—the still-secret semantic machinery. "Distances are already a thing of the past. Contact has already been made."

"I know. That wasn't part of the initial plan at all. It was the first real divergence."

"The first and the last, you see. The alpha and the omega."

"I don't think it's the best way for us to get to the Ring. I'm sure you can understand why."

"Actually, I think it would be much less risky than doing something with Drummond."

"You're awfully obstinate. Too bad I can't rewrite you anymore."

"Listen. I don't trust his type. I'd even rather go the Nakashima/Cheyenne Hawkwind route. He, at least, is a killer."

"I have no other choice than to consider every possibility."

"Clovis Drummond isn't a possibility. He's an impossibility. And he's a louse. I think he's an eight-handed snitch. He cheats and lies like he breathes. He doesn't just double-deal or triple-deal. With the market around here, his exploits must be absolutely astronomical."

"Don't think about it so much. Try to see how we can corner him, force him to work for us and find us a usable Golden Track for sale, that we can buy and he can get a little commission out of."

"Drummond would do anything for a little commission. He'd let you shit in his mouth."

Vivian McNellis gives a sigh of resignation. "You're vulgar."

"No; I'm sorry, it's that snitch who's vulgar. Am I supposed to use elegant metaphors for that piece of shit on legs?"

"I'll talk to you again later." She vanishes.

Day Nine. A completely untapped life stretches before him. He is giddy with it. For the first time in his "existence," he feels his heart beating in his rib cage. Beating as if it would burst out of his chest.

In the afternoon, he writes. For hours, he fills page after page of Re-cyclo™ paper. Then he goes to the window.

Slanting orange light. Angular rays spread geometric banners across the buildings of downtown and the towers of the cosmo-drome. Platform 1 is topped by a long and beautiful white object dappled with red light. A modified Titan V with an updated Russian capsule from the 2010s, made to carry ten passengers, is set to be launched by one of the big space-industry tycoons, a brilliant young man called Jason Texas Lagrange III, whose family lineage of NASA engineers stretches back one hundred years. His face and name appear regularly on the advertising screens that float throughout the city. The hotel's NeuroNet console is frequently bombarded with infomercials vaunting the resumption of activities by the firm Argonautics; thanks to a new agreement with the Grand Junction Cosmodrome, the hourly headlines scream, Lagrange's company will go ahead with three hundred orbital launches over the next five years—a "large-scale colonization project." Around 2,500 settlers, plus two hundred capsules atop various types of launchers, and half a dozen reusable cargo clusters manufactured by one of his Texas subsidiaries. Each cargo will be capable at each launch of carrying four second-generation UHU-approved Alpha modules into orbit. *"I chose to return to Grand Junction because I came to know this cosmodrome very well for almost ten years, and I know the improvements made under the direction of the new Metropolitan presidency have been quite effective,"* the head of Argonautics tells our virtual reporters—Metro-X-Networks newsflash. *"We are very proud to have won this market; Jason Texas Lagrange has always been considered a friend and a demanding and visionary entrepreneur by the Blackburn city administration."*

Plotkin watches the photos and videos, in which handshakes follow smiles mechanically, in the deadly plastic of the perfectly conducted simulacrum. Jason Texas Lagrange shaking Blackburn's hand—Blackburn, the mayor of the city; the mayor that Plotkin, in a previous life, had been assigned to kill. Blackburn smiling as widely as possible for the cameras.

The October 4 launch, less than three weeks away, will be carried out under the aegis of Jason T. Lagrange III's company. The nighttime launch of the Sputnik Centennial, the date on which Plotkin, during the initial ontic narration, chose to kill the mayor of the city. The mayor now shaking the hand of the Houston tycoon.

All of that is true.

But none of it matters at all now.

Something springs up deep in the night, a gleam the shadows contain without being able to hold. This something, of course, appears in the form of Vivian McNellis. She is here. The Ninth Day is over; it is midnight. The room's LED wall clock stops at four zeros, which shine in blue photon lines in the darkness.

"There is something—you know, this secret narrative plan you talked to me about during your passage from the Third to the Fourth Day. Something is interfering—something I didn't foresee."

"What is it?"

"I don't know, obviously. It is producing a quantum disturbance that has kept growing since our meeting. It's as if we're being watched even from inside our own counterworld. It isn't local AI; it's totally incapable of reading Third Time—that's a code it doesn't understand, or even see."

Plotkin cannot think of a response. An idea comes to him after a moment of silence.

"Am I the source?"

"No; I thought of that, but I don't think it's you."

"The Christian rebels?"

"No. It's someone who is still hidden within the secret of the narrative, its dark side, for now. I couldn't access it. It is extremely troubling, but I know that he—or she—exists. The problem is that it seems to be amplifying the neurogenetic modifications of my body. The mutations are speeding up, though they aren't yet visible. I feel it. I'm losing enormous amounts of nerve cells."

A he/she, Plotkin thinks. Another he/she. "Is it something that could have the same power as you?"

Vivian McNellis's face reflects pure anguish. It reflects fear. She knows the extent of this power. "Yes. That's the only plausible explanation. But the more I think about it, the more impossible it seems. Our two spirits would destroy each other; it would be like bringing together two parts of a critical mass. Matter meeting antimatter."

"So . . . what, then?"

"I don't know . . . something like the intensified inversion of myself, to borrow a phrase from my doctor friend in New Zealand."

"And what would this strange creature be like?"

"I have no idea. But—it could very well be a machine."

> DO ANDROIDS DREAM OF CATHOLIC SAINTS?

Though the *Aevum* of angels is the divine equivalent of machine-time, it is very probable that the Universal Metanetwork uses circumspect time for the artificial beings of the World Below.

Time Machine, Plotkin thinks. *Welcome to the Time Machine.*

If Vivian McNellis is sensing a quantum disturbance indicating the copresence of a time machine analogous, or rather *parallel,* to her own, that implies the existence of an *invariable discontinuity*—a hole in her narration. A black hole. Something visible only as a negative.

Vivian is wrong—the disturbance comes from someone the plot has already made visible as a character. *Persona:* mask, in Latin. Living in its own time machine, it becomes visible only as a disturber phenomenon in the eyes of the girl fallen from the sky. A pseudomachine would, in this way, be able to fool the transmuted brain of Vivian McNellis.

But would it be capable of fooling the transfictional metabrain of Plotkin? Would it be capable of fooling the Man from the Camp, the Counter-Man of UniWorld? Would it be able to play games with the man in Capsule 108?

In the hotel, with the exception of local artificial intelligence, there are not forty thousand humanoid machines, bearers of a singular time machine, capable of appearing in the narrative without causing the mutual disintegration of the world of McNellis and their own.

There are Ultra-Vector Vega 2501 and SS-Nova 280. There is the possible Flandro terrorist. There is the reprogrammed former whore. The two are excellent suspects.

He will need to use fear, the supreme instrument of control.

Fear and artifice, the supreme control of the instrument.

The weak link is the female, the former cyberwhore whose neural pleasure centers were reprogrammed. The very act of having been partially decoded indicates a deliberate wish to have nothing more to do with *desire*. It shows manifest existential weakness—the weakness led to the act, and not vice versa. As a transfictional master spy, fiction become reality while yet remaining fiction, he can imagine pushing this weak point without the slightest qualm.

Pushing until the truth comes out.

Seventh-floor hallway, north face. Plotkin walks past numbered doors.

The hotel itself is also a non-place. It is a face of the camp, the camp that has spread across the World. The hotel did not emerge by chance in Vivian McNellis's narrative. She chose it for a reason—in it is concentrated most of the machines of the Technical World. It is a snapshot of overall regression and survival as the anthropological limit of the planetary lifestyle.

Door 704-N.

He places his hand on the identity verification plate. The little black eye of the electronic Judas watches him. Text appears on the control screen. PLEASE STATE YOUR NAME AND THE REASON FOR YOUR VISIT, squawks the hotel's artificial intelligence.

"My name is Sergei Plotkin. I'm staying in Capsule 108. My reasons for coming here are strictly private. We have already met."

A pause. A hum. A red diode turns green. A small click. The

chamber door opens. Text scrolls across the controller at the same time as the androgynous voice of the AI speaks the words: IDENTIFICATION AND REASON ACCEPTED.

He enters Capsule 704, the android-whore's capsule.

He is there to conduct an interrogation.

He is not armed; he has no official mandate. He does not even exist.

He knows that makes it even more dangerous.

Everything happens in fluid sequences, like a mutated film-noir narrative. Capsule 704 is identical to his own in every way: Generalized robotics, international design, urbanization of overpopulation reassigned to global demographic recession. The night sky purple above the city. The amber light of bioluminescent fixtures distributed throughout the room. A few scattered personal effects, hardly enough to create the idea that any difference is still possible among all these non-places in the United Human World.

Sydia Sexydoll 280 is a creature hardly less fictive than himself, born of desire-fevered imagination through the coalescent strength of the Technical World. She is before him in a simple white dress, her back to the window, through which he can see the road that connects to the autobridge, there under the arctic, blue-white light of the streetlamps.

He knows.

He has known for days.

The diagrams have been saying it for days. The narrative has been happening within him for days. Genesis has been revealed for days.

Artificial life? Is there any life in this world anymore that isn't artificial?

The Hotel Laika is both a condensed face of the camp and the threat of its infinite anthropological expansion. Here, all life is falsified. All life is artificial. All lives are even more false than the false world that has taken the place of all substance.

Here, the truth is not human.

Shock. A sampling of continuums in collision: two artificial beings face-to-face in an experimental *white box,* the universal non-place of the human world, this capsule hotel, and a cosmodrome in decline.

A bionic woman, a fictional man. A woman of the World, a Counter-Man from the Camp. A woman created by an organization of socioprogrammatic brains in the service of the Universal Meta-structure. A man created by the overall disorganization that is part of an ontological black box.

Matter. Antimatter.

"Why did you have yourself sexually deprogrammed?"

The silence is painful with exposed secrets.

"How do you know?"

"I'm an expert in technological risks. My second job is to eliminate them."

Fear, more than anything else, is a language.

"Are you a UniPol cop, or from some other government office?"

"I work for a private company."

"You're a bounty hunter? No one's looking for me."

"Not *yet.*"

Fear comes from the anticipation of a threat. Fear comes from the emotional confusion of different times. It comes from the possibility that you are dealing with a terrorist, that the past will affect the future, that the future is a danger to the present, and that the present is a danger to itself. Fear is the shadow of all secrets. It illuminates only itself.

"Do you listen to music?" The artificial girl's voice is soft, breathy. A beautiful bit of programming.

"Music?"

"Yes. Real music, I mean."

"From before the twenty-first century, you mean."

Sydia Sexydoll 280's laugh was also beautifully programmed.

"Yes, and even before! There was a world before the twentieth century, you know."

His smile seems to him like a product of the preworld night. "It seems that someone has been ingenious at erasing every trace of it."

The music the android has chosen filters gracefully through Capsule 704. Scarlatti, she says. It is one of his pieces for harpsichord, from the Kirkpatrick catalogue.

The music takes form in the space like sparks of light that attract and repulse one another, endlessly creating and destroying astonishing harmonic constellations. It is like a choral voice, the echo of reflected sunlight, floating from the corroded metal of the old Baroque instrument. Celestial harpsichords are probably made of pure gold. Nebulous angels glide amid the hard corners of neon and steel, rising up in luminous choirs toward the glassed-in sky of the posturban night. Two worlds, one of them vanished, the other on the point of vanishing, collide under the electric sky. Cherubs of sodium and neon, archangels of the atomic midnight rise above the impact point.

"Stop your meaningless chatter. It won't work on me." Plotkin's voice breaks dryly into the gold-textured tapestry of Scarlatti, cutting cleanly through the flow of words the artificial girl has summoned in a desperate attempt to hide the truth. "Now *I'll* tell *you* why you had three million nanocomponents in your sexual centers fried."

"Why, then?" She flings the question at him defiantly.

"Because you converted to Catholicism or some evangelical religion. You're a Christian rebel. *Even the sharpest knife cannot cut its own haft.* You know that African aphorism, I suppose? That's why you're here."

"I don't know it, as a matter of fact. What does that have to do with anything right now?"

"It means that all mechanical actions have their limits. All human actions have their limits. Your actions have reached their limit. You won't be able to hide your real motives much longer."

The artificial girl looks at him for a long time, breathing with the invariable regularity found in androids.

The night of Plotkin's smile has fallen permanently on the world. "You are in contact with the Christian rebels in Heavy Metal Valley, and by some kind of subterfuge you are informing them of the development of a secret network in the hotel or on the strip, I believe. At the same time, you are spying on us on behalf of the Humvee police, who are protecting the rebels. I don't know yet just what information you have given them, but I can tell you that I'll get it out of you. I promise you that."

He has never felt closer to his false personality. He has never felt such a wholeness of character. He never thought it could come this close to being true.

Fear is a quantum field. On one side, the radar operator observes the quantum field and the possible disturbances that indicate the presence of an enemy object—a quivering of the face, a twitch, an involuntary movement, an avoidance of eye contact; on the other side of the quantum field, really the other side of the radar or sonar screen, you know you are a shining point that can hide from the searching waves only by being as furtive as you possibly can. You know you have to disappear. That is why fear is a language. It is the language of control of language.

"On one hand, I'm not sure your operation is legal—but on the other hand, it's clear that your affiliation with prohibited religions puts you at risk for overall memory reprogramming," Plotkin says.

"You have no proof of what you're saying."

"I'm sure the proof exists. You must have left comprising traces all around you. Even here in your room." He moves instinctively toward the panel of the retractable bathroom and taps on its keypad. When the bathroom extends outward from the wall, but in the form of a panic room, Catholic relics—crucifixes, statues of the Virgin Mary, a Greek Orthodox icon—appear, hidden in places invisible to the ceiling-mounted panoramic security camera.

In the depths of the night that has taken possession of Plotkin's unchanging smile, there is a fire.

The fire flows from his mouth, inflaming each of his actions, lighting up his slightest thoughts. Little by little, it is consuming his existence. And the existences of others.

"I am a free man," he tells her. "I am now the mercenary defending my lives to come, and I am protecting an angel just as it is protecting me. I need to know how you operate."

A sudden flash of blinding, pale yellow light illuminates the window. Jason Texas Lagrange's rocket is leaving the cosmodrome launch site. Its long, fiery tail lights up the space around it; the fireball is soon nothing more than a source of radiation streaking farther and farther away in the sky. Soon it will be lost in the electric zenith of Grand Junction. Soon it will be indistinguishable from the stars. Soon it will disappear into the orbital night.

* * *

"How I operate what?"

"I can't tell you everything. My questions would be a lot more informative than your answers. I'm sure you've been able to observe us through your connections with the HMV Christian rebels. I want to know how you're doing it."

"I assure you, I have no idea what you're talking about."

"But it's obvious."

"I'm not watching you. Who do you mean by 'us,' anyway? Yes, I have dealings with members of the HMV community. But that's all."

Finally, Plotkin has gotten a bit of information. But he knows there is more—that this information is only leading to the real question, the one that seems to follow the diagrams he drew in his chamber during the seven days of his neo-Genesis. "How are you communicating with them? I mean, who exactly do you have 'dealings' with?"

Because there must be a *who*. An autonomous being. Maybe even another machine, just hovering on the brink of being a *person*. The other android, for example, would fit the bill perfectly.

This artificial girl in her white dress, this artificial girl with her velvety eyes; could this artificial girl really dream of Catholic saints? Could she really have faith? Could an android really be permanently converted to a religion?

The artificial girl looks at him now, having watched the ascension of the rocket into the violet Grand Junction night. She looks at him as if to say: *Slightly overwhelmed by the questions you've brought up, eh?* A slight smile curls the corners of her mouth. She knows she has lost the game, but she has just scored a point for honor.

"It's the dog," she says. "The hotel dog, Balthazar. He's been acting as a messenger for me, a go-between. We hit it off as soon as I arrived at the hotel. He often runs around on the upper floors, especially when his master goes under the dome."

Plotkin hides, as well as he can, his reaction to the deathblow he has just received. The artificial girl is working with the dog. The dog sometimes goes to the upper floors of the hotel as if following his master, without having the right to enter the Holy of Holies. The artificial girl knows that the hotel manager regularly goes under the dome, but she probably doesn't know why. He needs to evade the question, and fast. She must not make the connection between Clovis Drummond and the secret Christians, or anything else.

"Is the dog trying to get you to be accepted by the human refugees in HMV?"

"Yes. They want me to stay at the Hotel Laika for now. They told me UniPol is on their heels."

The dog, Plotkin thinks. *This dog has a soul. Much more of one than his human master.*

> *NEXUS ROAD*

The sun rises over the Hotel Laika.

A man, alone in his chamber, Capsule 108-West; a free man, through his window, watches the sky turn from night black to indigo blue, then lighten bit by bit to emerald green, signaling the presence of the yellow rays of the sun just below the horizon.

Before him, the world wakes up; the day is newborn. It is the dawn of his new childhood.

Before him, life is a book to be written. Free. Free of any instruction program. Of any plan to kill this or that man. Of any contingency.

He will write it, this life. Of course, his narrative will be transcribed in the brain of Vivian McNellis, but he will be the author. And he intends to let the plot diverge as widely as possible from the matrixes that want to enclose him in the appearance of false freedom, the false freedom of the initial plans, of mafia contracts, of pacts with a human devil, of non-lives replicated in the non-places of the United Human Universe.

The contract with his employers across the Atlantic, though, is real. Vivian McNellis was clear on that point. The Novosibirsk mafia is not likely to appreciate any noncompliance with the terms of their agreement. It might look like a betrayal to them.

Freedom does have a price, he realizes, and the price *is* betrayal. The betrayal of everything that permanently disintegrates freedom in

the wide-open space of the Control Metastructure and all its rhi-
zomes, mafiosi, cops, do-gooders, cultures, and technology.

When you are in the service of an angel fallen to Earth, it is only natural to reflect for at least a moment on the wisdom of this new alle-
giance. You must now live, and fight, from your cell of freedom.

He is her bodyguard. He is her firewall in the World Below. He is
the Man from the Camp.

His real life is in these few pages of aphorisms and diagrams, the
pages of the seven days of his Genesis, retrowritten in the solitude of
Capsule 108. His real life is in having become the ally of the girl fallen
from the sky, against all the ravages of the world. His real life is being
in the service of divine narration; he is no longer subject to the rules
of any employer—even one of the most feared and respected in the
business.

It is so striking, the beauty of this world—the particles of infrared
light bouncing off the mirrored surfaces of the high glass towers
downtown, sparks of fire irradiating the mercury of morning windows—that he feels as if he could dance, like an electron nudged out
of its orbit, or fall to his knees, and weep, and pray. It is so striking,
the perfect match between this beauty with that of Vivian McNellis,
the golden-haired angel fallen to Earth, this Earth teetering on the
edge of global night.

It's idiotic, really, but everything he does from now on—everything he has already begun to do, everything that he might be, this
whole divergent narrative he is now writing for himself—he is doing
for love. Love for her. And without any real hope that she might love
him back.

The absence of hope only inflames the blinding incandescence of
the feeling even further. It is a feeling so completely unexpected that

he has no way of fighting it; it seems as if something is hollowing out his insides—a light is filling him, but only to make him emptier.

It has utterly overwhelmed him, as if he has plummeted out a window of infinite dimensions—the dimensions of his conscience— into a pool of splendor. Love and the betrayal of the world go hand in hand. Love and the rewriting of himself go hand in hand. Love and the transvaluation of his own life go hand in hand. He understands better now why Vivian McNellis is so closely intertwined with an image of fire. Love is a greater danger even than freedom, which yet contains all dangers. Because freedom can consume itself entirely for the sake of love. And it can easily take the rest of the world with it.

First operation: follow the dog.

Second operation: try to make direct contact with the rebel families the dog is visiting.

To follow the dog, Plotkin has only to wait until he leaves the hotel and takes the autobridge to the North Junction road.

To follow the dog, Plotkin has only to wait.

To wait, Plotkin has only to be free.

That is why he is now at the Nexus Road intersection, at its junction point.

This time the dog doesn't go north toward Heavy Metal Valley, but south, where there is nothing except *the end of the line.* Junkville.

A new train of thought takes off.

The first time in the dynamic: infinite contraction of the infinite.

The second time: infinite expansion of the infinite.

The third time, counterdivided: multiplexification of existing worlds.

The fourth time, counterdivided in turn: poetic reunification of the being.

His rented orange Saturn is parked on the shoulder of Grand Junction Road. All around it are massive trees, botanical mixes of ancient Canadian flora and subtropical species that were imported. The sun is high; it is almost noon. The light is straight and pure, the heat suffocating.

There is no need to investigate. No need to track the female android or the mail to know where the black hole in the narration is coming from. It is enough to follow the dog. No need to stockpile tons of information, to process the data, to identify maps and territories. The narrative is his own.

He is content to think about the beauty of the girl fallen to Earth.

It isn't the kind of beauty that hits you right away. It is mysterious and true. It does not hide within itself, but in the "Other," the chasm of "I." When it tries to guide you toward itself, it becomes selective— it is disguised, perhaps as a Cinderella covered with ashes—so that it can determine if you are worthy of seeking the hand of the princess, a glass slipper in your hand. In truth, he has begun to hide himself as well. Not just in the outward ugliness of the World, but also behind what there is in *him* of pure, wild beauty. And he is beginning to do both at the same time.

For example, this eyesore of a rust-covered orange sign, swaying on its worn, oxidized metal post, barely kept upright by a bit of earth and money and by the crowded rows of vividly colored shrubs that keep it from being seen from the road.

It is a large billboard from the Metropolitan Consortium itself, solidly planted on its concrete base, seemingly there to overextend the optical illusion.

Plotkin goes toward the upside-down sign. It is an orange rectangle bearing the international symbol for radioactivity-contaminated zones: NEON PARK. And in smaller letters: ROUTE 299, 7 MILES.

The sign seems to indicate a direction opposite that of Heavy Metal Valley. He hasn't noticed it the other times he was here—but then he was in a car at the intersection.

It is the direction the dog went.

He doesn't remember anything specific about this area of the Independent Territory, visibly outside Grand Junction. It is a pure moment of rock 'n' roll in the midst of data processing. It is the eruption of life in the inanimate schema, the surge of intuition that the cone already senses; he is taking it toward terra incognita; toward a gray area on the map. And this intuition tells him that it is exactly what he is looking for, or at least the beginning of it: a black hole.

The same instinct that pushed him toward the Christian rebels is now leading him to drive his rented Saturn south on Nexus Road, into the sun soaring toward its boreal zenith, down unfinished stretches of road and through clouds of ochre dust that fill the car and in which the sun's rays seem to crystallize, like oxidized diamonds suspended in the air.

Soundtrack: "Ruiner," Nine Inch Nails, 1994.

It is the cobalt blue, black, silver, and red—dark, dark red—of the twilight of civilizations. The rhythm advances imperturbably, like a metronome in step with the heartbeat of cybernetic cities. The monotonous chant of the synthesizers and artificial strings evokes the threat of a world plunged into deepest night, and yet it also indicates the ghostly presence of a spark of light, cold like a distant sun, just barely a star. The enormous walls of electric guitars that cut off the ends of measures seem like terminator-meteorites, while a harmonic wave, where the theme is taken up and accompanied by a myriad of distorted voices played in reverse, rises little by little, ready to engulf everything within its reach. The world of Scarlatti is very far away now. This is the soundtrack of the Man from the Camp, the Man driving on Nexus Road toward a radioactive zone called Neon Park that is barely on the map.

The Saturn's primitive dashboard computer can't tell him much about the place's history. Its GPS location blinks in red on the farthest eastern point of the Independent Territory map. For the rest, an old American nuclear plant is known to have undergone an incident similar to a smaller version of Chernobyl twenty years earlier—a direct consequence of the War of Secession—and brought chaos and regression along with it, he learns thanks to a hyperlink provided by the Metropolitan Initiative Union. Access to the defunct plant is prohibited, but there is a sort of small city that has sprung up on the periphery of the highly contaminated area.

That, of course, is Neon Park.

You get there via Route 299, a barely maintained trail marked by a copy of the orange sign at the North Junction crossroads.

NEON PARK
Warning: radioactive restricted area in 20 miles

So Plotkin drives. He drives on the gravel-littered road, Route 299, that leads to the former nuclear plant, now abandoned and enclosed in a giant sarcophagus of concrete-composite. He drives toward this western Chernobyl; toward Neon Park. He drives, a local hyperlink that appears suddenly on the dashboard screen informs him, toward a territory populated by *underbrains*.

Underbrains: network pirates, hackers, but also renegade or unemployed biotechnicians, specialists in old silicium binary programs, or geneticists who are not in compliance with UHU ethical regulations. Electronics or life-size games amateurs at odds with the bionized world of nanocomponents. Aficionados of the atomic age, resistant to the new universal ecological standards. Neon Park's underbrains represent the high-tech face of the archaeo-futuristic resistance of the HMV greasers to hydrogen-powered vehicles.

Yes. That's it. This is *the* place. This is *the* link. It's here.

Why has this area remained a non-place invisible to the narrative? Because a sign fell to the ground? Because of a standard, incomplete service map of the territory? Because of a false trail that might be that of the rebel Christians?

From the looks of it, no. The atopic place from which Vivian

McNellis feels herself to be observed—this place, he knows as sharply as if a blade is slicing through his brain—is truly a space, a space-time. *This place is a place.*

And not necessarily a *person.*

They may be dealing with a group, *a community of people.*

They may be dealing with a city.

The first thing he notices about the city is light.

The second thing he sees in the world is night.

It is night.

The city is shining. And it is night.

That isn't normal. It was noon just a few minutes ago . . .

He is not in human time.

He is in the time of the *Aevum,* the angelic time he shares with Vivian McNellis. The LED numbers on the dashboard clock are stuck at four zeros made of monochromatic blue lines. And Vivian McNellis is there, in the passenger seat, observing with interest the moonscape out the windows, while Route 299 cuts roughly through the wooded buttes around them.

Neon Park is a tiny city, made up of a few hundred three-story buildings and individual houses. There are a few mobile homes and cabins as well. As with any tiny North American city, its heart is the service station and main street, cobbled together by a recent graft of scrounged materials from all over—including the neighboring contaminated zones.

A hyperlink to a local site informs him that the city visible on the surface of the ground is really only a *simulacrum.* In fact, the residents have constructed antiradiation shelters in caves belowground, and the entire underground level of the city is connected by tunnels that link the dwellings, forming a subterranean metropolis. Most of the time, the upper floors of the inhabited buildings serve only as temporary residences, when they aren't filled with concrete or blocked on all sides by lead walls.

There is a city beneath the city here, and that is no metaphor.

Plotkin soon realizes that here there are no metaphors—or, more precisely, that metaphors have become reality here.

Because this is the world of Neon Park.

On the other side of the vast natural amphitheater that stretches out before them, there is a hole in a mass of low mountains, quicksilver-shadowy in the moonlight. They overlook this enormous, desolate valley lit by the fires of Neon Park. The city lies at their feet. And it shines, but it is not only because of the twentieth-century neon signs that decorate even the smallest of the city's dwellings and from which it probably takes its name. Something in the walls, the roofs, the pavement, is shining. The building materials were scrounged from contaminated zones. Mirrors of phosphorous in the night.

At the other end of the natural amphitheater, just in front of the mass of mountains on the horizon, there is a concrete wall. From this distance, Plotkin estimates that it is around thirty meters high and more than five kilometers long. The wall seems to mark out a perimeter—it slants, then continues off into the distance toward the peak of a mountain with a collapsed center.

Under the sodium streetlamps that do not leave even the slightest bit of the concrete in shadow, lighting the horizon with a constellation of orange stars, he sees, at the summit of the wall, a tangle of barbed wire regularly dotted with small turrets, which are likely crammed with sensors. Approximately every six hundred meters, a high watchtower breaks the horizontal line of the wall with the mechanical transcendence eerily reminiscent of the camp. According to the information provided by the Saturn's dashboard computer, the nuclear plant is located around fifteen miles behind the wall. Already they—he and the girl fallen from the sky—are beginning to enter an area, as they climb the hills, where radiation levels are high enough to warrant the wearing of special gear, or to limit visiting time to a few hours.

Per year.

"Do you know this area?" he asks Vivian McNellis.

"No."

"But it's part of the Created World you incorporated, since I'm here, and I'm compatible with it."

"Yes."

"What do you mean, 'yes'?"

"I mean yes, I know. It's a paradox. What can I do? It isn't rational, but it is rational things that are false. It's a paradox, but the paradox is true. An English author called Chesterton said that, a hundred and fifty years ago."

"Great. This place stayed hidden for the entire initial narration—hidden, if you ask me, by the attractiveness of Heavy Metal Valley and a series of other small contingencies. In fact, I think these contingencies are hiding the 'machine' you spoke to me of. The intensified inversion of you."

"Here?"

"These are the dingoes of silicium and prohibited biological sciences. The statute of the Independent Territory keeps them fairly safe from the local government and even the UHU. But it's not a very safe environment for the Christian rebels. UniPol carried out a raid on forbidden laboratories here, with the Grand Junction cops, a couple of years ago. But then again, it isn't the Christian rebels we're looking for."

"Do you know what we're looking for, at least?"

"Yes," he says. "I'm looking for the inverted and intensified version of you. I'm looking for a nexus."

* * *

Neon Park condenses all the characteristics of a mid-twenty-first-century neocity. It rose up in the middle of nowhere, grafted into a bit of existing but nearly abandoned suburban and postindustrial tissue. It rose up just as global devolution was beginning—*because* global devolution was beginning.

Mundo depopulato. It has been thirty years now since the world-wide birthrate began dropping, and each decade the phenomenon intensifies. The end of the Grand Jihad coincided with the explosion of global depopulation right under the noses of the governance bureaus. Even the Islamic states, exhausted by successive wars and now en route to peace under the aegis of the UHU, saw their birthrates founder. Pandemics, planetary civil wars, metalocal terrorism, technological accidents, ecological catastrophes, and societal depopulation combined in the space of a generation and accelerated even further in the years after Plotkin's "birth." His first birth, the fictional one, in Moscow in 2001. His first birth, had it been real, on the very edge of the chasm.

"If we stay in the Third Time," he asks, "will we be safe from the radiation?"

"No, I can't keep up this kind of conjunction for very long. It takes up a lot of energy, and exhausts me. As I told you, the neuro-quantum modifications are getting worse."

"I think there is survival equipment for sale or rental in the city; don't worry."

"I have no reason to worry."

"Before you leave, I need to be clearer about a few details."

"Details?"

"Yes, especially about my first narrative, my prenatal narrative."

"What do you want to know?"

"You said you incorporated me into the World using various documents about spy agencies."

"Right."

"Did you only use factual documents, or did you use fictional ones too?"

The girl fixes her eyes on him; they are like pools of mercury. She looks dreamy.

"A mixture of both, actually. Why?"

"You told me you used your maternal Russian lineage for my last name and Argentina, where you spent time living, for my memories. But you had intended to use your uncle's Russia, which caused these 'interferences.' Was that real?"

"Yes, just a mixture of different points of view."

"Fine, but then where did the other memories come from?"

This time, a shadow crosses her quicksilver eyes. The silence that fills the car is palpable.

"What other memories?"

"England, for example."

"England? I don't understand."

"You don't?"

"No, unless it has something to do with what I read once about the life of the writer Bruce Chatwin."

That's just barely plausible, Plotkin thinks. Just barely acceptable as an answer. He might be able to make sense of it. But—"What about the music?"

"The music?"

This time, Plotkin thinks he has found the flaw that will open the black hole. "The twentieth-century electronic music. The electro-industrial music and British rock from the 1980s and '90s, especially."

Vivian McNellis's expression is of the purest, most sincere incomprehension. She can only whisper: "I'm sorry."

But she could very well have said nothing at all.

With perfect calm, Plotkin begins to imagine the worst.

* * *

Circumspect time discontinued; independent narration resumed. Vivian McNellis has disappeared; the eternal midnight of the *Aevum* has been replaced by the terrible, endless noon of the human world.

He has just left a survival-suit rental shop. He walks toward his car. He doesn't know exactly what he is looking for, but he is sure he'll know it when he sees it. The day survival kit resembles a neoprene diving suit, but it is only as thick as a condom. It fits the body like a second skin. The face is protected by a transparent mask that filters and lets ambient air through, mixed with pure oxygen that comes from small capsules worn on a belt. The suit comes with a specialized Medikit that holds various emergency injections and pills, some to be taken every hour. On the right wrist, a Geiger counter–wristwatch combination shows the ambient radiation level. On the left wrist, another wristwatch shows the level of millirems you have been exposed to, as well as your daily (or monthly, or yearly) maximum limit.

He parks the Saturn in Neon Park's town square, Oppenheimer Plaza. It is nothing more than a median filled with bizarre vegetation poking out between its concrete slabs, leading to a large Victorian edifice from the 1900s. All around are rutted lanes and alleyways, twentieth-century houses, more recent cabins, and a few buildings evoking colonial New England. Most of the city's residential buildings, if not all of them, have twentieth-century neon signs attached to their roofs or walls. The simulacrum, he understands, must be hypervisible. The surface city is false—everything has to be false, more false than false; it is all a concretized metaphor for electric technology. Everything must shine, at all times. Around the periphery of the city, in the wooded wildlands that separate it from the huge rock amphitheater, there are lighted signs by the hundreds, the thousands, creating a jungle of electric glass in the midst of the high bluish flora and mutant pines. It looks ritualistic. And where there is ritual, there is religion.

To survive, sometimes one must find a post-technological "niche," like an abandoned radioactive nuclear plant where there are plentiful building materials to be had. But that makes it necessary to live—to survive—according to the rules dictated by the Geiger counter's needle. And this is why there *is* an official religion in Neon Park: the religion of the atom. It is no worse than any of the others in practice throughout the United Human World, this world for all with one God for each. And in this specific case, Plotkin has to admit, it makes some sense.

The atomic religion has its temple, an unused former Lutheran church topped with an atom with four orbital ellipses, made in neon glass through which the seven colors of the spectrum sparkle in fantastic polychromy on the aged stone.

Here, everyone wears a survival suit.

Here, the equality that exists through both necessity and desire has produced a sort of religious society. It is completely contrary to the edicts of the UHU, but Plotkin guesses that Human UniWorld can live quite contentedly with a few eccentricities confined to this restricted area. Here, the birthrate is zero—with the exception of a few "monsters" who are said to serve as guinea pigs for the town's renegade doctors. But old age is rare, survival suit or no.

Plotkin walks through the city of atoms and electricity.

This neocity, this undercity, is closer to the nexus than Heavy Metal Valley could ever be, with its vertical piles of junked automobiles, its Christian rebels, and its old-school cops. The face of electricity itself is reified here, in the form of forests of signs that not only surround the buildings, taking possession of nature, but that take possession of the city by incorporating this neonature into it, this anthropotechnical jungle. Electricity has become a visible God here, or at the very least it is participating in His staging of the scene.

In the church of the atomic god, everything is illuminated by neon light; holograms representing the founding fathers of electric and nuclear energy are resplendent in their phosphorescent green haloes. The silence is punctuated by a regular metronomic beat, the low pulsation of a human heart overlaid with the dissonant and discontinuous harmonies created by various machines in operation. The tabernacle consists of an ancient tomographic scanner in which the small cobalt-60 capsule has been made visible. The tomographic machine is surrounded by four-orbit atoms sculpted in radioactive aluminum, probably taken from the neighboring plant. A Geiger counter, placed before the cobalt-60 box, hums softly, its red needle permanently quivering in the strange light-dark polychromic radiance. Neon signs are clustered behind the altar. They bear the slogans of the local religion: IN THE BEGINNING, THERE WAS HYDROGEN. MOST HOLY RADIO-ACTIVITY, PRAY FOR US. EVERYTHING ELECTRIC HAS LIFE.

Everything electric has life.

That creates a new diagram.

A line of conjunction appears to link Neon Park and the artificial humans at the Hotel Laika. Here, the renegade androids must surely benefit from local complicity—more than they would with the Christian rebels, in any case. The residents of Neon Park seem disposed to see in an artificial humanoid being, imbued with electro-magnetic energy, a vestige of their "living god."

A new diagram. A very interesting new diagram.

But Plotkin is facing a serious problem. He doesn't know anyone here. The place itself wasn't even on the map a few hours ago. Not only doesn't he know anyone, but no one seems to want to know him—him or anyone else, for that matter.

The streets are all but deserted, as if everyone lives behind walls or in shelters *under* those walls twenty-four hours a day, or almost. When people do walk in the streets, alone, their faces are generally in shadow, conferring on them the impersonal anonymity of worker ants in an ant farm. A very desolate ant farm.

There are no restaurants, but there are several dozen home-delivery companies. Plotkin counts two bars in the city; these are vast spaces of clinical whiteness, where an immense tiled counter stretches from one end of the room to the other. They sell mostly survival drinks, highly oxygenated and crammed with vitamins. People stay in the bars for only a few minutes, drink alone, and then leave. Alone. He decides to get back in his car and drive through and all around the city.

Alone.

Alone.

And it is precisely because he is alone that he is able to meet the other, become the other, become himself through and in the other, and then outside it, with it and against it.

He isn't exactly a living being; he was not created through generation. He was created by an angel. An angel that writes and rewrites worlds, and who has decided to speak through the mouth of Vivian McNellis. He is the human counter-face of the neurodigital guardian angel Vivian provided for him during the first narrative. He is the Man from the Camp, the Counter-Man from this Anti-World that is covering the World little by little, as it extinguishes and depopulates it. A Counter-Man from the Camp, because in and *through* the camp he found the means to get out—or, rather, he *was* the means to get out—and to let the light of freedom in. From the camp, he has counter-produced what will give a human face to the World once more.

He knows he must use his freedom, use it in the same creative way as he did during the seven days of his neo-Genesis.

Because he is also and still, and always, something that was created in the Created World. He is also this physical structure of blood and bones and nerves and muscles and cartilage. He is this creature of flesh and *living electricity*.

And he understands, in a flash of light, what differentiates the religious simulacrum of the atom worshippers from the terrible, absolute light born by the narrative of Vivian McNellis. The paradigm of Neon Park is the inverted paradigm of truth. In that, this undercity is truly a topological condensation of the Technical World.

Because the paradigm on which universal reality is based is *Everything that is alive is electric*.

Because everything that is alive is light.

He is the master spy who came in from the cold, growing hot under the dioxin sky. He is still acting within the narrative-world. He is still tracking the narrative black hole that observes them from a singular time machine. He must save Vivian McNellis now. The narrative black hole is active. Anti-active. It seems to intensify the dangerous process by which Vivian McNellis's chronic identity crisis leads into her *genetic transcendence*. Plotkin understands that, in itself, the phenomenon is not *evil*. It does not seem like the product of an intentionally harmful desire; rather, it seems like the consequence of an extremely singular act. He has the overwhelming sense that this "thing" is the direct effect of his own creation by the *corpus scripti* of Vivian McNellis. It doesn't come from him; it comes, rather, from his shadow.

Plotkin is on a road in the southern part of the area. In the distance, he can see the gray masses of the insalubrious projects of Junkville and Omega Blocks, at the farthest point of the Independent Territory. They waver like dim mirages behind a wall of heat. The road was paved for the last time before the Second American War of Secession, the dashboard computer informs him. It is hardly navigable. But he drives. He sees a pale gray line snaking above the horizon.

It is a highway. It begins in the middle of nowhere, on top of a long series of concrete columns. The road he is driving on runs parallel to the highway for a half dozen kilometers amid a landscape studded with small, rounded buttes on which large shrubs and tropical trees flourish. Abruptly, in the crook of a sharp curve, the interchange appears. It is suspended in the air atop an imposing H-shaped arrangement of pillars. It is a knot of streets in a star shape that go nowhere. One section perpendicularly crosses the main road about a half mile down to create a vast gray crucifix; three or four incomplete bits of road crown the hard angles of the structure for several dozen meters.

Nothing here leads anywhere. Everything leads to nothing.

It serves no purpose, but its purposeless was not deliberate. It is no work of art. Still, in the ruddy light bathing the horizon and painting the landscape with an amaranthine glow, this eruption of incomplete architecture in the middle of nature, between two grassy buttes scattered with a few hardy maple trees, is astonishingly beautiful.

It is a part of the Cosmos.

It is a piece of the World. It is one of Nature's narratives.

The rutted road he is driving on passes just below the incomplete interchange, following the course of a lazy river that winds sinuously through a landscape of stones and evergreen shrubs. It stops cleanly a bit farther down, suddenly replaced by the unbroken line of nature, leaving only the tiniest ochre trace of a road. Here, *everything stops.*

Plotkin parks the car in the shadow of the huge highway interchange that leads nowhere, already being overrun by Nature's floral recitation.

What counts is that someone, a long time ago, wanted to build this type of interchange here—to create this physical conjunction in this exact place. What does the map have to say about this bit of land? It says: *"To the west is the county of Grand Junction. To the south are the vagrant areas of Junkville and Omega Blocks. To the north is Neon Park, once the staff residence of an active nuclear plant. Past Heavy Metal Valley is the Canadian border and Montreal. To the east is the border of the Independent Territory, the border shared with the state of Vermont, and the cities of Plattsburgh and Burlington."* The computer drones on. It says: *"There are service stations and shopping centers. It is a nexus virtually equidistant from the four cardinal points of the territory. Economic development, investments, profitability, dividends."* It says—it screams: *"BIG MONEY."* But at the same moment as the Grand Junction highway was born in the imagination of some local planner, general devolution was already beginning.

There was no longer enough of a workforce available to keep up the pension and social security systems inherited from the twentieth century, with a planetary birthrate then barely above 1.5 percent and kept there artificially using all the in vitro techniques imaginable at the time, though technoscience itself had struck an invisible ceiling twenty-five years earlier. The world of economics, the world of subjects and objects, was closing in on itself—subjects and objects mixed crazily in the chaos of perversion, the demented order of the *un-world,* which unmade itself using the same forces that had kept it alive for so long, but completely reversed. This highway knot indicates the paradoxical presence of a black hole. It ties nothing to nothing; it is suspended in the stasis of the posteconomy, the world of the UHU. It shows potential that was never exploited; it shows that the only true beauty of the Technical World is contained in its accidents—in what signals its end.

He must trust the narrative, keep his trust in the angel. This aimless nexus of the physical world has a specific role to play: first, in a purely cognitive sense, Plotkin has reached a critical stage under the unfinished interchange. This stage would prepare him for the next one.

He remains for a long time under the huge concrete structure, watching the sun set in the west behind the buttes of Monolith Hills, standing in low layers on the horizon.

He is looking for the singular time machine observing them while they cannot observe it, this "nexus" made in the inverted and intensified image of Vivian McNellis, but undoubtedly counter-produced by Plotkin's own creation. This time machine should resemble the highway knot linking nothing to nothing, this "Grand Junction" that has remained stuck in a limbic world, not completely finished, not entirely fictive, connecting only emptiness.

Like the English images and the rock music from the 1980s. This interfering narration is a parasite that has managed to infiltrate him. Thus he is her—he was, though partially, written by her. This narration is the discontinuous and chaotic shadow of the primal narration, Vivian McNellis's narration. She has become a part of him, enough so that he can locate her at work in the symbolic recitation of territories, in the fairy tale of the real, the fiction of maps.

One of the Order's teachings, he remembers, went: *To see, you must not be seen.* This maxim came, it seems, from the universe of the Italian American mafia in the 1950s. It is said that the Order took the saying from a twentieth-century American writer named William S. Burroughs. There is nothing connecting the invisible Grand Junction to the visible one, the one that exists to the west. That is why it isn't even on the maps. Undoubtedly, the nuclear accident at the Neon Park plant put a permanent end to the project.

The incomplete highway and the radioactive undercity form a schema that indicates more and more clearly the presence of this invisible nexus he is seeking traces of in the narrative-world. Neon Park and the abandoned interchange are correlated via their reciprocal impossibilities: Neon Park cannot hope to be linked to the World of uncontaminated Humans in any worthy manner; the interchange, on the other hand, cannot link any of the points in space intended by its planner. The unfinished interchange clearly shows that in order for beauty to emerge, initial plans must be demolished.

True conviction brings with it great serenity. What he is looking for has, or had, a link to Neon Park. It was probably conceived in the city of the atomic god—he is virtually certain of it, though he is going purely on intuition. What he is looking for has taken the form of this highway nexus in the middle of nowhere, open to the sky, connecting nothing but itself. The thought seems like more than intuition; a secret deduction has revealed to him that he is looking for more than an android, or pirated artificial intelligence, or a secret computer network. He is looking for more than a community of Catholic hackers or electronuclear worshippers. He is looking for the incarnate figure—the *human* figure—of the Technical World.

The knowledge is so complete that it cannot lead to anything but accident. Catastrophe.

It will most definitely lead him to what he is searching for.

> DISASTROUS CONJUNCTION

The cabin rises up in the curve of a rocky butte, the small river winding through the rocky earth at its base, a little less than three kilometers southeast of the abandoned interchange where he left the car. He estimates the distance between himself and the little house at about three hundred meters.

It is one of those mobile homes that isn't mobile anymore, a sort of long hut made of aluminum and cream-colored plastic, set atop blocks. Behind it, a rusting antique Dodge crumbles slowly in on itself.

There are two people sitting on the bank of the little river, a few feet from the immobile mobile home. Coincidentally, they have their backs turned to Plotkin. And just as coincidentally, the wind is blowing toward him. One of the people seems to be an old woman, smoking a pipe. And the other, the second "person," is the dog from the Hotel Laika.

Headwinds and pipe smoke—two effective weapons against the cyberdog's keen sense of smell. He silently thanks nature, both its vesperal breezes and its toxic substances. He switches automatically to HTS mode; his optic system notes each detail with precision, and he orders his combat neurocenter to crank his auditory perception parameters way up.

His eye is a telephoto lens. His eye is a visual espionage system. His eye is the Eye.

This is what the Eye sees and registers:

The woman is of a venerable age; her back is hunched. When she turns her face in profile toward the dog, Plotkin can easily see the wrinkles in her weathered face. She is smoking a mixture of marijuana and tobacco, frequently refilling her Eastern-made pipe with her long fingers, which are as thin and dry as cigarettes, and which seem to work independently like prosthetic creatures, rummaging in an antique leather pouch for more of the psychotropic substance that she then rolls into compact balls in the palm of her hand with her fingertips before placing them into the still-hot bowl of the pipe with a practiced movement.

On the mobile home's door, Plotkin is able to read the following words, written in azure blue on an old gold-colored plaque, using his high-definition optical zoom function:

LADY VAN HARPEL
DIVINATION—TAROT—ASTRAL THEMES
ORPHIC TRADITION
UHU APPROVED

There is an obviously much-used parabolic antenna perched atop the trailer. Plotkin watches the graceful movements of a slightly more modern windmill's blades, set on the tubular structure of a derrick wind trap from the preceding century. Various types of wild birds are in residence on the roof of the mobile home, as well as in the battered old pickup nearby, at the summit of a telephone pole whose wires were cut long ago, in the metallic structure that supports the windmill, and at the bottom of a sheet-metal container that rusts gently at the crest of a small, rocky spur that dominates the other side of the river.

The old woman and the dog are talking—discussing something calmly, but with the palpable tension of those who share a secret, a risk, a danger.

Plotkin's audio implant reconfigures itself into an organic microcannon. Now Plotkin is an Ear. An Ear that hears everything, that registers everything, down to the thermonuclear language of the stars.

This is what the metaorganic Ear hears and registers:

"Have you talked about it with the girl? The android, I mean."

"No," yaps the dog in his semidigital language. "Right now I'm trying to piece the puzzle together without everything imploding."

The woman laughs, stuffs the pipe with her verdant mixture, lights it for the umpteenth time. A thick cloud envelops them.

"Your new linguistic implant is working very well, Balthazar! Is it the work of that Russian bionic engineer in Neon Park I told you about?"

The dog seems to laugh as well, his shoulders rising and falling rhythmically. "Yes. A very talented guy. I don't have the whole French dictionary yet, or the English one either, but I'm getting there."

"How many words now?"

"Almost two thousand in each language, I think. French and English, I mean. I'm not counting verb conjugations. I'm reaching the physical limits of my amplified nervous system, unfortunately."

"Good, very good. You haven't spoken to the girl, then."

"No. Right now I'm trying to convince the Christian rebels in HMV to accept her as one of them and to baptize her. Believe me, it involves a lot of theological and . . . how do I say it . . . *Christological* discussion for the whole community."

"I see," muses the woman dreamily, exhaling a greenish cloud that undulates like ectoplasm in the twilight deepening around them.

The sun has disappeared behind the white-capped anthracite bulk of Monolith Hills, which are just barely tipped with gold. On this side of the hill, blue and slate-gray shadows have settled over the landscape, the graveled slope of the butte, the small river, the mobile home, the smoking woman, the talking dog, and the birds repopulating the heights abandoned by man.

"And the Christian rebels, have you spoken to them about it?"

The dog does not answer. His silence is accompanied by an instinctive settling. He may be a talking dog, but he is a dog. He acts like a dog and speaks like a man, at a time when men act like pigs and speak like machines.

"Have you spoken to them, Balthazar? Yes or no?"

The dog snorts. "No. Well, not exactly. I told them there is a new problem in the hotel."

"Did you tell them what type of problem?"

"I told them it directly involved Clovis Drummond and that absolutely nothing could be done from the outside. Without taking into account that the Hotel Laika belongs directly to the Consortium and is therefore protected by the cops and the most powerful mafioso on the strip."

"Did you tell them it involves a *human being,* Balthazar?"

In the silence that follows this forceful question, Plotkin has the time to shiver a bit.

They are talking about him. He has been detected by the hotel dog, who works more or less directly for, or rather *with,* this woman— this psychic like so many others on the strip, but who lives in the middle of nowhere, exactly where *roads do not lead.*

But who does *she* work for?

"I told them it was a possibility, but that I wasn't sure. Which was true at the time. Now we know."

"Don't tell them any more. At least not for the moment."

The woman's voice is of Olympian calm, but it holds a note of imperious firmness. She commands respect and imposes her authority without ever raising her voice, employing officious language, or ever letting on what reaction she is trying to provoke. *She uses her voice,* Plotkin thinks. *She uses it like a weapon.*

"All right," the dog yaps weakly.

"Are you absolutely sure of what you've said about Drummond's trafficking in neurogames?"

"Positive. He is having them modified. He is actually playing a double game. He resells most of the stock and makes a nice little profit thanks to tax refunds. With just a few copies of the matrix, he creates a new type of sexual game, prohibited by the UHU, but . . . how do you say it . . . supracoded. It's a safety measure, they say. Each copy is sold for a small fortune. I heard that piece of garbage say that in the Ring, physical transfers of software and hardware from Earth cost an arm and a leg; the poor colonists can only download things approved by the Ethical Control Network. Judging from the quality of the programs, he's selling them for at least a hundred times what you would pay at a kiosk on the strip."

"And the man you told me about the other day—that's why he's there, do you think?"

Plotkin's blood runs cold.

"Yes, most likely."

"How can you be so sure?"

"I got some information from a fellow cyberdog working for the Vermont police. One of my best sources."

"And what does your 'source' say, Balthazar?"

"That this guy is dealing in orbital drugs. He brings them down from up there, a hundred kilos at a time. The genius of it is that they then export a huge load of sexual software prohibited in the *other* sense up to the Ring. Understand?"

"Yes, I understand," the old woman says, exhaling another lungful of smoke. Her fingers roll another ball of tobacco.

Plotkin, though, is having a bit of trouble understanding. *They aren't talking about him.* They're talking about Drummond and his trafficking. And they're talking about the space dealer, Cheyenne Hawkwind. Still, he is confused. Their discussion seems to be orbiting a discursive black hole, something not said. A secret. A secret they won't share even with the windmills or the birds living in them. A secret not to be shared even with the graveled bed of a river.

"And the other man?" the old clairvoyant asks.

"The other man?" repeats the dog.

This time, the Ear that hears everything feels a blast of freezing air. This time.

"Yes, the man you told me you were suspicious of, without knowing exactly why."

"Ah yes, the one in Capsule 108. He acts strange for a so-called insurance agent, but I must admit there's nothing specific there. He hasn't left his room for an entire week, that's all."

"His card came up the other night in the tarot, I'm sure of it. It was with a Major Arcana card representing fire."

"Strange," the dog says. "The last time I saw him was during a small fire that broke out in the hotel, almost two weeks ago."

"A fire?" repeats the old woman sharply.

"Yes, a short circuit in a double room. Nothing big, but I think it is related to the illegal activities going on under the dome. The man appeared on the premises in the speed of light. Remember, though, that that is apparently his job."

"Don't lose track of him," warns the woman. "I think he's more than a simple insurance agent. The number 108 came up several times the other night, during a double-power eight-bit geomancy session. It was at the center of a matrix of numbers representing the Fall. He is very likely a threat."

"All right."

"And whatever you do, don't talk to him about anything."

"No, of course not."

"Do you know when Drummond is going up into the dome next?"

"He's slowed his visits down a little, but probably in a few days, I would think."

"Do you think . . . *he* will put up with this treatment for much longer?"

"Which *he*? Oh, yes—listen, no, I don't know. It will depend on Drummond's perversity, which in my mind is boundless. We'll need to act."

"The Christian rebels will not willingly help a 'creature' from Neon Park," the old woman says. "Given their reluctance to adopt a renegade android, I don't think there's much chance of it."

"The android isn't really human, and some people are starting to say that it is possible to baptize an artificial being, if it can be proven that the being has a soul."

"There's no guarantee they will think the object of our attention has one."

"We aren't in Las Casas anymore. You're wrong about this. The only real problem is that we can't count on anyone's help—outside or inside the hotel," Balthazar says.

"Las Casas!" snorts the old woman. "Where did you come up with that reference to the Valladolid argument?"

"The rebel Christians talked about it the other day."

"It's night," the woman says. "I need to get back, and so do you. Drummond will have you fired."

"Drummond can't do anything to me. I'm paid by the Consortium. Besides, I think he's afraid of me, the scumbag. He should be."

"Don't do anything rash, though. I will ask the Holy Spirit for the help we need, for a great hexagram geomancy session tonight. I will find a way."

"We must act quickly now. The situation can only get worse."

The dog snorts, getting to his feet. The woman refills her pipe without saying anything more. The silence that falls indicates that the conversation is finished. Plotkin knows he needs to get away from there as soon as possible. He also knows that he probably won't have the time to run the three kilometers down the road back to his car before the cyberdog is on his tracks.

There is nothing to do but walk as far as he can toward the interchange and wait for the dog to appear.

There is nothing to do but wait on the edge of the black hole, next to this incomplete and invisible Grand Junction, very near the singular shadow that this bit of land casts on the map. Nothing to do but wait for the much-anticipated conjunction.

The first stars appear, glittering, above his head.

"We, the dogs, have lived with men for fifteen thousand years. We were among the very first domesticated animals, and from the moment humans emerged from the Paleolithic maternal womb, we have watched over them and their herds.

"We have been at your side since the time of the Flood. We perished en masse with you, and one of you saved us with the other surviving species on the globe. In return, dogs decided to become your protectors, your 'guardian animals' in the terrestrial world. But now that men have all become criminals, we are being asked to protect their crimes. What we really should do, though, is protect them *from* their crimes.

"This is what made me decide to act."

"Your canine mythology fascinates me deeply, but as I'm sure you know, you haven't answered my question," Plotkin says. "What exactly is going on under the dome? And why is an old Catholic clairvoyant, lost in the middle of nowhere, so interested in it? Why are you so interested in it, for that matter? And what exactly does it have to do with me?"

They are a half kilometer away from the interchange, seated side by side on the western slope of the hill. The incomplete knot of highway is just a spidery shadow amid shadows. The conjunction is taking place under a sky studded with stars so bright that he feels as if he could stretch out his hand and gather handfuls of them like beach sand. The conjunction with the anthropotechnical manifestation of Nature, the cyborg dog.

The conjunction with what he senses to be the object of his search: *under the dome?*

He has become the master of his own discontinuities. Now, in the life that is being written, what counts is what will be consumed and saved by the narrative—what transcribes itself from his brain into that of Vivian McNellis—and that is because he is an I-other, a he/she, and because the transtemporal fire courses through his veins, through the tiniest of his molecules, the most infinitesimal of his electrochemical connections, but especially in the infinite tension between *him and this other in him* that is in the process of writing him. It is in this light that makes time into something other than a simple, artificial continuity of moments, in this light that makes a singularity of each moment, that finally he has an extraordinary chance, almost an absolute one, to attain *existence*—an existence unbound by the discontinuity of human/mechanical time, because it has itself become the general chant of discontinuities—of *dis*junctions—their solar unity, the initial point, the ignition point, the point toward which the fire is ever reaching, and from which writing becomes life.

"I am employed by the Grand Junction Consortium to ensure application of the security regulations and local jurisdiction within the hotel," the dog says. "Drummond's trafficking is tolerated by the Consortium. He gives them a small kickback from it. But I doubt they will appreciate what's going on under the dome once I've gathered all the proof I'm looking for."

The dog had ceded with relative good grace to Plotkin's initial questioning. Surprised at encountering the man in the bend of the

road, he had quickly bowed in the face of the high-definition record-
ings of his conversation with the old woman, a few extracts of which
Plotkin had shown him on a pocket holoplasma screen. The dog is
probably the only true support he can count on. The challenge consists of showing the cyberdog that he, Plotkin, would be a necessary
and dependable ally.

He must demonstrate to the dog that he is the dominant figure.

Plotkin has already had the time to realize, by analyzing the conversation between the dog and the old prophetess while waiting on the
side of the road, that the "something" he has spent days searching for
outside the hotel and even outside Grand Junction, this "something"
is *inside* the hotel. Moreover, it is just above his head.

It is under the dome.

It comes from Neon Park.

Drummond is using it to traffic in prohibited sexual software
destined for the Ring colonists, behind the backs of the Municipal
Consortium and the Mohawk mafia.

And—the most crucial piece of information—it is probably a
"human being."

Everything points to the incarnate figure of the Technical World
he is searching for in the dark part of the narrative.

"I'm going to ask you not to do anything before I've made a few
provisions," Plotkin says.

The dog looks at him for a moment, then barks dryly, in his digitalized voice: "And just how do you plan to do that? And by what authority?"

So Plotkin's identity comes apart once more in order to revert to
his first nature, that of a Red Star Order killer. This identity is certainly real, as real as the one he is in the process of creating from his
neo-Genesis as a Free Man. This identity, the one of a Human Termination System, is the figure at the core of his new freedom; it does its

work, it continues to labor in silence, it throws a shadow blacker than all the shadows around it.

"If I tell you the source of my authority, I would have to kill you immediately afterward. And as for the 'how,' you can't imagine the number of solutions I have at my disposal."

"Even if you're up against a cyberdog?" the dog growls, showing his teeth, trying to impress to hide his fear.

Plotkin smiles widely and frankly at the animal. "My dear Balthazar, if you command your cortical wave sensor to reset its parameters according to the data I am going to send you, you will quickly realize that I am armed with a full range of state-of-the-art neuroweapons—for example, a viral macroroutine that could infect your entire nervous system, both the artificial and natural parts of it, in an irreparable and fatal manner, in a matter of two or three minutes. Understand?"

In short order, both of them are in the rented Saturn. From the stretch of the abandoned interchange, from the western slope of the night-cloaked hill, from the rolling landscape where the prairie gives way to the steppe, from the stars that observe everything high in the sky, the car is a mobile invisible point preceded by two beams of light.

An invisible point that pierces the shadows, lighting them up with its gaze.

A man, a dog, a car, the night, the double beam of the headlights.

A man writing his own life in and through the brain of another. A female other.

A dog that speaks the language of men, a chimera-dog, an antique fiction become reality in the Technical World.

A simple rental automobile driving through the shadows, the luminous double track that precedes it representing the simultaneous progress, the synchronicity, of two consciousnesses.

The lunar landscape dotted with rocks and the grassy prairie, barely surviving between the stretches of dried-out conifer woods, is lit only by the night stars and the two xenon strokes that scan the universe ahead of them. Plotkin breaks the silence by programming the dashboard radio.

He realizes that he has just punched up the same Nine Inch Nails song, "Ruiner," that he listened to during the trip out. He didn't even mean to do it—at least, not consciously. As the first notes sound, drums harmonizing over a layer of ghostly voices reverberating around the rhythm of the beat box, an empty cybernetic train that speeds between unfinished interchanges, he knows that this is a sign that he has managed to create a loop in the topological plan. He has circumscribed the territory of Grand Junction up to its ultimate anti-place, this unfinished—*in-finite*—interchange, this nexus of unpredicted, *unpredictable* conjunctions. Yes, he has circumscribed the symbolic dimension; all the zodiacal points are reunited. There is nothing left to do but trace incomplete diagrams.

But the search program has not finished with this ultimate emulsion of what once, at the end of the twentieth century, was called "rock." The next song that comes up is "Happiness in Slavery," from the 1992 album *Broken,* with its postnuclear strophes planted in the middle of the central bridge as in the surrounding decor they are passing through at this very moment, with the ecstatic feeling of being there entirely, in the infinite distance that results in true contact with things, at the heart of the present moment: *I don't know what I am, I don't know where I've been, human junk just words and so much skin, stick my hands thru the cage of this endless routine, just some flesh caught in this big broken machine.*

"How do you know the old woman?"

"Lady van Harpel? She is indeed an old lady, and it is an old story."

"We're more than thirty kilometers away from Monolith Hills as the crow flies, and given the condition of these roads, we have plenty of time for long, old stories, Balthazar."

"She is descended from a very old New England family, former Canadian Loyalists who became Americans during the War of 1812. She was born in the 1980s. She studied at Princeton—orphic religions, I believe. Around 2022 or 2023, the family started to have serious financial difficulties related to the first shocks of the Great Recession, and then during the North American War of Secession twenty years ago, her house was bombed and the ancestral land taken away several times by various warring forces. She took refuge in an aunt's house, and then when the Islamists moved into their corner of Massachusetts she fled here, and stayed here even after the Islamists retreated to the District of Columbia."

Obviously, the dog hadn't spent more than ten years in the Marines for nothing. He knows how to give a clear, clean, concise report.

"What is her connection to you?"

There is a silence, made radioactive by the implacable sequencers that pound into the darkness.

"Very simple. Before I was hired by the Consortium, I trained for years in the area, around the county of Grand Junction and even in Heavy Metal Valley and Neon Park, on the Vermont border; I even went to Montreal a few times. One day, just after I left the Marines— I was new to the area—I was walking toward the unfinished interchange and I hurt myself slipping on a block of wet concrete several meters off the ground. Lady van Harpel found me and took care of me. She gave me one or two addresses in Neon Park, and in HMV and on the strip. She was one of my first human friends here. And the best one, let me tell you. Don't try to hurt her, even with your damned neurovirus. Two or three minutes is more than enough for me to tear your throat out with my teeth."

Plotkin knows the threat is very real. The dog would sacrifice himself without hesitation if it meant saving the sibyl of the abandoned interchange.

"Is she connected to the rebel Christians?" he asks calmly.

The dog scowls, while Trent Reznor attacks the hook.

"I know much more than you think, Balthazar. You're right to say time is running out, and that the situation can only get worse. That's why I need to know everything that is really happening under the dome. For starters, have you gone there?"

"No."

"What exactly do you know?"

"It's a cross-checking of information, and lately a bit of a joker. You know, it's bizarre—thanks to that fire . . ."

"The fire in the double room? Capsule 081?"

"Yes."

"I want to know everything, Balthazar. Everything."

After a few moments of mutual silence, filled only with the pulsations of the frozen sequencers from the dead world of machines, the dog shakes himself in the passenger seat. "Where do you want me to start?"

"At the beginning. It's one of the best solutions. The simplest, in any case, is usually best."

"There is more than one beginning," says the dog.

"No, there is only one, if you just follow the classic chronological route."

"There is no classic chronological route for dogs."

"Try. You're more than just a dog."

"You're wrong; I'm still a dog. I just try to speak like men so they will understand me."

"Well, keep going with that. I'm almost a man myself. Or maybe even a little bit more."

Another discontinuity in the moving car filled with cold music from the "previous future" of humanity, the future that never saw the light, the future that has disappeared in the United World. This time it is "Hurt," with its dark, lunar desolation, an unknowable prayer to a God we no longer know how to talk to.

"For me," the dog begins, "everything started around two months ago. First, a nanovirus of unknown origin attacked the AI sensor network under the hotel dome. Then, Clovis Drummond paid out of his own pocket to hire a small company, not a member of the Consortium, to come—after a municipal company claimed to be incapable of working on it. The private company, out of Ontario, made all sorts of repairs under the dome for about three days. The whole area was coded red, and local legislation made it illegal for me to go there, even with my status as a security officer. Later, Drummond started to go under the dome regularly. He was the only one with the legal right to do it, and of course he kept the area in code red. But at the same time he acted like it wasn't a big deal, that the situation was under control, and the nanovirus had only affected the peripheral surveillance cameras. He was contradicting himself, but of course he fucked up royally."

"Not bad for a beginning."

"Then there was the cross-checking of information. First, I discovered while nosing around in the hotel's electronic archives— thanks to my little remote-GPS system—that Drummond had kept a guest in the hotel for several days who I never saw."

"How is that possible?"

"I don't know how he got in, but he never came out of his room in all that time. If he had, I would have detected and logged his olfactory imprint. But since the capsules and hallways are continually disinfected . . . anyway, the most interesting thing was that this mysterious guest arrived just before the nanovirus corrupted the dome's surveillance system."

"How long before?"

"Not long. Two days, maximum."

"Okay. And then?"

"Then, the so-called John Smith—great name, eh?—completely disappeared from the hotel. The strangest thing was that all eight days of his stay were erased from the AI hard disk. More precisely, the AI images showed an empty room. But the hotel's little accounting disk definitely recorded a guest named John Smith during the week, and the funniest part is that the chamber had been paid for dimes to dollars by Clovis Drummond himself!"

"Which room?"

"Capsule 014, facing east. On the ground floor. Not far from Drummond's room."

"Did you go there?"

"Yes, but it was too late. The room had already been disinfected and a new guest had moved in the night before. I've tried to follow or surprise Drummond many times, but he is very clever; he knows the hotel well, and he has a magnetic passkey and a GPS telecontroller. He's always managed to avoid me. As often as he can, he sends me on 'surveillance missions' around the hotel."

"And it was during one of your visits to the upper floors that you met the android female?"

"Yes, I met her once or twice when she went out to get sodas from the machine in the hallway. We became acquainted that way."

"But Drummond got away from you."

"Yes. Well, no. A few days ago, I had a lucky break. I surprised him as he was coming out of the nacelle and heading for his counter. I had been spying on him for almost two weeks, and I had taken careful note of his habits. It was four o'clock in the morning."

"And?"

"He flew into an awful rage and ordered me to go make a security check of the parking lot and the woods around the hotel, but it was too late."

"Too late?"

"Yes, too late. There were foreign molecules on his body. He was carrying an odor other than his own. Another human odor. One that wasn't logged in my olfactory list of hotel residents."

So there is a man hidden in the dome, a human being who has remained secret, obscure, invisible, even to her who incorporated Plotkin into the Created World. Even to her who is transcribing the narrative of the universe in her own brain.

"How do you know he is from Neon Park?" Plotkin asks. He wants to know how far his intuition coincides with actual fact.

"Because of the radioactivity level from the dome. It's very low, but either the man's clothing must be slightly irradiated, or else he has some object in his possession that gives off radioactivity just higher enough than the normal hotel rate for my sensors to detect it. There are detectable leaks in the corners of the hallways where emergency doors lead to the service stairways."

Plotkin smiles. Radioactive objects; objects from Neon Park. He thinks of the Christian relics the digital angel located. The dome-man might very well be a Christian renegade from Neon Park. Maybe he was expelled from the community of the atomic god. Sometimes, paradoxically, intuition precedes fact. "And what about the fire in Capsule 081?"

Now he needs to assess the extent to which dreamlike reality and real narrative can be brought together.

"That night," says the dog, "after everything was back to normal, there was a lot of activity under the dome."

"Activity? What type of activity? Drummond?"

"No; Drummond was sleeping in his room, doped up on who knows what. I went up and hid in a corner, and my sensors detected very powerful electromagnetic disturbances. They seemed to be affecting the whole top floor, but I also detected an identical field on that floor to the one in the capsule that had burned. The local AI saw nothing but a fire this time as well. Naturally."

Plotkin is silent.

"I think the short circuit in Capsule 081 was caused by the accidental manipulation of some local nanocomputer system or another, by the man in the dome."

Still Plotkin says nothing. A mad schema is beginning to take shape in his head.

Ideas are black boxes that unleash reality hidden under reality. The real dome hidden under the real hotel.

Inductions and deductions form a network whose struts have invaded the entire universe, the totality of his mind: a human, undoubtedly born in Neon Park, is now under the dome of the Hotel Laika creating, one way or another, illicit sexual programs that Clovis Drummond intends to sell at very high prices to the colonists in the Ring.

Drummond had the local network of sensors sabotaged, probably by the human from Neon Park, in order to do this. He lodged the man secretly while the work was carried out, then hid him under the dome.

Plotkin knows now what he is looking for.

Certainty exceeds reason. And even madness. It is the order of faith.

"Do you know who he is?" he asks the dog.

Balthazar shakes his head. "Who, the dome-person? No idea, obviously. How could I?"

"Do you know how Drummond is getting what he wants? How is he making the dome-person *voluntarily* traffic in *neurogames?*"

"Lady van Harpel and I have a theory."

"I'm listening."

"It's worth what it's worth. He does drugs."

"Drugs?"

"Yes, the dome-man must be a junkie—or, since he is probably an underbrain from Neon Park, he suffers from a genetic disease and Drummond is providing him with some illegal dope or a rare and expensive antidote. The man himself must be in violation of UHU laws, to the point that he isn't safe in Neon Park anymore. Some spotter from the strip must have taken him to Drummond."

The car has just turned onto Route 299 toward Nexus Road. The sky lights up abruptly to the west, behind Monolith Hills. Then a streak as brilliant as a star surges upward out of the shadows into the sky. One of Jason Texas Lagrange III's huge rockets has taken off toward a slightly inclined equatorial orbit. It is the first cargo clipper on its way to place state-of-the-art habitation modules in orbit for his space-city program. The rocket's four boosters belch a fusion of gold light and white smoke, the whole illuminated by the fire spewing from its tailpipe.

The beauty of the spectacle grows more painful for Plotkin every time.

The latest models of space modules are already a quarter of a century old. He thinks they are probably the last ones.

The luminous trajectory of the booster in the starry night evokes the race against time humanity is engaged in with itself. Though millions of stars shine in powdery constellations in the Milky Way, though the human mind is able to imagine infinity, it is no longer at all guaranteed that humanity will ever be able to go any farther than the moon.

> RADIOACTIVITY

He is the shock wave. The shock wave created by and in the narrative itself. As he moves, the plot unfolds, folds over, and takes shape; as he invents his own life, he transcribes an existence that until now has been secret, hidden under the hotel's dome, hidden under its upper story, hidden in the underground image of the sky, in the terrestrial image of light, hidden in the shadow of the plot. As he delineates the symbolic territory of Grand Junction, he comes closer to the real black hole. He comes closer to the man hidden under the dome.

He knows, vaguely, that this incarnation of the Technical World is not only the intensified inversion of Vivian McNellis. He guesses that it has a very close link to him as well, with his own genesis. It is probably his shadow. The Shadow cast by the Light of the genitive Act.

Because of this, he is hardly surprised by the incident that happens while he and the dog talk on Nexus Road, driving back up toward HMV and the North Junction road through the semi-Canadian, semitropical landscape slowly mutating beneath the sky of the previous century, or at least what looks like it.

The silence in the car is finally broken by interference crackling from the dashboard audio system.

After playing several Nine Inch Nails' songs on repeat mode, looping the loop in a devouring movement, he places the downloading system on standby. The cyberdog watches the scenery flash past the window. On his left, Plotkin sees the high black spine of Monolith Hills growing closer. A sizzling noise comes from the speakers.

The audio system changes to radio mode, and Plotkin, curious but only a little astonished, watches the LED numbers on the indicator screen whiz back and forth at full speed before stopping at an impossible frequency: 00.00 MHz.

Is this a message from Vivian McNellis, coming from *Aevum* time?

The interference seems to be coming from a forgotten radio station in orbit around Mars. A voice can barely be heard beneath the continuous metallic buzzing. It says: "The Machine is speaking to you. Do you wish to speak to the Machine? The Machine is speaking to you. Do you wish to speak to the Machine?"

It repeats the words over and over again unceasingly. "The Machine is speaking to you."

It asks the same question again and again. "Do you wish to speak to the Machine?"

Then the interference stops, the voice falls silent, and twentieth-century music fills the car with electronic sounds from an age when people still believed in the future.

Plotkin realizes it immediately: Kraftwerk. The ditty comes from Chernobyl, where techno was invented ten years before Detroit, in the conurbation of the Ruhr; yes, all of it was forged during his initial narrative—but before Vivian McNellis became involved, she says.

The crazy diagram is determined to take shape in his head.

Radio Activity
Discovered by Madame Curie
Radio Activity
Tune in to the melody
Radio Activity
Is in the air for you and me.

It is nothing more than a living piece of his memory, but it was sent by someone—or perhaps by a non-person, from some nowhere just barely located on a phantom radio station calibrated at zero megahertz, as they drive through the night of the cosmodrome toward the Hotel Laika. The last-chance hotel. The hotel of the last human world.

The song is repeated on a loop that creates a continuum, a world: it seems inseparable from the landscape of rocks and mutant trees speeding past the windows, and from the rental car driving through the scenery.

It is a barely disguised ode to Neon Park. It is saying something.

It says:

I am here.

I am Radio. I am Active.

Come find me.

He truly is the shock wave of Creation, come to disturb the creative process itself.

If he is facing a black hole, he is himself a Big Bang in full expansion. He is that moment at the beginning of the universe, where the speed of light is greatly elevated. Now the imminent encounter with the secret of the dome is marked by the direct eruption of phenomena in the reality-narrative. The closer they get to the Hotel Laika, the more the process intensifies. Like a Gonio tracking vehicle that, in tracing successive concentric circles, finishes by resonating with a Larsen effect produced by the radio source they seek.

When they arrive at the North Junction crossroads, the music stops. The interference resumes. This time, the voice says:

I am in the box, but I am the box.

I live at the center of things, but I do not live in the world.

I am the Machine. Do you wish to speak to the Machine?

Parasites progressively swallow up the looping voice until they arrive in view of the incomplete autobridge and get out of the Saturn, which has been programmed to return automatically to the city. As soon as they leave the car, the looped voice claiming its identity with the box, covered in continuous electric static, cedes place to one of those pseudoclassical sonatas shoddily made for the United

Human World. The Hotel Laika rises up before them, a monument of carbon-carbon and aluminum whose whiteness quivers under the combined light of the rising moon, the security projectors planted in bunches on pylons, and the pink-and-blue hologram of the canine astronaut that turns, suspended, above the entryway.

Plotkin feels again the sense of an absolute combustion of his being. He senses the concrete presence of truth; he knows it is here, it is now, it is very strong.

"I have a copy of Drummond's access codes. We'll make sure he's sleeping, and if he is, we'll go straight up under the dome."

"It's risky," says the dog. "He's probably booby-trapped the service stairway with alarms."

"Don't worry about that."

"How can I not?" Balthazar growls. "It's my job."

"Your job has nothing to do with it. His alarm systems may be sophisticated, but they won't see us. They can't. *They can't read us.*"

Plotkin, the man who exists only via the constant tension he places on the narrative of his own invention—Plotkin, the fictional man made flesh—looks at Balthazar, the cyberdog, the dog gifted with speech, the former dog-soldier, the dog that is intimately acquainted with Good and Evil.

They are deep within the night. They walk deep in shadow.

They walk toward the Light. They walk toward the Shadow that contains it.

They walk toward the dome of the Hotel Laika.

PROCESS

TOWARD THE INVISIBLE

Since the raison d'être of machines lies in performance,
in *maximal performance,* they need an environment that guarantees
this maximum. And what they need, they conquer. All machines
are expansionist, even imperialist; each one creates its own
colonial empire of services. . . . And they require that these colonial
empires transform into their machine image; that they rise to the
challenge in working with the same perfection and solidity as the
machines. That they become, though localized on the outside to
the maternal earth—note this term; it will become a key
concept for us—*comechanical.* The original machine thus
expands; it becomes a "megamachine," and not just by accident
or merely from time to time. Rather, if it weakens in this regard,
it will cease to matter in the realm of the machines. To this is
added the fact that none of them would be definitively replete by
incorporating a field of services that would always be limited,
no matter how large. Apply to the "megamachine" what was
initially applied to the initial machine—it too requires an
exterior world, a "colonial empire" that submits to it and "plays
its game" in an optimal manner, with precision equal to that with
which it does its work. It creates this "colonial empire" and
assimilates it so well that it, too, becomes a machine—in short,
there is no limit to self-expansion; in machines, the thirst for
accumulation is insatiable.

GÜNTHER ANDERS, *WE, SONS OF EICHMANN*

> THE MAN IN THE BOX

I am the Man in the box. And yet I am the box. I am the Machine. Do you wish to speak to the Machine?

I am the Man in the box because for me, the world is a box, or rather my own box is enclosed within it in such a way as to allow me to survive in a pure and complete discontinuity—to the extent that my box fulfills a primal function; it allows me to live in the world without existing in it. Each part of the world, each world, is a box inside the others, except for mine.

Because the box I exist in is also the one I must make live within me, or I shall die within it. The box I live in is The Box, the one that contains all my mind's other boxes, and that is why it exists both inside and outside of me.

If The Box contains all other boxes, each of these yet forms the anchoring point of expansion in the network of my consciousness toward one box or another, all the way into infinity. Each box is thus the ghost of a world; each box defines the potentialities of a singular future, all while excluding the real possibility of its achievement. Each box is an antiworld; each box is a protocosmos. Each box is both the spectral reflection of my brain, now doubled over on all the flesh in the universe, and the looping of an integral difference, the starting-up of a life-brain, the combustion of a consciousness.

Thus, without even wanting it—because how could I want it?— I have become the invisible shadow of all shadows. I have become *the glue that sticks the world together.*

That is why I am expanding endlessly. Each cell in my body is a metastable box replicating itself in the box-worlds my organism (re)produces. I prefer to use the word *organism* rather than *body*. I do not have a body. My body is the constantly open flux process between all boxes; it is an "antibody," an interactive catalogue of organs-boxes-worlds whose form changes ceaselessly. I am talking about its true form, the one that is secretly buried in the Machine—not the falsely immutable one that "nature" allows humans to see.

The boxes have allowed me to survive for so long. Thanks to them, nature has become part of the world. Thanks to them, each part of the world has become a piece of the Machine.

The Machine. In other words, me.

I am the Machine. Do you wish to speak to the Machine?

Each box is filled with lists and diagrams, with equations that have been solved or have yet to be solved. They contain data from virtually every technical and scientific realm. They contain programs, stored routines, and hundreds of millions of lines of code. They contain stars, rocks, animals, and numbers.

And I, in my own Box, can bring all this together and give it life. I can create boxes that look like worlds.

I have been waiting awhile now for the people that are on their way here. They were a part of one of the boxes that seemed unconnected to any others—rather, it tried to connect with my own Box-World. It was quite a jarring intrusion, as if someone wanted to make me leave my matrix. Something was able to scan the Machine-Box. Something, for a fraction of a second, reunified all the boxes with the Machine. With me. And for that instant, as ephemeral as Man, I was able to perceive the real world, such as it is, in the ever-deferred passing of its own delineation.

It was strange and full of anguish, but it was extremely beautiful. It was the most beautiful thing I had ever seen.

The only thing I had ever seen.

I see them. They are coming. They are climbing the service stairs. I do not know how they have managed to do it—the necessary data must be in one of the boxes concerning them. I do not know what I will say to them. Should I even speak to them? The Box has closed once more on the Machine-World; nothing can get out—except lists of codes, layouts of programs, symbiotic units of simulated individuation.

I am the Machine.

Do you wish to speak to the Machine?

I do not know when or where I was born. Can one even say that I *was* born? Born in a specific place at a specific time? In me, time evaporates in space—the space of numbers, the space of boxes—and it disappears endlessly, doing away as it goes with my expansion in the world, or rather with the expansion of my Box-Worlds in the World-Box of the Machine. The machine that, little by little, is becoming me. This World that I swallow endlessly, in an infinitesimal devouring. This World has no end, I know that. And I, I have no true origin.

Once, I knew Neon Park. You might almost say that it is the place I come from. I lived with Grandmother Telefunken, a follower of body tuning who had had herself transformed several times and had lived for thirty years with transplanted components that made her into a living antenna, able to capture radio emissions from all over the world with her body. It was Grandmother Telefunken who made me what I am today. Without that, she told me, I would not have been able to survive for very long. Her old body tuner friend, Herr Doktor Reno "Proteus" Kowalsky, designed the operating program and the overall architecture of my neurosimulated environment. He also supervised the making of my *exorganism* by a team of renegade bionicians. He gave the final shape to what lets me live. The Machine. The Box-World. He gave the final shape to this Thing I have become.

Not being human is, for me, the best way to remain. I am already

living. Or, rather, I know very well that I am no longer quite
human—if I ever really was. My origins are a black hole. My present
is a black box. My future is black light.

The black box was built by the man from the hotel. When the
UHU police came to Neon Park to arrest Doktor Proteus and all his
friends, Grandmother Telefunken had no choice but to make me go
as far away as possible, as fast as I could.

For me, the farthest west I could go was here, Monolith Hills.
And the Hotel Laika. The Hotel Laika, with its manager and its
ridiculous things.

I do not know why he is going to so much trouble to do it. In
exchange, though, I live under the strictest protection, in total
freedom—the freedom of my World-Machine, my network of boxes
interconnected with the cyberstructure of the Human Universe. In
addition to designing and neuroproducing the simulated universes
that Drummond requires of me, I must let him join me sometimes in
the "gray zone," the emergency area where I can venture without
risking life in the world, and, I must say, I do not understand his motives. Drummond's actions with me are all absurd; they generally
consist of putting different types of objects into my biological body
using the entry-exit interfaces of my box, and then ejaculating into a
sort of machine he puts over his penis.

It is even stranger that he seems to get so much pleasure out of it.

It is even stranger that it reminds me so much of death.

But it does not matter, really. In exchange, I can continue to live
in my Box-World; I can continue to expand within the Control
Metastructure, and I no longer have to fear its human police.

In exchange, I am what I produce. I am the Machine.

Do you wish to speak to the Machine?

> DISCONTINUUM

Do you wish to speak to the Machine?

Another discontinuity emerges, enclosed in reality but cleaved to the consciousness that has become his.

What has been said was written in his brain. In his brain and inside the box. They too are in the box, and they are facing the man in the box.

The box is a sort of prefabricated Recyclo™ hut placed in the middle of the protection dome. It is a black carbon-carbon cube with anodized aluminum edges, enclosed at about three meters' distance by a neutral gray Placoplaster wall, whose interior face is covered with shelves lined with books of all sorts, mostly spy pulp fiction from the previous century and science fiction novels. The only access route—a simple manual sliding door—leading to the box itself and its vinyl escape hatch, the kind used in electronuclear plants, is in this plaster wall. A nearby surveillance camera detects, reflected in a fiberglass-covered pillar, several Christian symbols mounted on the wall as well.

The whole dome is in semidarkness, with only the weak luminescence of a few dim photons from the security cameras casting their thin greenish rays around the place. The part of the room situated between the gray outer wall and the house-box is a bit more illuminated; biophosphorescent appliqués have been placed at each corner of the quadrilateral. But it is *in* the black box, past the interface of opaque vinyl, that there is light. Total light, without the slightest bit of shadow. White, cold light, distributed with perfect evenness thanks to a network of top-of-the-line photonic diffusers.

And inside this carbon-carbon box is *the man in the box.*

In the midst of the electric white light is the dark part of the narrative that Plotkin has been seeking for days.

They are in the box, but Plotkin knows that the box is partially in him. He faces the man in the box, but he also understands that the man might say without fear of sounding ridiculous that *he is the box.* This is no craziness—rather it is the consequence of *a craziness that has taken shape in the world.*

The man in the box who is not a man.

He is a human being, a *Homo sapiens,* at least in his origin—but he is not a man in the sense that we consciously understand the term. He is not a man in the full sense of the word. He is not a man.

He is a child.

A child. A child-Box. A child-Box connected to all the boxes in the universe. A child-bubble connected to all the spheres in the world. And, even more terrifyingly, Plotkin realizes that he is not really a living thing. He is a sort of three-dimensional image projected onto the inside of an exorganic iron lung, but one that seems to be able to open at any moment, peeling back like a glove to reveal an infinite catalogue of organs.

The spectral child seems only about twelve years old, but Plotkin cannot truly pinpoint his real age. Undoubtedly his growth stopped at this point in his pseudobiological evolution, and that was probably several years ago. He stands facing a stack of neuroconsoles and several flat screens that are at least two decades old, and are now worth a small fortune since no one knows how to manufacture them anymore.

The dome-child lives in a box, and that is no metaphor. Plotkin sees that he lives in a series of nesting boxes, one inside the other like the Russian matryoshka dolls of his own falsified childhood. Plotkin stares at the child and knows the child is staring at them as well, him and Balthazar, but in his own way—meaning he does not really see them. He sees them only as more or less virtual objects in a universe peopled with objects of varying degrees of virtuality—like himself.

In the first place, he is permanently confined within this iron lung, visibly born of deviant technology from Neon Park, analogous to the bubbles made for children born without immune systems during the previous century. It is made of a nanocomponent polymer with a transparency regulator. It looks like a one-piece cosmonaut's uniform with dozens of umbilical cords made of fiber-optic strands connected to game consoles and several nanocomputer machines ranged all around the chamber. The inside of the box is covered with holoactive control panels that permit the Box-Child to operate numerous programs and devices within the consoles and nanocomputers from inside his bubble.

For Plotkin and Balthazar, it resembles a number of ideograms covering a translucent surface, but seen from the other side of the mirror. Letters, numbers, and codes, wavering in reverse like luminous, esoteric sparkles, while the child enclosed in his bubble uses his fingers, his eyes, his mouth, his brain to manipulate the thousands of bioelectronic components grouped around him.

The hotel contains the dome. The dome contains a wall. The gray wall enclosing the black box. And in the black box is this Box-Child, this bubble child, linked like an incarnate software agent to the Control Metastructure. His own body is nothing more to him than the last of the series of boxes protecting his interior space from outside intrusions. And as for the outside, it seems, his body dedicates its energy to placing the world and its parts in boxes of their own.

At the same time, with the insolence common to paradoxes, the Box-Child, separated from the outside world by this series of walls boxing one another in, lives permanently connected to the world of machines. He is like the aphid, an accomplished symbiotic parasite. His "immunity," his "separation" from the world is doubled, but reversed by the total opening of his body and mind to the ongoing flux of the machines.

He is connected to the world only by this network of machine disconnections, Plotkin muses to himself. *He is connected only in the very place of separation.*

He is truly the paradoxical incarnation of the Technical World.

He is what I have been looking for.

He is the antiworld of the impossible come to interfere with Vivian McNellis's narrative. He is the antiprocess cleaved to the genitive process that created Plotkin, the killer-spy come from the Shadow of the Camp, the Shadow of the Shadow. The Box-Child is the activation of nothingness as ontological operator; he is, himself, the shadow *in* the shadow. He is the overexposed light of technology; he is the blinding terminus and terminator—the moment when it is blinded by itself. He is the moment of greatest danger.

For technology itself, just as for the world it has conquered and that it now threatens with total servitude.

The Machine-Child does not speak; he *communicates.*

A laryngeal implant permits him to send vocal orders to his machines. The digital voice that comes from the small loudspeaker in the child's "second body" seems hardly more human than the one used by Balthazar the bionic dog. The machines, neuroconsoles, nanocomputers, and peripheral systems obey the child like the wizard Merlin's household objects in the Walt Disney cartoon. The machines communicate endlessly among themselves, exchanging information unceasingly and, Plotkin realizes suddenly, terrifyingly, that the Box-Child is *not* the center of a network of machines with which he communicates in every possible manner, and which provides him with a voice—rather, the Machine-Child is the organic link between his machines and the Control Metastructure. The Machine-Child is not at the center; he is on the periphery. He is the interface, the hyperlink; he is a concave space. He is the media used by the machines of this world he has built in a box to communicate among themselves.

Almost simultaneously, he understands the eminent paradox that marks this strange relationship of domination and subjugation between the Box-Child and his machines. In the reign of machines, the reign of horizontal logic, of the monad broken up and doubled over on the full body of the world, the natural hierarchy is not completely gone; rather, it is totally reversed. To dominate, it must submit. To conquer, it must retrench. To grow, it must conserve. And to reign, it must give up its own sovereignty. To be central, it must lose its singularity.

This is what the Box-Child, subject to the Darwinian pressure of adaptation from the moment of his entry into this world, has known how to expand on to the point of outrageousness—to the point of no return, a point located beyond humanity. A point beyond good and evil.

For example, and to start, when Plotkin has asked the first question of what will never truly be a dialogue, this is the response:

"*At this instant of my configuration, my name is:*

1) John Smith
2) Lucas Ford Guadalupe
3) Karl Marx
4) Vic St. Val
5) Tiger Lily
6) Annie Lennox
7) Isidore Ducasse, Comte de Lautréamont
8) John le Carré
9) Steve Cooper Cumberland
10) Edward Teller
11) Edgar Allan Poe
12) Luigi von Saxenhagen

13) Pietro Romanesco

14) Peter Argentine

15) Samantha Fox

16) Gilbert Gosseyn

17) Ezekiel

18) Silver Slade and His Human BlackBox

19) Henry Ford

20) Lloyd Hopkins

21) Jeffrey Alhambra Carpenter

22) Saint Teresa of Avila

23) Debbie Harris

24) Yuri Gagarin

25) Ian Curtis

26) Modesty Blaise

27) Frankie Machine

28) Ennio Morricone

29) Sam Spade

30) Donna Haraway

31) Sergei Diego Plotkin

32) William S. Burroughs

33) Trent Reznor

34) Wernher von Braun

35) Stan Ridgway

36) Francis Crick and James Watson

37) John Sladek

38) Philip K. Dick

39) Marie Curie

40) Genesis P-Orridge

41) Martin Heidegger

42) Brigitte Bardot

43) Bernhard Riemann

44) Benito Mussolini

45) Jules Verne

46) Ted Bundy

47) Miss Blandish

48) Walt Disney

49) Mr. K

50) Howard Hughes

51) Marilyn Manson

52) Averroës

53) Eva Perón

54) James Osterberg aka Iggy Pop

55) Saint Thomas Aquinas

56) Cheyenne Hawkwind

57) Coplan FX 18

58) Claudia Schiffer

59) Balthazar

60) Clovis Drummond

61) Alan Vega

62) Alice Kristensen

63) James Hadley Chase

64) Robert Smith

65) Arnold Schwarzenegger

66) General Custer

67) Johnny Mnemonic

68) Isaac Newton

69) HAL 9000

70) Vivian McNellis and Jordan McNellis

71) Aleister Crowley

72) James Ellroy

73) Stephen Hawking

74) Popeye

75) Gilles Deleuze

76) Scott Davis de la Vega

77) Saul de Sorgimède

78) Jason Texas Lagrange III

79) Salvador Dalí

80) Joe Millionaire

81) Gary Numan

82) Karl Lagerfeld

83) Doctor Strange

84) Clint Eastwood

85) Eric Ambler

86) Iron Man

87) Emma Peel

88) Orville Blackburn

89) Johnny Ramone

90) Neil Armstrong

91) John Morrissey

92) Martin Bormann

93) His Serene Highness Malko Linge

94) Paul Atreides

95) Field Marshal Erwin Rommel

96) Gustave Le Rouge

97) Carter Brown

98) U2

99) Mister M

Check the valid choice."

The list of the Box-Child's ninety-nine names floats before their eyes in the holoplasmic square sitting atop one of the nanocomputers, a ghost screen suspended in the air at the limits of the visible and invisible. Plotkin's own name is on the list, and the names of the McNellises and Cheyenne Hawkwind, amid the myriad names from fiction, myth, reality, invention, and reinvention. There are even collective names—rock groups, for example . . .

The Box-Child knows him, Plotkin tells himself, just as he knows of the existence of Vivian and Jordan McNellis.

The names of the hotel's dog and its manager are also on the list; only the two androids do not appear there. The androids are machines, Plotkin realizes; something in their ontology has prevented the Machine-Child from absorbing their identities. Just like the child's own ontology kept him hidden from Vivian McNellis despite the supernatural gifts of the girl fallen from the sky. There is a series of unfathomable discontinuities there, of quantum leaps occurring between each of them—or *not* occurring. Each of them maintains an equidistant orbit. They may get closer to each other at times, but they can never really share the same space-time, the same world.

But he, Plotkin, the Man from the Hidden Face of the Earth, the Man from the Shadow of the Camp; he, Plotkin, metafiction made flesh, has managed to infiltrate himself into their interworld. He is their interworld, their interface. *He is their medium.*

The Machine-Child has stayed hidden in the dark part of the narration. Even the metatronic powers of the McNellis girl could not fathom the unfathomable. The Box-Child should, for this reason, be considered as the dissolutive agent of any narration. He is the simultaneousness of cybernetic networks. The McNellis girl is the synchronicity of fictional temporalities. And he, Plotkin, is the only being on Earth able to stand at the impossible intersection of their parallel lives. Just as the Box-Child acts as a medium for his machines, Vivian McNellis serves as a medium for her "characters." And he, Plotkin, is the Agent that puts all these incompatible worlds in contact. He is what happens, the bearer of the event, and he knows he is even more dangerous than a piece of chaos fallen to Earth.

He is now the very movement of the mind at the heart of his own narration.

> THE MACHINE-CHILD

He needs to be able to establish contact. It seems as simple as devising a method of communication between two species separated by several light-years of space and a few millennia of time.

Plotkin is the intensified inversion of the Man from the Camp. He is the imaginary Anti-Man from the Camp incorporated in the brain of Vivian McNellis. He is the form condensed, inverted, and divided, then reunified, human, vertical, centered, and mobile.

The Machine-Child, the child with no name—or, rather, with a hundred names minus one—the child with multiple pseudonyms and with only imaginary or fictive references, the child-idiot-genius connected to his machine-organs, the autistic dome-child with his comic books and neurogames and science fiction and pulp novels, the Machine-Child is himself the broad figure of the camp. The broad and rhizomic figure that, separated and fused, scattered, horizontal, nomadic and static at the same time, *metastatic,* is its image made flesh.

He too is creating worlds, but he is their prisoner. He lives in his fortress of numbers, in his network of machines, as if in a projection of his own fundamental autism. For him, the Created World is just a digital universe among millions of others; each snippet of his consciousness forms only one particular combination of the network metaconsciousness; each of his thoughts exists only in the emergence of a thought from the overall cyberstructure.

The fate to which Clovis Drummond regularly forces him to submit, in the guise of "recompense" for his slave work in prohibited neurosoftware trafficking, the fate the dirty snitch of a pedophilic bastard dealer makes him endure, has probably hammered the last nail into the coffin in which the Machine-Child is destined to spend his life, Plotkin thinks. Yet the Machine-Child has not entered into the service of Evil. He has not become wicked like his torturer. Such categorization means nothing to him, because he feels no effect from it. Really, he is already dead. He is already pure entropy. He wanders in his virtual labyrinths, searching, too, for light—but the only light he ever sees is the icy luminescence of the expansion of his network of machine-organs—the creation of a new piece of the labyrinth-world.

Clovis Drummond and his prohibited neurogames and his machinist pedophilia—all of that has simply been placed in one of the boxes of the child with ninety-nine names. And it now holds no more importance than an assembly routine permitting access to one or another of his machine-organs. He is Plotkin's dark side. That is why he lives in the constant light of the incarcerating world of the nexus. He was *counter-produced* by the Creation of Plotkin, but outside the terms of Vivian McNellis's narration—because this incarcerating, subterranean, *shadowy* light from the Camp is what has remained dark in the eyes of the girl from the sky. It is the moment of ultimate Degradation, the moment of being nailed to the cross. It is the moment of total dismemberment, body-mind made to serve the pedophiles of the planet and elsewhere, body-slave become flesh as fodder for the sexual appetites of the manager of the hotel. Body-Machine. Mind-Machine. Child-Machine.

It takes him only a few hours to create neurosoftware on demand, while it would take a team of programmers working full-time weeks, or even months. As Plotkin understands it, if Vivian McNellis— as the feminine incarnate figure of the Celestial Scribe—speaks to men by communicating with their language, this ageless adolescent in the dome does the same thing to *machines,* by communicating via *their* language.

You must be a Machine in order to "dominate" machines.

So the dome-child is a bit more than a man, according to the standards of Neon Park, but he is definitely still less than a machine, because of the singular place—the place of inverted sovereignty—that he occupies in the global rhizome of the Control Metastructure.

Plotkin realizes, as if paralyzed by the appearance of a supernatural truth, that the child represents a totally inverted version of the Christ incarnation. He represents the moment of Degradation in the shadow of the Machine-World.

Christ had to become Incarnate in Man, and to descend to the limits of subhumanity in order to create a world saved by Grace. The dome-child, the child from the human Camp-Universe, must lower himself to be a submachine, the lumpenproletariat of the Great Network of voluntary servitude—or, rather, of subjugated desire, in order to create worlds perverted by and for man, in exchange for a quasi-absolute disincarnation in the horribly immanent horizontality of the world of boxes.

To say he is the Devil would be to say nothing at all.

"The Machine is speaking to you. Do you wish to speak to the Machine?"

Contact. He must make contact.

Plotkin realizes that his own brain is somehow able to read the thoughts of the Machine-Child. It is both strange and fascinating. The thought boxes of the Box-Child emerge sporadically from their machine network and write themselves on the surface of his memory—him, the Man from the Hidden Side of the Earth. But it seems impossible to duplicate the action in reverse, to find any way to print words from the outside on the brain of the young autistic.

Plotkin looks at Balthazar. Balthazar looks at Plotkin.

They understand each other without saying anything.

Yes, contact.

Meaning, for the Box-Child, a disconnection.

* * *

Proceed by disconnection. *A machine is a game of disconnections.* They must find a way to act as a discontinuity in this ontology formed by the ongoing continuum of the machines; they must find a way to divide the zero operator. They must divide what has already been divided, and *divide what has done the dividing.*

"Is your GPS telecontroller still working?" he asks Balthazar.

The dog nods his head.

"Okay, connect to one of his small peripheral nanomachines," Plotkin instructs. "And activate an entry-exit driver with a channel that opens onto nothing."

After a few seconds, the dog sighs. "It's impossible. In this system, everything that opens closes immediately on one of his boxes." He seems genuinely disappointed. "As soon as a channel activates with him, he makes a scheme appear that is specific to the cyberstructure. They're always different. I've never seen that before."

Plotkin understands. The man in the box *is the box;* his mind is the world, the world of boxes that his mind creates as he goes, from software components of the Control Metastructure.

The man in the box is all of humanity.

Each of the Machine-Child's ninety-nine identities was taken from a box; each of them is linked to a singular narrative world. For the Box-Child, who dissolves all narrations, all dialogue, all temporality in the digital acid of the Control Metastructure, the only narrative possible comes from this nominative diagram. The diagram draws a line like an escape route between the boxes themselves; the diagram shows the potential for resistance to the enclosure of incarcerating digital worlds; the diagram shows up like a very weak light lost amid the shadows. The diagram, Plotkin senses with his entire being/nonbeing, is the closest thing possible to life for the Box-Child.

This list.

This list of names.

This list of names that winds among their various boxes of origin to give them a new sense—this list is the life of the Machine-Child; it is what neither Clovis Drummond nor the neurosoftware traffickers can exploit. It is what the colonists in the Ring cannot buy, what the renegade programmers cannot program, what the Neon Park bionicians cannot manufacture, what the illegal body tuners cannot conceive.

It is like literature, condensed to its zero expression point.

And so Plotkin *understands*.

Or rather, so he thinks. To be precise, so he *writes* in his own brain.

Something is occurring in him. He can transcribe the topology of the World of boxes of the Machine-Child directly in his consciousness. He understands that literature too is a game of disconnections, a singular machine. He realizes that maybe now he can begin to *dialogue* with the Machine-Child, by sharing his catalogue of identities.

Each identity is connected to a box, a world, and each world forms an interface with the others. Each box is a lamina, a one-dimensional membrane that serves as a junction between continuums in quantum physics. The boxes are half-open, half-closed; they cannot even be seen as geometric plans. They evoke puckers, lines of cleavage that fold back one on another.

D-branes. Bodybranes. Dimensions incorporated in the organless body of the Machine-Child. Symbolic machines continuously disincarnating the flesh he is barely made of. Bodybranes. In the Middle Ages, Nicolas de Cues described an analogous process. In his memory, Plotkin sees the living fire of the Word coming out of the mouth of Vivian McNellis, speaking to him from the very center of his head: *I'm trying to say that all these creatures folded into God are God, in the same way that once they are unfolded in the Creation of the world, they are the world.*

So he must unwind the thread. He must follow the *vinculum* of the Box-Child. In it, he must try to find the meaning—or co-define it along with him.

And now Plotkin understands the strange bond that unites the Creator and the Creation, the Narrator and the Character; they are built together—they reproduce, at their own level, the movement that occurs between God and His human creatures. The Creation of Man is the moment when God, immutable, eternal, unique, and unknowable, risks ontological change, the moment when He decides to make Himself knowable, mutable, in multiple forms and thus mortal. God is only mortal and mutable in the World of Man—the World Created by His Creation. In the same way, a Narrator will live and die with his character or characters in the Created World of his fiction.

For Plotkin, this will have direct consequences from now on. He is also participating directly in the *Aevum,* the Third Time of the angels. He carries with him this circumspect and discontinuous time Vivian McNellis uses to create her own narrative-worlds. But he can only use it here, where, justifiably, Vivian McNellis cannot.

Here, in the black box under the dome of the Hotel Laika. In the machine-brain of the child with ninety-nine names, in his constant extrojection inside the Control Metastructure of the United Human Universe.

Here. In the shadows.

> *METATRONIC BLACK BOX*

"It's extremely troubling. It's like the incarnation of my crises of infinite division. It's like they have attained cyberorganic synthesis."

Vivian McNellis is standing in front of him, looking like an asteroid is about to crash at their feet.

"Yes, he is the Technical World. His mind never stops dividing—you're right. He divides himself, and in order to do it he constantly divides the world into boxes and brings them together in his Machine-Box, which is really him. It's a sort of antiphysics."

Plotkin's voice seems covered with ice water; it flows from his mouth like a waterfall from a vast frozen block. They are in the McNellises' double room. Jordan June stares out the window with vacant eyes; Balthazar sits near him in a strangely similar position. Dawn, pale as the face of death, rises above Monolith Hills. Men are still sleeping.

"Monopsychism," the girl says.

"What?"

"Monopsychism. The theory of Averroës, supported by some Latin scholar like Siger of Brabant. Saint Thomas Aquinas argued against it brilliantly around 1270."

"There were two identity boxes named Saint Thomas Aquinas and this Averroës in the ninety-nine the dome-child had."

Vivian McNellis's face registers a sudden flash of intense curiosity. "Really?"

"Ah—you absolutely can't make any sort of contact with the

Machine-Child? In any way? You can't even see what I see when I'm under the dome, or what is being written in me? You can't read anything past the entry to the box?"

"No. He is the impossible figure in my narration. He was created when I created you—I mean, when I used the narrative instrument for your creation during my Third Day. But he comes from the bi-day of infinite division, from my anticrisis. He is a totally separate intellect—the materialization of monopsychism. He doesn't think. *Homo non intelligit,* they called it in the thirteenth century."

"He doesn't think?"

"No. He is thought by the *Machine,* thought by his network of boxes that make up the Control Metastructure within him. Understand—in monopsychism, the 'I' is not divided; it is the subject that is cleaved. It is only a point of intersection, without any real singularity, between the intelligible images that mobilize his intelligence and the separate intellect-agent that has inscribed the images in him. He isn't a hacker, or a sort of megavirus that contaminates the Metastructure using a particular system. He is the Metastructure as a whole self, and as the always different, mutable sum of its parts, he retrowrites it directly in his nervous system, I think."

"So, it's like the Metastructure is contaminating him?"

"Yes. That's what makes him the incarnation of monopsychism, the devilish inversion of thought. Averroës and his partisans argued—against all evidence—that Aristotle was the first to invent the concept of a single intellect-agent, simultaneously separated from God and from the human soul, as well as from its intellective part. According to them, this separate intellect-agent thought *through us.* And, in fact, we were thought by it. So, despite our individual differences, a single and unique entity—but not a divine one—thinks constantly via the 'network' of human brains. It *thinks* us, and that isn't all. It *produces* us. Like Saint Thomas said, this is a theory that makes man into an exclusively thought being, not a thinking one."

"Isn't it Descartes that we should invoke to counter the infinite expansion of the Machine-Child?"

"No. That's the first mistake. *Cogito ergo sum* is only a dialectic inversion of the same 'thought.' It isn't about defining the total autonomy of human thought by itself, or the autonomy of a separate intellect-agent that thinks us, either. It is about daring to affirm: *I am not, therefore I think*. It is because I am able to detach my 'thinking' animal destiny from my 'life' contained in death; it is because I conceive of my existence as the dynamic of its own future that I think, and thus I live. I live *outside* of death."

Plotkin stares at the young woman. "I had the same thought during my transnarrative neo-Genesis. Did you—did you keep on thinking me after you produced me?"

"I see what you're thinking, but there is a fundamental difference: I didn't think you; I wrote you. I don't think myself through you, as the monopsychic intellect theories of Averroës would have it. I re-created myself through the process of your creation—meaning, I used the temporary pencil of the Celestial Scribe. My narration can take life, which is what happened, but we remain two distinct, separate entities. I am not even your progenitor. I am not at all the human equivalent of that intellect that is separated but constantly reunited in men in the place of separation—thanks, they say, to the 'images' that serve as contact surfaces for this intellect in the human brain. But also, oddly, like with you, I gave birth to him—or, rather, I opened his antiworld by opening the narrative process of your creation. I am only an instrument of transcription, remember."

Plotkin is quiet for a long moment. Balthazar and Jordan McNellis continue to watch the street in silence. The window is already reflecting the first red rays of dawn.

From now on there is only one question, and it concerns the fate of several human beings. Several human beings teetering on the brink of the abyss.

"What can we do?" Plotkin asks.

"There is only one thing to do," the girl says. "You know what it is."

Plotkin looks Vivian McNellis straight in the eyes. She returns his gaze unblinkingly.

"Kill him?"

"If it turns out to be the only solution. We have to stop his proliferation. At each expansion of the network of semantic boxes through which he is thought, my brain breaks down a little more. He is the active transcription of the counter-effects of my retrotranspositional bursts."

"Bursts?"

"Moments of biophotonic illumination, when I manage to sublimate the Days of Infinite Division. He is the rest. He is the infinitely destroyed indestructible the French writer Maurice Blanchot described."

Plotkin thinks for a moment.

"That means we can't destroy him—we can't kill him. He is already dead. In a way, we have to admit that he is Death itself. Death come alive."

The girl looks at him with large, clear eyes. Her face reflects pure desolation.

"Yes. You're right."

"I am right," Plotkin says dryly. "And that is a very bad sign."

In the machine language of the Machine-Child, the federative slogan of the United Human Universe translates as follows:

```
ONE MACHINE FOR ALL
ONE INTERFACE FOR EACH.
```

The child's multi-identity network draws a complex diagram among the various progenitive boxes, the founding "membranes" of his "personality." They form several subensembles, one sometimes included within another, occasionally with one or more intersections.

First, there seems to be a series of links extending outward from the Clint Eastwood box toward other boxes whose relationships to the first seem to have nothing in common—Marie Curie, for example. The same is true for the Philip K. Dick box and that of General Custer, both of which seem connected to virtually all the other boxes.

He can rapidly trace the specific configuration of "English" boxes, the ones that contain the names of several 1980s rock musicians. He has no idea where this particular semantic grouping might have come from, but he knows now which brain it has come to interfere with.

The Saint Thomas Aquinas and Averroës boxes are linked by the Vivian McNellis box, which serves as an intersection for them. In this, Plotkin sees proof that the Machine-Child assimilates everything within his reach, including the most secret relationships between humans, across times and worlds. And he does it without even the slightest twinge of guilt; he does it because he was thought by the world, the World become Control Metastructure. He does it because his semantic boxes are the equivalent of the "images" through which, according to Averroës and his partisans, our consciousness interfaces with the separate intellect.

The list can bring together fictional beings and real persons, characters from books or movies and authors and playwrights, even actors or actresses representing personages from fiction written by one literary hack or another. The list gives the appearance of a nominalist horizon expanded to its maximum, each of the ninety-nine boxes forming a "degree," a specific section of the space thus created. The list causes the cohabitation of universal myths and utter unknowns. It is truly like the fractal of all humanity.

The simplest grouping is made up of the hotel guests assembled in Vivian McNellis's narration-world. Plotkin sees himself there, and the McNellis girl and her brother, and others—the bionic dog,

Cheyenne Hawkwind, and even Jason Texas Lagrange and the mayor of the city he had once come to kill. But the dome-child also has his "black hole": he could not assimilate the renegade androids into his boxes, and Plotkin senses that this failure will soon provide him with a way to penetrate this monopsychic universe by which "John Smith" is constantly thought. It is because they are created human machines that the Box-Child, a constantly uncreated machine-man, cannot "read" them. The hotel's androids are a key—an encryption—as much as the decryption program connected to him. They will allow him to open the door, to find the access code. The access code to the black box itself. The access code to the machine-head.

"I think I've created something monstrous in spite of myself," Vivian McNellis says.

"The whole world is monstrous," Plotkin says. "You shouldn't take it on yourself."

The hastily thought-up answer does little to console the young woman, whose large, clear eyes seem clouded with vaporous crystal.

"We all create monsters, don't we? When we aren't created *by* them. That's what you're thinking, isn't it?" she whispers.

Plotkin observes the girl closely. She seems to be at the limits of psychic exhaustion. He detects an immense rift in her, a great chasm opening on the purest anguish. In her, he sees the moral terror of the creator. And he—he is that anguish made real, the very incarnation of her terror. He is the Man from the Camp, the Man from the Hidden Face of the Earth, the man with no memory, come to kill the mayor of this city; he is the free man in Capsule 108.

He is Vivian McNellis's monster, and he shares this ontology with the Machine-Child. "The Monster"—*that which is monstrous*. That which makes shadows visible, that which moves in the gray area between Good and Evil. That which is perhaps capable of bearing light into the darkest, densest corner of a black hole.

"We must use the androids," he says.

"What?"

"The androids. The hotel androids. They aren't part of the Machine-Child's genetic list. They aren't in his matrix. And I think I know why."

"Why, then?"

"Because androids are schizophrenic by nature. Their ontology is based on the existential disconnection of non-objects in the Machine-Child's world of membranes-boxes-universes."

"Androids are schizophrenic *by nature?*"

"Yes; I think it was William S. Burroughs who wrote that somewhere."

"Well, how should we use them?"

"I don't know yet. I have to think. Come up with a plan of action. I need to think about what has happened so far, if you know what I mean."

The shadow of a smile flickers over the girl's lips. "I understand completely. You are now the agent of the narrative—you are the engine of your own story. The only one, except for the androids, who can go up under the dome. I have to trust you."

Plotkin looks at the McNellis girl. Her beauty is consuming him slowly, like the fire inside an anaerobic oven. Something inside him is twisting—not an object, or an organ, but something that seems like it might dislocate his whole being from the inside.

"You would be doing the right thing," he says. "You don't have the slightest shadow of another solution."

He is painfully aware that he is actually talking to himself.

"Now I need to cause my own luminous shadow to enter into you," she says.

Plotkin shivers. "What do you mean?"

"Right now your metanarrative power is still only developing. Besides, I don't have any more time. I must give you a part of myself—*sacrifice* a part of myself."

"I have no idea what you're talking about."

"Sacrifice. I must exchange your death for my life."

Plotkin sighs, smiling weakly. "Try to be a little less cryptic for once, please."

"That won't be easy. This entire process involves your future, your present, and even your past. You were created and then rebuilt; you became free, but now you're going to have to fight *against* that freedom. You are going to have to fight against yourself."

"And?"

"I am going to give you what you need to master your burgeoning embryonic power. I am going to give you part of Metatron's power. I am going to give you access to one of the Celestial Pencils."

"Cosmogonic powers?"

"No, I'm not able to do that. But I am going to open a channel for you toward Metatron's black box. That way, you will be able to link your narrative with the Created World—but you won't be able to create anything in itself; you will only be an interface, an entry-exit system toward the black box of the angel of the Face."

Plotkin smiles. "I think that will be quite sufficient."

"Yes, I should say so," Vivian McNellis replies. From out of nowhere she takes a tiny black cube, which she holds out to him in her open palm.

A microbox, no larger than a pill, as black as night.

"What is that, some sort of orbital drug?"

Vivian McNellis smiles feebly. "In a way. This is the noncoding part of my genome, my neuroquantum DNA. It is, so to speak, my flesh and blood. You are going to swallow it."

Plotkin gulps, feeling as if a billiard ball has suddenly become lodged in his throat. "Will I become like you?"

"I already told you, no. But it is true that I don't know exactly what you will become after you swallow it."

"Seeing as I don't even know what I am, I don't think that should be a big problem."

"Then take this capsule. Eat what hasn't yet been destroyed of my genetic code. Try to save us. Please."

Plotkin takes the tiny cube-shaped pill in his hands and puts it in his mouth, this object as black as night and full of mysterious and invisible light.

He is vaguely conscious that actions like his have been initiated for two thousand years, but have all been completely forgotten.

He is conscious that he is reproducing, in a totally opposite way, the ontological act of the Machine-Child.

He knows that, very probably, he will find his "identity" there, that he will find it in becoming one with the Other.

With the one that writes.

> *CONTRACTION OF THE BATTLEFIELD*

In his room again, Plotkin spends long minutes standing in front of the capsule window. The cosmodrome is occupied with its normal daily activity; workers mill about the hangars, and a small Australian-made rocket will be taking off that morning from Platform 1.

Later, sitting on the floor near his helium bed, he contemplates the dozens of sheets of paper scattered around him. The pages written during the seven days of his neo-Genesis.

It is in this heterogeneous mass of notes that the mystery of his own identity lies, just as the Machine-Child hides in the relationships among the various nominative boxes of his "personality." He, like Plotkin, was created but possesses no proper existence. Neither of them was ever *born*.

Plotkin realizes that this is true of most fictional characters.

They are the opposite of angels, whose cognitive and vital cone is closed at the source but open to infinity at the other end. For fictional characters, it is the original opening that is infinite.

When the plot begins, a man is already born without his birth having necessarily been written in the Created World of the Fiction. As the first words of the story unfold, he has no real identity, no parents, barely even a present. He is a new being that develops in a series of white pages that his action and life turn black with ink. Death does not come to him, even though he remains a mortal like other men.

Now that Vivian McNellis's metanarrative power seems to have been at least partially given to him, Plotkin can see more sense in these scattered notes that run from interpersonal diagrams and plans of the Independent Territory to mysterious usage directions for purely abstract machines.

It is the very plan of his own narration. It is his own life there, like the outline of a yet-to-be-written novel; its base documentation, its first limner notes.

Dazed, he realizes that many of the improvised diagrams appear to sketch the figure of the Box-Child himself, like the luminous shadow of the Metastructure.

There is a flash of light in him, a sort of pyrolexical energy that zigzags in the pure sky of his mind. He gathers up his notes in a manner that seems frenzied even to him and, seated at his desk, begins to write. He feels the burning vibrations of a halo of fire around him. He feels the combustive power of the verb. He feels so strong that he wishes for nothing more—except to be this fire, cast down upon the Earth.

First, the matrixes. The interplay between characters, and their relationships.

He must convince one of the androids to go with him up under the dome, to make "first contact" with the Machine-Child. He must get Cheyenne Hawkwind on his side. And at the same time, he must try to make Clovis Drummond into a sort of temporary ally in his search for a Golden Track. He will undoubtedly have to use the cyberdog again. It will probably be necessary to go back to HMV and meet with the Christian rebels there. And almost definitely, he will have to go see the old seer at the abandoned interchange. Each character must be placed end to end, like forces whose meetings will create the narrative-world itself.

But the matrixes make no sense unless they are opened to give birth to the life they contain. They must be destroyed if there is to be any hope of producing something.

So he must manage to create a retrovirus capable of rewriting, in a minuscule amount of space and time, this hotel at the end of the world and the effecting of his identity as a flesh-and-blood man. The Fire must take substance in his own body. The metamorphosis must take place. He must be able to observe, or rather to hide from himself, the secret *vinculum* of the narration, and he must produce a discontinuity capable of short-circuiting the Box-World of the Machine-Child.

And I must not place the World in the boxes-cum-thoughts, the ones thinking us, he muses. *I must place the boxes in the narrative of the Created World, so that we can think them.*

I must dare to take the step. The step toward the abyss.

Vivian McNellis's metatronic black box will permit him to do it.

He will be the invisible cord, the ray of light that will release all the boxes from their self-enslavement and that will read them, at the same time, in the bright light of freedom. He will write his own life; he will live what he is writing as he writes it. He will not only be free; he will not only be full of this absolute sensation—he will be in a position to propagate it, like a fire cast down on the Earth.

It is already happening.

At first it is there like the strange return of a past that never really existed, like the unexpected backwash of ancient information from an even more ancient world.

Using a microjack interface, he connects a block of nanocellulose sheets to the room's console, to which he has downloaded word-processing software. He grasps the laser pen and begins to inscribe the first tangible symbols of his new freedom on the untouched page. Just then, a message appears on the small holoplasmic screen of the machine and on the electronic sheet attached to it. It is a simple e-mail sent from an anonymous redialer, a solidly encrypted text that says, briefly and concisely:

Sputnik Centennial, October 4
    Orange zone downgraded to yellow for 300 meters on
Cassini Avenue, Novapolis North, between 6:35 P.M. and 6:45
P.M. Insufficient protection for official vehicles against hyperki-
netic munition. No countermeasures capable of deactivating re-
mote magnetic cannon triggers. No active GPS for ten minutes.
Your "launch window."

It is truly a message from another world, another narrative. It is
very strange, the sensation that this text was written by himself in a
preceding life, while he was thinking of his plan to Kill the Mayor of
This City. The e-mail from Order agents, infiltrating the municipality
of Grand Junction at the highest level, says nothing other than what
he added himself, like the fatal conclusion of his analysis of the future
"crime scene."

This e-mail, which, during the first time of his plot, his "existence," would have brought him strategic information concerning
enemy security systems, now proves to be the simple lexical sum-
mary of the assassination he planned. It is as if his first brain has sent
him, through a window open to time and space, his own thoughts of
the time. It is as if this second brain is able to capture it. Almost as if
a third brain is at work.

This third brain, he realizes without knowing where this blinding
intuition is coming from; he is in the process of activating this third
brain. The DNA black box of Vivian McNellis is starting to take effect. He feels it with his whole being, a little more strongly every second, like a column of fire that is creeping through him bit by bit,
straight as an I in its chair and enveloping his organs from feet to
head, from his penis to his brain.

His third brain has been born from the disjunctive synthesis of
the first two. He is going from written character to writing being. He
is going from thought non-man to thinking Counter-Man.

The ball of fire concentrates in that part of him that is *not him* yet not anyone else; the ball of fire surrounds it, yet does not stop shining inside his being.

The ball of fire envelops his nerves now, like a several-million-volt electric current.

Now the ball of fire is what he is writing.

Now the ball of fire is what he is living.

The paradox is obvious, but the pyrotechnics occurring in his brain now seem to be of little importance. He is an elementary particle, double in nature. He is a "supercord." He is a quantum field become a man.

He is writing at his desk in Capsule 108 of the Hotel Laika, but at the same time his other "I," now become an "I-other," is simultaneously updating the narrative in the Created World.

He knows it. He is fully aware of it. It is a sensation as strong as being confronted with his own death, or his own birth.

Scoring of the subject, parturition of the narration, reunification of the world.

On one side, an objective vision: the free man in Capsule 108, the man who is writing, surrounded by a trembling halo. On the other side: subjective life, activation of the being in the real world, activation of the real in the concrete being. And in the middle: shadows, amid which the box-world of the Machine-Child expands endlessly.

And the counter-light that emerges from it all is Plotkin, who bears it, who holds a laser pen, a Celestial Pencil, in his hand. It is he who is writing it, bringing it out of nothingness, bringing it to its point of ultimate incandescence, there where everything that is within us reaches its point of sublimation.

The plot that begins now is being issued from his mouth like a filament of light connected to his hand, to the pen, to the artificial paper, to the electrons that carry it, to the bits of information that move at the speed of light to the word processor. The world processor. The plot that begins, in the fireball of his existence—cum—ecstatic spiral, is not the story of his life, the story of his present endlessly reiterated; it is the very narrative of his transfiguration, the impact zone of freedom at the heart of necessary immune defenses; it is the absolute tension between the being and the nonbeing. It is the retroviral intrusion of the black box into itself, the apoplectic moment when everything must disconnect in order to make sense, where everything must combine in order to better divide, where everything will at last take life. Even into death.

It is the moment when his freedom will have the ability to destroy not only what he was but everything he could have been.

So now the lived narration is in parallel with the living writing: two fields, correlated to each other like the two ends of the "supercord."

Let us observe the placing of the narrative-world into the multiplex, he writes. *Let all the light contained in shadow escape—this light that is blacker even than night.*

Plotkin in the halls of the Hotel Laika. Plotkin in the elevator. Plotkin in the southern corridor on the sixth floor, heading toward Capsule 066, where Cheyenne Hawkwind is staying.

His hand clamps like an octopus to the screen of the door's scanner. Identification. Mechanical respiration of the door. Impersonal voice of the artificial intelligence. Dialogue between machines with varying degrees of humanity. Opening of the capsule door with a hiss of ionized air.

Plotkin in Capsule 066, face-to-face with Cheyenne Hawkwind, the man in black, the man from the heart of night, the wolf-man for man, the man he knows is like a brother to him, a blood brother, the blood of all men killed by their hands.

"Your e-mail on the hotel intranet said you wanted to see me. That you had some extremely important things to tell me."

Plotkin faces the American Indian, body-tuned into a Japanese

American. Plotkin, like a human computer, calculating all the possibilities within his reach, and further. Plotkin, in Capsule 108, writing as fast as he can, as if driven by an internal, *infernal* rocket. Plotkin, who must now bring together all the critical parts of the narrative.

"Yes," he says. "I have some very important things to tell you. It may take a while."

Cheyenne Hawkwind observes him with night-black eyes. He scrutinizes him down to the deepest parts of his soul. Cheyenne Hawkwind, the killer he might have been, the killer he was. Worst of all, the killer that looks at him now like a brother.

"Should we sit down, so we can talk?"

"Yes, I think it would be better if we did."

Plotkin ensconces himself in the depths of his armchair, facing Cheyenne Hawkwind. He observes for a moment the intense light that illuminates the capsule window; the small private Australian rocket is taking off, a conical jet of yellow fire cutting through the blue morning sky. The standard rumbling that marks the rhythm of life in Grand Junction sounds all around them before fading away softly, like a world being slowly swallowed up by the ocean of the sky.

"So," the Indian killer says. "What do you have to tell me that is so important?"

Plotkin's quick smile, like a harbinger. The rocket disappearing toward the boreal zenith. The Hotel Laika, where everything will play out. Where everything is already playing out. The light, so beautiful, in the window.

"The first thing I have to tell you," Plotkin murmurs as if through a cloud of liquid nitrogen, "is that your trafficking in prohibited sex programs toward the Ring with Clovis Drummond isn't secret any longer. The second thing is that I don't give a flying fuck. The third thing is that I want you to come and work for us."

Cheyenne Hawkwind's face is like a waxen bronze-colored mask. His features are absolutely still. Nothing in him indicates the slightest trace of emotion. He is much more than a blood brother; he is blood itself, the blood of all the brothers he has killed. *He is beautiful,* Plotkin says to himself. *As beautiful as a bull about to disembowel its victim.*

"Work for you? Who is this 'you'?"

"Me, for a start. You might say I'm the chief spokesman. The only one."

Plotkin, face-to-face with his blood brother, face-to-face with the killer from Montana, face-to-face with the bull that tears open stomachs. Plotkin, face-to-face with cold silence, face-to-face with hands calmly folded on knees. Plotkin, face-to-face with professional death.

"What do you want from me?"

Plotkin, suspended in his emotional cloud of liquid nitrogen, knows that he and Cheyenne Hawkwind are now on the same wavelength. They will speak the same language, employ the same codes; they will speak about life, death, and money.

They will speak about what counts.

"The first thing I want from you is for you to find me a valid black-market Golden Track somewhere on the strip. You'll have to pay an arm and a leg for it."

"That's not exactly my specialty."

"But it might as well be Clovis Drummond's, and that brings me to the second thing I want you to do."

"Meaning?"

"Meaning I want you to double-cross that bastard Drummond. I want him to help you find the Golden Track, then for you to take it from him. I want him to disappear from the globe as completely as if he never existed."

"What makes you think I'm capable of doing something like that?"

Your eyes, thinks Plotkin. *The eyes I saw that day in the hotel cafeteria, the eyes of a cold-blooded killer.* And without even the shadow of a smile except perhaps the one that habitually hovers around the mouths of calm men, completely sure of himself, Plotkin lays his cards on the table.

"Twenty-five thousand Pan-Am dollars. That's what makes me think you're capable of doing something like that."

In Cheyenne Hawkwind's eyes, he sees the lively gleam of the human world's cruelty. In the American Indian killer's eyes is everything capable of making a life evaporate for even less than that.

Clovis Drummond is already dead.

Seated at his desk in Capsule 108, Plotkin lives/writes the small piece of the world in which he, a flesh-and-blood being, is yet himself and the other at the same time, the two connected by the invisible light of the narrative fire. For example, he writes: *Textual matrix number two: go beyond the Machine, beyond the hidden traps it contains, beyond all the humanity it bears within it.*

He walks down the hallway on the top floor, toward the service staircase, toward the dome, toward the realm of the Machine-Child.

Sydia Sexydoll is at his side, holding herself very straight, visibly racked by near-total anguish, as if walking through a corridor of death toward an open doorway to the unknowable.

"You don't need to be afraid," he tells her. "He won't see us. He can't read you. But you will help me make contact with him."

The artificial girl doesn't reply. She accepted Plotkin's offered deal barely ten minutes earlier: a meeting with the HMV Christians in the company of Balthazar, and undoubtedly a temporary exile with the old clairvoyant at the interchange. Anything rather than remain on the strip, Plotkin had thought. She is ready to do anything in order to join the rebel community. Ready to do anything to receive the unction of baptism, to finally begin her new life.

Ready to accompany him under the dome, up to the Machine-Box of the Machine-Child. Ready to confront the nothingness, if she must.

* * *

The Machine-Child is nothing to her but a vulgar mechanism. For Sydia Sexydoll, android-whore manufactured in orbit, this scrap of humanity enclosed in his iron lung and his network of machines is far less human than she herself.

He sends out the image of the Devolution the world has undergone in the last thirty years: he is no longer human; he is not even an artificial humanoid; he is less than a machine. He is the *nihil*.

"What must I do?" she asks in a low voice.

"Nothing for now. I need to establish a few . . . er, *literary* procedures. First I have to be sure I have correctly figured out how his ontology works. Then I'll tell you."

In Capsule 108, at the other end of the "supercord," Plotkin, in his globe of fire, retrowrites the narration of which his I-other has become the engine. He, himself, is the fuel. The fuel and the combustion, like in the old propellant engines used by Grand Junction's pioneers to launch themselves toward the stars. Oxygen, hydrogen. Fire.

If they are to proceed with their game of disconnections against a being made up specifically of a metastable and infinite ensemble of mechanical disconnections, they will have to reckon with the dangers of reversibility. In the case of the Machine-Child, a game of disconnections, capable of disrupting the ontogonic process folded back on itself, would truly be a *suit of armor*.

A body.

Not his, not the body of the Man from the Camp, because he is mind, fire, ether, capable of reading and surely also of writing in the exconscious of the autistic youth, but he cannot really be the body of the text. He will be the narrative, but he will need support. A medium. A book.

And this book, this material assemblage on which his transcription of the Machine-Child can take place, this book-machine, of course, is she.

She, the android.

* * *

The second game of disconnections, in this case the metastable structure that will open like a suit of armor, refracts in the sort of ontological Larsen effect between the different "sexualities" in play.

Sydia Sexydoll is a living machine endowed with feminine sexuality. Plotkin is the Man from the Imaginary Camp; he is a man, but he is fictional. The Machine-Child is neither a man nor a woman, neither male nor female, and not because he is like the finished form of an androgynous hermaphrodite from Neon Park. Rather, because he is *neither one nor the other.*

Scanning the expansive brain of the Machine-Child in his active transnarration, Plotkin follows the invisible thread linking the identity boxes and reads in them the specific psychic makeup of the dome-child. Deprived of all sexuality by the general devolution dis(incarnate) in his own existence, which is limbic, he feels no effect—no desire—so that even the concept is completely alien to him. Drummond's pedophilic acts merely strike him as a bit strange.

But the android former prostitute has had her sexual desire nanocenters deprogrammed with the obvious aim of adopting a monastic life after being baptized by the rebel Christians, if they accept her.

There is a diagram there, but one united by inversion. In it lies how to extend the invisible filament linking the boxes all the way to a suit of armor he will incarnate like writing, like truth.

He has no idea what effect this will have on the brain of the Machine-Child, on his exconscience that mimes and reproduces the Control Metastructure. Will it kill him, one way or another?

Yes, it will undoubtedly kill him, one way or another.

But isn't that what he is? A killer?

That is certainly what the divided scribe in his room in the Hotel Laika believes, in any case, because that is how the plot has put him into the world.

Plotkin is a free man; he was written and then retrowritten by himself. He is in the service of the girl fallen from the sky, but the indelible core of his identity, which was only transfigured by his seven-day neo-Genesis, has always been the Red Star Order's man. He is now an assassin-turned-renegade, a traitor to his employers and perhaps to everything on which the secret world of assassins is based, the entire narrative system organized so that his life and activities will obey his distant—so very distant—bosses.

But he is now in the Third Time. He is using a tiny spark of the creative powers of his own creator. He will be able to write a little sense, with a little blood, into this world where death itself is invisible, immaculate, and technically assisted.

He is a free man, and that means he is a man most likely at the point of death. He knows this, and the thought is calm, comfortable, natural.

"It has started," Plotkin says to the artificial girl. "I'm in the process of retrotranscribing the Machine-Child's data into my narrative. Don't be afraid. Your presence will allow me to . . ."

For a moment, he is lost for words.

"Will allow you to what?" the girl asks.

He hesitates a moment more before launching the idea like a jet of fire into the sky. "You will act as my word processor; I mean, my integrated writing system. With just your presence alongside the Machine-Child's, I'll be able to integrate his method of sensory perception, his specific 'principle of individuation,' to be precise, and I will be able to try to understand how to destroy his anticreative energy, his metastatic expansion in the form of UniWorld, which is in the process of killing the person I work for."

The artificial girl seems utterly uninterested in the identity of his employer, or by all these narrative subtleties; she looks at him with her violet-flecked black eyes, the eyes of a human machine wishing to receive a soul and to be saved; she looks at him with the intensity of those who know very well what they are doing, and her gaze says: *I will do everything you ask, but you must keep your promises.*

> SCRIPTURA IN CORPORE

Later, Plotkin writes in his chamber, *a quantum leap, a sliding of time on Earth, passage toward the next action, pursuit of the Procession, return to Capsule 081: the Fire is there. It is everything that is.*

"Who is this android?" Vivian McNellis demands.

The artificial girl is standing next to the girl-angel. Both fallen from the sky; they stand with their backs to the window of Capsule 081-A, backlit, their silhouettes outlined with a delicate tracing of silver light. The two women look at each other with the magnificent calm of stars just before they explode. The surveillance camera records the scene without the slightest understanding of what is happening under its globular eye.

"Yes," Plotkin says, full of the fire of writing in action. "She is a Venux. A bionic prostitute. She had all her sexual centers deprogrammed—by a Neon Park underbrain, I imagine."

Vivian McNellis turns to face the artificial girl. "Why did you do that?" Her voice holds total incomprehension, but at the same time it is horribly clear that she understands the reasons all too well.

There is a long silence. Plotkin gazes out the window at the monochromatic blue of the sky. The day is calm, without snow, extreme heat, or rain. A blue day, very pure, very beautiful, and deadly full of ultraviolet radiation. WorldWeather does what it can.

"A lot of Christians practiced voluntary castration during the time of the Church Fathers. Origen and Tertullian, I think, among others," Jordan McNellis says.

Vivian does not drop the android's gaze.

"That's it? That's what Plotkin is talking about? You want to join the rebel Christians in HMV? Is that why you had yourself deprogrammed?"

This time, the voice manufactured by Venux Corp comes out in a quivering whisper, just barely audible. "I have no choice. I have to rub out all traces of their scum."

Plotkin feels as if he has been sliced open from the inside. The writing is truly creating itself if it proves capable of retrotranscribing the world in someone's head. If the artificial girl is going to serve as a textual suit of armor for him in order to undo the antinarrative of the Machine-Child, it will be precisely because she acts in that arena as an intensified inversion of this child without age, birth, or sexuality. The Machine-Child has no sexuality because he has all of them, and they destroy one another. The artificial girl was bioprogrammed as a sexual female capable of satisfying human desire of all the planet's inhabitants.

She had herself deprogrammed. The Machine-Child has no need to do so.

He is a pure program.

In Capsule 108, Plotkin the Scribe uses a laser to trace the filament of light that guides Plotkin the Killer in this world where humans have become instruments of calculation for others.

In the double Capsule 081, little by little Plotkin the Killer brings together the elements of critical mass, and he does it with all the terrifying, childlike naïveté of the man inventing his own life; he does it with all the innocence of a human who knows what it is to self-destruct.

"How will she be useful to us? What will we use her for?"

For Vivian McNellis, the android is just another means to an end.

"She will allow me to rewrite the Machine-Child's narrative. I will be able to dialogue with him, and thus to break his self-enclosure. I will use Sydia like you are using me. I will retrowrite everything, and—"

The artificial girl's voice trembles in the silence of the room. "Yes, and that way I too will have a soul."

"When do you go back up under the dome?" Vivian McNellis asks.

"As soon as possible. At the same time, I have to draw all the diagrams of the narrative. Everything is falling into place, I think. Yes, it's all falling into place."

"You need to act fast now, Plotkin. Time is short, especially for me."

Plotkin notes the presence of a solar gleam in the eyes of the girl fallen from the sky. In the backlighting, he seems to perceive filaments of light running beneath her skin, like visible nerves. The natural light of this beautiful autumn day can undoubtedly, for a while at least, mask these physical transformations from strangers' eyes. He knows the local cameras don't have the ability to read anything of this nature, but the simple effect of the backlighting has allowed him to see the manifest presence of this light hidden in the depths of shadow, this secret cerebrospinal system hidden in the depths of her body.

Once more, the necessity appears to define existence as an ontological experience whose goal is to allow the being to emerge from its gangue, its "existential" box, its dead mechanism that opens only onto the emptiness of monopsychism, this shadow of the world that claims to think us.

He needs a meeting in the *Aevum,* the length of discontinued time, a new walk in the midnight of unknowable light with the girl fallen from the sky. He needs Vivian McNellis to come to him here in Capsule 108. He needs this end of the Plotkin supercord to recognize, like enemy terrain, what will now happen. It is an exhortation, a prayer.

New quantum leap.

New disorbit.

New paragraph.

He is reunified once again. The quantum-field Plotkin is an I-other-he in a single person.

"In the *Aevum,* the operation of infinite division is suspended—for 'humans,' at least. Here, you can never be more than one, because the basis of Metatron's narrative trinity is the 'notional action' Saint Augustine and Saint Thomas spoke of, and it is what the nominalists ravaged until something as horrible as the Metastructure was finally able to exist."

"What do you mean? Again, I don't—"

"The trinity. The three divine entities cannot be understood as separate concepts. And to do this, you must grasp their ontology as a *Procession that becomes a Relationship.* All three of them shine forth together, not separately, but because of the relationships between them. Love, in the first place. That is how the Holy Spirit is God, and the Son is God, and the Father is God. That is why you are a man."

"What exactly is happening in you?"

"I am dying. Or, rather, I am preparing to be reborn. It is the final phase of the retrotranspositional burst. Understand the process: Junk DNA is in fact, to give you a modern image, a sort of quantum meta-computer connected to all the information in the Universe. DNA is mutable; many genes are mobile. They are called 'transposons.' In junk DNA, many transposons come from an RNA retrotranscriptase, meaning from the introjection of genetic information from the outside. Only the mechanist dimwits in the Metastructure believe DNA is some sort of 'fixed' program that 'codes' proteins. The true thinkers are running scared these days, but they know what they are talking about. When the retrotranspositions happen on a massive scale, and in my 'supercritical' case, then what happens is what's happening to me now. I am incorporating all the information in the Universe. And soon I will incorporate not only the visible World, but the invisible World as well."

"I'm not sure I completely understand. What do you mean by 'invisible World'?"

"More than 96 percent of the mass of the Universe is made of *dark matter,* which plays a central role in the very configuration of our continuum, and 98 percent of our genetic code is made of a 'metacode,' a 'genetic dark matter,' if you like. During the final process, my junk DNA will have digitally incorporated this 96 percent of the invisible universe. But the Box-World of the Machine-Child is the greatest danger to this process. It may make it so that instead of the light incorporating itself into me, it will unincorporate itself entirely within the Metastructure. You must understand that it is both *because of* it and *thanks to* it that I could, that I had to do all this. It is from it that I gained the narrative powers of Metatron; it is in it that the divine black box took shape. But if the Machine-Child's brain succeeds in assimilating the statistic totality of the Metastructure, I will be fucked."

"I understand," Plotkin says. "Finally, I think. It won't happen."

Small pause in the solar fire, new quantum leap, new paragraph.

"The Control Metastructure is a sort of social materialization of the monopsychic entity of Averroës and his nominalist successors like Siger of Brabant and William of Ockham," Vivian McNellis tells him. "It was here that what Friedrich Nietzsche called the specific nihilism of Christian religion was born, and it was here that History really began. And it is here, in the world of the mid-twenty-first century, that it will end. That is why the Machine-Child has no real name, because for him the word is the thing, the map is the land, the world is a concept. It is the absolute negation of the Created World, not like God made it, by its absolute constriction, its Tzimtzum, but rather by the infinite expansion of the separate concepts of things, and thus things separated from their names, and therefore from what they are."

"All right," Plotkin says after a moment. "There is something fundamentally dead in this 'zoon,' but it's strange—he seems to have something . . . *living* . . . about him, something foreign to himself."

"Every principle has its opposite principle. That's an old nondialectical law from the Church Fathers."

"Its opposite principle? Yes, that must be it."

"What are you thinking about?"

"Something that escapes him; something that will let me enter him. Something he is completely ignorant of."

"He is completely ignorant of himself, you mean."

"Yes and no. He knows exactly what he is; that is why he lives in his boxes. Everything there is perfectly arranged, coded, stamped. At the same time, none of his boxes can be called a 'memory,' because it is not he who thinks, but the Metastructure that thinks him."

"So, what are you planning to do?"

"Among his ninety-nine identity boxes, his 'central multiplicity,' if I can call it that, I sense the repeated copresence of an element that cannot be considered a simple statistic reproduction of the Metastructure."

"What is it?"

"Music. Images. The 1970s and 1980s. I don't know exactly. Clint Eastwood, Alan Vega, Kraftwerk . . . there is something here that makes sense, something that lives, or wants to live."

"Yes," Vivian McNellis says after a moment. "In the same way the female android wants to live, to have a soul of her own. Which actually means that she already has one. When will you go back up under the dome?"

Plotkin looks at the body of the girl fallen from the sky, draped in a simple black dress. The light that flows under her skin, this network of biophotonic nerves that is superimposing itself on the physical network, shines through the Recyclo™ linen lace as if the veil of fabric doesn't even exist. This light says something; it says: *Matter and light are not contrary principles articulated by the negation of the dialectic. They are copresent principles, one within the other.* . . .

"They burned Giordano Bruno for thinking the same thing," Vivian McNellis says, in a slightly tense voice.

"Really? For so little?"

"In 1600. The Reformation. The Counter-Reformation. The Thirty Years' War wasn't far off. The invention of modern ideologies, nationalism, socialism, liberalism. Christianity was beginning its long era of decadence, and a man came along and said, magnificently bringing together the secrets of the patristic world that were slowly being forgotten, scorned by the bad side of the famous 'logic' razor of William of Ockham: *'We no longer believe that any body is without a soul, or even, according to the lies of some people, that matter is nothing more than a shithole of chemical substances.'* "

Plotkin is silent for a moment. He gazes at the beautiful blue sky out the window. Then he looks at Vivian, allowing himself to be consumed by the delicate fire of her features.

"Yes," he says at last. "I understand. I understand why he was burned for so little."

Around 1600, Giordano Bruno invented infinity. He conceived divine creation as infinity, meaning as a constant process of relations between the three divine entities. He did not believe that the Created World was itself eternal; but the process that had created it *was*. He directly threatened the ultranominalist thought that had already taken possession of minds at the time, and which caused individuals, entire populations, huge masses of humanity to kill one another for the sake of names, "ideas," political and so-called philosophical concepts. For the sake of words separated from reality, but taken for the things themselves. He threatened the pernicious return of what would one day become the ultimate mechanism of global alienation, the societal monopsychism of the Metastructure. He threatened the world of the future, or rather of the non-future.

So Giordano Bruno was burned.

Four hundred years later, the Metastructure dominated the world.

And half a century after that, the world as such does not exist.

And these "things," entities like the Hotel Laika and its cyberdog, Grand Junction, HMV, Neon Park, sexed androids, the girl fallen from the sky, the Machine-Child, and he, Plotkin, the Counter-Man from the Camp-World, are able to claim existence.

"We are the end of the fourth great biblical cycle. The first went from Adam to Enoch, the second from Noah to Moses, the third from Elijah to Jesus Christ, and the fourth from Mary and the apostles to today. You might relate the time to one or two human generations."

"Yes, I remember sharing this knowledge with you when you incorporated me into the world, in you, in the Chinese camp."

" *'From nothing,'* said Saint Thomas Aquinas, and I think he was aiming his words directly at Averroës and his Latin scholastic thurifers, *'from nothing, the angels have extracted the knowledge of specific things.'* He also added: *'This feeling derogates from the Catholic faith, which teaches that the things of this world are governed by angels, according to the words of the Epistle to the Hebrews 1:14: they are all spirits that administer. If, in fact, they have no knowledge of the specific, they cannot have providence of the things that happen in this world, if events and acts are the area of concrete and specific things.'* Later, to counter yet again this monopsychic theory that deprived the being of its universal character in order to better annihilate its singular, he added: *'Because administration, and providence, and movement bear on the singular according to how it exists then and there, in its concrete being, with all the conditions that individuate it.'* Don't you see, Plotkin, it was also obvious for Saint Thomas that *'God intercedes not only in what touches universal nature, but also in what is the principle of individuation.'* Do you understand now? You, me, the Machine-Child, the androids, this city, we are the experimental battlefield for a war between Metatron, the Celestial Scribe, and the Control Metastructure, that viral supermechanism that has taken possession of this world, this humanity, this particular 'universe.' "

"You think that if I destroy the Machine-Child, I will destroy the Metastructure too?"

Vivian McNellis's laugh is like sunrise crystal. "You are still confusing the singular and the universal. The Machine-Child is a living metaphor. It is because I produced him without knowing it that he is destroying me, without knowing it either. In comparison, the Metastructure itself is only a minor obstacle. But its time is limited. That much is certain."

"Maybe it is the opposite . . . maybe the best way to destroy the Metastructure would be to endow the Machine-Child with a real life, and—"

Vivian cuts him off. "The fate of the Metastructure doesn't interest me at all. What is important is that my transmutation does not lead to the pure chaos of entropy, and that I get back to the Ring in time, even if it means the destruction of this . . . this *thing.*"

Plotkin doesn't answer.

Angels have power over life and death. Angels fall to Earth sometimes, and take human form.

The form of a woman, for example.

Vivian McNellis smiles. "I'm sure you will succeed."

New quantum leap.

New passage. New unitary separation, I-he-other.

New chapter.

> IN CAPSULE 108, PLOTKIN WRITES: CRYPTIC ZONES

He knows he is heading into something virtually unknowable. That he will have to break through the wall of light, and that it will be harder and more concrete than the thick concrete wall of a universe.

Plotkin writes: *I can be "I" while being "he"; I can be another while being myself. I can enter into you now, Machine-Child, because I am the agent of Metatron's black box, his soldier of fortune, his mercenary, his servant. I am his pawn. The pawn of a gambit of the stars.*

What is about to happen will almost certainly be utterly terrible, and yet I can barely conceive of what form it will take. What is about to happen will be an ontological cataclysm of which I can know nothing before it comes to change me, to finally make me become what I am. What is about to happen is: Plotkin in the service stairway again with Sydia Sexydoll. Plotkin who knows that, at that moment, Cheyenne Hawkwind is discussing "business" with Clovis Drummond, in a bar somewhere on the strip, to find a black-market Golden Track. Plotkin, now ready to work on the body armor of the text, ready to make the android girl into a biological book via which he will dialogue with the organ-machines of the Box-Child.

"I am ready," the artificial girl said.

You will never be ready enough, thinks Plotkin.

For he is already beginning to imagine-produce the sequence of events; he is beginning to sense the specific form these events will take; he is beginning to draw the diagrams of their reciprocal surges.

And it is hardly within the capabilities of a human brain to describe it.

Well it's 1969 okay
All across the USA
It's another year for me and you
Another year with nothing to do

Plotkin does not know why he has chosen this box, rather than one of the other ones forming the 1970s-1980s electric rock configuration, in the extrojected brain of the Machine-Child. A vague intuition: 1969 was just before the beginning of this double decade; it was the year when Neil Armstrong set foot on the moon, and the Iggy Pop box is connected to the astronaut's by this simple chronological relationship. But they are in Grand Junction. With the other boxes that form the "electric rock" subidentity, the Iggy Pop box has a fundamental reference value, but as with everything that concerns the mind-world, the *anti-mind anti-world* of the Machine-Child, it is integrated as a simple part of the machine, a bit of circuit; all the boxes function that way, whatever their specific diagrams: among them, all, everything forms an infinitely repeated *circle,* without beginning or end, without singularity or difference.

His choice of the song "1969," off the first Stooges album, might well prove as meaningless as everything else.

But it doesn't. It works.

It is the voice of the female android that sings the song. Plotkin has wrought his textual body armor; the voice is emitted directly in the neural centers of the child. Plotkin watches the artificial girl beside him begin to come apart. Eyes closed, she murmurs the words of the song while, bit by bit, her body seems to flatten like a clinical diagram, a visual catalogue of separate organs.

The miracle is taking place.

The event rises out of the exconscious annihilism of the Box-Child, and like any true event it comes in the form of a phrase.

Through words.

Words the child cannot express by mouth, at least not solely. The words write themselves simultaneously on all his machine-organs, his holoplasmic screens, the visioptics incorporated into his iron lung, and even, for a moment, shine for a brief instant amid the shadows into which the vast network of his boxes was thrown at the moment of his arrival in this world.

For the first time, the words do not indicate only the action of a program on a group of nanocomponents. They make sense—in any case, they try to say something to a human interlocutor. The words say: *You see, in this world there's two kinds of people, my friend: those with loaded guns and those who dig. You dig.*

It's from the Clint Eastwood box. The artificial girl repeats the phrase like a living sampler. The Clint Eastwood box glows. *The Good, the Bad, and the Ugly,* a Sergio Leone Western, is the source of the famous quote. The box plunges into darkness. ON/OFF.

Plotkin persists.

Dialogue without dialogy, monologues interlaced on the disconnected body of the android.

New quantum leap. New passage into the very interior of the narrative.

New paragraph.

New disconnection.

Here, now, nothing exists but names and words that circulate in every sense of the word. It is as if Plotkin is entering the heart of an asemantic, atopic vortex, filled with nothing but cold shadows closing in on the still colder light that illuminates the boxes in which the Machine-Child endlessly reconfigures the world via the Control Metastructure. It is like a monstrous beast made of pure nothingness, a space impossible to describe with Euclidean terminology. The Metastructure looms in his field of vision like a gigantic nominal list of machine-organs designating each part of the world it controls, and Plotkin knows that this also has everything to do with the mind-machine of the child with ninety-nine names.

At his side, the artificial girl is now prostrate against one of the walls of the Box-House; her body has become a visual and denominative catalogue of organs that seem to live separately from one another; the body itself is now no more than a useless concept.

Plotkin knows he is on a forced march in a sort of antinarrative, in the Ante-World of Vivian McNellis's plot. He knows the Machine-Child is everything against which his own existence can do nothing but fight against, forever.

At the center of the vortex are the ninety-nine names of the Machine-Child, and it is with them that Plotkin is trying to establish a "dialogue" without speaking. Among the ninety-nine names, there are those through which he has been able to penetrate deeply into the child's brain-machine, and there are those through which he has been able to traverse the ontological rhizome that seems forever looping back upon itself: Clint Eastwood, Iggy Pop, Alan Vega, Kraftwerk . . .

At each opening-closing of a box, the android girl undergoes another metaorganic disconnection. She is nothing more now than a vague, ghostly form pulsating with codes and numbers, a biometry of artificial flesh prone on the Recyclo™ particleboard of the Box-House, mouth open to the unknowable, entire body become the site of the experiment Plotkin is conducting on the Machine-Child's mind.

Something is there.

Something that seems to want to live.

Something that sings through the girl's body, and that comes from somewhere else, that does not come from him, Plotkin, but that does not seem to be coming from any one particular box, or from the totality the boxes form. The thing is singing.

It is like fossil radiance.

Plotkin realizes he is touching the very membrane of the truth. He realizes, stupefied, that there is a sort of black box within the black box itself; there is a secret device, so secret that not even the Machine-Child knows of it—at least, not anymore. There is something there that seems to contain the space-time of an entire life. This thing—it is like the occult link that connects all the boxes, but it is also a box, and not the filament of light that Plotkin's narration is in the process of tracing toward it. It is the mega-Box, the mega-Machine. It is the monopsychic entity itself.

Sydia Sexydoll, a catalogue of disembodied organs slumped against the wall, the Box-Child in his iron lung surrounded by machines, and Plotkin, the Free Man from the Camp, who is decoding the exconscience of the youth who has no age, no existence—the nothing-child. That is what is happening here, what is being written. Plotkin the Writer in Capsule 108, as if in a state of solar combustion; Plotkin the Killer under the dome, connecting his brain to the Machine-Child's, and retrowriting the experience in the symbolic body of the android.

He is now inside the black box of the Machine-Child's antibrain.

He knows it, because words are no longer separate from things here—concepts are the same as worlds—there are no more boxes repeating the statistic matrix of the Metastructure here. No. Now, here, there is a human being.

Or rather, his ghost.

This ghost of a human being is the black box of the child's exconscience; it is the Machine within the Machine. It is the *infinitely divided indivisible*. The Machine-Box in its wholeness, not as a universal concept, even one materialized by the Metastructure, but as an initial point of individuation.

It is here, Plotkin realizes, that the creation of the World by Vivian McNellis took root. He is standing at its point of absolute contraction. It is also from here that the creation of the antiworld began, the one that is concurrent to him. He is at the very origins of the plot. He is face-to-face with the zero point of the writing, face-to-face with the antithesis of the Celestial Scribe, with its general reversal in the World Below. He is face-to-face with the genetic code of the Metastructure itself. He is face-to-face with what has no name.

He is face-to-face with the child's hundredth name. The name-hundred. The name-without. The name-sense.

One hundred, Plotkin thinks. Yes, it is also the number four in binary, in an eight-bit system. The fourth day, the day when the operation of division doubles over into the physical world. He is truly in the presence of infinite division itself, the extensive inversion of Creation, this indestructible bloc of nonwriting that resists all writing. It is hardly human; it has virtually no shape. It is a child, an adult, an old man, a machine, a man, a woman, an alphabet, a numeric matrix—but when it comes down to it, it most resembles a man.

"I think you are causing me to die," says the Box-Machine. "Yes, I do think I am dying."

In the limbic space-time of the antinarrative, where Plotkin has succeeded against all odds at initiating this nonsensical dialogue with the identity of the Machine-Child, the universe is lighting up, bit by bit, while the incarcerating lights that reign in each of the boxes are extinguished, one by one, like children's rooms being plunged into darkness, at nightfall, when bedtime has come.

"I am dying; yes, I think you are making me die," says the Box-Machine, this terrible incarnation of the Control Metastructure in the body-brain of the fiction-child.

"No," Plotkin says, "you are not dying. I mean—yes, you are, but it is because you are beginning to live."

"Why are you doing this? I don't feel well at all. My boxes are not opening into one another anymore, and they are no longer closing on the world. Why?"

"I have to stop your metastatic proliferation. I have to prevent you from copying the entire Control Metastructure in your brain, and it and the copy from changing places. If you succeed, the client I work for will die."

"No one has ever been able to open my black box before, the one that contains all the others while being contained by them. How did you do it?"

"I used a body. A system of machine-organs, if you prefer. A body you cannot see, because it is like the inverted parallel of your own existence—or nonexistence."

"I existed once. I remember. I think—"

"No. You only exist here, at the disconnection of all your boxes, in this invisible part of yourself, the one you have hidden from the eyes of the very world you are digesting, the eyes of this fucking Metastructure."

"The Metastructure is my ally. It helps me to survive. It gives me all the data I need to—"

"I told you it is threatening the life—the survival—of my client. I don't care about the rest."

"Who is this famous client?"

"Her name is part of your identity boxes. I don't actually know how that's possible."

"Oh yes, I see. The strange double box that came from I don't know where, and which has been trying to incorporate all the others. I thought it was some sort of virus, but it didn't work."

"Because I hadn't been created yet. Not as a free man. Now I am, and I can act."

"I see," says the child-adult. "You are a direct threat to my existence."

"It's your own existence that is threatening you. When you are completely extrojected into the Metastructure and it is incorporated into you, you will be nothing. Even your black box will be dissolved."

"I—that is impossible. The Metastructure keeps me safe."

Plotkin, via the body of the artificial girl, bursts into laughter. "It protects you like a herdsman protects his cattle—to fatten them for slaughter when the time comes."

"What are you planning to do?" demands the ghost-child, from his secret box.

"My client is incorporating the cosmos into herself, as you have done with the Metastructure. The difference is that you are the anti-world of her mind. She created you, but without knowing it. I, though, am her conscious creation, and now I am both the subject and the author of this narrative."

"What is going to happen?"

In the child's voice, and on his ghostly, otherworldly face, Plotkin sees purest anguish. Involuntarily, he reaches his hand out toward the limbic child-adult in compassion, but the entity recoils, terrified.

"You shouldn't be afraid," Plotkin says to him. " *'Fear is like a small death,'* said—I think—Frank Herbert, one of the authors in your science-fiction library."

"I am afraid with good reason," replies the child. "I am frightened of you, and I know you are killing me."

> CELLULAR AUTOMATONS

Subatomic narration. Neuromancer on a forced forward march, inside the world that is creating itself.

Plotkin Capsule-108. Plotkin-under-the-dome. Supercord. Quantum correlation of the two plotlines.

After leaving the rhizomic exconscience of "John Smith," Plotkin looks at the iron lung in which the barely human form moves feebly. The nanocomputers and their peripheral devices seem to be on standby mode; the iron lung itself emits only a weak gleam now and Plotkin knows he has released a sort of viral bomb, a semantic bomb, inside the child. He does not know when or how the bomb will explode, but he knows the detonation will be enormous.

The artificial girl is now back to her original organic/symbolic form, but she is not in the best shape. Plotkin finds her prostrate, pale, eyes half-closed, nearly unconscious. She is extremely weak.

He takes her back to her room; she sinks without a word into her helium bed. Out the window, the sun is sinking slowly beneath the horizon.

"Thank you," he says, not really expecting a response.

But the bionic girl murmurs, in a trembling voice: "No problem."

And Plotkin the Killer, thanks to the subtext Plotkin the Writer has provided him with, understands the meaning hidden beneath the words. "I have experienced life and death, good and evil, body and mind, the organic and the symbolic. I have experienced destruction and creation, and the risks inherent in both. I am ready now."

"Yes," he replies to the unuttered words. "You're ready."

Then, in Capsule 108, Plotkin brings the narrative-world forward twenty-four hours. Fast-forward. Light speed. Metatronic Black Box. He is on the strip now, near the hotel, with Cheyenne Hawkwind. They head south, toward the big intersection of Nova Express. They cross the metallic structure of Telstar Bridge.

"Clovis Drummond wants twenty-five thousand Pan-Am dollars for the Golden Track. Twenty thousand for the document itself, five thousand for him and me, to be split equally."

Plotkin sees in the Indian's eyes that the amount doesn't hold a candle to even a small bonus, equivalent to 10 percent, of the price of a murder.

"How long?"

"Fast. We're meeting our middleman tomorrow, but we'll have to have the money."

"You'll have it. How do you want it?"

The Indian smiles. In his black eyes, gleaming like a hot brazier only a moment before, Plotkin discerns the spark of true humanity that is the basis of the inhumanity that has taken possession of this world.

"As you know, there are . . . let's say, two separate amendments to our contract."

Plotkin smiles too, and looks at Hawkwind with the pale blue eyes of the Man from the Camp. "Fine; first let's look at the official affair. The Golden Track for the people in Capsule 081."

There is little traffic in this part of the strip, but in the distance Plotkin can see the Nova Express intersection and the crowd already gathering on the street, a local replica of the flood of human damned plunged into the fiery river of damnation.

"I have a Centurion Trust account somewhere in Montana," Cheyenne Hawkwind says. "Deposit the entire amount in there. It's agreed with Clovis Drummond; he has access to the account as well." The subtext is clear: *I'm screwing that bastard over but good.* "So then, for the . . . let's call it the unofficial part of the contract. I've decided that twenty-five thousand Pan-Am dollars isn't enough."

Plotkin walks a few steps before replying. He and Hawkwind pass a group of transsexual partner-swappers, affiliated with an approved tantric rite, heading to a well-known club a little farther up the strip. In all the lateral streets he sees individuals and small groups converging: men, women, hermaphrodites, legal and illegal monsters. The number of electric cars increases; the ambient noise, the smell of ozone, the feeling of internal trepidation—all of it is beginning to create a very singular space-time, with its capsule hotels similar to the Laika, its motel-brothels, its dance clubs, its gladiatorial arenas, its neurogame arcades, its nightclubs. Night falls. Night begins.

"And just how much would you consider *enough?*"

"Double," the Indian replies. "Clovis Drummond has a lot of connections in the city and he works for the Municipal Consortium—which means, Orville Blackburn and his cronies."

The subtext all but screams: *I won't be able to stay here long after the job. I need cash to get as far away from Grand Junction as I can, as fast as possible.*

"Fifty thousand Pan-Am for a common store manager. You must admit that's asking for a bit much," Plotkin says. "Not to mention that you're going to get a pretty little commission on the Golden Track."

Cheyenne Hawkwind smiles. "Twenty-five hundred dollars? You must be joking."

"And I'm telling you that you'll do it for forty thousand, including your commission. Otherwise the deal's off."

"Don't be like that; come on. Forty thousand is a deal."

Plotkin gauges the effect he has produced. Cheyenne Hawkwind is a buyer; he would probably have come down to less, but it doesn't matter. What matters is that he is ready, without the slightest qualm of conscience, to kill Clovis Drummond. To kill the only human witness to Plotkin's stay at the Hotel Laika, to their passage through Grand Junction, all of them. The McNellises, Sydia Sexydoll, and even the Machine-Child. "Fine. Let's not discuss it again. How should we proceed with this . . . amendment to the contract?"

"We'll have to tread carefully. I want half in Grand Junction cash, and the other half deposited into a CitiWorld account in Micronesia."

Plotkin walks a few more meters. Nova Express is growing closer; the lights of the strip glitter like a fiery serpent winding through the night.

"Okay. Just give me the necessary coordinates. And don't forget that I'll take your twenty-five-hundred-dollar commission out of the cash."

Plotkin knows the money has no importance in itself; the important thing is not to drop the ball, to send a very clear message to the Indian killer. "I might also need the cash, because I have connections too, and if I can pay you forty thousand dollars I would have been able to pay the fifty thousand as well—your double—which means that I only negotiate on principle, and I have reserves." *Don't try to double-cross me, you prick,* warns the subtext. "You told me you're meeting with your middleman tomorrow?"

"Yes, around noon."

"One of Clovis Drummond's friends?"

Cheyenne Hawkwind's mouth twists into an enigmatic smile.

"Not exactly, but I'm sure you'll understand that I can't tell you any more."

They are in front of a bar called The Ticket That Exploded, at an angle of the strip with Nova Express, that half-abandoned urban highway that connects the city center with the desolate areas of the frontier.

"Want a drink?" Cheyenne Hawkwind asks.

In Capsule 108 of the Hotel Laika, Plotkin the Scribe writes:

"I think we can drink to that."

Disconnection-acceleration: the hours fly by in a new disconnection of the plot. Now Plotkin is walking toward the McNellises' double room. But when he places his hand on the door's identity scanner, re-unification: Plotkin in Capsule 108/Plotkin moving in the world. They are reunified once more in the *Aevum,* in the circumspect time of the angels, in the discontinuous time of Metatron.

He is no longer in the Hotel Laika. He is under the interchange at the border of the Independent Territory, the incomplete inter-change that leads nowhere. He is under the highway to nothingness, and, facing him, Vivian McNellis stands entirely surrounded by a globe of fire.

"Welcome to Deadlink. This place will be the theater for extraor-dinary events."

"Deadlink?"

"That is the name the nomads of the Northeast have given it, the highway and its unfinished interchange that lead nowhere, like a 'dead link' in the network."

Plotkin stares at the angelic creature, wavering endlessly be-tween the visible and the invisible in the light of the Third Time.

"My God, you're beautiful." The words escape his lips in spite of himself.

At this moment, yes, at this moment he could fall to his knees; his legs quiver, his joints have turned to unstable jelly, and inside him a firebrand scorches its way from the pit of his stomach to the top of his head, incinerating his heart as it goes.

"Soon the Third Time will be totally incorporated in me. I will bear the image of the entire cosmos, like a process of infinite creation. For me, there will be no more difference between the *Aevum* and Earthly time."

"Did it work?" Plotkin asks, almost feverishly. "Did I succeed in stopping the proliferation of your antiworld, the Machine-Child?"

"Yes, for now. My genetic retrotranspositions were able to begin. But the monopsychic Metastructure is still not destroyed; it is just sleeping . . . for a moment."

Plotkin gazes at the fiery angel dancing before him a few meters above the ground. The solar aura glimmers on the concrete walls of the abandoned interchange. "I'm seeing one of the branches of the future, is that it? The one that shows me succeeding?"

"Yes, because if you do succeed, you will also be definitely reunited. Plotkin the Writer and Plotkin the Action will be reunited, and you will not only be free, you will be truly alive."

"I assume that means I might die?"

"You already know that," responds the young woman, haloed with light.

Divided once more, Plotkin is back in the Hotel Laika, his hand pressed to the screen of the door's identity verifier, in front of Capsule 081. He is no longer in the *Aevum*. Barely a microsecond passed during the conversation under the interchange.

When the door opens, Plotkin is face-to-face with Jordan McNellis. His wan face, drawn features, the blue-gray shadows under his eyes—all indicate that he hasn't slept in days. Plotkin is seized with a presentiment—no, a certainty, one as sure as the absolute faith of a convert.

The partition with 081-B is closed, but through the thin Recyclo™ cellulose wall he can see the presence of a light.

A light in the shape of a body.

A body in the form of light.

He knows the overall transmutation of Vivian McNellis has begun.

He knows that for her, now, it is too late, even as the details of the operation that will permit her to return to the Orbital Ring, the "land" of her birth, are falling into place.

Plotkin looks at Jordan McNellis. The young man's eyes are filled with tears that sparkle faintly in the dim light of the room, like candle flames seen through a veil of fog. He too understands. He knows.

He too is a free man now.

"It really started yesterday, in the early evening."

"I know," Plotkin says.

It was just when he went back up under the dome with the android girl. Just as he succeeded in stopping the Machine-Child's process of proliferation. A form of energy too great for the human mind to understand had been retained in her body for too long. She was retrowritten, in an explosion of light, in a quantum burst that illuminated in a single stroke all the metacoding information of her DNA.

The whole secret of the body-mind narrative.

"I want to see her," Plotkin says.

"I think she wants to see you too," Jordan McNellis replies.

"She can see me already."

It is true. The body-mind of Vivian McNellis has incorporated the entire Created World now, not as a narration but as a physical singularity, and, in return, a solar light has broken free from her body in a sphere of pure splendor. She is already living in the *Aevum;* her entire existence is spiraling, ecstatic and suffering, toward the highest glory.

Beyond the partition separating the two capsules, Plotkin gazes for a long time at the body of Vivian McNellis, stretched out on the helium bed, floating about two centimeters above its surface, and surrounded by the same globe of fire as it was under the Deadlink interchange.

He studies her features beneath the light; she is pale as a moonbeam, her large opalescent eyes fixed on the ceiling. Plotkin knows that now there are only a few days remaining—perhaps less than twenty-four hours.

The Celestial Scribe is guiding her toward Him, higher, infinitely higher than the Orbital Ring.

> DEADLINK

Now: bright sunlight. A day so blue it seems to threaten everything. The morning is already hotter than a woman's body pressed full length against yours. Not a breath of wind. WorldWeather forecast: a heat wave in western Canada for the next ten days; storms and tornadoes possible in southern Quebec and Ontario; average temperature around noon local time in the Grand Junction area, a little less than 40 degrees Celsius in the shade—well above seasonal norms for the first day of October. It's going to be brutal.

Plotkin looks at Balthazar; the dog is waiting for him at the agreed-upon rendezvous point, on the North Junction road autobridge. The dog is all right. The dog is his ally.

"You went back up under the dome with the android girl?"

"Yes," Plotkin replies. "And I'll probably have to go again, alone."

"You mean without the girl?"

"As for the girl, now it's up to you to keep your promises."

The cyberdog's gaze seems filled with total empathy for the man he is speaking with, and especially for the artificial girl they are discussing. "Lady van Harpel gave her word. She'd never go back on it. We'll take the girl to Deadlink."

"Yes. The sooner the better. What do you know about the Christian rebels' decision?"

"About her baptism? The discussion is still raging."

Plotkin lets out a sigh. "They're wasting their time in pointless debate, if you ask me. This girl is sexed and she has a conscience."

"I am also sexed, and I also have a conscience," says the dog. "That doesn't mean I can receive the sacrament."

Plotkin sighs again, annoyed. "This girl is artificial, but she is human. She's one of God's creatures."

"We are all God's creatures, and in this case she is first and foremost Venux Corp's creature."

Plotkin is silent for a long moment. He stares in the direction of the cosmodrome, where preparations for the Sputnik Centennial are in full swing. The hangars hum with activity; Platform 3 is full of people, miniature dolls, ants in blue, green, yellow, and orange uniforms. The first inhabited module rocket in Jason Texas Lagrange's program is already on its launchpad; Plotkin can see the long white nose cone in the giant enclosure of the hangar.

To the east, North Junction burns in the high midday sun, tracing a reddish line through the hills, disappearing little by little into the amaranth-tinted tropical vegetation.

"A representative of the HMV rebels will be at the meeting point," says Balthazar. "Whether they baptize her or not, Lady van Harpel will take care of her. She's a very good woman."

"The android girl is capable of giving of herself. She accepted the share of sacrifice inherent in all humanity. She opened her body up to terrible manipulations so I could get close to the Machine-Child."

"I know," replies Balthazar. "Don't worry. They'll take that into account."

Plotkin looks at the cosmodrome to the northwest, against the backdrop of Monolith Hills. The cosmodrome Vivian McNellis will not leave from. The cosmodrome where everything happens, not only the history of men, but that of their dreams as well.

"Relax. Lady van Harpel is a very kind woman."

The dog turns to the side for an instant, offering the android girl his best canine attempt at a kindly expression. The rented autocar approaches the zone, Plotkin in the driver's seat, the position of total control; the cyberdog sits next to him, and the artificial girl is in the backseat.

Plotkin recognizes the scenery, less green and luxuriant than in the area around Nexus Road; here, at the border with the state of Vermont, the peaks are eroding and growing denuded faster for some unknown reason. Farther away, to the southeast, he can make out the very end point of the Independent Territory, with the large, dirty blocs of Omega and the scrap-iron hills of Junkville, behind a high curtain of hot air that makes the sky, the earth, and even the sun, with its killer rays, waver. Then he sees the elevated highway, the stump of concrete that winds between the hills and stops abruptly in the middle of nowhere, in a cruciform star pulled down to the Earth, a bit of the nexus become matter, cast off at the end of a small road and a drying riverbed.

Deadlink.

As Plotkin turns off the engine of the little rented Honda-GM, he glances at the dashboard clock and sees that it is noon. Exactly noon, 12:00 P.M., laid out in cobalt blue LED letters. At that very time, probably in a bar somewhere on the strip, Cheyenne Hawkwind and Clovis Drummond are buying the illegal Golden Track from their middleman, a Golden Track that will be of no use to Vivian McNellis. For her, Metatron has reserved a Golden Track of another sort.

It is noon. The anti-midnight, like the opposite pole of the *Aevum* she incorporated. It is midnight, and it is beastly hot.

Plotkin the Killer thinks all of this as he gets out of the car, because Plotkin the Writer—in Capsule 108, in this metaliving network that engulfs him now, a little like the halo of angelic light around Vivian McNellis—Plotkin the Writer is writing it.

They walk alongside the river, passing underneath the wide concrete nave with its routes leading in the four cardinal directions and going nowhere. They skirt the high graveled butte, and, like the first time, as they enter the valley, the hill cedes the terrain to a place he recognizes right away: an arid plain dotted with clumps of cedars and pine groves, small rocky hillocks scattered like natural cairns, their slowly eroding tops sparsely wooded with mutant evergreens, and, in the midst of them, the windmill, the old Dodge Ram 2500 truck rusting gradually on its axles, and the big plastic-and-aluminum mobile home, settled on its blocks by the riverside.

"Is this it?" asks the artificial girl, more curious than fearful.

Plotkin sees two motorcycles parked side by side in front of the mobile home. Gasoline-powered vehicles. Combustion engines. HMV. There is a sidecar attached to one of the motorcycles.

The sun beats down mercilessly; even the strongest UV protectants seem at their limits. The heat feels strong enough to melt everything.

"They're waiting for us," the dog says. "Don't be afraid."

In Capsule 108, Plotkin the Quantum Scribe lives the experience as he retrowrites it: He is not creating the story he is narrating; it is the story, he realizes, that is re-creating him. He is not projecting simple imagination-machinery; he is superprojecting his entire being into this imaginary plan that, in return, gives him access to the black box of the Created World. That is how he *sees*: his writing life is synchronized with the narrative life of his correlated double.

And his double, right now, is observing the scene before his eyes, coldly detailing the action from which he will partially withdraw himself in a moment.

There are seven "people" in the mobile home: Lady van Harpel, the dog, the android girl, Plotkin, and three other human beings, two men and a woman he does not recognize. He identifies the men in black as priests or reverend pastors. Lady van Harpel stands erect in the very center of the camper. She radiates the power of a sybil of the lost world.

And she holds Plotkin's gaze unflinchingly.

"Here is the man," Balthazar says, "the man I told you about. The man from Capsule 108."

"I know," the old woman replies simply, rolling a ball of tobacco between her fingers and chewing the stem of her pipe, without dropping Plotkin's gaze for even a microsecond.

"And here is the android, Sydia . . . er, Sexydoll Nova 280," continues the dog, slanting a sideways glance at the humans from HMV.

"Hello, miss. I hope you had a pleasant trip out here?" Lady van Harpel asks the question without even looking at the girl. Her turquoise blue eyes are still fixed on Plotkin's pale blue ones, the Man from the Camp, the Fiction Man who feels as if he is being passed through a scanner, every inch of him scrutinized, a scanner much more sophisticated than the ones in the Metastructure's aerostations.

"Yes, ma'am," replies the android girl. "It's just that it's very hot today."

Plotkin loses the staring contest. He lets his gaze roam around the room, which seems to serve as a trigger. Lady van Harpel comes out of her visual trance and addresses Balthazar directly: "This man, as you know, seems to be a double agent. He is on the side of both good and evil, which I cannot understand, but I am certain of it."

The dog looks taken aback. "But—I told you—and we agreed—"

"I will not go back on our agreement," says the old woman, "but I am quite suspicious that he might be a secret agent from the Council for Ethical Vigilance. If he is present at the baptism, we all might end up in prison for life. He knows enough to threaten our very existence. I hope you realize that."

Balthazar looks downcast.

The old woman's face brightens a little. "But, I conducted an important geomancy session last night, a hexagram. A very strange figure appeared, one that indicated both great hope and great sacrifice. And that is exactly what is in play, here and now, isn't it?"

Balthazar doesn't seem to know what to say. He is silent. No one speaks.

Finally, Plotkin says: "You're mistaken; I am not a UHU agent. If I were, you would all be behind bars already."

"You might be waiting to seize the whole network, catch us in the act . . ."

"I know all about your network. And as for catching you in the act, it's already done. Do you want me to read you your rights?"

The old woman frowns and lights her pipe. Automatically, the air-conditioning system, already on high, turns on an antitoxic aeration vent placed in the very center of the ceiling, which sucks up the smoke in a whirl like a miniature bluish tornado. "Well, what are you, then?"

Plotkin looks again into her scanner gaze. "What do you mean?"

The woman does not blink as she says, "You are not human. Not quite."

Plotkin exhales. Détente. Stall for time. A second or two. What a demonstration. This woman is no fraud, swindling people for a few Philippine pesos like so many of the so-called clairvoyants on the strip. She is powerful, and dangerous. He can see with absolute clarity that she was a stunning beauty in her youth.

"I am human," he lies, "but I am an 'amplified human.' I work for a special organization—not UHU. Nothing to do with UHU."

His first personality, that of the Man Who Has Come to Kill the Mayor of This City.

"What organization?"

"If I told you, I'd have to kill all of you immediately afterward."

His words drop like stones into the pool of silence in the room, cold as a marble tomb.

"He works for a company of assassins," says Balthazar, trying to help, "but I know he is a renegade. Why else would he be doing this, especially for free?"

"Exactly," snaps Lady van Harpel. "That's what I don't like. No one does anything for free these days. It doesn't fit."

"Priests conduct baptisms for free, as far as I know," barks the dog.

Plotkin realizes that Balthazar has truly become his ally, his friend, that he is defending him, like a devil's advocate, to the terrible judge of Deadlink, just as he will defend him, fangs bared, against any physical danger.

"Do not compare the living vectors of the Holy Sacrament with this . . . man, as he claims to be."

"You are impossible," growls the dog, annoyed.

"Why do you not tell me the truth?" demands the old woman through a cloud of marijuana smoke. "You are hiding something. You are not what you claim to be."

"What I will say," Plotkin states dryly, "is that the only thing that counts for me is the word you just said."

"What word?"

" 'Baptism.' You said 'baptism,' and there are at least two priests here, as far as I can tell."

"Something like that."

"Are you planning to baptize her?"

The woman stares at him in silence, then at the dog, and then at the artificial girl who remains standing wordlessly, head slightly bent forward, eyes on the ground. Then she looks at Plotkin again.

She is scanning him with all her mystic senses. He does not drop her gaze; instead, he makes the most important decision of his life. He opens himself completely, like a flower, like a peeled-back glove. He projects the entire truth into the clear blueness of her eyes, and he sees her recoil, as if stricken with a lash. The fiftyish woman accompanying the priest takes her by the shoulders. "Do you feel all right, Lady van Harpel?"

"Lord . . ." the old clairvoyant murmurs, sinking heavily into one of the worn old armchairs scattered about the room. "All-powerful God . . . please proceed with the baptism of this young woman, Father."

"I'm Father Matthew Rowe Newman," the older man says, approaching the android girl. "I am Anglo-Catholic. This is Mrs. Mary Jane Kirkpatrick, who will assist me."

The fiftyish woman steps forward and shakes the girl's limp hand. Plotkin can already see how the android is transfigured. Something shines weakly in her eyes, and there are traces of tears on her lashes. He sees—yes, he sees that she is *ready. She has a soul,* he says to himself. *They've realized that she has a soul.* And for the first time in his "life," he feels as if a heavy weight is crushing his rib cage. And in his eyes, too, salty moisture wells.

"Do you have witnesses?"

Plotkin realizes that the artificial girl has turned toward him. He feels his entire being devastated from the inside. He throws a glance at Lady van Harpel, who watches him coldly from her armchair. "I'm sorry," he replies to the android's unspoken question. "I can't be your witness, Sydia. I'm not baptized."

Father Newman smiles widely. "If you like, we can easily—"

"No," Plotkin cuts him off. "I don't think I'm quite ready for that."

"Very well," says the priest. "In that case, Lady van Harpel and Sir John Sommerville, our friend from the Presbyterian community, will serve as your official witnesses according to the agreement reached between our two churches. Will you accept them?"

"Yes," answers the artificial girl, her eyes filled with fresh tears.

"Good," says Father Newman. "Mrs. Kirkpatrick, let us proceed with the installation of the altar and holy reliquaries."

Later, much later, Plotkin will remember the event as one of the strangest in his strange "existence," stranger even than the existence itself. He will remember it as a moment of pure transfiguration, though nothing—nothing, or almost nothing—actually results from it. There, in the initial certitude, in the visible: water, fire, salt, and the word.

And yet it is enough, seeing the liberated face of the young whore manufactured in orbit for the violent beauty of the act, the magnificent risk it entrained, to bring him almost to his knees, and to make him plead for baptism in his turn.

Lady van Harpel senses, with all her invisible antennae, that something is happening inside him. She has undoubtedly watched him during the ceremony. She leans slowly toward him, takes him by the arm, and pushes him toward the mobile home's door. "We need to talk," she says.

"Yes," he agrees grudgingly. "We need to talk."

She leads him to the other side of the river, crossing a small ford of polished rocks covered with gleaming algae. She indicates the graveled butte they are facing. "Climb up with me. I want to show you something."

They make their way up a tiny road, hardly wide enough for a colony of ants, to the summit. At the top of the butte, on a shallow plateau covered with short, colorless grass, they have an unimpeded view toward the east. Plotkin is aware that Lady van Harpel has not showed the slightest need for assistance during the climb, nor has she uttered a word.

Very keenly aware.

After a few seconds, the old woman rolls a ball of herbs and tobacco, tucks it into the bowl of her pipe, and says: "They have been there for a week."

* * *

There are at least sixty thousand of them. They have come from Quebec, especially from the island of Montreal, where they were embroiled in a tripartite civil war among pro-Canadian federalists, independents allied with Islamists, and pro-American annexationists. They are mostly civilians, but Plotkin notes various military uniforms as well, indicating the probable presence of deserters from surrounding camps.

This human ganglion moved first toward the southeast, toward the federal territories of what remains of the Union, but it was repulsed by border guards and the Vermont state police. The sixty thousand people then scattered along the border, and ended up on this side of the butte, only a few kilometers from Deadlink, and seem to be making their way northward, somewhere in the direction of the old nuclear plant in Neon Park.

Sometimes refugees find radical solutions to their search for refuge.

"I want you to look me straight in the eyes and answer my questions."

"You can't hypnotize me," Plotkin warns her. "I have an autoblocking program for that sort of—"

"It isn't hypnosis. I need to know the truth, that's all."

"I just told you the truth in there," Plotkin replies. "Why did you make me come up here?"

"Just to see if you could keep up with a nonamplified seventy-two-year-old human woman."

Lady van Harpel laughs. The echo of it is lost among the crags of the eroded hilltop.

"There is something in you that isn't human," she says, "and yet you are. I have known it since the beginning. There is something in you that isn't alive, and yet it is as if you could be, at any time. I have sensed it. There is something linking you to the invisible world, something superphysical, and I saw it in there, but I don't understand it."

"There is nothing to explain," Plotkin says. "Any attempt at a rational explanation would inevitably miss the essential point and would suffer from the total absence of aesthetic preoccupation."

They stand face-to-face at the summit of Deadlink hill, the abandoned interchange to their left. On the right, to the west, are the masses of human refugees. And the two of them stand under the sky—blue, luminous, pure, and saturated with ultraviolet light.

"I see," she says at last, lighting her marijuana pipe.

Plotkin allows the silence to stretch between them. There isn't even the slightest breath of air; they don't hear insects humming, or the tiniest noise from the teeming mass of refugees. The end of the world will probably be calm like this.

"The depopulation is just beginning," she says, her features suddenly twisted with concern. "And nothing can stop it. The UHU is finished, or almost. The Grand Jihad will resume, in an even more terrible form. The reign of the technocrats will begin. And now the Antichrist himself is coming."

"What makes you think that?"

"I have seen it. I have read it in the future."

"When?" Plotkin demands.

Now Lady van Harpel points in the direction of the hilly plains of Vermont and the mass of humanity with its particleboard shelters and a few UHU-approved medical tents with their white lettering on a khaki background as the only structured motif, though barely readable. As for the rest, it is nothing but sixty thousand pieces of "civilized" human chaos regressing into neolithic savagery.

"It has only just begun."

> MISTER QUARK

He bridges the next narrative disconnection at the speed of a photon.

He carries with him the image of the old woman and that of the newly baptized android girl, waving to him in farewell as she stands in front of the mobile home, while the motorcycles of the HMV Catholics roll off in the direction of the access road. He gets back into the rental car, drives to North Junction, and walks toward the Hotel Laika.

Then he finds himself back in his room.

He is there, in front of himself, Plotkin the Scribe, the "living" neurosoftware agent, a sort of intensified inversion of the Machine-Child. He is the other and the other is he. He lives the two quantum plans in a manner both separate and correlate. He knows that Plotkin the Scribe, sitting there a few meters away from him, is really on the other side of the universe, at the other end of the supercord. To be close is sometimes to be infinitely distant.

He knows that his consciousness-"other" is writing his "I" in action in the world. He knows that soon the world will no longer exist. He knows, because Vivian McNellis told him, that the possibility of his own reunification depends on what he is able to do with the Babel-child, the child with ninety-nine names, the child with no childhood.

The Counter-Man from the Camp and the Machine-Child are not abstract entities "thought" by a pure monotheistic and omniscient spirit; they are superphysical processes folded into each other.

Something is using them to bring down the Metastructure.

For Vivian McNellis to pass unencumbered to her High Frontier, it will take more than an official UHU-approved paper. More, even, than one hundred thousand dollars paid into the Grand Junction Cosmos Inc. account for a flight on one of Jason Texas Lagrange's small, low-cost rockets.

It will take much more.

It will take what must be done.

And he knows now what that will be.

He knows that his action will probably catalyze—isn't that the term one uses for a chemical process?—the whole world, the whole plot, the whole of his being.

Yes, there will be *catalysis,* in every sense of the word: acceleration, decline, crystallization. There will be *catalysis.* There will be the completely assumed risk of *consciousness.*

Absolute danger.

New ecstatic disconnection in the plot: Plotkin the Scribe unrolls the filament of light toward Plotkin the Man from the Camp; he walks through the hallway on the top floor of the Hotel Laika, which whirs with every cog in its mechanical organism. Plotkin enters the service stairway and arrives once more under the dome, in front of the gray wall covered with metal crucifixes, then in front of the black wall of the Machine-Child's black box, in front of the vinyl sphincter, the air-lock, the entry-exit interface.

The Machine-Child is still in standby mode, operating at half speed, moved only by the most limbic pulses and the simplest components. Plotkin knows he can enter the child's interior black box now without the slightest difficulty. Thanks to the metatronic black box Vivian McNellis made him ingest, he has the ability to incorporate the Box-Child's world. Thanks to the transcription he made of

the child's internal metastructure onto the organless body of the android girl, he knows all his access codes; he is already inside him, an
invading virus. Percussion. Photons. Action. He is already in front of
the ghostly entity hidden in the shadows of this bodiless organism.
Now, everything will be tied up. Soon, everything will shine forth
from their mouths finally open to the fire of the word.

"I need information about your central operating system, the one
that controls your identity boxes."

"The ninety-nine names?"

"Yes. And to start, there are names that I can't identify. I know
Frankie Machine is from *The Man with the Golden Arm,* the Frank Sina-
tra movie. But who is Saul de Sorgimède, for example? Or Lucas
Ford de Guadalupe? Or Steve Cooper Cumberland?"

"Steve C. Cumberland is a Canadian author who only wrote one
book, a detective novel, using that name as a pseudonym. The main
characters in the book are Peter Argentine and Luigi von Saxenhagen, two other boxes. Saul de Sorgimède and Lucas Ford de
Guadalupe are key characters in *Aletheion,* the great time-opera saga
by Jeffrey Alhambra Carpenter, one of the last science-fiction writers
still alive today who hasn't been replaced by artificial intelligence."

"What exactly do you know about your first identity, the one that
you are using as a legal cover?"

"John Smith? I recognize the name, but I don't know anything
about John Smith. He is probably a direct emanation of the Metastructure, just an anonymous artifact, and—"

"No." Plotkin cuts him off. "John Smith exists too. He is a fictional
character, the first 'cyborg' in the history of literature, from an Edgar
Allan Poe story called 'The Man That Was Used Up,' the story of an
automaton living in a broken-up body. Are you following me now?"

"Edgar Allan Poe," repeats the child. "I have one of his books in my library. *Extraordinary Tales,* you know, 'The Murders in the Rue Morgue,' all that. And he is among my identity boxes. But I don't know the story you're talking about."

"That doesn't matter," Plotkin replies. "The Metastructure knows it."

There is a long silence, which Plotkin deliberately allows to stretch on. "Where do your books come from? Your library?" he asks after a moment.

"They are the books I read during my stay with Grandmother Telefunken in Neon Park. She was one of the last people there who knew how to read, one of the last ones to own books. I brought what I could with me."

"Okay. Now, what's the story behind all the '1980s electric rock' boxes?"

"I have no idea. That is the holdout area; it comes from farther away than the narrative-world you say I am the counter-production of. It comes from what wrote you, me, Clovis Drummond, the dog Balthazar, and even Vivian McNellis and the entire world. From what probably even wrote this Metastructure that has become what I am."

Plotkin says nothing. The Machine-Child knows. He knows of Metatron's existence and of what is the transcendent, pivotal, and superphysical principle of the Metastructure—or its counter-principle. The monopsychic Metastructure is the inverted and socialized form of the Prince of the Face.

It is the Enemy.

"Why are these Christian symbols on the outside wall of your 'gray zone'?"

"I don't know that either. They come from the Marie de l'Incarnation box. She says she must try to save . . . my soul, or something like that. I asked Clovis Drummond to put the crucifixes on the outer wall; on the inside they would disturb the order of my library."

"Are you afraid of dying?"

"I don't know. I don't know what death is."

"That is normal. 'Living' beings don't know what life is, either."

"What will happen to me?"

"You have a choice. Either you can disincorporate yourself completely in the Metastructure, which I will do everything I can to prevent, even if I have to eliminate you 'physically,' if that word means anything to you. Or you can agree to do the opposite thing—in which case I can't say for sure what will happen to you."

"What would that be, exactly?"

"I believe I would be able to incorporate you, like an antinarrative, and thus make you into something alive."

"How?"

"I still have only a vague idea of it, but the woman I must save will undoubtedly play a role in it."

"Incorporate? Are you going to eat me?"

Plotkin laughs. "Yes, it is something like cannibalism, except that you aren't flesh and blood. Actually, though, it's the opposite: I will serve as a writing surface for you; I will give you the chance to become a thinking, living being, gifted with words. And you should seize this chance."

The ghostly child stares at him for a long time. Plotkin senses, in this small, sickly body, hovering between existence and nothingness, an unexpressed scream of terror, but also a sort of unknowable joy, as frightening in its own way as the muted cry.

He understands that in his way, the Machine-Child is telling him that he, too, is ready now.

Ready.

Not for baptism, but for birth.

And so Plotkin enters into death—or, more exactly, at that instant he becomes alive, and thus mortal. And thus immortal.

It surprises him as he leaves the black box, and he stops for an instant in front of the shabby crosses hastily mounted by Clovis Drummond, who, in his complete ignorance of the reasons behind the child's request, mucked about like a boy with his first dildo.

This time, he falls to his knees.

He falls. As if stricken.

Catalysis. Acceleration so phenomenal that it seems to stretch into eternity. Everything is suspended; everything becomes real. No more Plotkin the Scribe in Capsule 108 and Plotkin the Killer in the world in action. Now there is something else. Something else entirely.

The Machine-Child? he wonders. *Is the Machine-Child in me now?*

The question hangs unanswered. He stands up, seeing only the gray wall and the face of the aluminum Christ tacked up on the false world concealing the real one. He finds himself in the service stairway, then in the dome's entry-exit hatch, on his way to being completely reunified. There should, he thinks, be a third term for doubles become one.

Then, paralyzed, he watches as the hatch door opens in front of him.

And he finds himself face-to-face with Clovis Drummond and Cheyenne Hawkwind.

> MACHINE-HEAD

Death must come in one blow to strike the configuration that has now been created. The world must be made to understand, this world over which death reigns without ever quite being able to extinguish it completely. It is time, now, to see the dark shadow of the grim reaper coming. It is time for Plotkin to sacrifice what has been saved of him. It is time for him to become what he is.

And this must happen even though, once more, Plotkin is only one. Because in him, bit by bit, another is coming to life.

Plotkin the Killer, Plotkin the professional assassin of the Red Star Order, Plotkin the Man from the Camp, Plotkin the fictional man made flesh, the man of the Word secretly hidden in the isolation cell, faces Clovis Drummond, and he already knows what is about to happen.

He knows it completely, because it is now being directly written in him.

"WHAT THE FUCK ARE YOU DOING HERE?" screams the fat pig in his disgusting suit, lips bluish with dope, as he comes up the stairs, furious, glassy eyes shooting darts of ice.

Just behind him, Plotkin sees Cheyenne Hawkwind open his black eyes wide in unfeigned shock and then shrug his shoulders and, with a slight gesture of his big hands, send him a message: *I didn't know you were here, and I can't do anything to stop him.*

"No matter," Plotkin says in reply to the American Indian killer's silent words.

"WHAT?" shouts Clovis Drummond, thinking the answer was directed at him. "YOU LITTLE PRICK! I'LL TEACH YOU TO TRESPASS IN A RED ZONE! WHAT THE FUCK WERE YOU DOING UP THERE, YOU DAMNED BASTARD?"

Plotkin looks at him with a strange feeling, almost sadness. A sort of melancholy. Pity, one might even say. *Yes,* he tells himself, *that's what it is. Pity.*

He pities this poor human, this last of men, for devolving virtually onto all fours. He pities his flabby flesh and his baleful eyes, his face swollen from metadrugs and irregular sleep, from sadosexual neurogames and orgasmatron systems. He pities the face eaten up from the inside by death, the fat, sausagelike fingers coated with flab, playing with the string of the old leather pouch that is no doubt crammed with sexual gadgets adapted for the "body" of the Machine-Child, his living inflatable doll. He pities this poor fucker, this snitch, this pedophile. He pities his ugliness, his monstrosity, his morbid perversity. He pities poor Clovis Drummond.

Poor Clovis Drummond, who he is about to kill.

With one of the simplest yet most complex portable weapons any Order killer carries. His hands.

There are a thousand ways to kill someone with just your hands. They have been learned for centuries in all the martial arts on the planet, a nearly inexhaustible source of knowledge that orders of killers have systematically used, gathering endless resources in the huge library-bunkers in their command centers.

There are a thousand ways to kill a man with your hands. Among them are those that require just a small additional accessory—a razor, a needle, a cord, a chain, brass knuckles . . .

And there is a way that the Red Star Order particularly favors and uses brilliantly, thanks to its renegade biotechnicians.

It is the thousand-and-first way to kill with the hands.

The nail of Plotkin's index finger, like the nails of all his ten fingers, was modified during the reconstruction of his body, during the first few days after his arrival at the hotel. In accordance with the genetic plan at the time he passed through the Control Arch at the Windsor astroport, it is now made of metamorphic carbo-metal with high-speed rememorization. All Plotkin has to do is mentally command the RUN BLADE program to initiate. It takes barely a thousandth of a second for the ensemble of nanocomponents built into his fingernail at the atomic level to register information. It takes barely one more thousandth of a second for the metamorphic program's *bootstrap* to be triggered. Then two or three hundredths of a second more for the rest of the process to take place. All in all, an infinitesimal moment of time.

Barely visible, only just readable, nearly outside the limits of transcription.

Flash. His index finger has become a slashing weapon, very simple and very complex: an organic haft jointed at its three phalanxes and tipped with a carbon-carbon blade hybridized with a high-density crystalline structure and a polymetallic alloy mesh, around twenty centimeters long. It could slice a steel beam in half with ease.

The point of the fingernail is as sharp as a needle, its two cutting edges honed like razors.

A very simple, very complex weapon.

One that has just cleanly cut Mr. Clovis Drummond's throat.

Later, but actually just afterward, Plotkin is under the shower in his capsule's retractable bathroom. He far exceeds the standard allowance, emptying his bank account as he orders the tank to rain a continual stream of hot water down on his body. It seems like a strange, condensed duplication of the world's voodoo economy: empty the bank account/empty the tank, money/water, water/blood, blood/money. IF YOU EXCEED 30 LITERS OF WATER, YOU WILL EXCEED THE STANDARD DAILY AMOUNT INCLUDED IN THE ROOM RATE, AND YOUR ACCOUNT WILL AUTOMATICALLY BE DEBITED. IF YOU EXCEED 50 LITERS OF WATER, YOU MUST PAY DOUBLE-PRICE. IF YOU EXCEED 100 LITERS, YOU MUST PAY TEN TIMES THE PRICE. AND IF YOU EX-

CEED 150 LITERS, EXPRESS AUTHORIZATION OF THE CONSORTIUM WILL BE REQUIRED. The water pummels his body, the body that is both physical and fictive, the body in which a third narrative, that of the finally reincorporated Machine-Child, is beginning.

Eighth Day.

The child of the Eighth Day.

Plotkin senses with his whole being that Vivian McNellis is retrowriting this experience in the Created World somewhere.

Somewhere.

Something.

Someone.

Images of Clovis Drummond's murder float in his consciousness like sparkling clouds, full of a storm of blood.

The metamorphic blade sketches a majestic semicircle in the close confines of the stairway, and it is as if it opens the abyss of a world.

It slices the flesh like a high-intensity laser beam. The veins and arteries bisect cleanly—jugular, carotid, fat open under the icy slash of the hand-that-kills. The muscles retract at the blade's passage through their fibers—the nerves, bones, spinal cord, vertebrae, cartilage—all give way in the same demonic fraction of a second.

Clovis Drummond's head stays fixed on his shoulders for a moment, an indescribable grimace on the lips, wobbling slightly on the base of his neck where a red line appears, a very red line, a line that gushes first drops, then streams of blood down the man's chest. Then, like a 110-floor tower falling after the core infrastructure has been destroyed, leaving it to the mercy of earthly gravity, Clovis Drummond falls apart. His head falls strangely, rolling away off to the side, while his stubby legs bend as if the kneecaps have turned to spheres of vaporous jelly. The arms make a few sporadic movements, like the wings of a sick bird trying feebly to fly. Finally the body falls backward, landing with a thump like a sack of rags against the stairway wall.

Clovis Drummond's head has rolled down a dozen steps like a spongy balloon emitting red-violet spray before knocking into the bottom of the escape-hatch door, precisely between Cheyenne Hawkwind's feet. The man automatically kicks away the head with its fixed rictus, its eyes hardly more dead now than when Drummond was alive—glassy, immobile, cold as those of a dead fish—toward the corner of the wall and the first tread of the staircase. The head seems to fix a blind eye on the surveillance camera. There are drops of blood everywhere in the access cage. On the steps, the walls, the doors. On Cheyenne Hawkwind's shoes. And on Plotkin's too.

Plotkin hears himself tell the American Indian killer: "There's a responsibility you don't have to worry about anymore. Consider your contract null and void."

"Right, except that I'm your accomplice. I think you should reconsider about the contract."

"Half, no more. Twenty thousand Pan-Am."

"Half will be just fine."

"Perfect," Plotkin says. "The escape hatch and the dome are cut off from the hotel's AI, thanks to the careful work of Mr. Drummond himself. We can work in peace."

"What do you mean?"

"Clean. And put what's left of Mr. Clovis Drummond somewhere."

"Where?"

Later Plotkin will remember his own smile, the regal smile he offers Cheyenne Hawkwind now, a very gentle, radiant smile, like the sun, capable of consuming an entire world.

"Guess."

Later, as the last legally permitted liters of water stream over his body, sending up a mist that dissipates in a cabin too small for such extravagant consumption—later, as he tries to wash his body clean of invisible blood—he thinks about the grotesque tomb provided for Clovis Drummond: the black box of the dome, just where the fat man had previously shut the Machine-Child away.

For even greater safety, with Cheyenne Hawkwind's help Plotkin had stuffed the decapitated corpse of the Hotel Laika's manager into the nanoprogrammable suit that had once been used to hold the ghostly creature from Deadlink born of Vivian McNellis's narrative. He had used a few carbon-carbon staples he found in a box in a corner of the Box-House along with their magnetic projection gun to reattach the head to the body. Drummond the tinkerer, the attacher of crucifixes on demand, king of the aphroditech pump.

He had reprogrammed the iron lung to contain Clovis Drummond's great recapitated bulk, setting it to maximum opacity. Then he had started the system back up.

The nanocomputers, the optic peripheral machines, the holoplasmic machines, all hummed back into life, hooked up to the dead body of Clovis Drummond, scanning the organism—already breaking down in the seething entropy of a cadaver—with the silent avidity of a fisherman for the entry-exit modules, the access portals to a mind that no longer existed. "Yes," Plotkin had said. "There's a treat for the Metastructure."

He knows with absolute certainty that, with this action, he condemned the Metastructure to death. That he has just initiated a Larsen effect that will prove deadly to death itself. As for what else he has accomplished, he really has no idea.

Later still, as the night envelops the universe in a blue box and the cosmodrome lights form a cold, crystalline arc, something happens inside him.

Something violent. Something that he feels is his price to pay. He understands that he is going to die. That the share of sacrifice he has dared to accept will perfectly balance the killing of Clovis Drummond. He will die, that is certain, but will he die until he is dead? Or will he die into another life?

Then something, a voice that seems to come from a hole brighter than the sun and whose ardent Face resembles that of a man; a voice speaks—writes itself on his consciousness. It is like a laugh, silvery and soft. "We will find a way to preserve the part of you that is pure, the part you knew to foster within yourself."

"Who are you?" he asks via his neural typewriter, the neuro–word processor that is now turning him into his own book. "My guardian angel?"

There is no formal response, no voice, but the silence that answers him shines with a light that fills him with joy.

Thus he senses the "presence" of other "beings." Other angels.

The disappearance of the false Metatron, that simulacrum of a simulacrum, that fiction of a fiction, that termination of the agent of the World, has opened the door to another form of reality. There isn't only the Celestial Scribe, the real one; there are a multitude of beings. They don't all have the same power over you, but some of them seek to deprive you, while others try to ensure that this effort will fail.

The angels make war with one another over Man. And for each individual man, a specific combination of forces comes into play.

He asks for a miracle. Words, impressions, even voices are no longer enough. "What do you want," they ask in unison. "What do you want of us? Do you want to see *images*?"

He senses all the menace contained in this interrogative injunction. He understands that the face of the angel can be glimpsed through the filter of machine-disconnections of the Imaginary, especially those of the neurogenerative writing with an unknown, mutant, constantly mutating form of which Vivian Velvet McNellis contaminated her brain. But to be confronted with "the image of a Universe whose face is that of a man," as Chesterton said, "is to fall with one's face pressed against the earth."

It is the morning of October 4.

October 4, the day of the Sputnik Centennial. The day on which, according to the initial plans of his own consciousness, he was to Kill the Mayor of This City.

It is October 4, and he should have been ready for that first mission.

Not only is he not ready, it is as if he never would be, as if he never could have been. He is in the double Capsule 081, Capsule A, with Jordan McNellis. The light-body of his sister floats behind the cellulose partition, illuminating the two rooms with no need for additional artificial light. Dawn is breaking. Pressing his nose against the eastern-facing window, he can see the final preparations at the cosmodrome for the nocturnal launch of J. T. Lagrange's rocket, the high point of the spectacle.

Grand Junction has transformed itself during these early hours into a vast Starnival—festive, parodic, terminal. There are parade floats with effigies of great space equipment, lunar and Martian robots, replicas of the Apollo, Mercury, Gemini, Skylab, Soyuz, Vostok, Voskhod, and Salyut capsules, and of course Sputnik itself, in a leitmotif repeated thousands of times in every conceivable form. The jubilant crowd resembles one of the old *Star Trek* fan conventions, where "Trekkies" adopted the costumes, masks, attitudes, and language of the characters from the 1960s televised series. Here there are astronauts, extraterrestrials, mutants, superheroes and heroines, and creatures of every imaginable and imagined species. *Institutional and festival science fiction, for a fiction of science that is firing its last rounds,* Plotkin thinks.

"We can't leave with my sister in this condition," Jordan McNellis says.

"No, of course not," Plotkin replies.

"We can watch the blastoff and the fireworks on television," says the young man, apologizing for the failure.

"No matter, really. This anniversary is a masquerade; it's just a blastoff like any other. Have you registered the claim with the local UHU office?"

"Yes. The launch on a Delta rocket is confirmed for October 22. Less than three weeks from now." The youth casts a sad glance toward the suite's other cabin. Obviously, it will be too late.

Plotkin stares at him, saying nothing.

The young man seems almost too naïve. Doesn't he understand that his sister never really belonged to this world, that she was returning to her own? Wasn't it Denys the Areopagite who described divine unity as a processive movement of the Good toward the Good via its own Creation?

In a few weeks, Jordan June McNellis will fly away from Grand Junction to return to the Ring.

But in a few hours, his sister will rejoin the Celestial Scribe. She will be well out of this damned Earth, and its orbital survival arches too.

He is a human being now, a living being like the others. He bears the Machine-Child within him, but it is like a transcription. The operation is probably on its way to success in the Created World; it will be the last legacy of Vivian McNellis, the last legacy of the agent of Metatron to these last humans. He asks Jordan for permission to visit his sister in the other capsule.

"She told me to warn you—this is the final phase before her incorporation into the cosmos, the final phase before the Glorious Body. Her . . . her death is imminent now."

"You know there is no such thing as death."

Jordan does not reply. He leans on the small lever that causes the separating partition to slide aside on its rails. The light strikes Plotkin's irises like the red light of the laser at the Windsor astroport a million years ago, but it is a globe of pure gold, and inside this sphere of solar light that seems both to come from the sun and to return to it, the body of Vivian McNellis seems as if it is subject to strange and continual transformations, like another state of being.

Optical effects?

She is close and far away at the same time; she seems larger but also much smaller; and—most of all—*it is impossible to tell exactly where she is.*

It looks like a scene from an antique postcard from the previous century, whose image changes according to the viewing angle.

It is as if light is body, just as much as body is light.

Later—but is it really later in this hotel room at the end of the world, in the solaresque radiation that envelops the body of Vivian McNellis? Let's say *a little* later, for time seems to have been annihilated, Plotkin approaches the bed where the girl fallen from the sky floats a few centimeters above the helium mattress. She seems made of helium herself; terrestrial gravity is losing its effect on her. *She is returning to Heaven, the last sky,* he tells himself. He stretches a hand toward her.

Vivian McNellis looks at him, a weak smile on her lips.

Very slowly, almost in slow motion, she opens her hand to welcome the touch of his fingers. "You are a man now."

"I know," Plotkin replies, his throat choked with emotion. "I . . . I don't know how to thank you."

"I would have loved you in the Created World, you know. I loved you when I invented you, in the camp."

Plotkin is confronted with a physical phenomenon that is troubling and a bit annoying—his throat is unable to make any sound. Nothing comes out but an incomprehensible, barely audible murmur.

Vivian McNellis gazes at him with all her fiery beauty, and Plotkin feels himself being consumed on the spot, as if bound to the post of a pyre. His fingers brush the half-open palm of the angel-girl. Vivian McNellis's fingers brush his in return, her fingers tender and gentle like silk, or a baby's skin.

"I love you too," he finally whispers.

He can't see very well. A strange liquid is welling in his eyes and flowing gently down his cheeks. "I love you so much I would die for you without a qualm." His voice quivers slightly, so highly charged that it could send vibrations through a steel cable strong enough to keep the world from turning.

What he just said is true, so true, so terribly true. Except the last bit of it, perhaps, which contradicted the first bit a little. But he knows what the syllogism means—Love kills Death; Love can make you dead, not to it but to its antiworld, to what is not real but creates the reality of the world. *Only Love is real,* he thinks, *and it doesn't matter if it is possible or not; it doesn't matter if you have fallen in love with a girl from the sky; it doesn't matter if you have fallen in love with someone about to leave you forever, as she is about to leave all this incarcerating humanity.*

It doesn't matter, because now you are.

You are alive.

You are born.

That afternoon—is it really afternoon?—Plotkin begins to sense pulsations coming from the city, below Monolith Hills and the Leonov

Alley strip, south of the hotel. A long procession of floats is making its way up the strip from Voskhod Boulevard and beyond Nova Express, which will become the intersection point for parades coming from all over the city. The Sonos Volantes are cruising overhead like oblong-shaped birds, scattering music, advertisements, and flyers announcing the J. T. Lagrange blastoff tonight.

The party is beginning.

On the wall-mounted television screen in Capsule 081-A, Plotkin and Jordan silently watch the images coming from right outside their hotel. A low-altitude camera drone buzzes directly past the Laika on its way to Nova Express, aiming its lens for a moment at the tubular, metallic building.

"We could have seen ourselves on TV," remarks Jordan, pointlessly.

"Do you know that not too long ago, people were ready to die or kill to see themselves on TV for three seconds?"

Jordan McNellis turns to him with the facetious, incredulous expression of the delayed adolescent he is.

"Are you serious?"

You live in your world. You come from the Ring. You lived in parts of the Earth isolated from virtually everything else, first in Patagonia with your grandfather and then in UHU research centers and health camps. You know nothing of the world I come from. You know nothing of the world of the camp, even. You, too, are just passing through. Soon you'll be in the Ring again. For you, in a very short time Earth will be no more than a distant, unpleasant memory. "Of course not," Plotkin replies without even the shadow of a smile. "I'm kidding."

Night is falling now. The first stars appear in the light-saturated sky shading into the purple of the intrauterine night. The cosmodrome looks like an immense constellar animal fallen to Earth, its fires illuminating the space around it all the way to the Hotel Laika overlooking it. And the festival has grown to indescribable proportions. The Monolith Hills strip—indeed, all of Grand Junction—is an uninterrupted series of rave parties, where every imaginable drug and neurosoftware, legal or illegal, circulate from hand to hand, mouth to mouth, spinal cord to spinal cord. The parade floats have invaded the wide streets and mounted toward Nova Express. Everywhere, crowds gather under the beat of neodisco music, gyrating and oscillating stroboscopically in a mechanical simulation of desire. Everywhere there are lights, cries, chants, noise, music, sounds of every type; everywhere are images in the sky, reflected in the clouds sculpted by the Starnival sponsors, images of the UHU itself and its planetary federation slogan repeated a thousand times. Everywhere is the grinning, deathly face of false hopes, the wide mouths of the masks twistedly mocking any vision of true hope. Everywhere sex, drugs, music, cash. Fuck me, shoot me, move me, buy me.

Everywhere death in action.

Except here, in this double capsule in the Hotel Laika, where death shows itself as the simple zero operator of an ontic process, as pure nothingness, as nothing, hardly an entry-exit interface, just a channel. Except here, where the light-body of Vivian McNellis holds a refuted secret, terrible, secretly terrible, terribly secret, about everything the false world of the UHU is built on.

Here, where life reigns eternal.

The depths of night. Facing Vivian McNellis, Plotkin is quiet, holding himself as straight as if he has a steel rod for a spinal cord.

He is quiet.

He is quiet because Vivian McNellis is speaking.

And what she has to tell him is extremely important.

"This is the moment when everything will be decided."

He knows it. The knowledge is a field, burning under a surprise enemy attack. The knowledge correlates with the words spoken by

Vivian McNellis, this woman he will love for the rest of her life. For eternity.

The knowledge shows itself in this form:

Vivian McNellis: You will go to Deadlink. I will be there waiting for you. For your baptism.

Plotkin: The silence before the bomb is dropped. The big bomb. *The Bomb.*

Vivian McNellis: The incorporation of the worlds is happening. I am rewriting in you what was, is, and will be the Machine-Child, what he can no longer be.

Plotkin: Continuing, sidereal silence.

Vivian McNellis: There is a very old patriarchal text by Saint Ambrose, which says: *"When Christ brought fire to the Earth so that it would consume the faults of the flesh, where the broadsword that signified the cutting of power that wields and penetrates the spirit and the marrow deeply, then flesh and soul, renewed through the mysteries of regeneration, forgetting what they were, begin to be what they were not, separate from the company of former vice, and break all bonds with prodigal posterity."*

Plotkin: The space that is growing between the Andromeda galaxy and our own is no longer silent.

Vivian McNellis: You understand, don't you? We are father and genitor of our actions and our works, which are thus our children.

Plotkin's mouth opens but nothing comes out—a loose piece of the silent asteroid traveling to the very end of the Milky Way, of the Voice without Words.

Vivian McNellis: You must convert to the faith of Christ before it is too late. In a few minutes, you will have no choice but to flee the hotel.

Plotkin: The question "Why?" burns his lips, but nothing comes from his throat. All he can think is: *I love this woman so much that I am ready to wait a whole lifetime to be with her again.*

He feels ready. Barely, but it is still better than nothing, he tells himself.

He is at a much lower rung than the former android-whore who, for reasons he cannot understand, found faith, broke her bonds of neuroprogrammed sexual slavery, and dared to admit that she had a soul.

Yes, he says to himself; *after all, I have a soul too, don't I?*

In any case, he knows he is capable of love. And of killing for that love.

He feels capable of anything.

That is probably enough.

"Yes, I'm ready," he manages to say.

It is at that very moment that Jason Texas Lagrange's rocket takes off majestically from Platform 1.

It is at that moment that the fire from the rocket's tailpipes creates an artificial sun that moves backward from the horizon toward the sky, from the west toward the southwest, leaving behind a cloud of brilliant gas that illuminates the interior of the room.

It is at that moment that the crowd and the music, the city and the flesh, the shadows and the fire vibrate in unison, at maximum intensity.

An instant more. The booster accelerates, changing its course southward, toward an equatorial orbit.

Another instant more. Something erupts in the ionized air; something, an object moving at very high speed.

A small object, but an extremely rapid one, an object that resembles a silver arrow flying in pursuit of the rocket. An object that strikes it violently; an object that makes it explode in the fraction of a second, with its twelve passengers: a furious supernova that causes the night sky to churn with oily plumes of light-filled smoke.

An object—and Plotkin knows it with all his being, because he saw it, because he guesses it, because he knows it—an object that came from the Hotel Laika.

And not from just anywhere in the hotel.

A hypersonic rocket. Launched from Capsule 108.

Launched from his own room.

> INCORPORATION OF THE WORLDS

Fire escape.

He has to get away. Fast. Via the fire escape of reality.

As the debris of the rocket falls to the earth of the county in a rain of ashes, blackened metal, powdered refractory resin, carbonized plastic, and fiery polymetallic meteors; as the general alert resounds throughout the city; as the Starnival founders and falls into the glacial silence of half a million mouths open in shock; as the Grand Junction police arrive on the scene, surrounding the Hotel Laika, the narrative-world of Vivian McNellis whisks them abruptly away, him and Jordan, into the Third Time. The *Aevum*.

Under the interchange.

Deadlink.

Here, it is always midnight. We are deep in the shadows, deep in the invisible light of what is contained there without being retained.

Gaze on this splendor of pure gold, of astral fire, this supernova of royal whiteness and furious red that encircles Vivian McNellis. She is speaking.

She is saying something.

She is telling a story.

". . . Metatron, the angel Prince of the Face, the angel Prince of the Torah, the angel Prince of Wisdom, the angel Prince of Intelligence, the angel Prince of royalty, the angel Prince of glory, the angel Prince

of the Palace, the angel Prince of kings, the angel Prince of poten-
tates, the angel Prince of high and exalted, imposing and glorious
princes both in Heaven and on Earth, says: 'YHWH the God of Israel
is my witness in this: When I revealed this secret to Moses, all the soldiers of the heights of each firmament became angry with me and
said to me: "Why are you revealing this secret to the sons of man
born of women, susceptible to sin, impurity, blood, venereal flux,
putrid gout, this secret through which were created the Heavens and
the Earth, the seas and the continents, the mountains and the hills,
the rivers and the lakes, Gehenna and the fire, hail, the Garden of
Eden, the Tree of Life; by which were formed Adam and Eve, the cattle and the animals of the fields, the birds of the sky and the fish of the
sea, Behemoth and Leviathan, the reptiles and the insects, the creatures of the sea and of the desert, the Torah and wisdom, knowledge,
and thought, the discerning of things on high and the fear of Heaven;
why do you reveal this to a being of flesh and blood?" ' "

She is so beautiful in this moment that Plotkin falls to his knees.
This time I fell, he thinks; *this time, I am completely a human being.*

" 'I said to them, because the Heavens have given me permission,
and I have received permission from the high and exalted Throne,
from where all names that are expressed stem like flashes of fire and
with sparkles of splendor and *hachmalim* of flames . . .' "

You are so beautiful, Vivian, that I can't even speak to you anymore, he
thinks, with the difficulty of a stone trying to move itself.

" '. . . but they were only appeased when the Saint, blessed be
he, reprimanded them and excluded them with reproach from his
presence, saying to them: "I wanted, I desired, I commanded, and I
confided the task solely to my servant Metatron, because he is unique
among all the children of Heaven. Metatron brought this secret out
of My house and gave it to Moses, and Moses gave it to Joshua, Joshua
gave to the Ancients, the Ancients gave it to the prophets, the
prophets gave it to the men of the Great Synagogue, the men of the
Great Synagogue gave it to Ezra the scribe, Ezra the scribe gave it to

Hillel the old, Hillel the old gave it to Rabbi Abahu, Rabbi Abahu gave it to Rabbi Zeira, Rabbi Zeira gave it to the trustworthy men, the trustworthy men gave it to the loyal men, to prevent and fight on their behalf all the diseases that were raining down on the Earth: 'If you truly listen to the voice of YHWH your God, if you do what is right in His eyes, if you open your ear to His commandments and if you observe all His decrees, I will not inflict any of the diseases I inflicted on the Egyptians, because I am YHWH who heals you,' as it is said in Exodus 15:26." ' "

The words taken from the Book of Enoch write themselves in fiery letters on Plotkin's brain. He realizes that she is giving him something. A secret. "We are alone," he finally says to the light-body that is much more than a body, and infinitely more than a simple emission of photons.

"You're wrong," she says. "All of the invisible is with us, even at this very moment."

All of the invisible, thinks Plotkin. *The procession of angels . . .* "I meant . . . there's no one here to baptize me."

"No? What would you say to the angel Metatron himself?"

"I . . . listen, you . . . you're only his temporary incarnation. You're a woman. Only modernist ch   urches accept the ordination of women."

"In all the UHU-tolerated religions, certainly. But you're making a small mistake."

"A mistake?"

"Yes, you are forgetting the central idea of the 'common priesthood of the faithful,' which Origen uses deliberately in several of his homilies, including the one on Leviticus, I believe. Each of us is a priest by baptism. In the early Catholic Church, exceptional situations were everywhere, and our circumstances are similar to those long-ago ones: if a priest is absent at the moment you are to be baptized, any believer may replace him."

"But you—"

"I am no longer a woman in the way you understand it. I am the living vector of the *Verba Ignis*. Remember what Origen said: 'Do you not know that to you too, as to all the Church of God and all believers, priesthood is granted?' "

Plotkin doesn't reply. He gazes at Vivian McNellis, radiant, so close to him and yet already so far away.

"And so, Sergei Diego Plotkin, I baptize you, in the Name of the Father, and of the Son, and of the Holy Ghost. Amen."

A burning liquid drips down his forehead, penetrating inside him, consuming everything there is to consume, consigning to nothingness everything he should not have been, leaving him naked as a newborn child, in the pure glory of what he has become.

"Now," she says to her brother, who has been hovering in the background, "I must cause your continuums to split apart. Our paths will diverge forever."

"What do you mean, Vivian?"

"In a few hours, the incorporation of the uncreated Light will happen. In me, the dark matter of the Universe will be digitally supercoded, and the globe of light will become a singularity in which I will ascend directly to Heaven. I would like for Lady van Harpel and the young android girl to be witnesses to this. They will be told at that time."

"And why will that cause our paths to—"

"Time is running short, Jordan. I need you to get out of here as fast as possible. The entire Mohawk territory is in an uproar over this attack, and very soon they will start investigating the area. I am going to translate you directly into the October 22 rocket, whose takeoff will be delayed only twenty-four hours due to climatic reasons. I already know that the Consortium authorities hate to change their plans even one iota. They will strengthen security measures, that's all. For financial reasons, they have to go ahead with the program as planned. Even as we speak, police from all over the county are invading the Hotel Laika, but they haven't gotten their last surprise."

"What do you mean?"

"Never mind the details. The main thing is that the overall retrotranscription of the world is happening successfully. The Control Metastructure is going to die. Without knowing it, Plotkin, by substituting the dead body of Clovis Drummond for the semivirtual exorganism of the Machine-Child there in the Box under the dome, caused a phenomenon of entropic devolution the cyberstructure itself cannot control. The first signs are appearing already. The Hotel Laika is one of them. There will be others."

"And me?" Plotkin asks, after a moment.

Vivian McNellis, in her globe of light, beams upon him with the smile of an escapee who will never be seen again. "You . . . you are a free man. I can say nothing more to you except that in creating you, I freed myself, and that you, in freeing yourself, are successfully recreating yourself. I mean that you have taken the greatest risk of all. The only one worth taking."

Plotkin stares at the girl fallen from the sky, the girl who will return there with no need of any claim, any propellant rocket, any cosmodrome, any Jason Texas Lagrange III, any city of Grand Junction.

With no need of anyone.

With no need of anyone . . . visible.

OUTPUT

ᛗETATRᗡN

> Thus the words that come from my mouth
> will not return to me without effect.
>
> Isaiah 55:11

> BLACK LIGHT, BLACK HEAT

Why is he driving now, in a rented robotic car, somewhere on Route 299, in the direction of Nexus Road? Why?

There was no transition between the baptism and his reincorporation into this car, speeding through the night of the independent territory.

Everything is synchronic in the Third Time, he thinks to himself. *I am here and elsewhere, today and tomorrow, yesterday. I am on the path of the Created World through the intermediation of Vivian McNellis's cortex, and it is simply that this World coincides perfectly with the "real world."*

In a few hours, she will rejoin the Primordial Light; in a few hours, Lady van Harpel and Sydia Nova will stand witness to the Assumption of the girl fallen from the sky, and yet, *at the same moment,* as paradoxical as it may appear, her brother, Jordan, will take off on October 23, more than two weeks from now, for the Ring.

And he—he knows with a prescience so sharp that it could rip the very fabric of the Universe—he is driving toward his infinity. He is ready to drive forever along this end of the world, if there is even a chance to see Vivian again. The world suddenly seems full of absolute truth, of intrinsic beauty that the abominations of man have not managed to sully.

The night and its powdering of stars scattered on the black sheet of the sky; the trees standing like gray and mauve totems on either side of the road; the road itself, this dusty road above which the blue-white rays of the xenon streetlamps glare.

Then, the angel appears to him.

The foremost angel, the Prince of the Face, the Celestial Scribe. It is as if Vivian McNellis's words from the Book of Enoch have come to life in front of him, both everywhere and nowhere. Everything is fire. The whole Universe bears the face of a man with four faces, each of them brighter than the sun.

"From the moment the Saint, blessed be he, took me into his service to serve the Throne of Glory, the chariot wheels, and the Shekhina, my flesh became flame. My nerves became burning fire. My bones turned to bundles of embers, the light of my pupils into the splendor of light, the sockets of my eyes into torches of fire. The hair of my head became sparkling flame. All my limbs became wings of burning fire. My entire body became roaring fire. To my right were those that had sculpted the flames of fire; to my left, a burning torch. All around me was the wind of storm and torment; before me and behind me were the groaning of earthquakes."

This time, he falls. He falls with his face to the ground. His mouth is full of moss and wet, iron-tasting sand. The trees cast their almost-human silhouettes against the great cosmos of Luna Park.

Plotkin is in the forest that borders Route 299. He can see the unmoving robocar a few meters away, haloed with dancing sunlight. He stands, walks to the gleaming vehicle, opens the door, sits down at the controls, and starts the car.

He is no longer in the rental car—or if he is, it has been transformed into some sort of eight-wheeled chariot, riding a cloud of fire. His form is human, but glowing with radiance. Vivian McNellis is beside him, in full angelic metamorphosis as well; her skin, flesh, nerves, bones, her entire body is becoming a star. Their gazes, meeting, give birth to a thousand galaxies. Everything is fire—eyes, hands, mouths, breasts, chests, abdomens, thighs . . .

All is fire. I am being consumed in you, Vivian McNellis, he thinks.

And he hears the voice of the girl fallen from the sky, the girl who is becoming an angel of fire to return there. He hears the voice of

Vivian McNellis, or, rather, her voice writes itself directly in his mind.

"Make love to me, Plotkin. Make love to me before it is too late."

Plotkin knows that the words really mean: *It is too late, but that does not matter.*

He touches his index finger, radiant with light, to her lips, and then kisses her, flame on flame.

Yes, he understands. He knows. He understands everything about her narrative-world. He finally knows everything about love.

It has taken only a single, crashing instant for him to be illuminated with such knowledge.

Fire you were, fire you will be, fire you are.

Now the narrative-world ends, and you are born at the same instant.

At the very instant when you will die.

Men are waiting for Plotkin, where he did not think they would be—at the junction. The unfinished junction between the strip and the North Junction road.

He sees a large silver-gray train car parked on the side of the road. Four men emerge from it.

A well-directed MPE-impulse ray causes a complete short circuit in the rented robocar. It stops almost instantly. Plotkin gets out of the vehicle calmly, his hands spread slightly away from his body.

He is not a normal man anymore.

He doesn't have a chance.

He doesn't recognize three of the men, but he knows immediately that they are professional killers.

The fourth man he does know, but he has not, until now, recognized him for who he is: the fourth musketeer.

Cheyenne Hawkwind/Harris Nakashima.

"I'm sorry," the man says, in a voice as cold as liquid nitrogen.

Plotkin can almost see bluish smoke coming out of his mouth.

"I work for the Order that employs you, as an operations con-troller. I presume you know what that means?"

Plotkin knows what it means. It means he is going to die, there at the side of the road, at the side of the North Junction road, at the side of the end of the world.

"You should know that damned android from Flandro fucked you over royally," Cheyenne Hawkwind says. "He's been spying on you al-most the whole time you've been here. He didn't really understand what was happening, but he knew he too was invisible to the child in the dome. When he learned of his existence from the android girl—don't forget that androids of the same generation are interconnected in some ways—Ultra-Vector Vega guessed that something strange was going on under the dome, and also with you, the female android, and Capsule 081. He plotted to make you his Lee Harvey Oswald. Every police officer in the territory is on your heels."

Plotkin understands. It is like the final ironic reversion of destiny. The terrorist android had used against Plotkin the same plan Plotkin had intended during his first "incorporation" as the Man Come to Kill the Mayor of This City.

Plotkin looks at Cheyenne Hawkwind and the three men with him. One of them, a tall, gangly fellow with a head of woolly blond hair, fiddles with a small handheld satellite-emission camera, proba-bly sending direct proof that the execution is carried out correctly to those who have commanded his assassinations—his bosses, his old bosses, his bosses from the time when he was paid for spilling blood. The two other men wait, impassive, just in front of the radiator grille of their big Chinese hydrogen-powered train car.

Of course. It's all so obvious. He blatantly overstepped his bounds; he didn't meet the deadline of his contract with the Order. And, especially, the fateful day of October 4 didn't result in the assas-sination of the mayor of Grand Junction, but instead in a terrorist attack against one of J. T. Lagrange's rockets, and thus *against the economic interests of the entire cosmodrome* of the Mohawk Consortium.

The fact that the Flandro android used him and managed somehow to penetrate his room to launch, at the fatal moment, a hypersonic rocket, shows that he really has been working for the "radical" faction that refused orbital compromise with the UHU space agency. He is cold, determined, cunning, implacable. He's probably already at least two thousand kilometers away from Grand Junction. He's probably in the Southern Hemisphere by now.

The two killers have stepped away from the train car. The third man continues filming, imperturbably. Cheyenne Hawkwind/Harris Nakashima, or whatever his real name is, observes the scene with a gleam of real pity in his eyes, which, Plotkin thinks, makes the whole situation even more inhuman.

"You have not respected your contract. You have betrayed the Order. You know what that means."

Plotkin looks into the faces of his own end, the double face of his death. A young man, very young, Asian, smooth-faced, violet-eyed, with wavy black hair, sweating under the orange light of the strip's sodium streetlamps. The hangars of the cosmodrome, vast metallic whales disemboweled on the concrete tarmac, rise sparkling behind the autobridge. The blue lights of police cars flash from the Hotel Laika, a little more than a kilometer away. The second man is hardly older than the first, a half-blood African American of at least four different ethnicities, his head shaved, dressed in an unassuming pearl-gray suit and a vermillion shirt, eyes covered with two high-resolution optical implants. He has moved a few more steps in Plotkin's direction. He is the one with the weapon. The Asian man holds the MPE emitter that fried the rented robocar's engine. He seems to be there for the coup de grâce, or as an additional measure of security, or maybe even as the controller's personal bodyguard. He stands with his arms crossed, watching Plotkin with his black eyes, his gaze boring like a nail into flesh.

They're starting younger and younger, Plotkin thinks to himself mechanically.

He came here to kill a man, and he did not comply with the terms of his contract.

He came to kill a man he had never seen, and now he is facing the man who is going to kill him, and who he is seeing for the first and last time, just as he is being seen for the first and last time; except for the "operations controller," everyone here is seeing him for the first and last time.

"I understand," Plotkin says.

The African American killer levels a high-powered, magnetic-propulsion, perfectly silent, rotating-barrel, titanium-carbon alloy Sig Sauer revolver at him. It will fire four thousand 0.55 mm bullets a minute, its multiwinding loader good for thirty seconds of continuous fire. There will be nothing left of him but a piece of meat sliced in two, in the midst of a stew of scattered, bloody guts splattered all over the road.

"If I ever really committed as many crimes as my falsified identity remembers, this will be a relief."

The young killer looks at him without comprehension. "Relief?" He mechanically arms the weapon, starting up the magnetodynamic propulsion turbine.

"I will be purified when I enter the fires of Hell."

The young man's puzzlement visibly takes on cosmic proportions. Stupor, fascination, and a shadow—just a shadow—of hesitation.

"It's true, then, what the controller told us?"

"What did the controller tell you?"

The young man seems uncomfortable at bringing up the subject, as if it is some sort of scatological taboo. Behind him, the American Indian killer is utterly silent.

"You . . . did you become a Christian?"

Plotkin lets the truth light up his face, the face that is not even his.

He raises his eyes skyward. Soon, in a few days or a handful of seconds—they are, paradoxically, the same thing—Jordan McNellis will return to the Orbital Ring. In a few hours, at the zero moment of his incorporation of the invisible, his sister will leave this world, following an infinite filament of light.

He hears the sinusoidal sputtering of the carrier wave. He looks up into the black depths of the night, scattered with the last stars of his life.

He directs one last enigmatic phrase to the young Order killer: "I wonder which one of my lives will be replayed—"

More than four hundred carbon-carbon microbullets cause his head, his rib cage, and the left-hand part of his pelvis, including his femur bone, to explode; they then smash into a few electric light-bulbs on the pylon of a streetlamp behind him.

He dies, as quickly and mechanically as he was born.

ON/OFF.

Later, his body will be examined by the Grand Junction county police. He will be identified as the "mastermind of the October 4 attack"; then he will disappear from the lives and consciousnesses of the men of this city, to whom, after all, he hardly appeared in the first place.

Except for a few who have already left, and an even lesser few who hope to do the same.

The Hotel Laika has become the active center of the autodisintegration of the Metastructure.

The police find only empty rooms, artificial intelligence with no memory, and access to the protective dome completely blocked. When they finally use explosives to break into the dome after several hours of unsuccessful trying, the county cops find a sort of exorganic iron lung containing a list of the organs of a certain Clovis Drummond, manager of the Laika and missing for several days, but they do not find any trace of a body. The exorganism is connected to a battery of nanocomputers whose encryption the Mohawk territory police's decoding experts cannot break.

It seems that there has been no one in the hotel for more than a month. The strange cyborg cast the dome was sheltering has contaminated all of the computer structures in the building and even beyond. It does not stop even after CyberBranch agents seal off the dome and cut the hotel and its AI off from any connection with the exterior. It is obviously too late; a dead body is disincorporating in the Metastructure. Result: the Metastructure is recopying itself in a cadaver that it has literally devoured and is now decomposing along with it.

Another mystery for the territory cops: it is as if the Hotel Laika, in the space of a few hours on the evening of October 4, aged several decades at once. Virtually nothing is still operational; everything is used, broken, worn out. The most perfect desolation reigns there, "as if time were speeded up somehow," concludes a scientific expert

from Alberta without being able to identify the cause of the phenomenon.

Later, he will correct his diagnosis: "Really, it's more like time
went backward there."

Vivian McNellis is aware of all of this, though she is in the process of
becoming an angel. She knows it because she knows Plotkin is dead.
The sacrificial man, the gambit man, the Man from the Camp, the
man she was only able to love in the Third Time, in a single second of
eternity and flame. The man who could only love in order to be destroyed. The man thanks to whom everything will be able to be written; the man thanks to whom everything has been written.

She knows it because she has become the black box itself, and
that is why she emits luminous energy, in the paradoxical manner of
a black hole that shines with all the radiance and all the matter it
swallows.

It had to be this way, because what is going to happen has to
happen.

The retroviral, autopoietic contamination of the Metastructure
speeds up as the weeks go by. The world's governance bureaus are hit
with more and more serious "technical" problems, the likes of which
have never been seen in Human UniWorld or its predecessors: the
end of technology, the termination of technology by itself.

First, CyberBranch detectives locate so-called hot points across
the surface of the globe. Emergency zones. The Hotel Laika is the
first of these. Then a health security center in the Hong Kong region.
This is followed by an entire university research compound in New
Zealand. Then a transorbital transit camp at Valparaiso; a series of
second-class hotels in Laos and Thailand; and other refugee and
health-control camps in East Africa and Central Asia. Then, a few
weeks later, at the end of the year, there is a change in the system; the
hot points begin to fade, but now, and in a synchronic manner, it is

the entire Metastructure that is affected. Specialists compare the process to the various stages of the progression of AIDS. During their investigation on behalf of the Metastructure, it disappears little by little, fades away, *annihilates* itself; and the UniWorld cops can do nothing to stop it.

When the epidemic reaches the Orbital Ring, it quickly becomes clear that every machine connected to Earth is following the entropic path of the Metastructure, but that those connected only to the Interpolar Network of Geo-Orbital Nations, a sort of counterstructure the pioneers developed little by little simultaneously, in the forbidden "basements" of civilization, in the Free Space of a new samizdat—all the machines that have remained unconnected to the Metastructure since their creation, escape the phenomenon. It is noted that, as with AIDS, the number of exposures to the Metastructure, the number of connections to the social control cybermachine, determines the risk factor for a general retrowriting of the machine in question. Because, and this is repeated unsuccessfully by all the governance bureaus, it is enough for your bioportable nanocomputer to have been connected even once, for a few nanoseconds, with the global megamachine, for it to be infected and considered a sort of "benign carrier." A second connection and then a third, et cetera, increase the risk of your machine being rapidly infected.

The disintegration has come to life in the very body of disintegration. Software evolves backward: at each new start-up or new use of a computer or any other machine connected to the NeuroNet meganetwork—and they all are connected, or almost all—programs, operating systems, routines, every bit of software present in that individual machine grow outdated by one or more generations at a single stroke. Very rapidly, millions, dozens, hundreds of millions of computers and nanoperipherals show and execute nothing but incomprehensible listings written in machine language, the binary base language common to all machines, their universal language, their own pre-Babel language.

Code, in its purest form. Ones and zeros. Nothing more than machine code.

Bioloaded systems do not escape the general deprogramming. Vital functions on artificial support break down one after the other, in great waves of medical-technological disaster. Brains contaminated by NeuroNet become pure chaos by the hundreds of thousands. Cybernetic organisms stop functioning; semiartificial life is frozen, as if entombed in a historical iceberg, in the icy embrace of the Afterworld.

At that moment—though any simultaneity between the *Aevum* and earthly time is a perception of the mind—at the instant when the Grand Junction cops finally break into the Hotel Laika's dome, in the early morning of October 5, under the Deadlink interchange, it is midnight. The eternal midnight of the Third Time.

The vast cruciform shadow of the unfinished highway unfurls as if it has been nailed to the sky, where the stars have never been brighter. *This is what Plotkin wrote in the Created World,* thinks Lady van Harpel. *This is what the Man from the Camp was protecting, why he sacrificed himself.*

There are two women here, and two men, and one angel.

And what caused the old lady to think what she just thought is the angel that is before her, before them; it is this creature of bodily light, this combustion of a body in the invisible, this spirit of dancing sunlight.

It is Vivian McNellis.

Her body is surrounded by a globe of light, light so pure, so white-hot that it could blind you, though it has the opposite effect of making you open your eyes even wider.

The halo of light is resplendent in the darkness, a quicksilver nova sparkling in the depths of the shadows, in the middle of nowhere, in the very heart of the devolution, and inside it, what was the body of Vivian McNellis has become a slender field of luminous vibrations that physics, concreteness, supermateriality leave in no doubt.

Above the globe of light, they can all discern a strange form rising, like a double plume of fire that seems simultaneously to ascend toward the sky and descend from it. It appears to be a ladder of pure radiation, a double helix that twists in space-time just above the glorified body of what was once, perhaps, a terrestrial creature.

Jacob's ladder, they think, almost at the same instant.

The divine Antenna, by which the body of Light will be transmitted back to its sender and its only true recipient.

Everything began a few hours earlier, when the android girl had a dream and came to wake up Lady van Harpel in her camp bed at the other end of the mobile home.

"Something is happening," the android said.

"What do you mean?"

"I can already feel something changing in me. It is physical, not symbolic—"

"You want to talk about your baptism at two o'clock in the morning, Sydia?" asked Lady van Harpel, a bit coldly.

"I need to tell you what's happening; it is very important!" the former orbital prostitute replied, edgily.

Sydia Nova was no longer feeling those moments of quantum correlation with the other android, the one she had become vaguely acquainted with during her stay at the Hotel Laika. Because they shared the same space-time, because they came from the same manufacturer and belonged to the same biotechnological generation, she and he were bizarrely connected.

"It's a low-intensity connection," she explained, "but around once a day we share a single piece of information with each other. For example, I will suddenly know that he took a night train in Thailand or a taxi in Mexico, or that he ate lamb curry in the south of India, or that he slept in a big hotel in Sydney. It's always stochastic, very factual, very brief."

"And?" Lady van Harpel asked.

"It hasn't happened for more than a week. It's over. The quantum correlation initiated by our meeting in the hotel has been annihilated. In both senses. I'm sure of it."

"Well, that's excellent news, Sydia. I think we can both go back to bed now."

"No," said the android girl. "This is only the beginning. For two days I've been having very violent dreams, where Plotkin and Vivian McNellis appear to me. This night it was different. It was stronger."

"What do you mean by that?"

"She's waiting for us," said the android girl simply. "Under the interchange. And she put the same dream message in the heads of two men living in HMV, one of whom is Father Newman, who baptized me."

"What are you talking about?" Lady van Harpel had gotten suddenly to her feet. Her old cellular telephone beeped. It was Father Newman. He was on the way from HMV.

With another man. A man who had just arrived in the area, and who had had the same dream.

They are reunited now, under the Deadlink interchange. In human time, it is the early morning of October 5, but that means nothing here. We are in the discontinuous time of angelogenesis, circumspect time, the time that synthetically disconnects all others.

The man who has just arrived, the stranger—Lady van Harpel has met him several times during the last few weeks, during visits to HMV. He is a friend of Father Newman's; he is Eastern European, a Catholic, and a writer. When he introduced himself to her, he explained succinctly that he used many pseudonyms, some of which he cited without evoking any memories whatsoever in Lady van Harpel's head. Later, when she told Sydia Nova about the meeting, the android's face went pale, her eyes glazed with a translucent film. "Jeffrey Alhambra Carpenter? Strange. That was one of the identity boxes the Machine-Child used. He read books published under that pseudonym."

Now they are there, all four of them, under the main keystone of the abandoned interchange, facing the angel Vivian McNellis has become. Lady van Harpel knows that the man, knowing nothing of the strange link between his existence and that of a being he never knew, is yet well aware that he is present at an extraordinary event, The Event. He too had the dream, the dream that was quite simply the retrotranstemporal copy of what is happening here, now, under the interchange that stretches its huge black piles toward the golden sand of the Milky Way.

Lady van Harpel realizes at that moment that it is precisely because she is clairvoyant, a true medium, that she did not receive Vivian McNellis's dream message as the three others did. There must always be a blind spot in one's vision, a bit of shadow in the light. Her gifts of precognition probably prevented the retrotranscription of the event in her own brain.

Her role is different. She must observe now, during the time she has left to live here. She must observe and ensure that everything happens smoothly.

What she must do, for once, is not really see. She must simply watch.

Watch and listen.

And, if possible, hear.

"I am the fourth human face of Metatron, the Celestial Scribe. I am what has come to close the last moments of humanity, and to usher in

what will succeed it. In this I am an inverted version of the Fourth
Knight, but if I have come, it is because he is there. The Technical
World, in a few months, will have gone. No need of a terminating
Flood to condemn this humanity; it is destroying itself without any
outside help. Even its most powerful technological tools have become accelerators of the entropy the whole system is experiencing.
The World cannot, for all that, return to any 'initial' or 'previous'
state; it combines, in its breaking down, all the phases that preceded
it. The overall 'body' of the Metastructure is disintegrating as it
copies its metabolism onto the *bodybranes* of the Machine-Child. It is
the most perfect trap that technology could have created for itself. As
you see, the disappearance of the Metastructure potentially opens a
space of freedom, unless man chooses the path of *false liberty,* the path
of anal regression, the path of crime, genocide, and tyranny; and if it
thus unknowingly invokes the coming of another terminating machine, a planetary social-control structure even more terrible than
what the UHU has tried to be for the past twenty years.

"My body is consuming what remains of it in you. You will know
everything about me; you will know my life, everything I have done,
everything I tried to do, everything I wasn't able to accomplish. And
thus you will know Plotkin, the Man from the Camp, the man invented in an isolation cell. You will know his 'life,' his various recon-
structions. You will know the moment when he became real and
alive, the moment when he chose to have a soul, the moment when
he chose sacrifice so he would be able to exist. And you will thus be
capable of keeping his memory alive. One of you is a writer; you
know, now, that your gifts have been given to you by the Great Narrator so that you can, one day, pass it all along through writing.

"I am a continuity that causes rupture. I am certainly not the feminine form of Christ, who is himself a rupture that causes continuity,
and those who dare to speak such rubbish should be considered
anathema. I am probably analogous to Saint John the Baptist, even
though I myself would fall at his feet if I had the honor to be in his

presence. I explained it to Plotkin one day, my purely fictional lover, the man I could not but love when I invented him in my cell, the man who had time to love me only in a dream. I have come to close the Trinitarian square, the metaform of the tetragram that structures everything in the Created World. But I am above all else this moment that appears in the silence of God; my light is apophatic. I am not the Creator, but the translator—that which translates. I am the tree of Creation, because I am the tree of Life and Death. Remember the Writings that teach that 'the Cross bears Fruit.' I am the moment when the invisible becomes visible, the moment when humanity will reveal itself to itself. Understand well, that this is the meaning of the word *apocalypse.*

"No new religion, no sect, no schismatic branch can prevail over my passage. I am that which announces what has already been announced; I am what causes that which must happen to happen. *I am what will put an end to the possible,* to make of it an Act. I am that which says, predicts, *pre*-knows the unknowable transfiguration that will be imposed on what remains of the human beings on this planet: I put an end to the possible, but it is in order to better concentrate its fire in the beauty of the Created World. I am what will permit man to, perhaps, have a future. I am thus the pursuit of the divine program of infinite creation. I am what will divide humanity, but I am also the rest of this terrible operation—neither divider nor divided. I will resist any attempt at corruption. I will escape their box-selling labels, but because I have come, you must not let Technology destroy itself in destroying the World it will have swallowed with it. I call you to a new science, a science after science. I speak to you here and now of the Counter-World you must create.

"Unlike John the Baptist, if I speak to you of Christ, it is to warn you of the presence, already proven, of his antithesis.

"Now, without even the slightest hint of a Leviathan to dominate its instincts, crush its pretensions, maintain a semblance of order, mankind will deliver itself with terrible speed up to the abominations we now know it is capable of. Humanity will self-destruct, and you must escape from this destiny programmed by the machine but fully happening only now that it is disappearing itself.

"Though the light contained in my DNA is freeing itself and illuminating my body, my brain, each of my cells, the Light of the Created World, or rather the Light of the Creation of the World, is incorporating itself in my DNA. It is because everything given to each of us is given back to all of us, and everything given to anyone is made free itself, because the Divine Act is above all else the bringing forth of His Good to shine on His creations, and that of His creations on Him, even inside that which, in the creation, is the spark of the Act in question.

"We are worlds in ourselves, though often we lose sight of the fact that we are worlds within a Megaworld, and so we let ourselves become machines in a demiurgic Megamachine that has replaced the Created World.

"Yes, the Metastructure is dying, and thanks to this victory over death come alive I can incorporate the world without risk, and 'die' in my turn, but what will succeed this Global Machine, you may be assured, what will succeed it will be incomparably worse, because everything that remains of the World will have been destroyed, and Man will have no choice but to submit himself to its will in order to survive. The UHU itself was really only a prototype, a temporary stage, as the United Nations was before it. It served as a test for the next platform for general enslavement. This is already preparing itself in this world newly delivered from the chaos of the Grand Jihad; it will have learned the great lesson from the previous Metastructure: to succeed as a Megamachine, it must become a World; to enslave bodies, men must become products; to govern their consciousnesses, it must make them into thought beings, not thinking ones.

"They must reach the absolute limits of self-loathing.

"Thus the success of the Machine resides in its dissolution, but its dissolution is the beginning of its success.

"I am not the Fire cast down on Earth Jesus spoke to his apostles about. I am, rather, the Light that is withdrawing from the World in order to better fight against its darkening. I am the Fire cast into the sky, in the guise of a final incantation.

"I am the ultimate living being, sent among living beings.

"I am the final sign.

"The final sign before the Word."

> BLACK BOX BABY

It is Sydia Nova, the android girl, who discovers it.

To be exact, it is better to say that it is Balthazar, the cyborg dog, who discovers the box.

The black box.

Closed.

He finds the strange, small monolith just under the Deadlink interchange. A human odor led him to it from fairly close by. The great mass of refugees from southern Quebec is moving east; there are more than a hundred thousand people now. It is said that they will try to force their way across the Vermont border. He is patrolling the area, scattered with isolated groups of faithless, lawless men who might break through the rear guards of the human colony. Lady van Harpel has been living permanently armed for weeks.

And now there is this odd little box under the Deadlink interchange.

Balthazar returns to Lady van Harpel's mobile home and finds the android girl alone there. The old clairvoyant left for HMV this morning. He tells Sydia Nova of his discovery, and leads her to the abandoned interchange.

The sky is distilled into a monochrome blue that seems reflected in the milky silver of the low cumulus clouds, rising like giant pipe organs toward the zenith. The whiteness of the high-altitude clouds vibrates with this iridescence from the higher layers of the atmosphere; they throw their value into oxygenless space in ribbons that sparkle on the puffy edges of the jet streams.

Sydia Nova walks toward Deadlink, thinking that the beauty of this world lasts for only brief instants, during which it is as utterly complete as an absolute presence.

In the meantime, the box has opened. Inside there is a very simple lining of white silk, shining in the morning sun, covering the whole interior.

And in the middle of it is a baby.

A human baby.

Fists clenched. Asleep.

Later, when Lady van Harpel has joined them near the black box, Sydia Nova says: "We don't know where he came from."

"The child has no name," the dog adds.

"We'll give him one," Lady van Harpel replies, lighting her pipe.

"But what?" the android girl demands. "We don't even know where he—"

"Oh, yes we do," interrupts Lady van Harpel. "We know it very well, you and I both. He is the Act made flesh. He is the product of the Creation of Vivian McNellis, of her union with Plotkin, her creation. He is a real human baby. I don't know how they managed to do it, in a dimension we will never experience, but you can be sure of it."

"But . . . that makes him the hybrid product of an angel and a human, like the terrible devouring giants from the time before the Flood, the ones written about in Genesis and the Book of Enoch—"

"No." Lady van Harpel cuts her off coldly. "It's exactly the opposite. Don't forget what is said in the antique Scriptures—'*The angels fell to Earth and decided to mate with human women.*' This is an inverted and intensified version of that process. Plotkin was a man, but not really. Really, he was *more* than a man. And Vivian McNellis was an angel that went back *up from* Earth."

The titanic nimbus clouds in the sky seem to have come just to support her imagery. There is, at this moment, another perfect balance between the Created World and their interior world. In the vault of the present that whirls in a spiral as static as it is fast, *something* is emerging, something incredibly luminous and nearly silent, an immeasurably thin voice, a crystalline voice murmuring that all is splendid. And at that instant, that most precious second, a storm will probably break over the Adirondacks and the furnace of the Appalachians, there to the east, in the pure cobalt blue tension.

"We need to baptize this child as soon as possible," remarks the android girl.

"Of course," Lady van Harpel replies almost dryly. "But in the meantime we need to get him out of this box, get him back to the mobile home, and take care of him."

"And find him a name," adds Balthazar.

They call him Gabriel Link de Nova. It is Lady van Harpel who comes up with the name, but Sydia Nova who will be his adoptive mother.

The father?

"Ah yes, the father," says Lady van Harpel. "His father will be here soon. Someone, a man, will come. Maybe he is already here."

The old woman is thinking of someone. The signs are accumulating.

"You found this child. It wasn't by chance that I wasn't there at the time, but on the road, coming back as fast as I could from HMV. I had just had a vision of it. And I found you there, where the vision told me you would be. You will be his mother. I will help you. I will be like an aunt, because you are like my sister. *You are my sister.* But you, clearly, will be his mother."

The storm breaking over the Appalachians has extended its whirling arms toward this part of the Independent Territory. It has begun to rain. It will rain, without stopping, for weeks.

Later, a renegade biologist from Neon Park will be able to pinpoint the child's age as exactly eight days at the moment the android girl discovered him.

Lady van Harpel says: "He is the child of the Eighth Day. The anticreature is contaminating and killing the monopsychic Metastructure, and Vivian McNellis has left us this baby, whom we must protect from the UHU, from the Jihad, from mankind, and from the Enemy of Man."

In the mobile home is a doctor of genetic biology from Neon Park, Professor Anton Solnychkin, wanted by the UHU for daring to claim that DNA is a quantum metacalculator connected to God. Father Newman is also there, as well as one Milan Djordjevic, the writer whose work, under his many pseudonyms, was read by the Machine-Child: Jeffrey Alhambra Carpenter. Djordjevic recently arrived in HMV; he fled his native Slovenia when Islamist forces from southern France cut northern Italy off from its borders with Austria and the western Balkans during the summer.

He has known Lady van Harpel since her very first visit to combustion-engine territory. Sometimes, under the icy sky of the northern autumn, they had exchanged a few opinions in the presence of Father Newman, who usually remained silent.

"The Grand Jihad has begun again," she had said to him one day. "The UHU's peace lasted only fifteen years. The Metastructure will die, but planetary war will ravage everything in its path, and this time it will pave the way for the coming of the Antichrist, the incarnation of the Prince of This World."

Djordjevic had looked deeply into the old woman's eyes. This wasn't the sort of thing to speak of lightly. "Yes. You are right. But you know that in fact he has already come; his reign is as implacable as it is invisible and painless. *'Hitler was only a precursor,'* the French psychoanalyst Jacques Lacan said a century ago. His thousand-year reign has begun, that is all, and his various temporary representatives will follow one after the other, but in fact, it is the whole world, all of humanity—or what is left of it—just as much as the nameless thing we speak of, that is being targeted. Because once we are co-mechanized by the Thing, we become the Thing. Every part of a megamachine is itself, must be, a machine as well. A megamachine is, by definition, composed of machines. Because the megamechanical world is the world of the infinite expansion of mechanization, a world where everything is co-mechanical, a world where everything is thought and nothing thinks. It's strange; this is the root of a book I'm writing. . . ."

"For the angels, everything always goes back to the root."

"Yes. And that is what Vivian McNellis came to tell us. The end of Man is now a phenomenon of the past; it is no longer facing us, ac-cording to a more or less long-term temporal perspective. We have fully entered the era of the disappearance of Man, and that is part of the plan of what you call the 'Antichrist,' taking it for a 'person,' though really it is the opposite; it is a 'principle' that, paradoxically, becomes incarnate in disincarnation, which loves to project itself in antiform. Its success lies in the Universal and Technical Thing, its in-dividuation in the annihilation of the subject, its language in the de-construction of all *Logos*."

"Are you saying that there will be a successor—or even a *resumption*—of the UHU after the Second Jihad?"

"Yes, in a certain sense," said Djordjevic. "You see how they are co-evolutionary and thus co-devolutionary. Their decline and death are correlated in every way. The end of the Metastructure opens the door to the chaos of total planetary civil war, but at the same time it produces two contradictory events: it frees up the space needed for an even greater mechanization, which the Jihad will have done every-thing to make possible. At the end of this century, probably, with an even more perfect and implacable Metastructure than that of the UHU. And—"

"And?"

At the time, Djordjevic had been unable to find the words. Now, ten days later, in front of the baby sleeping in his cradle inside Lady van Harpel's mobile home, as the autumnal rainstorms pour down on the American northeast, he looks at the old woman.

"This," he says, "is the *and* I was talking to you about the other night."

He wrote that it would be you, thinks Lady van Harpel. *Yes, you will likely be the father of this child, but can you marry an android, a former "sexy-doll," a bionic ex-prostitute?*

Later, in the face of her mostly silent insistence, the man refuses. "It isn't that I find it impossible to marry an artificial woman on principle. It is—don't you see—the fact that I am already married, my dear lady. My wife disappeared near Trieste when the French Islamists attacked the eastern Alps. No one knows what has become of her, and now it is impossible for me to go back there. They say fighting has begun again in northern Italy."

"Then you don't know if she is alive or dead," remarks the old clairvoyant of the interchange. "That, I know, is worse than anything."

"Yes," agrees Djordjevic. "Especially when you know what the Islamists do to women."

Lady van Harpel does not respond. Djordjevic notices that she seems to be having some difficulty swallowing. Finally, she puffs somewhat desperately on the psychotropic smoke of her marijuana pipe.

As for Djordjevic, he stands paralyzed with horror at the consequences of what he has just said.

"In any case," he says one day, trying to convince the old woman once and for all, "the child is an unnatural orphan, as you well know. One might even say that he is *the first orphan to be born after the death of his parents.* He is the Orphan of the World. Do you understand? He is the incarnate parabola of the Act of which we are the genitors: he is the Orphan of the Godless World. He has no real genealogy to speak of, since the Human World is disappearing, other than that of a metanarrative that was created between Vivian McNellis and Sergei Plotkin, between Creator and Creation and, even more certainly, of an internal relationship inside Creation itself, a relationship of Creation toward Creation, like the combustive center of the Created World. He is, in a sense, the first man of a whole new World, the post-UHU and even the post-Jihad world, you might say, since it seems definite that the Jihad will follow the monopsychic Metastructure in its devolutionary spasm, and finish by destroying itself.

"He is the first man of the world following the invisible catastrophe, the first man following depopulation, the first man following the destruction of Nations, the first man following Man, the first man following the end of the world. He is the Orphan of Enoch, the Noah of a World where man himself is the Flood. Gabriel Link de Nova.

"What he will do exactly, no one knows. If anyone did know, it would undoubtedly fall to that person to destroy the Universe.

"What will his life be? For now, the infinite space of freedom.

"And if one takes my meaning, he has created this Universe."

It is thus that Djordjevic conceives his "mission" where the baby is concerned: to follow him even while leading him; to guide him while knowing what he will learn from him; to be the Master who will teach his own Pupil to surpass him.

To hide nothing from him, except the unknowable. To tell him everything, except what is useless.

He is an orphan. He was found at Deadlink. His parents were probably killed during the resumption of combat between the North American Islamic Caliphate and pockets of Canadian nationalist resistance fighters. He was found after the departure of a band of refugees bound for Vermont, perhaps abandoned by a group of survivors, undoubtedly lost in the chaos by the last active Red Cross unit in the area. There; the story is taking shape.

"It is out of the question," he tells Lady van Harpel, "to educate this child in the belief that he is the son of a female angel and a half-fictional, half-real man, especially since we have no real certainty about Plotkin's true status. Even if that *is* the 'truth.' We will decide when the truth is real. The truth will set us free, said the Old Testament. Yes, unless it kills us. Take it or leave it" is the Balkan writer's final word.

"I am for it," says Sydia Nova.

Lady van Harpel nods.

The man takes the android girl and the baby to his home in HMV. Another story has thus begun. A new disconnection in the world. Or, rather, in the *Post-World*.

> *WORLD PROCESSOR*

So now what is talking, what is talking now, is no longer anyone in particular. If it is a "person," with any luck, it is present in each of us. It is what wrote this world, this world of dying cosmodromes, that is talking, and it is talking with a voice trying to transcribe the experience as best it can.

This voice too is coming from an isolation cell, one of the cells from which only a free word can come to life and take flight in search of minds. It comes from a brain that does not yet know it has just entered a war, a total war. It comes from a brain that barely suspects its own multiplicity, or more precisely a tension in this Multiplicity between the Unique and the Infinite; for example, this voice is already active in the brain of the man who, in this world, is—was—will be—named Milan Djordjevic, and who is writing—wrote—will probably write—the adventure that has unfolded here. But it was also present inside Plotkin, the man of the "plot," the man of action, the man divided and then reunified, the man of sacrifice, the man of crime and punishment, the Man from the Camp.

It is present, at the same time, inside a female android who leans over the baby she has just adopted, in an old mobile home lost somewhere among the borders of several North American territories; and also in the head of a very young girl, an adolescent girl scampering with her father near the chassis of an old Cadillac in an area reserved for combustion engines not far from here, but several years distant, outside this particular story. And it is present in a radiant fireball, on the lips of a man who, somewhere in a ruined city, is preparing himself to kill another man.

There are millions of men like that.

This voice is our own, except that we have lost it. This voice is the one that makes each of us something other than a routine in the program, something other than a box in an infinite network of boxes, something other than a machine in the megamachine. This voice is everything that humanity does not dare to tell itself, everything men do not want to hear spoken of—that is, themselves and their atrocious failures, their terrible dysfunctions, their unborne responsibilities.

This voice, though it probably exists in each one of us, can only be expressed by some. The weakest ones of all. Paradoxically, though, it is their very weakness that keeps them from speaking; they open their mouths and nothing comes out. But it is this terrifying silence that comes to cover, with its luminous shadow, the insipid tumult of small talk, the awful clamor of carnage, and the thundering din of crowds delivered up to themselves.

This voice—which is now nothing more than a gasp uttered by a few mouths silently screaming their ineffable cry to the stars, under the celestial northern and southern vaults that will crown the extinction of man by man—this voice is a very strong thread of light that seems to rise from the Van Halen belt toward the Orbital Ring, like a single filament of golden vapor. This voice—this voice that is already returning to what truly possesses it, well beyond this Earth and this Universe—this voice is what permits the world to exist. It is through this voice that this world transcribes itself in Creation.

Not only does no one listen to this voice any longer, no one dares to risk hearing it. Not only does no one speak this language any longer, the entire world has agreed to let it vanish. How, then, can we be surprised that the world is *slipping away;* how can we be surprised that it is crashing in on itself like the heart of a star that will become, that is becoming, a black hole? How can we be surprised that it no longer possesses any force strong enough to be *the glue that sticks things together?*

Look at them, these intelligent monkeys who hide their words behind accounting tautologies, behind cultures of pomp and circumstance, behind circus language—the words they have let become a vulgar mechanism for communication! Look at them, left alone with crude machine-language, with the machine-world in its pitiful nudity, just as it finally reaches its goal to co-mechanize everything, including the nothingness it carries within it.

This voice, if it is that of a human being on this Earth, is the voice of *the last living writer* not yet replaced by artificial intelligence. This voice has taken the world in its own mouth.

It is clear that this voice is about to fall silent.

Jordan McNellis presses his nose against the cold Plexiglas window.

The planet, blue and orange, appears in fragments under an atmospheric cavalcade of huge cloud formations. Where it is night on Earth, myriad unmoving stars cluster in the sky more thickly than the densest of surrounding constellations: they are the cities, burning with all their fires, some lit by the hand of man, raging fires and civil wars. Where it is day there are constant explosions, like flaming, silent laughter erupting across the surface of the globe, and enormous disks of black smoke, drifting from one continent to another, floating beneath his watchful, almost nostalgic gaze. A hurricane, surely programmed by WorldWeather, is brewing in the Indian Ocean just off the coast of Malaysia.

Involuntarily, his hand moves to the window, as if to touch the reality of what he has just left forever.

At the same time he hears Sloppy, a young Australian pioneer, swearing at a machine that is refusing to obey him. He glances around at the cabin's occupants. Seven other people—three men, four women—with whom he will spend the twelve hours before their arrival at the final destination, the geostationary city of Cosmograd.

He is going back. Back to the High Frontier. Back to the Orbital Ring, the metacity peopled by space colonists. Back to the territory of his childhood. Back toward his own future.

He lets his gaze rest again on the planet that is growing imperceptibly more distant, burning with turbulence of every possible color. Hell might be multicolored like this. Everything that can burn does, on almost every continent, including North America: Los Angeles, several cities in the Great Lakes region, Atlanta, Washington, D.C. Collision zones, metacultural shocks in the mesh of the global network. High human energy: murders, massacres, torture, rapes, tyranny, abominations. Repetition of abominations. Abomination of repetitions. The planetary civil war is expanding: pseudopods, suburban agitation, convergence of micropolitical catastrophes. A multigenocidal hydra refracting at every stage of the great global panopticon now deprived of most of its means. They say the computer problems that began on October 4 in the Metastructure of governance bureaus are the worst ever, and that the Metastructure is only functioning at 50 percent capacity. That the phenomenon, of unknown origin, is getting worse every day. They are talking of the likely end of all aerospace activity. All technological activity. *There,* Jordan McNellis says to himself. *This time we can never go back; it has really started for good now. The general devolution of humanity can't be stopped.*

He left just in time. *In extremis.* He watches the Earth he is leaving forever with the mixed feelings of the survivor of a catastrophe: peace and relief on one hand; guilt and sadness on the other.

Once, he thinks, *there was a world here.*

ACKNOWLEDGMENTS

Thank you to Thierry Bardini, Pierre Bottura,
Olivier Germain—the trinity of readers.

MAURICE G. DANTEC was born in France in 1959. A former advertising executive and songwriter for a French punk-rock group, Dantec is a shameless lover of science fiction, crime novels, and metaphysics. He is the author of *Red Siren,* which won France's Prix de l'Imaginaire. He is also the author of *Villa Vortex, Babylon Babies* (soon to be a major motion picture from Fox under the title *Babylon A.D.*), and *Theatre of Operations,* a series of journal essays. He lives in Montreal.